Yonder

&

Far

THE LOST LOCK

MATTHEW C. LUCAS

Yonder & Far

Matthew C. Lucas

Ellysian Press

www.ellysianpress.com

Print ISBN: 978-1-941637-78-4
First Edition, 2022

Editor: R.A. McCandless, Maer Wilson
Cover Art: M Joseph Murphy

DEDICATION

In loving memory of my mother, Dolores Lucas, and all

the fortunes she foretold.

PROLOGUE

The offices at the end of Merchants Row were . . . odd. Nothing about their outward appearance, mind you. The building that housed the offices was a sensible square of red brick and timber set within a fashionable part of Boston Town. Upright, unostentatious. No one had ever remarked upon any impropriety with the house on the end of Merchants Row – indeed, few had remarked upon the building at all, except to use it as a point of reference to distinguish between the Episcopal church and Masonic lodge with which it shared a corner. In every respect, it would have seemed a proper place of commerce in a good and upright Federalist neighborhood.

There was nothing at all strange about the shape of the chambers within. The single floor had been neatly halved into two adjoining rooms. Each office was well apportioned, neither smaller nor larger than its neighbor. A narrow stairwell in a foyer led to an attic. The stairs wound upward, just as stairs should. The railings wore a coat of unremarkable white paint.

Nor could one charge that the offices were not suited for their ostensible purpose. Walking through the entry and past the stairwell, at a casual glance, one would behold an eminently serviceable lawyer's den. The ceilings were high. The walls all made of polished wood and plaster. Both rooms had a beveled glass window. There were more than ample bookshelves, rugs, chairs, and furniture to serve the needs of clients. All of it was laid out in a manner just as one would expect for a barrister's workplace.

But if one were to pause in any of the rooms, if one stopped long enough to consider the surroundings more carefully, if one leaned in close enough to give anything a good squinting, a veneer would begin to peel away. One would notice little things, trifles, which, collectively, would exude . . . oddness.

First, there was the oak partner's desk in the center of the first office chamber, which had been crafted into a shape that resembled an unfurled shamrock. And the draperies carelessly thrust aside on their rods, they were almost colorless – except at a certain moment every dusk, when they would suddenly and inexplicably refract the setting sunlight with a gleam as startling as fireworks. The lone portrait in the second office was centuries out of date and it portrayed a truly loathsome looking fellow (clutching a bloodied halberd, of all things), while the floral illustrations that had been hung in the first office all depicted plants much too vibrant, too exotic, for a place ostensibly devoted to the solemn business of courts. And though none of the stoves within the offices had ever been lit nor any of the windows ever cracked, the air in each of the partitioned rooms felt, at all times and in all seasons, like a dry, comfortable autumn.

But perhaps the most disconcerting feature of the law building was the matter of its legal papers. Which is to say, there were none. Not a solitary writ, demurrer, pleading, or complaint could be found within.

It was as jarring as coming into a church bereft of Bibles.

The door that led into the offices was drab and featureless, save for a handle and a brass knocker. There was a shingle hung above the knocker, a small plaque in faded green with white script that was rather embellished in its cursive, and it read:

Yonder & Far,
Attorneys and Counselors
of Custom

CHAPTER ONE

"Like a proud father, your author has ambitions for the progeny of his writing. I will share with you, dear reader, one in particular that I hold for the little tome you now have in your hands. A select few of you, I dare hope, may come to relish as much as I the fascinating intricacies of CUSTOM – that vibrant canon of laws, principles, and animating spirits which governs the Realm of Doldrums (a place as misunderstood as it is misnamed). I have spent the better part of my life studying Custom in Doldrums, I have canvassed its every nook and cranny, and its contemplation intrigues me more today than when I first discovered it. Such a beguiling subject, Custom! Once its contours are discerned and its boundaries ascertained, one begins to see Doldrums in a new light. For Doldrums can be a charming place, despite its reputation."

—Wherestone's *Commentaries on Custom*,
Introduction

The morning of the 30th came on gray and cold and wet, not unlike all the preceding mornings had in November of 1798. The raindrops fell hard as dollops, more or less straight down, and exploded like cannonballs within the puddles and ponds that enveloped the streets of Boston. A month of deluge had turned the roads into a slurry of mud. It was nearing the latter half of ten o'clock, and an oily glow had deigned to peek through the clouds. More a half-light, one that had the feel of an eclipse, so that the elm tree that grew crooked near the streetlamp, and the hitching post, and the empty coachman's stall were more shrouded than illuminated.

John Yonder looked out from the beveled glass of his office window and scanned the stretch of Merchants Row it overlooked. Seeing no one in the rain, he returned to the fussing that had engaged his attention for the past half an hour.

The chairs should be closer, he decided. It would connote confidentiality. He hurried over to the shamrock-shaped table and inched two armchairs nearer together, the same ones he had moved further apart not a minute earlier.

For a chap who looked to be in his fifties (and, it must be said, verging into portliness), he moved with a preternatural grace. His footfalls made not a sound against the wood paneled floors. His chair did not at all squeak when he sat down to gauge how he would look in it. And when he tipped the spout of a tea kettle to freshen his cup, it was with a flourish, so that the line of steaming liquid seemed to almost dance from the pot to the cup. He was dressed smartly with a crisp linen shirt and a heavy, slate-colored waistcoat tailored to his frame. His shoes were buckled with silver and carried a generous heel, for John Yonder, Esquire was (it must also be said) on the shorter side of most men.

He took a sip of tea. He wound and unwound a napkin in his fingers and unbuttoned and buttoned his coat. Ten more minutes passed.

"She's not coming," he murmured under his breath.

No sooner had he spoken when he heard the sound of footsteps outside. They stormed up the front stairs of the office building.

He was out of his chair and at the front door before they reached it.

Yonder threw the door open with a lurch. He offered a broad and unctuous smile to the woman who had only begun to raise her hand to knock.

"John Yonder, at your service, my lady."

Judging by her bearing, she was unquestionably a lady of importance, for she held her head proudly. The wind and rain had not dared to stir so much as a strand of gray hair she had tied so primly to her head. Her dress was a sensible cut of fine wool dyed in midnight blue. Her face was taut, severe, but unblemished by any spot or wrinkle (though one was still left with the impression that she was frighteningly old). It was a plain, well-worn visage that reflected the bleakness of the day as vividly as a mirror. It had one emotion etched upon it: displeasure.

"I've come for our appointment," she said.

She kept her hand poised for the knocker as if to express her distaste at having been deprived of the propriety of engaging the door on her own terms.

"A pleasure, my lady." Yonder made a fluid bow. "Do come inside."

He ushered her through the small foyer and into his office, where the two plush cushioned chairs he had so carefully positioned awaited her arrival. She accepted the seat as well as Yonder's offer of tea.

It should have been curious (though it was not to Yonder), that the lady seated before him, who had until a

6

minute ago been caught in the grips of a thumping New England downpour without so much as a shingle or a stick to cover her head, looked as dry as if she had just come from her parlor. No puddles followed her steps, no drips of rainwater marred the carpets. She did not even have to bother to wipe her shoes.

Yonder tried to appear at ease, though sitting this close to her ladyship made him regret his final choice of chair placement.

"You may call me Jane Otherly," she said stiffly.

"An excellent name. I trust your journey was not unpleasant?"

"I loathed every moment of it."

"I am very sorry for it. It is rather gray here, I suppose."

A howl of wind beat against the window, causing one of the shutters to thump against the wall. Otherly sat as erect as a statue, her hands clasped tightly about the blue-flowered ceramic cup she held. Yonder took a long sip from his, smacked his lips, and exhaled a pleasured sigh.

"Such a delightful drink."

He waited a suitable time for his guest to respond, and when she said nothing, his smile never faltered.

"You know," he said, "it wasn't so very long ago the locals here went to war over it. Tea, that is. Absolutely slaughtered each other." He shook his head, chuckling. "A war over a drink." He drew another languid slurp. "One understands the motivation."

Otherly scarcely seemed to be listening. Her face had pinched into a scowl.

"I have come on business, Yonder. I would prefer to dispense with the chit-chattery."

Yonder dipped his head obsequiously. Otherly scanned his office.

"Your partner should join us," she said.

"Ah," Yonder tried to sound apologetic without actually admitting to a fault. It proved difficult. "Ah," he repeated. "My partner. Yes. I suppose that would be appropriate for him to join us. Quite the proper thing . . ."

He shuffled his feet and busied himself with a long draught from his empty teacup. "I'm afraid Captain Far is engaged on another matter at the present."

"Indeed." She said the word with profound disapproval.

"A very pressing matter. If you understand my meaning."

It was clear she did not.

"But as I am the senior partner in the office," Yonder continued, "and the one most learned in Custom, you may trust that your matter will receive the utmost attention." He paused and added, "I presume you seek counsel on Custom."

"Why else should I have sought you?"

Yonder bobbed his head.

"Very good. And may I also presume this is your first visit to Doldrums?"

"My first and hopefully my last. Dreadful place. The air here is every bit as noxious as they say. I desire nothing more than to leave this wretched realm at once." The corner of her mouth went up into a wicked curl. "As I have it in my power to leave. Yes, when I am done here, I shall draw a doorway in the first oak I come upon and return home."

For the first time since Otherly's arrival, Yonder found himself incapable of maintaining his delighted expression. But not for long. A moment, and the bright, earnest, jasper colored face returned in force.

"How wonderful for you," he exclaimed.

Otherly glowered at him.

"So I should like to conclude this business as quickly as possible," she declared firmly.

"Of course you would. Let us turn to your business, then. Pray tell me. How may I be of service?"

"I require you to fetch something of mine."

She set her teacup down, folded her hands neatly in her lap, and sat quietly, leaving Yonder to wonder whether he was supposed to guess what it might be. For Otherly would say nothing more. After a time, one of Otherly's long fingers began to tap against the arm of her chair impatiently. The two of them sat in silence. The muted patter of raindrops upon the roof was the only sound within the office until Yonder cleared his throat politely. He ventured that it must be a singularly important item she had lost.

"I've lost nothing," she replied icily.

"Stolen perhaps?" Yonder inquired.

Otherly rolled her eyes.

"Stolen? From me? Do you not know who I am?"

Yonder bowed in acknowledgement.

"Forgive me. I lost my senses for a moment." He furrowed his brow in concentration. "Well, well. An item you would have returned that was neither lost nor stolen, must have been one . . . you have given."

She gave the slightest nod.

Yonder leaned forward, his hands pressed to his knees, his lips drawn tight, his face angled just so – the portrait of a lawyer poised to receive the confidence of a client. With the gravest, most respectful tone he could muster, he pressed his query.

"What have you given, Lady Otherly?"

Otherly began to wipe at her dress absently, as if the very intimation of this matter to Yonder had already sullied her person.

"I am a lawyer," Yonder assured her, "your secret is safe with me. I shall keep whatever you tell me in the strictest confidence."

She glared at him with equal measures of contempt and defiance. Eventually, though, a crack appeared.

"Have I your Word?"

9

"I told you I am a lawyer."

"All the more reason. Do I have it?"

Yonder considered for a moment, shrugged, closed his eyes, and parted his lips. A single whisper escaped, one that was so faint it barely passed as a breath between them. He gave her his Word. She took it within her grasp, like plucking a wisp of smoke.

It must have satisfied Otherly, for her shoulders relaxed. She drank her tea and began to speak more freely about her business.

"A certain individual," she began, "was welcomed at the court of Her Majesty, the Queen of the Grove. He was one of those Traveling Fellows."

"Ah!" Yonder brightened. "I am intimately acquainted with that society."

"Glorified vagrants, if you ask me. Licensed roguery. One should know one's place, not flutter about from realm to realm like a butterfly."

It would be proper to bow to her opinion, and so Yonder did, though this one came off a tad stiff.

"He was quite handsome," Otherly continued, oblivious to Yonder's gritted teeth. "His cheeks were particularly fine as I recall. But it was his charm that set him apart. His grace, his wit, his poise – perfect in every regard. Quickly, he became a fixture within her Majesty's retinue. This individual – note, I've not called him a gentleman – led many in the court to believe he had come in search of a match. A high match, if you understand my meaning."

"I believe I do. But allow me to interpose a question here. When was this individual first introduced to Her Majesty's court?"

Otherly waved a hand in the air with annoyance.

"However does one mark time in this place?"

"It can be disorienting here. The folk in Doldrums use a device called a calendar, which, I believe, has something to do with the sun, or the Romans, who—"

Otherly interrupted him with a sudden recollection, "It was just after you had gone. Yes. I remember it now. The talk of the court was still abuzz about you and your friend's caper that led to your banishment. Then he appeared, beguiled us all, and everyone quite forgot about you."

Yonder sat stock-still, his mouth locked into a grin of an almost maniacal dimension.

"A little more than a year ago, perhaps?" he offered, grinding his teeth.

"If you say so. It was long enough for him to weave his spell over every one of the ladies of the court – all of them, high and low. I daresay even Her Majesty found him to her liking."

"What of the gentlemen of the court?"

"They despised him, to a man."

Yonder hesitated, unsure how to broach a delicate topic.

"And what, if I may ask, was your opinion of this individual?"

But much to Yonder's relief, Otherly took no umbrage at the inquiry.

"If Her Majesty succumbed to his enchantment, what chance did I have?"

Otherly heaved a wistful sigh and gazed out the office window. The storm had weakened from its earlier deluge into a light, misting rain. Tiny rivulets of water cascaded down the beveled glass, clutching at the surface like long crystal fingers. The wind died down to a hard breeze.

"I'll confess, Yonder," she said at last, "since I have your Word to keep this conversation in confidence – I was taken with him. Why shouldn't I have been? He is the comeliest man I've ever laid eyes on. A perfect admixture of sharp wit and soft manners. As if he knew all of my inmost fancies, my desires, and could play them like music on his flute."

"Did he profess to return your affection?"

Otherly's face darkened. Her voice dropped to a low, almost feral growl.

"He all but said he would marry me. If it were in his power. He said he required a token of my love, to show the seriousness of our commitment. He said without it, Her Majesty would never approve the match. He said . . ."

Otherly clutched the rails of her chair so tightly her knuckles turned white. Yonder tried to exude a pained expression and asked, as gently as he could, "What did you give him?"

She held her chin up defiantly.

"A lock of my hair."

"Oh, Lady Otherly!" Yonder exclaimed. "My dear Lady Otherly. I am so very sorry for you. To have put so much of yourself in the hands of such a rascal. Oh, my."

"I do not desire your condolence for my loss," she said, "only your service in restoring it."

"Forgive me, my lady. You're quite right. What's done is done. No sense wallowing in lamentation over it. So, this rake has come to Doldrums then?"

"Yes. He jilted quite a number of ladies in his time at court, and it's stirred the pot to a boil. Alliances have frayed. Betrothals broken. Duels fought. The court was becoming ungovernable for all his shenanigans. Finally, one of Her Majesty's chamberlains – you know the gentleman of whom I speak – informed him he had worn out his welcome. That, apparently, left an impression. For at the last moon, he slipped away from court without even a by-your-leave to Her Majesty. I have since learned he has fled to this place," she said, and tapped her finger upon her chair's edge. "He's in Doldrums. Trying to lay low while the turmoil passes."

"And you've followed him to retrieve what is rightfully yours. Have you been able to make contact with him yet?"

"I know he is here," she replied archly. "But he is

beyond my power to reach. He refuses to acknowledge my summons. That is why I've come to you. Can you find him and get my lock?"

"I suppose a replevin action might serve, since what you seek is the return of your personal property . . . Hmm. Let me think on this a moment."

Yonder arose from his chair and began to pace about in a circle with his hands clasped behind his back. He clicked his tongue and fluttered his eyelids. It was a practiced gesticulation of his; one that was meant to convey deep and scholarly contemplation. It only seemed to irritate Lady Otherly, however, for after little more than a minute of the spectacle, she snapped at him.

"Well?"

"Yes." He came to a halt and began to sway back and forth from heel to toe. "I believe I can help you with this matter. That is, there may be a course in Custom we can pursue on your behalf. I shall have to consult my treatise. And the work will assuredly require the joined efforts of my partner and me." He let out a contemplative breath and nodded. "But I'm certain we can handle the matter for you. If this fellow is indeed in Doldrums, and all goes right, we should have your hair returned to you within, say, a fortnight. Give or take."

"Really?" She leaned forward in her chair. "And you'll bring it to me? The lock of hair?" For the first time, her voice seemed tinged with the faintest trace of emotion. "Once you've gotten it, you'll give it to me?"

Yonder smiled. He went over to a small table caddy to serve himself another cupful of tea from the kettle. A lone tendril of steam broke free from the brim, twined in the air, and settled upon his cravat making an undulating silver pattern within the colored silk. He slowly took a sip, and his eyes met Otherly's gaze from over the edge of his cup.

"I shall," he said. "But before I do, there is the matter of payment."

Otherly rolled her eyes, as if she were about to launch into a fresh complaint, but she stopped herself.

"Yes, of course." She gave a curt wag of her hand. "Your kind won't lift a finger to aid a lady unless it yields a four-fold profit." She withdrew a dainty silk purse from a pocket of her dress. It was as dark as moonless midnight and seemed empty, for it fell into her palm as a feather with no sound at all. She began to open the clasp. "Gold or jewels, then?" She paused a moment and considered. "Or do you prefer those scraps of paper?"

Yonder gestured for her to put away her purse and explained that he had no interest in gold or jewels, and that the currency that circulated in these parts was no better than a continental. He and his partner had ample trinkets and funds lying about, thank you.

"However," he said, and drank again from his cup, "we are in the market for favors. Particularly those from well-connected courtiers in a certain Queen's court . . . As I hear, you are a lady-in-waiting, and quite close to Her Majesty."

"She listens to my advice."

"Just so." He nodded. "If you would give your Word that you will speak to her on our behalf. Advise Her Majesty that she has two repenting servants stranded in Doldrums who could render her invaluable services if she would only grant them leave to return. In short, put us back in her favor, Lady Otherly – that will suffice as payment for my firm's services here."

Otherly's thin face screwed in thought. Outside, the sound of the rapping broke the stillness. The rain had stopped, but the wind began to howl with a renewed intensity.

At last, she gave him her Word, in the same fashion as he had given his.

14

"We shall also require a retainer," he added off-handedly.

"Oh, come now! How am I supposed to pay you a portion of a future favor?"

"A retainer is different. It is something more substantial, more corporal. A Bond." He set the cup down. "I've got it. For this matter, I believe one of your hairs, Lady Otherly, would serve as adequate security. Adequate and apropos. If you'd be so kind."

She shrugged indifferently and fumbled with the knot of ashen gray above the back of her neck. But as she tried to pluck one out, Yonder burst into a loud, fruity laugh. His face turned from orange, to umber, to apple red, then back to orange. His whole body shook.

"No, no, no, my lady," he said, wiping a tear away. "I apologize, for I should have made myself clear. We require a strand of your *true* hair."

"Eh? Oh . . ."

Otherly hesitated. "You'll return it once we're finished?" She regarded him suspiciously. "I damned well don't want to have to come tramping back here again—"

"I'll give my Word again," Yonder assured her. "You'll have it back so long as you keep good faith to your obligations. We've made a Bargain."

She eyed him a while longer. A debate seemed to rage behind her dark eyes. At last she gave an indignant huff and slowly, very slowly, Otherly reached once more for the back of her head. Only this time the gesture was one of perfection, done with the grace of a young maiden performing a midsummer dance. Her arm arced into a curve. Her fingers, though knobbed from arthritis, seemed to dance, lithe and fluid and perfect in their every motion. Another pin, like a brooch, fluttered down to her shoulder, and the office was suddenly filled with a brilliant illumination.

Yonder caught a glimpse of Otherly's hair – her true

hair – when a curl hidden beneath the mound of gray tumbled out into view. It pulsated a red glow that shone with melancholy, like the sunrise before a hanging. She drew a single strand of it until it was taut, plucked it out, and handed it to Yonder, who locked it away in a small, enameled box he carried in his vest. He smiled at Otherly and gave the box in his pocket a reassuring pat.

For the remainder of the cold, dreary morning, in that odd law office on the end of Merchants Row in Boston Town, the lawyer and his client worked through the particulars of a very odd business.

CHAPTER TWO

"It must be acknowledged that the people of Doldrums are, by and large, an obnoxious folk. They move slowly, speak dumbly, and think poorly. In their dealings with us, they often seem as befuddled as cows."
—Wherestone's *Commentaries on Custom*, page 8

Captain John Far sat on his camp stool and let his gaze wander across the shadows of a benighted forest. It was cold and dank and, except for the patter of rain falling on the leaves, utterly still. All around him, the trees stood at attention like sentinels. Moss-draped limbs held high, as if in salute, twined through a canopy of branches that swayed with each passing rush of wind. Absently, he extended a finger to touch the bark of a nearby oak. He traced a long rectangle over the soft lichen and jagged bumps of wood, withdrew his hand, and studied the tree trunk.

A tiny gray spider scurried through the space of the

rectangle he had drawn on the bark. Far watched it impassively and wiped a streak of rain from his face. Nothing had happened. As usual.

Dawn would be breaking soon. Cheerless, gray, a stillborn sun trapped behind the cover of clouds, but it was coming. Far felt the first hint of warmth intrude into his wooded sanctuary. A powerful breeze gusted in the dark and made the ceiling of branches shudder. Far glanced up and watched a flurry of droplets and a dead limb plummet into the brush. He let out a long, frustrated breath.

He was seated beneath a tarp he had strung over an elm bough. Not a true encampment, for what he had brought comprised of nothing but the tarp, which kept the better part of him more or less dry, the camp chair he sat upon, a round table with a linen cloth, a plate, fork and knife, and a napkin. No lantern or candle for light, but a small fire burned close by. Above the crackling embers was an empty spit.

He shifted in his seat, a broad-faced, broad-shouldered man in his prime years, trying to find comfort on a hard stool. He wore no hat, he seldom did, but kept his mane of black hair tied into a ponytail, not caring how unfashionable it appeared. Though the air was biting, he only wore a light, pea-colored coat and left his shirt open at the neck. A loose pair of green trousers was tucked into riding boots. At the moment, one of his feet bobbed in rhythm to a tune he had in his head, while his fingertips tapped absently, rat-a-tat, across a dampened edge of the tablecloth.

He waited another's arrival. Far did not mind the elements, or the dark, or the discomfort of sitting in a forest, but he very much minded lack of punctuality. And the man he was supposed to meet was late.

At that moment, though, there was nothing for him to do but wait and listen and drum his fingers. In the space beyond his tarp, the drenching went on, and the more the rain fell, the more he became annoyed. He debated whether it might be worth a venture from his camp to look around, or whether he ought to just give up on the meeting altogether and head for the nearest tavern. But a loud clatter caught his attention. He peered around the trunk of the oak, shading his eyes from the rain, and shook his head with disgust.

Two gentlemen groped about the trees like lost, newborn calves.

Each held the other up, though it did nothing to keep them from tripping over one another in the dark. Every other step they took was followed with a stumble, or a twisted ankle, or a painful scrape from some unseen branch. They were both winded, and cursing, and the finery they had chosen to wear was as soaked as the forest floor. The one on the left was short-legged, round-bellied and, it was quite clear, ill-suited to the rigors of forestry. He wore a traveling hat that kept a channel of rainwater flowing more or less directly onto his bulbous nose. The one on the right looked much like his companion, but with the added disadvantage of carrying a long, unwieldy package of some kind wrapped in waxed canvas.

"Damnation!" the man on the left cursed. "Bastard's chosen a fine place for it, hasn't he? Why the devil wouldn't the Common have served?"

"Come, Dr. Danforth," replied the other. "The choice was his. We're almost there, I think. Just a few more yards. Mind that root – oh, dear."

A loud splash, and the one on the right stooped to lift the fallen Dr. Danforth from a leaf-covered puddle. He paused mid-hoist and squinted through the rain in Far's direction.

"I believe we may have arrived," he said. He called out to Far, "Sir. Sir! Are you there?"

Far shook his head.

YONDER & FAR: THE LOST LOCK

"I am," he answered.

The two men both startled like hares at the bray of a hound. Only when the echo of Far's voice had faded did they resume their trek through the brush. It took some doing, but once they had caught sight of the campfire, they managed a fairly straight line into the clearing.

Far did not bother to rise at their arrival, nor did he acknowledge their presence with any greeting. For a long, awkward moment, the two gentlemen shivered before him in complete silence. At last, the one who had first spotted him cleared his throat.

"We have arrived."

Far's eyes narrowed.

"So you have."

The man sniffed, made a feeble attempt at brushing the damp from his greatcoat, and angled his chin a few degrees higher. "And may I presume you are Captain Far?"

"You may," he answered.

"My name is Robert Coombs. I believe you received my card and letter?"

Far shrugged in such a way as to convey that a card and letter from Mr. Coombs could not possibly have intruded upon his memory.

"Well," Coombs continued, "I had them sent to your office on Merchants Row. In due form, with all the proprieties . . ." He stopped and made a pretense of inspecting Far's tarp and the surrounding clearing, though it was obvious there was nothing more to see. "Where is your second, sir?"

"My what?"

"Your second. Your appointed representative."

Far watched the rain fall upon Coombs with a blank, uncaring expression.

"Oh, this is absurd!" Danforth spat. "Look here, Far. If

you're not a gentleman, just own up to it already, apologize, and be on your way. No point carrying on the pretense."

"I'll be on my way," Far said evenly, "when we are finished here."

Before Danforth could reply, Coombs held a restraining hand to his shoulder:

"Doctor, please. Recall yourself. Allow me to fulfill my role in this affair." Turning to Far, he addressed him with a reproachful tone: "Your station is no trifling matter, sir. And to be perfectly candid, your conduct thus far raises questions about your station. No appointed second. No surgeon." He surveyed the clearing. "This . . . curious selection of grounds. Your ignorance of the Code Duello, the gentleman's code of dueling, would suggest . . . well, it is not for me to say or to speculate."

Far's fingers drummed, while Coombs strained to stand as tall as his meager limits would allow. He clasped the bundle he held to his chest, as if to shield it from an affront.

"Before one's honor can be satisfied," he declared solemnly, "one must hold a proper claim to it. As Dr. Danforth's second, I am duty bound to enquire of your status. You claim to be a captain. I ask you: in whose service? Not this Republic's, I can tell by your accent. Certainly not His Britannic Majesty's. How were you made a captain?"

Far paused a finger in midair where it hovered above the empty plate. An eyebrow tilted into a bemused expression. For the first time, the ghost of a smile broke across his lips, one which, if it had manifested itself more fully, might not have been an unpleasant thing to see. For a moment, his eyes caught the flickering glow of the campfire, like two wistful sapphires sparkling in the dark. A raindrop hissed as it fell in the fire's ashes. Far spoke softly, almost to himself:

"I was proclaimed," he said, "by my warriors when I flew my banner over the Mad Queen's carcass. I hoisted it over the bitch's dead eyes, right after I gutted her. My flag of bloodied skins flapped in the morning breeze, and the warriors blew their horns and hailed me as their lord captain. Then we feasted on her flesh in the sight of her followers." He stared at the burning logs for a while. "What a day that was."

There was a long silence broken only by the crackling fire and the patter of rainfall that was beginning to subside.

"Ahh, so you're German," Danforth concluded. "I don't think that counts."

"A lesser breed of gentleman," Coombs acknowledged, "but if the Hapsburgs made him an officer, he would have the right to an officer's honor under the Code Duello. Very well, Captain. I'll proceed through the customary forms."

Coombs cleared his throat once more and began to recite a vignette he had obviously rehearsed at some length:

"Sir," he said, "it is reported that yesterday morning in the common room of Holland's, in plain sight of several reputable gentlemen, you did bump into Dr. Danforth's person causing him to spill his coffee. An innocent accident, but you refused to beg his pardon. To the contrary, you insulted Dr. Danforth quite loudly in front of those assembled and proceeded to call the Doctor a vulgar term that no gentleman should ever express in public, nor any gentleman ever have to endure. If that were not enough, you then threatened Dr. Danforth with bodily harm of a most gruesome form that, as a man learned in the medical sciences, Dr. Danforth could only take particular umbrage at. Construing your threat as a challenge, Dr. Danforth has come to this place, the ground of your choosing, for the satisfaction and preservation of his sacred honor."

Far laced his fingers behind his head and said nothing. All he could think of was how much this man's voice reminded him of a goat's.

"This is a sad affair." Coombs heaved a sigh that sent a

small cloud of raindrops from his lips. "And needless. As a second, it is also my duty to mediate a peaceable resolution if one can be honorably obtained. Come, Captain Far. If you're a man who knows the horrors of battle, surely you must appreciate how senseless bloodshed would be over a matter as trifling as spilt coffee. As a gentleman, as a Christian, will you not spend the few words needed to bring about peace? All my principal seeks is for you to beg his pardon for bumping into him and apologize for the hard words you spoke to him in public. The loss to his honor far exceeded yours. Will you not repent of words said in the haste of anger and make an honorable peace?"

Far glared at Coombs and began to seriously wonder whether both of these louts were in fact nothing but livestock animals wearing men's skins. Coombs began to fidget. Without a word, Far rose from his chair and stepped out from beneath the tarp to stand at his full height. His footsteps thudded in the mud, his long limbs unfurled, like a tree coming to life, one that carried all the dark intentions of the surrounding woods. Far watched as Coombs and Danforth quavered beneath his shadow.

"You're wrong on three accounts," Far said quietly, counting off his fingers before Coombs. "First, I never bumped into this man. He bumped into me as he tried to leave. His fat ass was too wide for the aisle. Second, I am no Christian. Third, your man has lost no honor, any more than a nag could lose honor when the plowman has to give her the whip. As I told him before in the coffeehouse, I do not beg the pardon of livestock."

Danforth began to sputter in a high-pitched voice, for Far's insult apparently had the effect of not only renewing his ire, but a large measure of his courage. A warning tinge of pink rose in the gentleman's cheeks. He waved a chubby finger before Far's impassive face.

"You are an insolent pup! A foul-mouthed, gutter-born

23

Hessian blackguard! I'll make you eat those words!"

Far smiled, dipped his head, and replied,

"And I'll make a meal of you. I'm a bit peckish."

"Gentlemen, gentlemen!" Coombs called out for order. "Remember yourselves, please. The Code's forms must be followed . . ."

With that, Coombs proceeded to direct Captain Far and Dr. Danforth to opposite ends of the clearing. The rain had paused, and a few lonely shards of opaque light had managed to filter through the forest canopy; enough so that the men could see the ground and avoid the worst of the roots.

Coombs marched around the periphery, dropping handkerchiefs every few feet to mark the boundary of their field of battle. As he did so, he explained, "This duel shall be fought under the rules of gentlemanly combat – English gentlemen, I should say. Dr. Danforth has chosen sabers for weapons, which I shall produce momentarily. Combat commences and ends upon my signal. If one of you should trip, I shall call for quarter. The ground here is treacherous, I'll not have a slippery shoe deciding the winner. The *flèche* is permissible, but if you should strike anywhere beneath the waist, anywhere at all, it shall be deemed a forfeit. Do I make myself clear?"

Danforth scowled at Far who grew increasingly bored.

Coombs stepped into the center of the clearing where he had set the canvas package down upon an old oak stump. He untied a cord, flipped the waxy cloth back, and drew forth two long, curved blades. They were ornate, almost ostentatious, the blades polished to a mirror's sheen with guards that were carved to look like twining ivy. Coombs held each one by the handle and approached Far.

"What are these?"

"Sabers," Coombs replied stiffly. "You may choose whichever one you prefer."

Far scoffed at the sight of the weapons:

"Am I supposed to carve a chicken with this? Or pick my teeth?"

"Those sabers," Danforth's voice carried across the clearing, "were crafted for my father, who was a baronet, I'll have you know. That's Sheffield steel. The pommel's worth more than you. I've brought them down from my family's hearth where they've hung these many years—"

"They look like spits if you ask me. But if that's what you want to fight with, I suppose I'll take this one."

He scarcely bothered to inspect the blade but grabbed it brusquely and gave it a couple of perfunctory swipes in the air. It was a pretentious little utensil, he could tell right away. Covered in a film of dust, all polish, not a drop of blood to its credit, spending all its days hanging on this jackanape's wall.

Once Danforth had his own saber in hand, Coombs withdrew to the edge and addressed them a final time.

"I remind you both, this is a gentleman's duel for honor. You shall fight only to first blood. At the first *touché*, you shall each withdraw and give leave. One strike and the duel is ended."

"Yes, yes," Danforth croaked, "Let's get on with this already."

Far poked at the ground with the tip of his saber, made a swirling motion with some twigs and shook his head.

Coombs called out, "*En garde . . . allez!*"

Dr. Danforth crouched into a fencer's stance (as well as any man in his fifties, with a soaked set of pantaloons could be expected to manage). He crept forward two paces and awaited Far's approach. A cloud of mist curled about his head from his panting breaths. His tongue licked at his lips nervously.

Far let out a yawn.

The doctor took another cautious step toward him, his

feet squelching in the wet leaves. He twirled the blade before him, gave a jab, then set back in readiness to parry.

"Captain Far!" Coombs chided.

"Eh?"

"Your opponent awaits you, sir. If you would kindly engage him."

"Oh."

Far let out a tired breath through his nose and sauntered across the clearing. Such an easy gait, one might have thought he strolled through a park, a pleasant morning amble toward the waiting sword of Dr. Danforth. As for his own blade, Far let it bob along at his side, using it as a walking stick, which was probably all it would ever be good for.

Danforth's shoulders tensed. At Far's approach, his button eyes rounded, and a smirk broke the corner of his mouth. For this, he must have imagined, was going to be an easier match than he could have hoped for. Far was walking right into his blade with his chest, his whole body, completely open and defenseless. Just when Danforth drew his elbow in to strike, there was a quick and unexpected flash of light.

Far had flicked his hand from one side of Danforth's shoulders to the other.

A flash of steel. A glisten that almost seemed to lag behind the metal it accompanied. A soft sound of air and flesh rent neatly in two. Followed by the muted thud of something falling into the mud.

Far stood at his ease in the center of the clearing. He drew his saber up before him, turned it slowly, with a look of mild interest. A streak of crimson stained the edge of the blade.

"Well, what do you know," he breathed.

"Good . . . *God!*"

Coombs had collapsed right into a puddle of frigid

rainwater. His face blanched as white as his shirt, while his hands and knees shook uncontrollably, splashing his already well-soaked derriere. Coombs' mouth hung open wordlessly, bottom lip aquiver. He could only make a wheezing, gasping noise. High above, the wind rustled through the leaves.

"I may owe him an apology after all," Far continued, scarcely taking notice of Coombs' apoplexy. "Perhaps this could serve as a weapon. In a pinch. I still say it looks more skewer than sword. Perhaps it is both? I should like to see for myself."

"You-you-you've . . . *killed* him," Coombs managed. "C-Cut off his . . ."

It was so tedious, these people's habit of observing aloud the obvious.

"Yes," Far nodded. "I did."

"Good God . . . Good God . . . N-n-not proper. H-highly — n-not proper. Oh, God . . ."

"Eh?" An annoyed grimace clouded Far's face. He stepped toward Coombs, who recoiled, shuffling in the muck and letting out a piteous whimper. Far pointed the saber accusingly. "Here now, Coombs. You said one strike. Stop at first blood. Keep it above the waist. I followed every one of your damned rules. They're dense as Custom, but I followed all the rules, didn't I?"

"B-but you – cut off – *his head!*" his voice squealed. "How – how could you . . .?"

It struck Far as an especially odd question, and he answered Coombs with the most perplexed expression. His eyelids blinked thoughtfully, then he shrugged. Another quick step, and another, even quicker sweep of his blade, and Far replied:

"Thusly."

Another jowly, Bostonian's head tumbled to the forest floor. It was soon followed by a lifeless body. Dr. Danforth and Mr. Coombs, principal and second, were splayed on the soggy ground but a few feet apart, so close that the blood coursing from their severed necks soon mingled together. A silver tendril of steam rose in the cold air. The wind moaned. It stirred the collars of the dead men's cloaks, which flapped freely. The gaze of their owners' heads – one haughty, the other horrified – remained frozen, the raindrops streaked down their cheeks like tears.

Captain Far glanced at his blade thoughtfully. Only for a moment, though, for having made up his mind, he began to drag each of the bodies across the ground. When they were within ready reach of his campfire and spit, he put Danforth's saber to the test again and was, once again, pleasantly surprised by the blade's usefulness. For though its garish handle made it a bit awkward, the little sword quartered flesh and bone as nicely as a butcher's cleaver.

CHAPTER THREE

"One may draw a portal to travel between the realms as readily in Doldrums as anywhere else. There is an abundance of suitable trees here (live, matured oaks are the most preferable). One draws the door in the usual fashion, using the finger to demarcate the portal's boundary. Of course, the door should always be closed once it has been used. Although Custom prohibits making portals apart from a tree's bark, it is, in theory, possible to effectuate a window into elsewhere upon any surface in Doldrums. I would advise against doing so, however."
—Wherestone's *Commentaries on Custom*, page 18

The cabin of the hackney coach rattled loudly. Wedged within, his bottom planted firmly on a cushionless bench, Yonder sat with his feet spread wide apart and a hand on either side of the carriage walls to keep his balance. Even with the precautions, he was in danger of tumbling over. It was a poor ride by his usual standards; but he had been somewhat rushed to hire a driver. The cabin was wet, mildewed, rutted, not unlike the road they traveled. The air inside was intolerably warm.

He sat about a foot across from Far, who did not seem to mind the closeness or the discomfort. The carriage jostled, and his knees bumped sharply against Far's. Yonder loosened his cravat and smiled apologetically at Far, who responded with an annoyed expression and an exasperated sigh.

"I really don't know why you bothered to come out here," Far grumbled. "I was fine walking back to the office."

"We are not going back to the office." He rubbed the throb welling up in his knee. "There's no time—"

The coach took a sudden, perilous drop and Yonder's body seemed to float above his seat for a moment before it landed with a painful thud. "Damnation! Has he lost the road? Take care, there! As I was saying . . . we have a client. So there's no time to waste."

Far made no reply but gazed out the coach's window disinterestedly. They rattled along in relative silence, watching the countryside through a glass that was fogged over and looked to have been last cleaned with an oily rag. Yonder could just make out the last vestiges of the forest fade into the haze of the horizon. The land turned into pasture, monotonous squares of gray and green undulating by like an old quilt. At last, he spotted a broken well overgrown with ivy and a small road sign, the first familiar landmarks. They would be home within the hour.

"Would you care for lunch?" Yonder inquired, reaching into his coat. "I brought the makings for sandwiches."

Far stifled a belch.

"Thank you, no. I ate a big breakfast."

There was a loud crack outside, followed by a curse. The coachman swore at the horses for not spotting a pothole. The cabin began to sag.

"Where'd you find him?" Far asked.

Yonder leaned to his left to try to compensate for the new angle he found himself. "The Golden Goose. The tavern's filled with coachmen starved for work. What with all this rain lately, no one's been traveling much, it seems. That one," he tapped the wall behind him, "was willing to work for gin."

Far craned an ear.

"He's drunk as a lord."

"I'm sure he is."

They came upon the first run of houses that marked Boston and with them, thankfully, a roadway with a solid firmament. The ride began to smoothen.

"So who's this client?" Far asked with a yawn.

Yonder brightened in an instant.

"One who orbits within the Queen's innermost circle. I don't claim to know her well. But I do know her star is bright. Trust me on that. She is well placed – exceedingly well placed – to bring us back into her Majesty's favor."

Far nodded impassively.

"Here in Doldrums," Yonder continued, "she calls herself Otherly."

"She's left already, then."

"Of course. For obvious reasons. However," Yonder said and leaned forward with a conspiratorial grin, "she gave a retainer – something of herself. This lady is thoroughly invested with us now."

"Well, well." Far extended his hand in a mocking gesture. "Congratulations. I never thought this Custom counseling enterprise of yours would amount to much. But here we are . . . in a hackney. On the edge of Suffolk County. Why, we're practically home."

Yonder could never be certain when his companion indulged in sarcasm or was in one of his tempers. The difference was often subtle, and he had no wish to provoke Far's ire.

"Oh, now," Yonder began cautiously, "I might not go so far as to say that . . . not yet, at least. We've a bit of work ahead of us." Yonder tapped his fingers excitedly at the prospect of their coming labor. "I've already laid the groundwork. As much as I could from the office. But if I've read my Wherestone correctly, we'll require some outside assistance. Certainly, for the first part of what I have in mind."

"And whose assistance are we seeking again?"

"I told you, she calls herself Blessed Mary. Though I doubt she has any connection to the Church of Rome. More of a muddled pagan, probably. She's a fortune-teller. And a bit unhinged." Yonder tried to reposition himself on the bench just as the hackney hit a rut in the ground. He rubbed at the stinging bump on his temple. "But I'm sure we can make good use of her."

Far could not decide which he despised more, the mass of trinkets littered throughout the apartment or the apartment's owner. He stood stiffly within the doorway of a filthy suite of rooms that had been neither scrubbed, nor dusted, nor aired out for what must have been the better part of fifty years. He stood for he could find no chair within the common room that didn't teem with cheap bottles, feathers, broken bits of twine, and the like. The floor was little better, though at least a heavy film of dust lent it some sense of uniformity. Scores of glass and ceramic bric-a-brac twirled from wires that were strung from the ceiling rafters, several of which kept the captain stooped. A tipped over cauldron barred the door from opening all the way. Far kept his hands in his pockets so that he would not have to touch anything and sighed.

32

Here he was. In a woman's apartment above an opium den, in the South End of Boston. With Yonder. The glow he had felt from his duel faded fast.

He scanned the room. A fire smoldered from a hearth at the far end. A slate board hung from one of the hearth's bricks. Its blurred chalk letters announced services for "Oracles," "Fortunes," "Séances," and "Fertility Rites," at escalating prices. Nearby a rise of clutter from within the debris indicated the presence of a table. Seated there, beneath the empty gaze of a painted cow skull, was Yonder, his teeth flashing like pearls in the light of the fire. Across from him, a squat, earthy woman with a mop of frizzled, mouse-colored hair smiled benignly. She nodded her head in agreement at whatever it was Yonder had said. She must have noticed him lingering in the open doorway. The woman's round face pinched with annoyance.

"For heaven's sake, come or go already." She waved at Far with a clanging set of bracelets indicating both directions simultaneously. "In or out. Nothing's worse for a séance than a half-open doorway."

"Quite right, Madam Faulkner," Yonder agreed. "Captain Far, pray close the door behind you, and come and join us. There's room for you by the hearth over here." He tapped a spot of rock that was covered over in soot.

Far felt his jaw clench. "Certainly," he replied. He tiptoed his way across the floor to join them.

As he approached, Yonder introduced him to Miss Mary Faulkner. She sniffed her delight and straightened a cloak that had the look and wear of an old stage prop. Besides the cloak, she wore a faded blue apron, which covered a shapeless, gray dress that was much too long. She had a habit, when she was not speaking, of constantly probing her tongue across her teeth, as if in search of some long-lost crumb. And every motion she made, no matter how slight, was accompanied by the tinkling of countless little baubles and glass jewels festooned all over her person. Far was instantly irritated with the woman and offered her the curtest of bows as he slid down into his seat.

"In this sacred circle," she announced, "I am called Blessed Mary." Her necklaces jangled as something occurred to her. "Or the Horned God's Consort. No . . . better stick with Blessed Mary."

Yonder dipped his head.

"As you wish, Madam – uh, Blessed Mary."

"You have five dollars?"

"Of course." Yonder reached for his pocket purse and produced five silver coins which he dropped into her waiting palm.

Mary pocketed the money and motioned for silence, though neither Yonder nor Far had made a sound. With a flourish of her hands, she brought forth a velvet bag from some hidden crevice in the table's clutter. When she had managed to open it, she began to spread the bag's contents before them. She laid each item in no particular order or scheme but with all the solemnity of a priest consecrating the Eucharist. There was a rabbit's foot, a brass crucifix, a number of old corn kernels, a shilling coin, four cards from Etteilla's tarot deck, and a poorly drawn charcoal portrait of Voltaire. There were also several blackened chips that Far suspected had once been hen's beaks. While Yonder surveyed the eclectic offerings, Mary lit three tallow candles and placed one before each of her guests and the last on top of a stack of pamphlets just beneath her chin. She muttered a soft incantation with each lighting. When she had finished, she blew out the taper and folded her hands solemnly on top of the crucifix.

"You've come from far away," she declared.

Far sighed, while Yonder eagerly replied that was just so.

34

She fixed the candle in front of her so that it would cast her face in an eerier light. Her eyelids fluttered, and she lifted the palms of her hands high over her head so that her bracelets clattered down to her elbows. One of the hen's beaks spilled to the floor.

"You have come," her voice rose dramatically, "because you seek something."

"Right again!"

"Well aren't you a clever heifer," Far quipped.

"Silence in the sacristy." Mary tried to sound ominous, though she was plainly flustered by the interruption so early in her performance. Far shook his head.

"Two strangers show up at the door to your shithole," he said, "and you figure that they're looking for something – how bloody clever you are."

"Silence!"

"Captain, please," Yonder chided. "You must forgive the captain. He's a bit of a skeptic."

"A nonbeliever?" She began to gather up some of the clutter, as if to leave. "I don't know if I can help you then. Discordant pieties could trouble the divining spirits. What with Mars' alignment—"

"Stay, please. I beg you, Blessed Mary." He gave Far a warning look. "He'll be quiet, I promise."

Two more dollars passed from Yonder to Mary, and the stars and spirits were sufficiently propitiated.

"And you were almost entirely correct," Yonder continued. "As it happens, we are actually looking for some*one*."

"I know you are." She paused and cast a challenging smile at Far. "I know all. The spirits speak to their own . . . Hark! Give heed . . . They are speaking to me now . . ."

With that, Mary fell into a fit of sorts. What began with tremors in her hands soon became contortions of her arms that gradually spread up and down the length of her body. She threw her head back, and loosed a long, husky note that could have signaled either pain or ecstasy, and which, by the time it had finished, had sent a train of spittle over Monsieur Voltaire's sardonic smirk. Throughout the performance, her jewelry rattled. Her mouth let out more groans and more saliva. She shook like a pudding until she nearly fell to the floor.

The spectacle ran on for nearly ten minutes, and Far had never known time to draw on so slowly. By the time the fire in the hearth had burned itself out, he could no longer contain himself.

He clenched his fingers in a choking gesture, and whispered at Yonder, "Can I just end this nonsense now?"

Yonder seemed to consider the proposal for a moment. "If she's still . . . oh, wait, hold on."

Mary's fit seemed to have come to an end. Her head lolled and suddenly lifted. She fixed a few loose strands of hair that hung before her face, revealing a tired but serene expression.

"The inner sanctuary is consecrated," she said with a heavy breath. "The portico cleansed. I have been given the light of the three wands to guide my path to the feet of Artemis. Mars will vouchsafe my passage. I am the line of the pentacle. The arc of the golden compass. The curve of the heavens. Follow me to truth."

Mary folded her hands expectantly.

"Ah. How, um—" Yonder struggled for an appropriate response. "How nice," he said at last.

"What is the name of the one you seek?" she prompted.

"His name? He calls himself John Wylde."

"John. Wylde." Mary intoned each word.

"Yes, but that really doesn't mean anything. You could just as easily call him Oliver Shambles, or Abigail Titmice, or Pontius Pilate—"

"John Wylde," she repeated and held her fingertips to her temples in a posture of concentration. Her eyelids quivered shut.

Far started to get up from the hearth.

"Now?" he asked, reaching for her exposed neck.

"Sit down," Yonder hissed at him. To Mary he said, "I say, Blessed Mary? Can you hear me?"

"I hear all."

It clearly pained Yonder to intrude upon her performance, but he pressed on.

"This really is a lovely ritual. We're quite enchanted, aren't we, Captain Far? Well, at least I am, but, um . . . your wondrous oracular power is not what has brought us to your abode."

An eye popped open to regard Yonder.

"You needn't bother with all this." He gestured at the splay of props she had laid out. "If you'll forgive my saying so, it was quite unnecessary. We desired only to secure your assistance."

One of Mary's eyebrows arched imperiously. She drew her arms tight across her chest.

"My assistance?"

"Yes. You see I have my own method of divination, paltry though it may be, which requires the—"

"I am the granddaughter of a Salem witch!" Mary gave her cloak a loud, meaningful shake. "I have traveled to Fae. Learned lore from a druid in County Clare. Completed a spirit quest with a Nashaway shaman. President Washington once sought my counsel. I do not play the second fiddle to anyone! Certainly not to a dabbler."

Yonder held up two placating hands. A soothing smile quickly followed.

"But of course you wouldn't! I would never deign to ask this of the Blessed Mary . . . at the price I've paid thus far."

Yonder reached for his coat pocket, and there was the

clink of a great many more silver dollars. The indignancy that had flared so briefly was just as quickly mollified. Her shoulders relaxed, her arms went wide and, to Yonder's apparent surprise, she reached across the table to pull him into an embrace. The side of his cheek turned from orange to pink, as she pressed it against hers.

"Very, very kind, Madam," he sputtered. "Too kind of you, really. Thank you. There we are." As they disentangled, another eight dollars changed hands, and Mary inquired how she might be of help, any help at all, to the gentleman's prognostication.

"If you will indulge my reading for but a moment, I must consult my material. Captain Far would you mind bringing that candle closer to my chair?"

The little flame guttered as Far pushed the tallow candle next to Yonder. Its soft light brought Yonder's features out of the falling shadows and revealed an expression of concentration. He reached into his coat and brought out a small, solemn-looking book.

Of course he would have brought the damned book, Far thought.

The tome had an emerald-colored binding. There was no lettering anywhere on the book's face or spine, but it had a curious fixture upon the cover – or, more accurately, *within* the cover.

It was an oak leaf.

A green oak leaf, as alive as any that ever grew from a branch, and yet still as much a part of the book as any ink that had ever been written upon a page. Its jagged edge caught a shimmer of candlelight that reflected a faint, olive glow. Mary let out a gasp at the sight of it, but quickly collected herself. Yonder's fingers pried the book open to a section that had been marked with a twining ribbon of ivy. He thumbed through the pages.

"What is that?" Mary breathed.

"What, this?" Yonder replied distractedly. "Just an old book I keep around."

"It's practically his lover," Far jeered. Yonder made a face at him but didn't disagree.

As Yonder turned the pages, a small cloud of yellow pollen wafted into the air. Yonder's eyes darted down, up and about in a circle, wandering in no real pattern of any kind, his face alight with excitement.

For her part, Mary stared at it dumbly. Far knew that the script written on the pages was of a language only their kind could read – though few, besides Yonder, ever did because this particular book was the most tediously boring one ever written in his realm.

"Ah, here we are!" Yonder declared. He leaned into the book, so close that his nose brushed against the paper, as he read softly to himself. Mary's curiosity must have overcome her, but when she stepped to catch a peek at the book's contents, Yonder slammed the pages shut and began to survey the cottage room.

"Since you're up, Mary, could you please fetch a glass of water, a clear one if you have it."

"Did you say a glass of water?" She sounded disappointed.

"Yes. And that hand mirror over there in the corner."

Mary shuffled across the room, heedless of what she knocked over, and soon returned with a chipped glass jar that was half-filled with a liquid which, it could only be said, was relatively clear. She had also brought the mirror Yonder had pointed to. It was in a gilded, gold-painted frame that looked suited for a brothel. She set them both on the table with a clatter.

"Thank you," Yonder said. He tucked the book away into the recess of his coat pocket. "Now, this is where it becomes a bit challenging. We shall need a second mirror to face the first. Then while keeping the water betwixt the two,

I shall . . . well, I shall do my best. Blessed Mary, can you rummage up a second mirror and place it here? So that it faces thus? Perhaps we could use that little portrait to hold it upright."

Mary seemed quite eager to scurry after Yonder's directions. She hurried into her bedroom to retrieve another mirror. As soon as she was out of hearing, Far broached a cautious step toward the table. He whispered from the side of his mouth.

"I don't know how the devil this-this—"

"Custom. It's all covered under Custom. We are trying to crack a window, so to speak."

"Fine. It's Custom." He jerked his thumb over his shoulder. "Does it require having one of them lugging around mirrors? I thought we were supposed to avoid those. And how is she possibly any use in this work?"

Yonder draped his arms behind the back of his chair. "That is an old, hackneyed notion. If you'd bother to read Wherestone, you would know that mirrors are perfectly safe, so long as they are handled properly. As for Miss Faulkner, yes, she is nine parts an idiot. But the remaining part will be quite useful to our purpose here. She has eyes, and ears, and a mind that can be utilized, with a little direction. I am quite optimistic this will work."

Far scowled. "The last time you said that to me," he said coldly, "I ended up banished in Doldrums."

"Completely different circumstance. Apples and oysters. No one could have foreseen how faithless that scoundrel would – oh, let's not have this argument again. Look, here she is."

Mary had returned to the common room brandishing a wicked shard of polished glass. She smiled and jabbered on about how fortunate Yonder was to have elicited her aid with his work. Her skill, her "calling," would assure the success of this metaphysical endeavor – whatever it might be.

She brushed past the gentlemen and elbowed clear a corner of the table, sending a small avalanche of various trinkets to the floor. She propped the mirrors more or less as she had been instructed. The hand mirror was against a vase, the broken piece of dressing mirror glass was balanced against the frame of the charcoal Voltaire.

She placed them so they faced each other. The two surfaces reflected an endless repetition of a stain on a tabletop, a sputtering candle's flame, and the Frenchman's naughty smirk.

Yonder dabbed at a film of sweat that broke across his forehead. Far watched from behind, unblinking, and not at all liking the feel of those mirrors. Whatever Yonder said, mirrors were dangerous. Everyone knew that. For her part, Mary seemed oblivious to her guests' discomfiture. She adjusted the mirrors' angles this way and that, as if she knew of some precise measurement that was required, until Yonder intervened.

"I believe you've got it placed perfectly, Mary."

She nudged the broken piece a quarter of an inch to the right.

"Now it is perfect," she said.

"Just so. And now, if you will kindly place the water in between."

Mary set it down, and the hazy glass joined the procession into infinity.

Yonder licked his lips. "I must ask that you please step back and remain perfectly still. And don't touch anything."

Mary nodded but pulled closer to Yonder. Far laid a hand on her shoulder, and she came to a halt. For good measure, he gave her shoulder a pinch, and Mary squealed in pain.

"Thank you, Captain," Yonder nodded.

Yonder reached into the kerchief pocket of his coat, but instead of a gentleman's silk, produced a small vial of salt.

He held it up to his nose and inhaled deeply, though as Far knew it was not at all a savory odor for their kind. Yonder held the salt out before him and gave it a long, studied glare. His head cocked to the side, he brought it to his ear. He gave the vial a rub between his thumb and forefinger. At last, he poured the contents into the water between the mirrors.

For a long while, they all watched a glass jar with a cloud of salt floating within like a cloud.

They watched, and nothing happened.

Another minute passed. A burnt-out log in the hearth collapsed in the ashes. Outside, a lone mockingbird began a mindless pattern of chirps.

"Blessed Mary," Yonder said at last. "I believe I can try my craft. Would you be so kind as to lean your head between those mirrors? Then look into one of them, it doesn't matter which, and tell me if you see anything – besides your lovely countenance."

Mary shrugged, but before she could do as she was bidden, Yonder made her pause.

"Might I whisper something to you first?"

He leaned across the corner of the table and breathed into her ear.

While Mary gaped at Yonder, he made a gesture with his hand. It was a familiar one to Far, though he had never seen it done on anything other than a tree trunk. Yonder drew a rectangle upon Mary's forehead. He gently guided her head down onto the table and angled her face so that she could gaze into her hand mirror.

A violent, horrible shriek rent the room.

"Don't let her fall," Yonder ordered.

Far hurried over to Mary's side and hoisted her slumping body upright.

She had nearly collapsed. Her body shook violently. A trail of saliva ran from her lips. Her dull eyes were ablaze and rolled about madly. Yet, at the same time, she listened for something, as if there were a distant strain that she wanted nothing more than to hear.

Tears welled in her eyes. Far hoisted her roughly back into the position Yonder had her in before.

"It may feel uncomfortable," Yonder said to her in a kindly tone. "To your people, I suppose it would be like becoming stuck in a doorway, with the door slamming shut. Unceasingly slamming shut."

"Oh, God," Mary wept. "I can't bear it . . . I can't."

"Look, my dear. Look with your eyes for just a moment."

Far drew closer. This was a spectacle he had not at all expected.

"I-I-I can't," she sobbed.

"Of course you can," Yonder replied calmly. "You're the granddaughter of a witch."

"Ooaahh . . ."

"What do you see?"

Mary quaked feverishly in her chair. Her tiny reflection shone pale in one mirror's surface. As Far watched, he caught a glimpse, as if from the corner of his eye, of an image in the other mirror. A glow. A windowed building made of red bricks. With a cupola. And a golden grasshopper blowing in the wind. When he tried to study it, though, it disappeared.

"Help me," Mary whispered hoarsely.

Yonder clasped his hands together.

"I can't help you just yet, Mary. But once you tell me what you see . . . it will all be over shortly. What do you see?"

She gasped for air.

Her strangled voice replied between gulps of breath, "It's . . . it . . . looks like F-Faneuil . . . Faneuil Hall."

Mary's head sank to the table. Her eyes remained open, though, unblinking, riveted to the dirty glass of water, the mirrors, and the vision that held them together.

Far let out a long, low whistle. "Well done. So your man's right here in the middle of—"

"Boston." The smile on Yonder's lips curled as high and as crooked as a jack-o-lantern's. "Our very own Boston."

CHAPTER FOUR

"The gods enjoy a peculiar life in Doldrums. Custom serves to veil their presence and affairs (which, I am told, is very much to their preference). This obscurity has had a curious effect on the local denizens. For some reason it inspires them to fervor. And to writing—the most bizarre, convoluted, and voluminous claptrap – which is neither close to the mark nor, in my opinion, worth the candle to read."

—Wherestone's *Commentaries on Custom*, page 30

Faneuil Hall.

Two floors of Georgian pretension, it had never fit in with the neighborhood. Too grandiose with its brickwork and copula to serve as a proper marketplace, but too mean and cramped for proper society to ever congregate, Faneuil Hall had become that most pointless of places in civilization: it had become a venue. A venue that was filled to bursting since the drenching rain had come to an end.

Yonder and Far had spent the past fortnight within its walls hoping to catch the scent of a fellow countryman traveling under the name of John Wylde.

From the moment the hall's doors were unlocked each morning until their closing late at night, the gentlemen took shifts, one on the bottom floor, the other upstairs, and kept a watch out for their man. Mingling among the crowds, lingering in the back seats along the walls day after day, they watched and listened to the sundry of Boston's middle-class drone on endlessly about . . . whatever it was Bostonians droned on about. Debate societies, soirees, prayer meetings, essay readings, it all began to blend together. The only break from the tedium was when, each afternoon, Yonder and Far would share a lunch before they returned to their reconnoitering.

It quickly became a drudgery, even for one of Yonder's almost limitless patience.

For Far, it was unendurable. By the third day before Christmas, Yonder began to detect those telltale signs that a foul temper had settled upon his partner. Far sat on a threadbare sofa in a small antechamber devouring the last of a cold lunch, a dark scowl etched in his face. He clinked his knife against a pewter plate, shoved in a mouthful of a basted hen, and clanked the metal again, as if he were trying to replicate the sound of a sword banging against a shield. Yonder sat next to him, twiddling his fingers, watching his partner nervously. A gray bar of sunlight fell between them from a window slit.

The room's only door was closed, but outside the clamor of chairs being rearranged and two crowds trying to exchange places cut through the wall. Far smacked the flat of the knife's blade hard against his plate, gouging the edge.

"I believe that will be the Anabaptists gathering now," Yonder observed. "Yes, I can hear Parson MacLean. He's calling his flock together. I'm fairly sure it's him."

Far ripped the last bite of chicken from a drumstick and tossed the bone at a baseboard. Yonder gave it a disapproving glance.

"So perhaps we ought to resume our investigation? Now that you're finished with your lunch."

Far did not move. He stared at the frost-covered window.

Yonder rose. "Shall we?"

"No," Far murmured.

"I beg your pardon?"

"No," he repeated louder. He fixed Yonder with a hard look. "I can't take it anymore."

Yonder offered an indulgent nod.

"You're strained. I understand completely. The Doldrums air has a tendency to induce lethargy in some—"

"It's not that," he snapped. Far craned his head and gestured toward the door. "Listen to them . . ."

A loud chorus of "Amens" echoed from the outer hall. It was followed by sustained applause.

"How they *bleat*. Like sheep – Bleh, bleh-bleh, bleh! Ach, if I could kill every last one of them, I would. If only to give me—" He thumped the heel of his boot against the wooden floorboards with each word. "Some – damned – peace – and– *quiet!*"

No one seemed to have heard him, for the noise outside continued unabated. Yonder started to reach toward his companion to offer a sympathetic pat but caught himself. Such overt sentiment could bring the poor fellow to blows in his present state. Yonder changed his tack. He lifted his chin, clasped his hands behind his back, and assumed what he hoped would pass for a militant expression.

"Captain Far, must I remind you of your duty? Our client has entrusted us with her affair. We have work to do, sir."

Far's eyes narrowed, his nostrils flared. He made a

sweep with his arm, sending his plate crashing against the wall next to the chicken bone. "You call this *work*? Slogging through Doldrums so some jilted bitch can find her court whore. What kind of work is this?"

Yonder leaned close and dropped his voice low.

"The kind that could finally gain us our freedom to leave Doldrums. A place you've complained about aplenty."

Far had the look of a man poised to strike, but Yonder was able to keep himself steady.

"Or perhaps you have a better prospect to secure our way home, one that you've not shared with me? I'd be eager to hear of it."

A fire smoldered behind Far's eyes, one that was on the cusp of burning over.

"Fine," Far said at last. "But I'm done skulking in Faneuil Hall. Sitting around on our asses all day in hopes we might overhear something. We're going to try my way now."

Yonder frowned. "What do you mean?"

Far leered at the doorway. "Round up a couple of the regulars and bring them in here. I'll have a little chat with them. If anyone's seen this Wylde fellow . . ." He flexed his fingers. "I'll find out."

Yonder shook his head emphatically.

"Too soon for that kind of thing." He paused to find the right turn of phrase and brightened at what he came up with. "We mustn't flush the quarry before the snare is readied."

"What the devil are you talking about?"

"If you start thumping heads about and hollering 'Fetch me John Wylde!' 'Fetch me John Wylde!' he'll surely get wind of it. And then he'll simply leave Doldrums."

Far frowned, as if offended by such an obvious point.

"Listen to me." Yonder smiled indulgently. "This part of the endeavor is delicate, more suited to my talents. Rely on me. For the time being."

There was a stirring of muffled voices in Faneuil Hall.

It gradually subsided as one voice – an angry one, with a Scottish lilt – rose to bring about order. Yonder glanced over Far's shoulder at the window of the antechamber. The first snowflakes began to pile on the sill. Far's shoulders sagged.

"One more day," Far said as he rose wearily. The sofa creaked as he stood. He rubbed his temples and ran his fingers through the length of his dark hair.

Yonder opened the door, and the roar of an Anabaptist worship service washed into their space. He lifted himself onto his tiptoes to offer a word of encouragement as Far brushed past him.

"Chin up, my friend. It's the only way we'll survive here."

The chairs had been arranged like a horseshoe, three rows deep, but not nearly enough for the crowd that had gathered in the formal ballroom. Women mostly, and a sprinkling of men, they were all dressed in starched, somber Sunday finery. Most of the throng stood, even those who had laid claim to a seat, as if to forsake the venial sin of modest comfort during the penance of a church service.

The faithful in Faneuil Hall's grandest rented room swayed, though their knees creaked painfully. A Mrs. Crowder addressed the assembly. She conveyed to her fellow congregants that they were all in imminent danger of hell fire. Flames, which Crowder illustrated by flitting her fingers uncomfortably close to her neighbors, were licking at their groins.

"Who can keep us on the path of righteousness?"

A chorus of replies answered her.

"Reverend MacLean!"

"God's chosen!"

"The Reverend! God bless the Reverend!"

The gentleman who was the subject of the crowd's shouting, MacLean, quietly stood and cast a long meaningful glare around him. As one, the entire gathering grew still. He buttoned a black waistcoat around a trim torso and strode to the empty podium. A set of eyeglasses balanced on the end of his nose reflected whiteness, hiding his eyes.

"Brothers and sisters," his Scottish brogue was all the more piercing among the flat, heavy-tongued Yankee accents of the congregation. "The Holy Spirit is movin' amongst us. Yes, indeed. Can ye not feel it?"

They all responded that indeed they could.

MacLean continued, "but now we must turn to the matter of music. 'Tis a topic indeed worthy of prayerful consideration. On the one hand, it is meet and right to lift our voices in songs – about Christ's righteous judgment, an' the pains He will inflict upon the damned. We may also sing certain psalms, which would not be displeasing to the Lord. But the venal playin' of musical notes upon instruments is a different matter entirely. A tune without the Word of God to sanctify it? What else can such a noise be, but the trumpet of the devil!"

Once again, the flock voiced their unwavering agreement with the shepherd.

"Why, just the other day," MacLean's voice rose with indignation, "in this hall, in this very room, I heard tale of the perfidy of profane music. A certain man, a Negro of all things, played a flute in here an' it had a most diabolical effect upon the sinners who heard him. 'Twas like a sorcery. The men staggerin' about the floor like drunkards. Women swoonin' in the aisles . . ."

Yonder jabbed an elbow into Far's side to gain his attention.

"What?" Far snapped.

Yonder held a silencing finger before his lips and whispered.

"This may be worth a listen . . ."

"An' the whole time, he's struttin' about," the minister's spit rained down on the front row in a flurry, "dark soul burnin' in his dark skin. Playin' that cursed witch pipe on his flapping, lecherous lips like a modern-day Pan. I heard he led that poor audience down the path to the bowels of hell. I heard – heard, mind you – that he had the whole lot of them . . . *dancing!*"

A low wail swept across the chamber. No less than four women curled onto the floor as if in pain..

But Yonder did not care a whit about that. He had only one thought, something the parson had said: *'Twas like a sorcery.*

"Come, Captain." Yonder rose. "I believe we've picked up the scent."

In the commotion, no one noticed the two quiet strangers who had lingered by the fern pot slip between the shadows to leave the hall. As Yonder and Far made a hasty exit, MacLean's voice cried over the cacophony.

"Hear me, oh Israel! Mrs. Crowder, if you'll write this down. Hear me! A revelation for God's people. It is settled that the wickedness of instrumental music . . ."

The sun had dipped behind the rooftops. A walled off alley separated the backside of a line of warehouses, taverns and hoteliers' houses. The last of the daylight fell into a soft, amber tint. Yonder trudged on, his pant legs hoisted above his shins to keep them from getting any more soaked than they already were. All about him, a dusting of snow fell steadily, mixed with the sleet puddles and made the cobblestones treacherously slick. The further he went, the more the place reeked of rotting hops and urine. Yonder shook the ice from one of his shoes and tried to pick up his pace.

"Men of study seldom have occasion for exercise," he panted to himself.

In the distance ahead, he caught a glimpse of Far's silhouette. His long legs moved at a steady stride, darting around the alley's turns and twists without the least trouble. Nothing seemed to slow the captain's heeled boots.

The man is part hound.

"Captain," Yonder called out. "A moment . . ."

Far paused and threw an annoyed glance over his shoulder.

"He's making for the south side," he yelled back. "Come on."

"Yes—" Yonder puffed, "good places there – more discrete – ooaah . . ."

"Hurry up."

Yonder bent over. His sides felt like they were gripped in vices. He dripped sweat in the frigid cold. He waved his partner on.

"Stop him . . . I'll catch up."

Without a noise, Far disappeared. As the snow and the soft din of the town's alley life began to settle over him, Yonder propped himself against the side of a haberdashery store for a moment of rest. Every breath he drew sent pinpricks in his chest. Slowly, however, his heart's drumbeat began to subside, his lungs felt less labored, the aches in his legs and feet became more bearable. He thought he might chance pressing on. But he felt a curious sensation come crawling like a worm from within his chest.

It was a tingling. Faint, neither painful nor particularly pleasant, but it seemed to reverberate with his breathing. He drew himself up, turned around, and bent his head close to the side of the building to inspect the wall he had leaned against, as if it might have passed some malady on to him.

Plain, ordinary brickwork was all he saw. Covered with a thin sheen of frost. Yonder's mouth puckered in thought. He gave one of the bricks a tap with his fingertip.

"Something in the air here, no doubt . . ." he said aloud. "No need to worry—"

He coughed. A small one, little more than a clearing of the throat, but it rattled whatever had settled in his chest.

Yonder looked about his dingy surroundings. The gray-tinged icicles dangling off the gutters from the doorways reflected gloom in the dusk's dying light. Heaps of ice and slush were shoveled over trash piles. A smoldering fire burned itself out in a barrel. A mangy cat huddled close to a stove pipe. Yonder tilted his head and watched the vapor of his breaths rising. Rising then disappearing. While the snow fell on him, silently, relentlessly.

A shudder rippled down his spine, and with it, a renewed sense of urgency. He set out after Far at a much-hurried pace, trotting, as best as his short legs could, working his stocky frame over and around the obstacles that Far had managed so easily. At last, he came to an alley, which opened up into an oblong courtyard. It was small, lit by a lone streetlight that revealed the shadowed fronts of a collection of shabby buildings. The windows were mostly dark even though night was coming on, and the doors were all closed. *Likely barred as well*, Yonder suspected.

The closest doorway bore a tavern sign, which was really just a warped bit of ship's planking someone had hung from two rusty hooks. Flecks of blue and gold paint revealed a passable depiction of St. Edward's crown offset by a sable hairbrush.

There were two other men in the courtyard: Far and the man he held by the throat.

That had been a disappointment, Far thought ruefully.

He stood beneath the globe of a streetlight, with his quarry squirming in his grasp. It had been a decent enough chase, once the man knew he was being followed, but he hadn't offered the slightest fight. Not even when Far had backed him into a corner. Not a punch, not a kick. Nothing but a slurred and desperate plea for mercy. The man might have a fire in the pulpit, but he had porridge in his guts.

The Reverend MacLean dangled from Far's hand, his gangly legs hung limply in the air beneath him.

"Oh, good," Yonder greeted Far, "you've found him."

"He's not answering my questions." Far shook his head. He clenched MacLean's neck tighter. For a man who should have been on the verge of strangulation, MacLean made surprisingly little noise.

"I suspect that's because he finds himself short of air," said Yonder. "Note the purpling in the cheeks. The glazed eyes. The tongue lolling helplessly around the lips."

"What, the devil got your tongue?" Far teased. He hoisted his captive a few inches higher so that the top of MacLean's head was almost in the streetlight's flame.

"I wonder," Yonder continued, "if the gentleman might be more inclined for conversation indoors."

"It's quicker this way," Far answered. "He'll tell us what he knows before the end."

"Yes, but I fear that won't be very much at the rate he's expiring. Please, Captain. Let's at least try my way first."

Yonder's way. It would surely be tedious. But Far had to allow that MacLean would indeed be dead soon, and that it seemed unlikely he would share anything useful before his passing. Reluctantly, Far set him down and loosed his grip. As soon as he did, MacLean crumpled to his knees, gasping for air like a newly caught fish on a wharf. The waft of cheap spirits made Far's nose crinkle.

"Th-the devil!" MacLean croaked.

He curled into a ball in the snow, rubbing his neck with one hand, pointing at Far with the other.

"K-Keep 'im away from me!" MacLean tried to shrink away, but Far took one menacing step and the parson froze in place. To Far's disgust, MacLean began to weep in a slurred brogue.

"Devil – devil he is . . . he's-a – he's a devil, come to *kill* me. Oh, God save me . . ."

Yonder crouched down next to the disheveled minister and slid an arm around MacLean's shoulders. He helped him to his feet.

"Now, now, Captain Far meant you no harm whatsoever." He fixed MacLean's collar and paused at the sight of the welts swelling around the bottom of his neck. "Well, no lasting harm," he corrected himself. He tidied MacLean's coat, brushed the snow off, and smiled. "Truth is, we would very much like to buy you a drink."

"Y-you . . . you-wish to, to wha—"

Wisps of MacLean's hair stuck out in odd angles, shining silver in the luminescence of the streetlight's candles.

"I . . . I dunnae drink," he said reflexively, as he straightened his glasses on his nose.

Yonder let out a fruity laugh.

"Ho, ho, that is rich! My dear sir! A Scotsman who won't imbibe? On someone else's tab?" Yonder leaned close to MacLean and gave a long sniff.

"It's penny whiskey," Far pronounced.

"Indeed," Yonder agreed.

Before MacLean could protest his innocence, Far thrust a silver flask that had fallen out of the minister's coat pocket into his limp hands.

"You've been drinking swill," Far said.

"A gentleman such as yourself deserves better fare," Yonder added. "Come. Won't you join us in the Crown? We'll share a proper bottle." He winked at MacLean, and tried out his best Scottish accent, "Aye, but sure it'll be grand!"

As Yonder chuckled at his joke, Far brought his hand down on MacLean's shoulder and let the weight of it make clear that this was not an invitation he should decline. MacLean trembled all over as Far half-carried, half-guided him toward a tavern door. There would be no question that Reverend MacLean would be anything other than delighted to join Far and his companion for a drink.

The strangers bunched around the corner table by the stove would have elicited stares, and more than a few disapproving murmurs, in any establishment more reputable than the Crown & Comb – which is to say, any public place under honest management. Among the denizens of the Crown, however, it was nothing of note. To them, the sight of a frightened maypole dressed in a minister's garb, what looked to be a confidence man, and a hired thug sharing a bottle together was entirely unremarkable.

For the Crown had served drinks, and related services, to Boston's passers-through almost since the town's founding; and it generally catered to those who desired discretion but did not necessarily have the means to pay for it. It had a long, narrow public hall with a low ceiling which seemed to encourage folk to drop their voices, and a set of grimy walls that had never been washed. There were a scattering of tables and not nearly enough lamps. The air inside was always thick with the haze of burnt charcoal and bad tobacco. It felt a trifle warm, despite the night's snow.

"Another glass, Mister MacLean?" Yonder offered.

"Reverend, if you please," he stifled a belch. "Aye, I'll have another. Jus' one more, though."

An arc of amber liquid flowed from the bottle's spout and filled MacLean's glass to the brim with the tavern's best bourbon.

"Your health, Misser Yonder." MacLean's hand trembled and sent a splash of his drink to the floor. With a gulp, he drained half of the glass' contents and let out a satisfied sigh.

They had been drinking for well over an hour, and in that time, MacLean had warmed to Yonder considerably. Which was quite remarkable, given the awkwardness of their initial acquaintance.

But then, Yonder thought, *my purse has thus far been bottomless for the good reverend.*

The serving woman knew MacLean well, calling him by his Christian name, Adam. She was told to spare no expense for the minister's food and drink. Since the lady happened to be married to the owner, she obliged in both the letter and the spirit of Yonder's instruction. At one point, Yonder had passed a small donation across the tabletop to MacLean.

"A widow's mite," Yonder offered demurely, "to help cover the many expenses of a new parish. A more befitting gift will be forthcoming. I daresay something on the order of an endowment."

That had actually elicited a peel of laughter from the dour Scotsman. As the evening wore on, MacLean grew very comfortable indeed.

For his part, Far had not uttered a word, and thankfully sat as far from Yonder and MacLean as he could while still remaining a part of their company. A couple of times, Far shot the minister a dark look, but mostly his companion leaned back in his chair against the wall. He drank a glass of port and read the latest edition of the *National Gazette*.

MacLean finished his drink, while Yonder studied him

in the table's candlelight. The man was as oiled as he was going to get.

"Reverend," Yonder began.

"Aye?"

"Something you said during the service earlier caught my attention. And I'll confess," he gave MacLean a wry smirk, "it's what brought me to seek your esteemed acquaintance."

"An' what would that be?"

Yonder scooted his chair a little closer.

"You mentioned a concert in Faneuil Hall. A flute concert. You said you had heard about it."

"Aye, I did. Hear of it, I mean. 'Twas terrible devilry."

"Indeed . . . Apparently, the story of it distressed you greatly." The smile did not waver from Yonder's lips. His voice fell to a whisper. "But I suspect you did not hear *of* this concert, Reverend MacLean. You actually heard it. You were there. Unless I'm very much mistaken. Which I seldom am."

MacLean's eyes rounded like two bloodshot moons.

"I-I-no . . . No. You are mistaken, sir." It was a sheepish protest, belied by the man's every twitch and shudder. The pink in MacLean's cheeks shone as bright and revealing as a burning censer. "A third-hand rumor, thas' all it was," he shook his head. "I'd ne'er partake of such ungodly diversions. You've got the wrong of it."

Yonder leaned back, laced his fingers behind his head with a reflective look, and recited, "*Excusatio non petita, accusatio manifesta.*"

"I've nothin' to be ashamed of, ye goddam Saracen!" MacLean spat. There was a lull in the tavern's hum of conversation, as several heads turned. MacLean tried to resume in a more dignified tone.

"What you're suggestin' would be a slander to an ordained minister such as myself. If it were true – which it's *not*."

"My dear Reverend," Yonder consoled. He slid his chair so that it touched MacLean's and offered the most disarming grin. "My most pious sir, I'm afraid you misunderstood my intent."

"Eh?"

"It makes no difference to me whether you indulge in spirits, or in sonatas. It certainly is no affair I should ever publish to a third party. I only wish to learn more of this flutist. My companion and I may have some business with the gentleman."

MacLean eyed him suspiciously, while Yonder filled his empty glass. The moment he set the bottle back on the table, MacLean drank it down in a quick, practiced pull. MacLean's face winced, but he held onto the fire manfully, with scarcely a shudder. His eyelids flitted, and Yonder began to worry if he might have pushed the man's endurance too far. For several long moments, MacLean withdrew into himself and began to hum the same somber measure of music over and over, oblivious to anyone around him. When he came out of the reverie, his words were thick. To anyone else's ear, the liquored brogue would have been impenetrable, but Yonder was able to wade through the slurring.

"Simply stunnin'. It . . . 'twas grand. Grand . . ." A tear began to brim at the bottom of his eye. He glanced around the table, and MacLean gestured for Yonder to lean close, as if the walls and windows might try to eavesdrop on the story he was about to tell him. MacLean's heavy voice rumbled softly, while Yonder listened intently, not bothering to write any of it down, for much of what was described was precisely what Yonder had hoped.

Reverend MacLean had attended a flute concert in Faneuil Hall. It had been a private affair sponsored by several ladies and gentlemen in the higher strata of Boston's society, those who were rich enough that they could openly embrace a moderate level of hedonism without any loss of face. MacLean had only come as a missionary, he assured Yonder. "I was like John the Baptist," he explained with utmost earnestness, "come to preach to Herod."

The comparison was marginally apt. At some point in the concert, it seemed the minister did indeed lose his head. For the rest of his story became a rambling morass. A tangled string of impressions, feelings, sights, and sounds all garbled with knots of incoherence. There were a few moments of lucidity, though. MacLean remembered clearly a handsome looking Negro walking into the hall. Or he might have been a Malay. Perhaps an Indian. Whatever he was, he was dark, that much MacLean was certain. He held a golden flute. Before he began, the fellow addressed the small gathering, and his voice was like – like his music. What had he said? MacLean could not recollect anything in particular, but whatever it was, it had been delightful, thrilling, a trifle sinful. The fellow brought the flute to his lips and played. What had he played? MacLean's story ran aground, for he could no more describe the sound of the music than he could describe the feel of wind, or the smell of jasmine, or the color red. It simply was. An irreducible experience.

Where words failed him, though, sensations flourished. These, the minister hinted, were pagan in the extreme. First, the audience swayed. Then laughed – stupid, intoxicated chortling. Which eventually devolved into dancing. And from dancing . . . writhing. All of them together. Touching each other. At some point, one of the ladies may have become disrobed and from the leer that spread across MacLean's lips, it was plain the man had done more than gaze upon the woman's beauty.

The minister's eyes closed again. Yonder gently shook his shoulder and asked the name of this silver-tongued, dark-skinned musician.

"Eh? His – his name . . ."

MacLean muttered to himself a bit, for his head had become heavy. His words came out as grunts. He had slid into a stupor.

"The name, Reverend," Yonder insisted. "What was his name?"

Before he slipped into unconsciousness, MacLean murmured a name, softly, reverently.

"Iss Misser Wylde . . . Wylde, from a faraway isle, said he . . ."

MacLean was asleep, his chin cradled in his arms on the tabletop, snoring.

Yonder nodded. He felt tired but no less pleased. Opposite the unconscious Reverend Adam MacLean, Far folded his newspaper and drained the last of his port.

"Sounds like our man," Far announced, stretching his shoulders. "I don't know how we're any closer to finding him, though."

Yonder reached across the table, draped the minister's coat like a blanket over his shoulders, gave him a kindly pat, and emptied the last of the bottle into MacLean's glass.

"Closer than you think, Captain," he replied.

CHAPTER FIVE

"For those, like your author, who are Traveling Fellows, who eschew the fortune and fame of serving a monarch or in a court, you may be surprised to learn that our fraternity of freethinkers has a chapter (of sorts) among the Doldrums folk. Rumor has it that a while back one of our number thought it would be a lark to initiate some of the locals into our society. One might frown upon his sense of humor, but these 'Traveling Doldrums Fellows' follow all our customary forms. They call themselves Freemasons."

—Wherestone's *Commentaries on Custom*, page 60, footnote

A half-moon lit the walkways of Merchants Row in its soft, marble glow. Dark windows stared down upon a nearly empty street. Two trails of misted breath hastened around the gray, somber cornerstone of the Universal Lodge and passed quickly by the cross of St. Andrew's Church. Yonder was in a hurry to get out of the cold. He scarcely saw the lamplighter on a ladder or the terrier that barked up at him. Yonder made a quick march for the doorway of their office. Far lingered behind, indifferent as always.

A single light still flickered in the chandelier of their foyer, but it felt no less warm within. The air in there, at least, remained as constant as it was refreshing. He rubbed his hands together and let the comfort soak into his bones. Far came inside after him, threw his coat in a corner, and locked the door.

Both gentlemen carried the stains and stench of a long evening spent in a shabby, smoky tavern, so a bath and a change of clothes were the first matters to be attended to. For Far, a short affair of splashing his face in a crystal basin. For Yonder, a more thorough scrubbing with soap and brush. Far changed his shirt and found a new coat, while Yonder went through his closet to replace his entire wardrobe.

As Yonder made himself a cup of tea, a tiny visitor perched upon his desk.

It could have passed for a finch. If such a bird had been born with a rainbow's array of incandescent feathers. And a platinum beak. And an unmistakably haughty expression. The bird scratched its tiny metallic feet against the wood of the desk in a gesture of irritation and chirped at Yonder with a sound that could only be likened to the echo of a pipe organ.

"Message from home," Far observed off-handedly.

Indeed it was. Clutched within one of the bird's talons was a furled slip of paper.

Under the finch's orbicular glare, Yonder unfurled the message, read it closely, let out a sigh, reread it again, and rolled his eyes.

"It's from Lady Otherly," he said. "Our client desires to know what progress we've made thus far. She wishes to have an update. Demands it, actually. I'm instructed to send my immediate reply with this messenger."

Far shrugged, as if the matter were no more concerning to him than the lamplighter's work outside. He straightened his new coat, a brass-buttoned cavalry jacket, and stretched it across the width of his shoulders. "What will you tell her?"

Yonder flipped the note over to its blank side. "The usual lawyer's reply."

He opened a drawer from the partners desk, retrieved a feather pen and a clay pot that was filled with black, dampened earth. Yonder sharpened the quill tip and plunged it into the pot. He sat down to write, a flowing, looping script that seemed to bleed into the fiber of the page.

He spoke a summary of what he wrote: "Progress is steady. Confident we are well on our way to achieving a satisfactory outcome. Should have it any day. No outcome can be guaranteed. May require a more substantive advance."

He made a flourish at the end, then stabbed the feather into the paper.

Far looked over his shoulder and frowned.

"You're implying we have her man on the run. That's stretching the truth, don't you think?"

"Not at all. Consider this." He began to count his fingers. "We have traced our man to Boston. Verified that he is still traveling under the name of Wylde. We know he disguises himself as a flutist. And now, at last, we know where he is likely to be." He folded his hands together, as if he had just finished a closing summation in a trial.

"You have no idea where he's likely to be," Far retorted.

"Of course I do. He's dark skinned."

"So what?"

Yonder gave Far a placating smile. He turned around in his chair to face him fully and assumed a professorial tone, for Far was still regrettably ignorant of the affairs in this realm.

"I can understand why you might be confused. Whether Wylde's skin was brown, or blue, or floral printed, would seem an utterly innocuous detail. To us. I suspect that's why our client neglected to mention it before. But such triviality matters mightily to Doldrums' folk. In fact, it's going to be the key to our finding Wylde. You see, in Doldrums, those born with lighter skin do not live amongst those who have darker skin. They don't even mingle. It's very much frowned upon. As a matter of fact, there are quite a few laws against it."

Far's jaw dropped a fraction of an inch. He shook his head in disbelief.

"That's absurd. Not even dogs sort themselves by their color."

"Dogs have a good deal more sense than men."

"But – but why?"

Yonder threw up his hands.

"Why do spiders eat their mates? It's how they are made. What they do."

He carefully folded the note he had written to Lady Otherly, sealed it, and handed it back to the bird, who plucked it rudely from his fingers. The finch hopped over to the windowsill, and off it flew, carrying the little packet along the night breeze, eastward, until it disappeared.

"I admit it's a bizarre custom." Yonder shut the window again. "But there it is. As laggardly as these people's senses are – and you really wouldn't believe the depth of their blindness when it comes to perception – the one thing they can sense very clearly is color. And they do not tolerate its variations in their skin."

"So . . ." Far pinched the bridge of his nose. "Since Wylde's dark, he'll be somewhere . . . that's set apart? A place just for darker-skinned folk?"

"Precisely. I believe we'll find he's as close as a carriage ride now."

They did not hire a carriage, but an old farmer's wagon that Far spotted by a storehouse on King's Street. True, there were plenty of coachmen for hire, and they had ample funds, but Far liked the open wagon. If he had to endure this business of Yonder's, at least he was entitled to be conveyed by a means that offered him sufficient legroom and a clear view of the weather. He sat with his back against a board with the open sky above him. The frost bit his cheeks, the wind tousled his hair. The weight and chill of metal was hidden beneath his jacket. He felt relatively content. There was little to be said in favor of this realm, but the landscape was not unpleasant. Once one was past all the inhabitants. Far watched as the steeples and rooftops of Boston's skyline faded behind a plain of rolling hills and farmlands. He found himself reminiscing on other bleak and blighted heathers he had known.

An indigo sky started to break. The snow had stopped, but the wind still cut across the countryside with a knifing cold. The world remained draped in frost, across the fields, atop the empty branches of elm trees and dead rhododendron, and on the cart path they followed. A sheen of gray, slowly turned white.

In a corner of the wagon, Yonder shivered beneath a saddle blanket. To Far, he had the look of an unhappy pumpkin that had been wrapped head to toe in worsted wool.

"I wish Gilead would show a little haste," Yonder grumbled.

Their driver was named Gilead. He was a devout, old, and surly Quaker, the kind that seemed to proliferate in these parts, and who was inclined for neither talk nor haste. His mules were cut from the same cloth as their master. They scarcely moved faster than a walk. Even the creak in the axles and the crackle of earth beneath the hooves and wheels sounded ponderously slow.

"Why?" Fonder asked. "The folk here sleep at night. Like animals."

"They do," Yonder agreed, "but he does not. Remember, Wylde is one of us."

It made no difference to Far. This was a fool's errand. He only wished to enjoy the quiet desolation of the landscape and the reflections it brought him. His gaze began to wander until it fell on a distant hillside, still shrouded in shadow. With the jagged brambles growing wild at the summit, it almost looked like a crown of thorns, and it brought to his mind the vivid memory of an old battlement. One he had climbed and found defended by a host of warriors, armed with glory, aligned in splendor. They had all fallen like stars . . .

The wagon crawled across the countryside for a while, Far in his thoughts, Yonder in his discomfort, until at last they came within sight of a hamlet and Yonder brightened.

"I say, Gilead?"

The hatted, silver-haired Quaker slowly turned around from his driver's seat at the sound of his name.

Yonder pointed to one of the buildings. "That little cottage there looks to be an inn."

Gilead glared disapprovingly at the house.

"Verily, it is," he said and returned his attention to the swishing tails of his mules.

"Perhaps I could prevail upon you to stop for a minute? Since we don't seem to be in a hurry. I for one could use a mug of tea."

The driver shook his head.

"Thou ought not to drink such brew. 'Tis dark and

twisted." He tucked the reins as the wagon trundled into a frozen dell, and added under his breath, "Like the place ye travel."

With the prospect of tea having been dashed, Yonder returned to his silence. The wagon dipped once more. A crow called from a fence post and flew off toward the bramble hillside and the horizon beyond. Far watched it until it disappeared.

"My friend." Yonder leaned close, as if to speak in confidence.

"Hm."

"Are you – are you confident with what you've brought?"

"Yes," Far answered without looking at him.

"What I'm saying is, do you think it will suffice? What you've brought? There's time to go back if we need more armaments."

Far made a face. "For the deadly flutist?"

"Don't underestimate him. He's not been here as long as we have. The air won't have tired him in the least. Wylde will still have much of his potency left."

Far patted his coat. It made a muted, metallic clink.

"I have what I need."

"We may only get one chance at this. It would be a shame . . ." Yonder's voice trailed off.

Yonder fidgeted with his pockets, and his eyes blinked rapidly. He looked as nervous as a maiden on her wedding night. The wagon inched its way over the wintry road, its taciturn driver cradled a horsewhip he never bothered lifting. While one of the passengers wrung his hands beneath a moldy blanket, the remaining passenger reclined at his leisure, watched a gray dawn break, and fingered what was concealed in his jacket with fond familiarity.

Morning passed, giving way to a drear and dire afternoon. The wagon plodded through the snow. They had ridden for hours. Yonder feared they might press on through lunch, when without a word of warning, the driver brought the wagon to a halt.

"We are come," Gilead announced.

Yonder surveyed the area. The snow-covered clearing looked no different from the fields they had traveled across since leaving Boston. There were no other carriages, no persons about, not even a posted sign. A lonely log cabin with an empty pen and a smokeless chimney was the only feature that caught his attention.

"This is West Chesterton?" Yonder inquired.

Gilead grunted it was. He brought the wagon's brake up and turned around in his seat to indicate that he had earned his fare, and this was where the trip ended.

"I had expected something more urbane," Yonder observed.

A passing wind picked up a flurry of snow. It blew across the wagon, dusting the mules and their cargo, and then disappeared into the unbroken whiteness of the landscape.

"This be the boundary," Gilead replied, brushing his hat clean. "The village art naught but a mile farther up the path."

"Couldn't you just—"

"I'll not draw another foot nearer," Gilead growled. "Not for thy three shillings, nor three hundred. Off with ye."

Feeling vexed, and slightly cheated, Yonder clambered over the side of the wagon. Far hopped down after him. While the driver began the tedious work of turning his team about, Yonder pulled his coat tight over his belly and started up the path, right into the teeth of a biting wind.

Despite the chill, they made good time, for the road, though little more than a rut in the earth, had at least been kept free from stones and was fairly level. With their course set, Far overtook Yonder, so that Yonder soon found himself having to pump his squat legs to keep up with his companion's long strides. It was a hard exertion, one that brought a measure of warmth back into his limbs – as well as that creeping tingle back into his chest. Whenever he was sure Far's attention was fixed elsewhere, Yonder would discretely tap his breast with his fist, as if to shoo away this pesky malady in his lungs. It did little to help.

Eventually they came to a stretch of wooden planks that bridged a dried-out gulch. On the other side, the landscape began to change. The shrubs had been cleared, the trees kept pruned, and dirt gave way to granite paving. A run of low houses came into view. These were built in even rows, frame and brick, and all well-kept with brightly painted doors and clean glass in the windows. Smoke rose from the chimneys. Yonder could almost feel the warmth that glowed within. They came to a square of buildings, where the first townsfolk were out. Men and women of all shapes and ages swept snow from porches, pulled carts filled with firewood, and brought feed to livestock. Farmers, carpenters, millers, and tradesmen. Like any other in Merchants Row.

Only they were all dark skinned.

"They're yeomenry," Yonder murmured to Far. He glanced up at his companion, and added, "Try to blend in."

The people of West Chesterton chatted freely, but not one was so occupied that he didn't spare a moment to gawk at the oddly matched, peculiarly dressed, pale-skinned strangers who strolled through their town in the dead of winter. Yonder could feel eyes bore into his back as they passed by. He dipped his head at a mother with three children in tow passing by, never seeing her making a sign to ward against evil. He did, however, notice a small throng of farm hands pointing at him with looks that were less than welcoming. One of their number hissed, "You don't belong here . . ." loud enough that it could not be ignored.

Far stopped suddenly and tilted his ear to the air. "Do you hear that?"

With all the noise of a town square, the doors opening and closing, the livestock braying, and the fractious threads of conversation and whispers around them, Yonder was not at all certain what his companion could have meant.

"A robin," Far explained. "About a half mile from here."

Yonder cupped his hand to his ear. He caught the sound. It was a faint distant chirping.

"So it is. Well. That's . . ." Yonder scratched his head. "That's quite odd, isn't it?" He shut his eyes to listen more. "That doesn't sound at all like a robin's song."

"Because it isn't. Come."

Far was off like a hound on the scent, heedless of whoever was in his way, leaving Yonder to beg the pardon of the ladies and gentlemen that he nearly knocked over. They said nothing in reply but glared at him in such a way to ensure that Yonder knew he had better not return the way they had come.

He had no time to fret about it, though, for Far was already across the square and raced down the length of a long, narrow street. Yonder hurried after him. The chirping he had heard had stopped, but its echo still hung in the air. Far ran after it, past the northern edge of the village, and a campfire circle, until at last they came to a wooded lot with a picket fence.

The snow lay thick on the ground. But a collection of recent footprints had left a path that led to a windowless frame cottage set beneath the canopy of six twining oak trees. The cottage had an open front porch held up by two columns that had been painted gold. A single wooden door looked to be the only means of ingress. Above it hung an azure sign emblazoned with an amber "G" bounded by a white square and compasses.

As they crept closer, music burst forth through the walls of the cabin. It almost knocked Yonder to the ground.

Someone was playing a flute.

It was only a warmup, some runs through the major scales, but the timbre, the tone – it seemed to shake the winter air. A sound that was as delicate as a songbird – indeed, it easily could have passed for a boisterous robin – but with the bombast of a cathedral pipe organ. The vibrato resonated through skin, through bone, down into the heart, as if it to re-forge the pulse and make it its own. Gradually, the notes turned into a song, as seamlessly as a tide coming in. It was, Yonder felt, an enigmatic melody, part dirge, part reel, a contemplative *divertimento*, a purposeful exercise. There was something prescient in it, though he could not lay his finger on what it could be.

Most of all, though, he no longer felt the cold, or the cough that had been prodding his chest. Even Far seemed taken by the music. His heavy arms hung limply at his sides. A breeze stirred the leaves on the ground and brought them both back to a measure of their senses.

"That's got to be him," Far said softly.

"Yes," Yonder nodded, though he hated to break the spell of the music. "Clearly, the malaise of Doldrums hasn't settled over him. We shall have to be all the more cunning. But as it happens, I'm familiar with this lodging."

Far gestured for Yonder to lead the way, but Yonder paused, unsure how he should broach a somewhat awkward point.

"I should say," Yonder began, "I'm familiar with this lodging's sect. You see, they're something akin to Traveling Fellows—"

"I knew it." Far blew out a disgusted breath. "I knew he'd be one of your vagabond friends."

"Yes." Yonder ignored the jibe. "I neglected to mention it earlier, but Wylde is indeed a Traveling Fellow. The fraternity can be a bit touchy about who we admit within our lodgings. I think I can gain entrance. But there's no way we can slip you by, not without raising a commotion. I was thinking if I could lure Wylde outside, perhaps over to that little knoll over there," he pointed to a clump of frost covered spruce that was overrun with brush.

"An ambush." Far nodded with approval.

"You don't find that distasteful?"

To Yonder's surprise, Far actually seemed pleased with the idea. "It is a fine tactic in battle."

"No battles," Yonder cautioned. "Remember. He might not have the lock of hair on him. You must not kill him. Promise?"

"I'll be as gentle as a kitten," Far said with a murderous glint and went off to hide himself among the trees.

When he was sure Far was completely hidden, Yonder approached the cabin's entrance. The porch steps creaked as he climbed. A final glance at Far's hiding place and he gave the door three hard knocks. There were some scuffling noises from the other side; someone grumbled. He heard a bar slide off, and the door swung open.

A barrel-chested, middle-aged farmer stood in the entrance. His hair was cropped close, pepper colored, and he had wide, dark, and piercing eyes. An otherwise rough-spun set of clothes were offset by an intricately patterned apron and a silver chain that hung around a neck as thick as a tree stump. At the end of the chain was an emblem of a sword. In his hand, he held a cutlass.

The doorman's voice cut over the concert in the room behind him. "Who goes there?"

Yonder held his arms wide, as if greeting a dear friend. "My brother," he exclaimed warmly.

The doorman lifted the tip of his blade to Yonder's

scarfed neck. At that moment, another man joined them at the doorway. He was also aproned and had a silver chain around his neck. He was younger and a trifle darker than the doorman and wore a trim set of city clothes.

"Is that the ale finally," the newcomer inquired. Seeing who was at the door, he stopped in surprise. "Oh," he said.

"It ain't no ale," the doorman said from the side of his mouth, never breaking his gaze from Yonder. "And it sure ain't one of us." His eyes regarded Yonder with an almost feral scrutiny.

"Who are you, sir?" the younger man asked.

"I am Brother John Yonder. If I may?" Yonder extended his hand.

Both men in the doorway stared at it, until the younger man, seemingly more troubled by rudeness than awkwardness, slid past the doorman and grasped Yonder's hand. At the same moment, they each placed their free hands over the grip they shared. Their eyes met, and Yonder noticed that the man's necklace bore a cross.

And so Yonder made the acquaintance of a brother of sorts, a chaplain by the name of John Marrant.

While the music played on inside the lodge, Marrant posed a few questions, which Yonder answered easily and, apparently, to Marrant's satisfaction, for when he had finished interrogating him, he ushered Yonder into the foyer. It was a courteous if not enthusiastic invitation to come in from the snow and warm himself by the fire.

The doorman, whose name was Thomas, never took his eyes from Yonder, nor did he set his weapon aside.

Yonder found the interior to be a welcome reprieve from the elements. It was spacious, a long hallway lit by a fireplace and three small chandeliers, with plaster walls that bore paintings of palm trees, desserts, an unfinished pyramid, and an all-seeing eye. Another set of doors separated the lodge room, where the flute concert reached a crescendo. Marrant kept his voice down so as not to disturb the performance.

"Are you from the St. John's Lodge in Boston?"

"Loosely affiliated," Yonder replied. He surveyed the interior admiringly. "Beautiful lodge you have here, brother. But I had no idea the Craft had reached this far beyond town."

"We're a new charter."

"Ah. Have you picked a name?"

"We call ourselves Prince Hall," he answered with what Yonder detected was a note of pride.

"Very good. Very good." Yonder paused as the flute landed into a finale. He whispered, "You have wonderful entertainment."

"Oh, yes." Marrant's face brightened. "The brother is a virtuoso! Says he's never studied or taken lessons. As natural as a songbird. He happened to be passing through town, though I feel as though we've met before. Hopefully, he'll stay on as our musician. He can play anything. Anything at all. I . . . well, I've never heard anything like him."

They listened by the lodge doors as the final note hovered in the space between them. When it ended, Yonder nodded knowingly.

"I'm sure you haven't."

The inner temple of the Prince Hall Lodge was small, rustic, and lovingly kept, the chairs all lacquered to a glow, the black-and-white tiled floor swept clean, the ceremonial candles neatly trimmed. In the center of the room, a handmade mahogany altar was trussed up with a bolt of azure silk that shimmered in the candlelight. To the side, a less ornate table held a series of platters that had just been uncovered. The smell of roasted beef and potatoes and the friendly hum of chatter filled the hall.

Around forty of the lodge's brethren mingled about. Most were dressed in plain work clothes and carried themselves with the self-assured air of men who were used to tilling their own earth to make their living. A good-humored group, for whom laughter seemed to come easily. They kept their heads uncovered, of course, revealing a mosaic of brown faces. All wore white aprons, but each was festooned with its own individuated collection of stars, suns, moons, pillars, squares and compasses. One, however, stood out.

Near the back of the room, next to a music stand, an apron gleamed with a light of its own. It was double tied around the waste of an impossibly slender black man. He was impeccably, almost garishly, dressed in a set of tailored pants, shirt, vest, cravat, and coat that were all dyed the same hue of royal purple. The body the outfit covered seemed inclined to bend at all times, like a long reed on a windy riverbank. He threw his head back to let out an uproarious peel of laughter. His hair jingled merrily about his shoulders, while the knot of brothers who lingered about him echoed in his mirth. In his hands, the man held a partly disassembled flute of gold. He cleaned the head joint with his shirtsleeves.

Foppish, carefree, arrogant – the exemplar for why courtesans held the Traveling Fellows in disdain. It was a view Yonder occasionally shared when it came to certain of his brethren. He suspected Wylde would be among that number.

Yonder had hoped to gain his man's attention discretely, but the moment he had passed the entryway, Wylde seemed to attune to his presence. The flutist paused midway in an anecdote and began to look about, and when he spotted Yonder lingering by the door, his face lit up and he let out an excited whoop. The rest of the lodge room fell silent.

"A countryman!" Wylde cried. "There's no hiding it! I see through your ridiculous disguise!" He winked and flashed a smile that radiated like a sun. He threw his spindly arms open and loped across the lodge room to embrace Yonder, who found himself unable to match such aplomb. The entire lodge stared at him.

"Mr. Wylde, I presume?" Yonder greeted him somewhat stiffly. "I pray you'll forgive the unannounced intrusion—"

"Tut, tut, tut!" He drew Yonder into another firm, and terribly awkward, embrace. "Native formalities in a stranger's land are as pointless as they are presumptuous. To think I should be found in Doldrums by a fellow countryman all the way out here in this rustic little lodge of – but wait . . ." Somehow his grin broadened and brightened even more. "You must be a Traveling Fellow, then?"

Yonder took his hand and showed that he was, and Wylde cried, "But this is absolutely *delicious*!"

"A pleasure," Yonder replied, remembering his manners.

Wylde laughed and slapped his side and clapped Yonder's shoulder much harder than Yonder liked. "My brother, let me say I absolutely *love* your disguise. Why, you almost had me fooled. With those ridiculous rags you're wearing, and the way you mope and hang your shoulders, and shuffle your feet, you almost look like one of the locals. It's a splendid masquerade . . ."

While Wylde effused, several of the other lodge brothers began to complain, and not subtly, about Yonder's presence in their lodge. Some had their arms folded across their chest, while others shook their heads, or scowled. As they started to close around him, Yonder overheard Marrant trying to explain that Brother Yonder had shown all the proper signs, that he had proven himself to be a brother, and that he was entitled to the hospitality of the lodge. It was an accurate point, morally, legally, and procedurally, but it did little to mollify the air in the room. The junior warden of the lodge, a bald, pot-bellied little man with a shrill voice interrupted Wylde.

"Beg pardon, Brother Wylde, but this, um, fellow here." He jerked a thumb at Yonder. "His lodge won't recognize us. He may be a Mason, but we've got no bond with him." Several of the brethren grumbled in agreement..

"I don't like the look of him," one of the other lodge officers said. "Looks like a lawyer. Bet he's here to dun somebody."

"Oh, come, come, come!" Wylde made a sweeping flourish so that he could address the entire assembly. The sound of his voice brought every mutter and murmur to an end. "I will vouch for this brother," he continued. "He's from my home country. As fine a fellow as you'll ever lay eyes on. There can be no question that he should be given every courtesy. Indeed, I must insist upon it."

There were a few scattered complaints, but they quickly abated when it became clear the flutist really did know the strangely dressed, orange hued stranger. Yonder was grudgingly accepted to remain inside Prince Hall Lodge. The brethren returned to their refreshments. Wylde rejoined Yonder, threaded his arm through the lawyer's, and led him over to a pair of chairs a little removed from the others. His dark eyes seemed to take Yonder's measure with a single blink, and for the first time, there was a note of sincerity in what he said.

"You look tired."

Yonder waved an absent hand.

"It's the air."

Wylde nodded. "Dead, drear fare. Yes, I've felt it, too. I should return home shortly, but I'm having so much fun here, and now that you've arrived, I couldn't dream of leaving." He let out a contented breath that carried an aroma of pollen. "There ought to be a word for running into a countryman when you're abroad. It's like finding familiar wine in a foreign land, a fortuitous discovery that renders both the new and the known that much more delightful."

"Indeed." Yonder locked his hands together in his lap and clasped them tightly.

"So." Wylde's smile dimmed for the first time. "I take it your little, um, misunderstanding back home still hasn't worked itself out?"

Yonder drew a startled breath.

"You – you know who I am?"

Wylde fixed Yonder with a shrewd look. He shook his head and *tsked*. "Feigned ignorance is veiled insult. I shan't pretend to be deaf, blind, and dumb to you and your fall from grace, if you'll extend me the courtesy of not assuming I'm an idiot. Who else *but* you would be wandering about in a Doldrums lodge?"

"I hadn't realized I was so infamous."

"My dear fellow, for an entire season you and that captain's exile were the only talk of the court. Even the scullery maids were nattering about it. The two of you managed to restart a war. Don't look at me like that, now. I cast no aspersions. I wasn't there at the time and, from what I gathered, your misdeeds were completely inadvertent. If anything, I would say you had been dealt with over harshly. You in particular since you are a Traveling Fellow."

Yonder heaved an exaggerated sigh.

"Harshly doesn't begin to cover it. Are you familiar with the temperament of Her Majesty?"

"Ho, ho, ho, ho!" Wylde lurched over, seized with laughter. When he had regained himself, he wiped a diamond sparkle from the corner of his eye. "Oh, goodness.

I am *intimately* familiar with that woman's moods. Ho, yes. She can be a tempest."

"One that never blows over, it seems. All this time, and still she remains adamant that I, *I* of all people, was a cause of her harm. It borders on obduracy."

Yonder fell silent, and the two of them listened to the soft murmur of the lodge finishing their meal. This had not gone at all how he had planned, but perhaps he could try a different tack to gain Wylde's confidence and lure him outside. "I heard that you were well received in her Majesty's court," he began.

Wylde dipped his head.

"I was hoping . . ." Yonder continued, "that, um, we could speak about your acquaintance with her." He lowered his voice as if divulging a secret, and just as he expected, Wylde took it like bait. "You know her moods," he whispered, "the wiles of her court. Perhaps we could discuss what I might do to regain my standing. As brother to brother?"

Wylde extended long, bony fingers and slowly brought them together in a contemplative gesture. "One must proceed carefully when discussing matters of the court, even here in Doldrums. But I do love to talk. Yes. We shall have a nice, long chat about your problems with her Majesty. Not here, though. And not just yet. First, I promised these fine brethren an encore, which I am obliged to deliver." He chuckled to himself. "Oh, who am I kidding? That's not the real reason for the encore." One of his eyelids slowly fell, like a great avalanche, a conspiratorial wink that would have made the Iscariot blush with shame. "The truth is . . . there is one in here I am hoping to impress."

He made a longing look at the Reverend Marrant, who, in the middle of licking his fingers from a rib, caught Wylde's gaze and returned it with an innocent smile.

"You wouldn't believe the marvelous notions that

beauty has floating about in his head," said Wylde. "The sovereignty of the soul, the perfectibility of man, rights that rain down from the heavens like giftwrapped presents. *Private* property. Ha! So radical. So feral! Like a panther who makes poetry. I could dine on him for days. Mmm . . . but I could."

CHAPTER SIX

" 'Doldrums air, the dead drear fare.' Is there a more oft-recited, or more hackneyed, saw about Doldrums? For most of our people, this banal little rhyme represents the entirety of what they know of Custom and of Doldrums. How drear, indeed. Yet the Doldrums Air couplet did not spring forth ex nihilo. For many of our people, it must be acknowledged, there does appear to be a deleterious effect from overlong exposure to the air of Doldrums: malaise, torpor, irritability, lesions, loss of hair, death. I have witnessed the phenomenon in visitors on numerous occasions. Many travelers will indeed fall ill if they overstay their holiday in Doldrums.

Many, but not all.

Personally, I have never felt off in my many years in Doldrums, not in the slightest. Perhaps the fervor of my intellectual pursuits has inoculated me from the noxious humours, or perhaps Custom shields those of a higher intellect when we remain focused on our endeavors . . ."

—Wherestone's *Commentaries on Custom*, page 19

Far stood back to admire his work. What had been an overgrown tangle of briars and barren branches growing wild were carefully woven together into a serviceable blind. One that was tall enough to accommodate his stature so that he wouldn't have to crouch in the snow while he waited. He took a few steps around the barrier to inspect it from another angle.

The sun had filtered through the sheet of clouds above the wooded overhang. It set everything below in a gray haze, a half-shadow that seemed to smear the distinctions between ground, and trees, and air. The wind had died. He could hear every stirring in the snow, every twig's movement. Good weather for an ambush. Far crinkled his forehead in concentration. One of the branches looked slightly out of place, a bit too contrived. He brought it down half an inch and rubbed his blistered hands together.

Really, this was servants' work. Building blinds, digging trenches, hammering bulwarks together. Servants did this sort of thing; servants or young pages who had shirked their duties and needed to be disciplined. He would never have let his warriors see him stoop to such menial work on a battlefield. Still. Far found a kind of peace in the endeavor. For the span of an hour, he had felt a little more like himself again. Pulling up scrub, bending it into shape, turning the cluster of deadwood to his advantage, in preparation for . . . well, he wasn't entirely sure. He hoped it would be conflict, though. A violent clash. Preferably, one with blood and bones. He had thought on the prospect all morning.

A faint smile stole over his lips. A good fight would be just the thing. It would almost make up for being dragged along this ridiculous manhunt of Yonder's.

Far spread the snow carefully across the ground to

cover the signs of his work and crept around the blind to wait.

After a while, he caught the sound of the flute playing once more from the cabin: a reel. One he recognized. Though Far seldom went in for courtly entertainment, he had always enjoyed a dance. So long as it required vigor. The tune was one that would have warranted somersaults. Without realizing it, Far's feet tapped along in rhythm. He even hummed the chorus. The fellow had talent, he had to admit.

Far paused. A noise broke through the music. A sound as clear as crystal shattering on a tile floor. From the far side of the clearing, a few hundred yards northeast from where he was hidden, Far heard twigs snap in succession. And a branch cracked. It was followed by footsteps crunching through the snow.

Far shifted his position but stayed crouched behind his blind. He pressed his eye up to a gap between the limbs and scanned the grounds. The light shimmered from the snowfall, a lonely vine of smoke rose from one of the cabin's chimneys, but otherwise the woods and the clearing were still. He squinted at the farthest line of trees, past the shadows, as the first of the men appeared.

They barreled through the brush, at least a dozen of them, clustered with no order. No scouts, no watchmen, no caution in their approach. Several looked like they were cackling jokes. They were dressed as city men taking a stroll through a park. But instead of canes, they carried clubs. And axes. Iron glinted from a pair of muskets. Far grimaced.

As the troop of armed men emerged from the trees, they fanned out and surrounded the cabin. Eleven, twelve, thirteen . . . fourteen in all. An officious looking clerk of some sort barked an order at the three men standing closest to him. The clerk drew some papers from a satchel and promptly proceeded to drop them. Glancing angrily to ensure no one mocked him, he picked them up and stormed up the stairs to the cabin's door.

Far's face grew taut. Whatever their purpose could be, the men seemed bound to complicate his plan. The plan he had been looking forward to executing. Complications rarely troubled Far, however. They were like changes in the weather. Something to be acknowledged and attended to. This would be no different.

Without looking he reached behind his back, felt for his folded coat, and calmly retrieved what he had brought with him from his office.

From the comfort of an armchair, Yonder watched as the brethren of Prince Hall Lodge were whipped into a frenzy. They shouted, stomped their feet, and performed whirling twists in mid-air, grinning like madmen. They clapped their hands and some shook with tremors. Dances from a faraway continent, recently forgotten but now remembered, had come back to them as naturally as breathing. Reverend Marrant had his eyes shut tight and held his palms high in the air, swaying like dandelions, while he kicked his feet together.

Wylde played on. His fingers traipsed across the tiny golden circles and arms of the flute keys, making them dance along with his audience. It seemed a part of him, the golden tube that touched his lips. He blew, and dipped, and pranced, and all the while his roving gaze kept returning to the chaplain. A predatory gleam seemed to shine from Wylde's face.

Yonder wondered if Wylde hoped to send his cleric into ecstasy, when suddenly the music's mood changed.

A mordent turned into a trill, as light and seamless as a mockingbird changing its song, which Wylde let carry across the room. He stood erect, as still as a statue, only his ring finger shook as his breath held out the flourish for an impossible length. He lifted the end of the flute to signal a new movement was about to commence.

The lodge's inner doors burst open with a crash.

The spell broke with them. Throughout the hall men stood, dazed and blinking, wondering what had happened . . . and why their lodge included four wary-looking townsmen armed for a war.

One of the strangers, a clerkish man stuffed in a suit vest, pants, and coat that were much too tight for him, fixed a pair of spectacles to the end of a bulbous nose, fumbled a paper open, and spoke in a grating, officious voice. His three companions leveled muskets and a heavy blunderbuss at the lodge brothers.

"I am Robert Sullivan," the man announced, "duly appointed tax assessor. I am come to execute a warrant that has been signed by the Honorable Theophilus Bradbury." Sullivan waved a heavy sheet of parchment in his hand, revealing an official wax seal and a bit of silk ribbon. The lodge members gaped at the ridiculous little man and his paper but said nothing.

"Is there a Negro in this chamber by the name of Wylde?" Sullivan demanded.

Slowly, every head in the lodge room turned to face the purple-clad flutist. He held his flute aloft, as if in salute, offered a gracious "hello," and made a courtly bow.

Sullivan motioned for one of his men to fetch him. Sullivan cleared his throat and read his warrant, his voice growing louder and more pinched, as he went on.

"In the Name and by the Authority of the Town of Boston, it has come to our attention on the complaint of a most honest and respected citizen, the Reverend Adam MacLean, that a certain Negro by the name of Wylde has of late been unlawfully residing within and about the town of

Boston. It is averred that said Negro Wylde can give no account of his lawful status, whether he be freeborn or slave, nor where he has come from, nor whither he is traveling. Said Negro Wylde, while enjoying the protections of the laws of Boston and the Commonwealth of Massachusetts, has as yet rendered no service to the local militia by virtue of his status as a Negro, nor has he rendered manual labor for the good of the town. He is, therefore, upon information and belief, a public charge, a vagabond, a drain upon the public doll and a threat to the peace of the town. The bearer of this warrant is, therefore, charged with deputizing such upstanding men as he deems necessary for the purpose of taking said Negro Wylde into custody and to bring him before the overseer of Beacon Hill to give a full account of his lawful status."

Sullivan had finished reading the warrant, but unable to slide it neatly into his coat pocket, he made a pretense of smoothing the paper out on top of the lodge's altar. That he had covered the Holy Bible with an ink-stained government document apparently did not trouble Sullivan in the least, though it bothered the lodge brethren a great deal.

For a long moment, the men in the lodge, dark and pale alike, stared at one another with equal measures of wariness. When Sullivan prompted his deputies to attend their duty, and one produced a set of iron shackles, the room burst with a torrent of indignation. As Yonder scrambled to get out of the way, a crowd of the lodge's brethren formed a ring around Wylde. Reverend Marrant was at their lead, which Wylde seemed to find both bemusing and touching. Next to Marrant was Thomas, the doorman, and his cutlass.

Marrant approached the deputy with the shackles, clasping the cross of his necklace close to his chest, as if to ward off evil.

"Get out," Marrant commanded.

The man blanched, not at the chaplain, but at the sight

of Thomas and his sword. Yonder could see him swallow hard. The chains rattled and nearly slipped from his hands. The other two deputies looked just as unnerved, for there were quite a few more targets than there were guns. And, gauging by the way they carried themselves, Yonder thought it likely none of them was entirely sober.

Sullivan was up in an instant, chiding his men and wagging a pudgy finger.

"Here now, what's going on? Stand down, stand down!" Sullivan gave a snarl at Marrant. "I'll have you taken up for interfering with a warrant's execution. You men, there. I said, stand *down*!"

"Who the hell does he think he is?" One of the lodge brothers demanded. A companion suggested that they "blackball the little fatty," an idea that was met with a roar of approval.

Marrant's voice rose over the din.

"Get out of our lodge, Mister Sullivan. Now. And take that scrap of litter off of our altar."

"D-did you say l-litter?" Sullivan fumed. "Damn you, man, that is a warrant. I can have you in chains for its obstruction. You have no right to—"

"The right of the people," Marrant cut over him, "to be secure in their persons, against unreasonable searches and seizures, shall not be violated."

"Hear, hear!" Wylde cried and clapped his hands.

Sullivan's face purpled over, and he screamed. "Put them both in chains!"

This would come to no good. Yonder called out to Wylde to flee, to run out the back door and wait for him outside, but the fool was just standing there grinning with delight. Apparently, he thought the prospect of being chained to Marrant would be delightful. He even held his wrists out helpfully.

"Wylde, no!" Yonder cried.

The deputy charged with taking Wylde into custody took a step toward him. That same moment, Thomas stepped between the deputy and Wylde. He raised his cutlass in warning.

There was a clap of thunder in the lodge room. A dense plume of smoke. A terrible shriek of pain. The acrid tang of gunpowder. And gradually, through the fog, arose the sound of weeping.

The man with the blunderbuss blinked. His face was flushed. He lowered the barrel, a squat metal pipe still belching out a white cloud. It seemed that with the sight of a Negro storming with a sword, and his flintlock already clicked, without meaning to, without any intention at all, he had squeezed the trigger.

Far heard the boom's report, stood upright, and calmly broke into a run. The echo still bounced across the tree trunks when it was followed by a lighter crack and another. That would be the muskets, Far reckoned.

He ran with a purposeful gait, swift, sure-footed, but not over-hurried, straight into the clearing, his boots floating over the snowfall. His dark hair billowed behind him like a mane. The air whistled past his face.

The men in the clearing would never hear Far's approach. Never know what struck them down.

They all mulled around outside the cabin, meandering in a stupid daze, no doubt wondering what to make of the gunfire they had just heard. As Far suspected, none of them would have any idea what they were supposed to do, what to look for. As stupid and confused as lambs left in the forest with the wolves. Though one of the stouter fellows did hazard a couple of steps that were vaguely in the direction of the front porch, only to retreat again. Another withdrew a few yards, watched the door and licked his lips nervously. He would be the first to fall.

Far came up behind him, never slowing his pace, and lifted his weapon.

A long metal rod that ended in an orb, polished, perfect, without the slightest blemish. The ball held the wan daylight for an instant, captured it and dimmed as it descended.

The mace's blow shattered the man's skull into a pulp. Still apace, Far moved on to the next guard. The corpse of the one he had just killed remained frozen, as if unsure where it should go, lingering on its feet a remarkably long time after its demise. A gust of breeze blew over the ruined lump of flesh that had been a head. A gray scarf tied tight around the neck became drenched, turning red then brown. A wood axe hung limply from a lifeless grip. Still, the dead man stood there, rooted to the same spot. Uncertainty his final legacy. By the time his corpse toppled to the ground, Far had finished off every one of the man's companions in much the same manner.

Tiny feathers of steam rose from nine lifeless bodies lying in the snow. The last one had spotted Far, but too late; he held up his hands to defend himself and died just as quickly. The only distinction between his corpse and the others was a shattered forearm. Far spun on his heel, scanned the area to make sure there were no more enemies and readied himself to charge the porch.

He was, however, thwarted by a new complication.

The front door swung open, and out came the group of townsmen who had earlier entered, leading a tall, dandily dressed gentleman, his hands bound behind him in manacles. The clerk and his three deputies hurried their prisoner straight for the farthest line of trees. They never noticed Far, nor the absence of their companions, but kept glancing over their shoulders at the cabin they had just left. As they skirted away, two of them tried to reload their muskets. Most of the gunpowder spilled to the ground. The only voice that spoke came from the one in chains, a lovely baritone, who kept repeating the same observation over and over.

"That was terribly rude of you. Terribly rude . . ."

Far watched them, considered for a moment, and made for the lodge, no longer at a charge, but with his mace still at the ready.

The smell of blood and smoke hit him before he reached the doorway. Far pushed the door open and crept inside to the lodge's inner temple.

A faint haze of smoke still hung in the air. But Far could see the carnage plainly. Several men lay on the floor, while others scrambled in different directions, tending to wounds, hollering out curses and pleas. A body lay next to the altar, the blue altar cloth draped over his face. A cross necklace peeked out from underneath the covering. The black and white tiled floor around it was smeared from feet running through the pool of his blood. As Far came into the light, the lodge brothers stopped and turned to glare at him.

One of them reached for a cutlass. As he gripped the handle, though, he let go of a rag he had been pressing to his stomach, and a trickle of blood flowed out.

"Aww, damn." The man winced and let the blade clatter to the floor. Hands grappled around his shoulders to keep him from falling headlong. "Another cowan in the lodge room," he said. "Get my weapon . . ." He tried to pick up the sword again.

A distant voice stopped him, "No, don't. He's not one of them. He's a friend."

"Here." Far pulled a kerchief from his pant pocket and tossed it down to one of the men helping the wounded. He scanned the room. "Yonder, where the devil are you?"

A hand went up, pale and stained in red.

Far hurried across the chamber and found his

companion slumped against a corner, alone.

"You should be after Wylde," Yonder hissed.

Far's eyes went wide at the sight of Yonder. He set his mace down.

"What happened?"

Yonder's tartan coat was stained in blood, his blood. Which was strange enough, but what Far found most disconcerting was how Yonder shivered all over, how his teeth chattered uncontrollably. He looked cold and very ill.

"Don't worry about me." Yonder grimaced as he clutched his side. "It's Wylde we're after. Get Wylde."

Far felt Yonder's forehead, unbuttoned his coat and vest, and gently prodded the wound. Yonder let out a yelp of pain. Three tiny trickles ran like rivulets down an amber expanse of skin. Stray shot from the blunderbuss. Far's eyebrows tilted in wonder.

"Why didn't you get out of the way?" Far asked.

"Wylde," Yonder repeated. He tried to push Far away from him.

"He can take care of himself." Far tucked his mace underneath his arm and crouched close to Yonder. He slid his hands underneath his shoulders.

"No." Yonder shook his head. He struggled for breath. "No. The fool. He can't. Not now. The poor fool . . ."

A shadow fell over Yonder, and he said nothing more.

CHAPTER SEVEN

"It is unfortunate that so many of our people will experience malady from Doldrums air. Fortunately, the tried and true cure for this affliction is simple: the traveler need only return to her country for a time. The waning constitution is restored within minutes of breathing the air of our realm. But could there be another antidote within the bounty of Custom, one that does not compel the forced exeunt from Doldrums to relieve the distress of Doldrums air? Rumors abound (none that I will vouch for). The most prevalent is an old canard of one of our poets, a Traveling Fellow who was able to remain for some years in Persia, who once claimed:

> 'If of thy spirits thou art bereft,
> And from thy slender purse two coins are left,
> Pay both, and with thy dole
> Buy flowers from home to feed thy soul.'

Some would read this as a homeopathic cure for the maladies of Doldrums. Most, however (including your author), dismiss it as sentimental tripe."

—Wherestone's *Commentaries on Custom*,
page 19 (cont'd)

"**H**old still," Far grunted through his clenched teeth.

"Sorry," Yonder replied.

"Almost finished—"

Yonder watched the thread that hung from Far's bottom lip quiver as he spoke. Slender and glistening, it ran from Far's front teeth, down to a couch, and into Yonder, where it wove a pattern of perfectly aligned crosses within the sagging skin of his belly. The line went taut, and Yonder could barely stifle his cry. He had endured three lines of stitching. Though his companion was surprisingly dexterous, even gentle, with his heavy fingers, the pain had become almost unbearable.

"Don't move," Far repeated.

Yonder repositioned his grip on the arm of the couch, squeezed his eyes shut, and did as he was bidden. He was stripped to the waist, lying lengthwise across the cushions in Far's office. A fire burned in the small iron stove by the wall, the first one either of them had ever lit in their chambers, but it did little to blunt the chill Yonder felt. A blanket was bundled tight around his legs. The light through the window bevels dappled against his body. He seldom paid much attention to his form, but he found the sight of all these fiery wounds marring a pale stretch of goose pimples – disconcerting.

Searching for something to distract him of his discomfort, his gaze began to drift about the space of his partner's office. It was Spartan, no rugs, no trifles, hardly any furniture, and but one decoration. In the center of a white plastered wall, Far had hung a colossal portrait of Alaric the Visigoth. With wind and fire blowing across a sea of bodiless hands begging for his mercy, the spoiler of Rome seemed aglow with contempt for the weak and the wounded.

Yonder turned his head and let out a muffled whimper

into a pillow as Far gave the stitch a final tug. With a quick flick of his knife, Far cut the line and tied the thread's end into a perfect suture.

"There we are," Far declared. "Your first battle wounds all stitched up. You'll have a scar or two, but they should look pretty enough once they've healed. Though you might want to come up with a better story for how you got them."

Yonder nodded and pulled the blanket back up underneath his chin just as a tremor of cold shook him. He tried to reach for a serving tray and winced. Far slid the waiting cup of tea into Yonder's hand and took a long pull from his own glass of port.

"Thank you," Yonder exhaled.

Far waved away the gratitude. They sipped their drinks while the burning log in the stove crackled and hissed. Alaric's wrath burned above it, unrelenting.

Yonder worked to sit himself upright so that he could face his partner fully.

"I suppose you're wondering how this happened?"

It had been a topic Yonder had pointedly avoided and would have preferred to continue on doing so. However, the questioning looks Yonder had caught from Far were as pronounced as the sutured wounds underneath his blanket. And in fairness, Far was entitled to know. The man had gone to the trouble of carrying Yonder's bleeding, unconscious body miles across the countryside in the dark of night and ministered his wounds as skillfully as a surgeon. It would be ungracious of Yonder to leave him with the enigma of how Yonder had let himself become hurt by specks of Doldrums gunshot.

"I admit, I'm curious," Far replied offhandedly. "I mean, they move so slowly here. Why you didn't just step out of the way . . ." He shook his head.

"Yes." Yonder's face stretched, a fresh wave of pain rolling over him. "Well, it seems I've slowed some, too." Far looked at him quizzically and Yonder sighed. "I might as well admit it. I've breathed too much of the air."

"Oh. So this was Custom's doing."

Yonder nodded weakly. "Around five in six of our kind will suffer maladies if we stay too long in Doldrums. Distemper, illness, lethargy. The effects are wildly variable, and no one's really sure why some are afflicted while others are not. Wherestone discusses the phenomenon at some length . . ."

Far watched him closely, as if at any moment Yonder might combust and turn into a pile of ashes.

Yonder snapped at him, "I'm not going to die."

"Are you sure?"

"Yes."

"Oh, good."

Yonder's gaze settled back upon the Visigoth king's painting again. A terrible rendering of an irascible subject, he decided. But it jostled a memory.

"Wherestone wrote, 'the longer some stay there, the less they may be here.' Something like that. I dismissed it as amateurish wordplay on a bit of useless advice. Don't spend all your time in Doldrums or the folk back home will forget about you, that sort of thing. But he may have meant it literally." He settled the back of his head into the pillow and let out a long breath. "I intend to try a remedy that he suggests. Or at least, I *think* he suggests. It's hard to tell. He can be infuriatingly obtuse sometimes."

"Blasphemy," Far chuckled. "More tea?"

"If you please."

Far refilled Yonder's cup and poured a decanter to top off his port. Far gave his glass a swirl, making the liquid sparkle like a ruby.

"I am not dying," Yonder repeated, "but I think I am . . . lessening. I'm less *here*, as Wherestone put it. I don't know how else to describe what I've felt of late." He glanced at Far for a moment. "Have you – have you felt that way at all?"

Far seemed to scarcely give it a thought.

"I'm certainly weary of this place. It would bore any man to madness." He drank deeply and wiped his mouth with the back of his hand. "For the life of me, I cannot imagine why anyone would willingly come to Doldrums. But no. I don't feel any less like myself. I certainly haven't slowed so much that anyone here could do me harm."

"Ah. Good. That's good to hear."

Yonder had to turn away to hide his dismay. He needn't have bothered, though, for at that moment, Far stiffened and tilted his head as if he had heard something mildly displeasing. The first drops of rain began to patter against the window outside. Far set his port down.

The knocker on the front door rapped three times.

It was midday. The curtains in the front office on the end of Merchants Row had been thrown open. But it was still dim inside, with no more than a faint dusky light creeping through the window. Long shadows stretched from the furniture and spread across the floorboards and carpets. Far stood ankle deep in the one by the partners desk. He tapped his foot on the shadow impatiently.

Lady Otherly leaned forward in her armchair, sniffed, but said nothing.

She was dressed in an indigo dress with a matching handbag, and her steel hair was bound as tight as a bowstring. As yet, she had not uttered a word since barging into the foyer and helping herself to the seat. Cold, haughty, put-upon, she held the demeanor of a landlord come to collect a tenant's overdue rent. Far would have gladly wrung her neck.

The rain came down outside in sheets, peels of thunder rolled by, and neither Far nor Otherly would speak to the other. It was as if the two were locked in a contest of impertinence that neither one wished to yield by acknowledging the other. Somewhere, a bell tolled one o'clock.

"So . . ." she deigned to speak (and it pained her, plainly it pained her to be the first, Far thought with some pleasure). The word hung in the air with a stony timbre and her mouth slowly curled into a snarl. "So you are the man who murdered Her Feral Majesty."

"The Mad Queen, you mean," Far replied. "Yes. I slew her in battle."

Otherly sniffed again.

"She was a dear friend of mine," she said. "Until that unfortunate misunderstanding between her and my Lady. Tragic affair. Before that, I held her as a very dear friend."

Far said nothing but looked at Otherly with unalloyed indifference.

"She wasn't mad, either," Otherly continued. "Driven, yes. At times manic. But when she was lucid, she could be charming and quite gracious. She had the sweetest heart."

He thought for a moment. "I found it a bit salty."

What darkness that lingered in the room seemed to flee before the shadow of Otherly's frown. The two glared at one another as the sounds of the rainstorm filled the space between them.

Half-past one rang. Otherly let out an annoyed grunt and turned her head about to survey the entirety of the room. When she returned her gaze to Far, she showed a hint of mock surprise.

"And where is Yonder?"

"Indisposed."

"When last I was here, it was the junior lawyer who was

indisposed. Today I'm told the opposite. I think I prefer to suffer the former."

Far pulled out a chair from the partners desk and sat down. He stretched his legs before him and propped one foot on top of the other. "What is it you want?"

"My letter was clear enough," she quipped. "I would have a report on your progress."

"He sent you a report, by return letter."

She opened her handbag, removed the paper that Yonder had written her and crumpled it in her hand. She tossed it at Far's foot. "This is lawyer's drivel. He's told me nothing of what he's actually done, yet has the gall to ask for further payment. I find that unacceptable."

Far glanced at the mess on the floor and folded his arms across his chest.

"Your partner holds something precious of mine," she continued. "Yet all I receive in return are platitudes and hollow assurances. Which, you know," she said, and a wicked smirk spread across her pale lips, "were what got him, and you, into your present predicament."

Far felt a flush in his cheeks. His fists clenched, and he might have come to blows with the woman there and then, but in limped Yonder. He was dressed and groomed, his hair oiled, his coat ironed, shoe buckles polished, but it did little to conceal the pallor he exuded.

"My dear Lady Otherly." Yonder flashed the briefest smile as he made straight for the nearest empty chair in the room. He collapsed into it and slipped his hand between the buttons of his vest. A line of sweat beaded down his forehead. As he dabbed a handkerchief at it, he noticed the discarded paper Otherly had littered on the floor. "Oh, good," he said, "I see you got my letter."

Otherly studied the lawyer and made a face.

"You look wretched."

"A temporary malady. Came on last night. After I was

99

exposed to some noxious vapors outside of town." He stuffed his kerchief back into his coat pocket. "While working on your case, actually. I'll be quite alright by the end of the day. Then it's back to work."

She shook her head disapprovingly. "If you're not well enough to attend to my matter, then say so. And return my retainer to me. I'm sure I can find someone else who can—"

"My Lady, please." Yonder held up a hand. He grimaced with some discomfort, but quickly mastered his features. "I am nearly recovered already. Besides," he added chidingly, "who else would you entrust such an important matter to? We are the preeminent firm on Custom."

Otherly's eyes narrowed.

"So you say. You seemed eager to keep me from returning. From your letter, it almost seemed as if you had bad news you were trying to hide."

"Not at all! Quite the contrary, I had hoped to surprise you with an early fulfillment. Save you the bother of coming back to Doldrums before we had your lock of hair. And we very nearly had it, didn't we, Captain Far?"

"Mm-hm," Far grunted.

"Really?" For the first time, the scowl that seemed sculpted into Otherly's being chipped apart, as if something were trying to shine through it. Her fingers twitched with anticipation. "Did you – did you see him, then?"

"Indeed, we did. And I would be pleased, Lady Otherly . . . nay, *delighted*, to share with you a full account of the extraordinary progress we've made with your case. For it is nothing but good news." He set his hands on his knees and tried to come forward to the edge of his seat but had to abandon his lawyerly pose. "Would you care to hear it?"

Otherly was ravenous to hear it, and so for the next half hour, Yonder proceeded through an account of their doings over the past few days. It was, Far reflected, a relatively honest, if not heavily stilted, recollection. He might not have described Wylde's unexpected abduction as "a cowardly flight from justice," nor did Far necessarily agree that they were a "hair's breadth from capturing the rogue." Personally, he had only caught a fleeting glimpse of Wylde, with at least sixty yards of wooded clearing between them. But perhaps embellishments that would have warranted a flogging had they been delivered in a report to a commanding officer could be countenanced when they were between an attorney and his client. What Far found more interesting was how the moment Yonder mentioned Wylde's appearance, Otherly perked up and peppered Yonder with a volley of questions on the most trivial of details. With each answer, Otherly's countenance brightened, and her bearing softened, if only ever so slightly.

"So you see," Yonder concluded, "we have him cornered now. He has nowhere to run. Soon we will close the net. And then—" he snapped his fingers and gestured as if he were holding something delicate. "We shall have your lock of hair."

"My, my." Otherly tapped her fingertips together in a rare display of enthusiasm. "My," she repeated. "I am surprised, Yonder. In a not unpleasant way. I had expected something more along the line of that letter—"

"A hasty note, Madam. I should have taken more time with its writing."

"Yes, you should have. It gave one the impression of dawdling and wheel spinning. I was almost of a mind to have my retainer back from you. But, no." She studied Yonder appraisingly with her dark eyes. "You've made progress. You have actually seen him. Of that, I have no doubt."

"Seen him – and nearly taken him."

Otherly dipped her head tersely and rose. "You may carry on, Yonder. I shall expect the matter concluded shortly. If everything you say is true."

"Depend upon on it, madam," he said, rising with her. Far did not bother to move.

"Um, my Lady?" Yonder ventured.

She paused and the displeased glower settled back over her features like a returning tide.

"A small matter," he continued, "a trifle. You may recall in that hastily written letter, I had made a very minor request . . ."

Otherly exhaled a long, annoyed breath. "I do recall that."

"I hope, madam, having now been apprised of all our remarkable progress and how dutifully we are managing your matter for you, that you could see fit to advance that inconsequential payment I had requested. A payment that, I can assure you, will only redound to your benefit, as it will help hasten along the remaining pieces of work that must be done."

She threw her hands up in disgust and launched into a rant about being fleeced with attorney's fees, and the burden of receiving a bill on short notice, but, in the end, after a little more cajoling from Yonder, she relented. She opened the handbag again and tossed something onto the table.

It was a cluster of thorny stems, each stalk the color of coal and topped with a button-sized petal. The buds were as black as a hole in a mountain.

"Baby's Death?" Yonder asked.

"You requested a payment of flowers, did you not?"

Yonder made a pretense of considering the forlorn clump of scrub lying before him. Far could sense the profound disappointment just beneath the semblance of pleasantry.

"Thank you, my Lady," Yonder said at last, "my deepest appreciation. But, um . . ."

"What?"

"Well, it's just . . . and please do not misconstrue this

for ingratitude, but . . . well, I was hoping for flowers of a more, how shall I say? A more substantive variety."

Otherly fixed him with a frigid glare, to which Yonder added hastily, "Not that Baby's Death isn't a charming – plant."

Far would have called it what it was: a roadside weed, good for kindling campfires and not much else.

"I had in mind," Yonder continued, "one of the more traditional flora of our realm. Souldrop. Canker-o'-king. Even Banshee Bloom would have served. They're all in season, and could be gathered without the least—"

"Do you take me for a *gardener*?"

Otherly's eyes blazed, and her nostrils flared.

"Not at all, madam," Yonder half spoke, half sighed. "Not at all. A misunderstanding, on my part. I accept – I appreciate – your payment, of course. Thank you. I shall put these to work straightaway and hope to deliver our next report by the next moon."

"No more reports," she said. "No more letters. I shall come to Doldrums one more time. To retrieve my hair. Get it before spring returns, else this bargain is ended. Ring for me the moment you have it in your hands. Here."

For a final time, she reached into her handbag and placed into Yonder's palm a plain and miniscule silver bell, no wider than a fingertip, of the kind that was ordinarily used by courtesans to summon their inferiors. Yonder slipped it into his pocket.

Otherly added icily, "It summons my butler. He has instructions to find me when he hears it."

"Very good."

"I take my leave of you now," she said. "If you hope to take your leave of this realm . . . don't dawdle."

She swept out of the office and slammed the door behind her.

When she had gone, Yonder loosened his cravat,

unbuttoned his coat, and sank back into his chair.

"Damn clients," he breathed.

"They're worse than queens," Far agreed.

Yonder made a face at the weeds Otherly had left for him. "I hate to impose on you again, but I can't bend over. Would you mind getting that for me?" He gestured at the table.

Far went and picked the bundle up and brought it to Yonder, who set up a tea kettle and cup. The clump of plants looked and felt completely unremarkable.

"What kind of payment is this?" Far asked.

Yonder cupped the flower buds to his face and inhaled. Carefully, he picked some of the petals and began to crush them between his thumb and forefinger, pinched them into dust, which he sprinkled into his cup.

They made a small flash, a paltry waxy glint of light, in the cinnamon-colored tea.

"A very poor one," Yonder answered.

He drank deeply from his teacup. As Far watched, the first traces of his partner's former orange glow began to return to his cheeks.

They ate breakfast in Yonder's usual booth at Holland's coffee house. A tucked-away alcove where someone had left a castoff pair of mahogany benches and a rickety table, it was seldom occupied except when Yonder came to dine, which was frequent enough that the proprietor had made it known it was "the squire's preferred table" for the few who ever asked for it. The hour neared nine o'clock and the bustling common room of Boston's fourth most popular coffee house thrummed with noise. A crowd of workers dispersed to their respective labors, while a statelier crowd comprised of the town's gentlemen came inside to take their place. In the shaded space of their booth, Yonder gave only a passing notice of this changing of the guard, while Far paid none at all.

They were each engaged in private pursuits. Far had his nose buried in the latest edition of the *National Gazette*. Yonder read the same line over in his green book of Custom. A plate of salted herring, eggs, and buttered toast sat between them.

Far propped his legs up on his bench and picked at his teeth, while Yonder returned his attention to the page of Wherestone he had been reading. He managed to finish it, let out a vexed sigh, and slammed the book closed.

"What was *that* about?" Far asked from behind his paper.

"I'm beginning to wonder whether I've completely misjudged Wherestone. His prose, the way he turns his phrases, it's almost . . . I don't know. Like he's having a joke, at his reader's peril." Yonder shook his head. "He confuses me."

"Better not let your client hear you say that."

"Our client," Yonder corrected him. "Obviously, I will not burden our client with my private misgivings. She only desires to be possessed of her lock of hair. How we bring that about is of no concern to her. Nor should it be."

A group of bankers filed inside, laughing much too loudly about some private jest that pertained to commerce, something to do with the rising price of gold.

"The problem is," Yonder said, more to himself, "there's nothing to go on now. There's no record of Wylde in the court or in the steward's office. His captors seem to have spirited him away. And I have nothing of his that we could use to track him down. I fear the trail's gone cold."

"Pity," Far grunted and turned a page.

"You could at least pretend to be concerned," Yonder

snapped. "Otherly didn't leave us much time to find him again."

Far set the newspaper aside for a moment.

"Face it, he's gone. Wylde's drawn a door and left Doldrums. That's what I would have done."

Yonder shook his head intently.

"He can't leave. The idiot let himself be bound. He gave his hands to them. I saw him. I'm sure he thought it funny at the time, but there's no jesting when it comes to Custom. 'Beware your bargains,' Wherestone says. Wylde's trapped himself here. That I'm sure of."

"What, just because they clapped some iron bracelets around his wrists?" Far scoffed.

"No. Because he willingly placed himself in those iron bracelets. That makes all the difference in Custom. Mark my words, Wylde is stuck in Doldrums. If we can only find him."

"I'm sure you'll come up with something," Far yawned and flipped over his newspaper to begin the back page.

Yonder groused and poked at the fish on the plate with his fork. It was an absent gesture, and not proper etiquette, but it suited his mood at the present. Yonder wracked his thoughts, but nothing would come to him. At last, he turned his attention back to Far and frowned.

"I don't understand you," he spoke to the front page of the *Gazette*. "You won't spend a minute to learn Custom, but you'll waste a whole morning reading the drivel in a Doldrums news sheet."

"I've acquired a taste for it. Like you with your tea."

"They're nothing alike." He plunged the fork hard into the herring. "But I do find it curious. For someone who loathes these people as much as you, to hold such preternatural interest in their affairs. Very curious."

"Not at all," Far grinned. "It's the tone I enjoy. Here, listen to this . . . 'and if His Excellency, the President, Mr. Adams, should not find this humble essay sufficiently seditious (presumably after an aide were to read and explain its contents to him), then let me add, if only to bring myself fully within the ambit of his tyrannical laws (and to join the esteemed company of Representative Lyon in his unjust imprisonment), that I propose another Revolution. Yes, to arms! Once more into the breach. Only this time, there shall be no treaty. Not for our Little King John the Lesser. This time, we shall have the tyrant *burned upon a pyre*, and his own seditious enactments *shall be the fuel.*'" Far shook the newspaper with fondness. "It's the damndest thing! They're as docile as sheep in person. But put a pen in their hands, and they're ready to burn the world down. I find it very entertaining."

Yonder chewed his fish, pre-occupied in his thoughts.

"Oh, look here," Far set the *Gazette* down between them.

"I'm not interested in that gentleman's invective. If you ask me, the Sedition Acts have been completely misunderstood—"

"No, not that." Far pointed to a small column near the lower corner of the page, the last article before a series of smudged legal advertisements. "Seems the local militia is to be called out to that little village we went to, what was that place called?"

"West Chesterton," Yonder replied, turning the newspaper around so he could read it. His eyes darted swiftly through the splay of words, when all of a sudden he spotted something that seized his complete attention. Yonder brought the newspaper near the tip of his nose.

"It says they're going to burn the place down," Far summarized.

"Of course they're going to burn it down," Yonder retorted. "I didn't need a newspaper to tell me that. Did you see the announcement underneath that article?"

"Eh?"

Yonder flipped the newspaper back around on the table and pointed at two lines of miniscule typeset.

"It's a court notice," Yonder declared, and were he not in a gentlemen's establishment, he might have let out a whoop and a whistle. "It concerns a certain Mary Faulkner. A maniac, the paper says. Who finds herself in custody. Our Blessed Mary has survived her ordeal with Custom!"

Far made a face. "I thought you said she would die."

"She should have." Yonder laughed in amazement. "A most resilient witch. I can't wait to see her again." He hopped to his feet, called out for their bill, and hurriedly drank down the remnants of his tea. "Come, Captain. We have a court appearance to make. There's no time to waste."

Far stretched his legs across the floor, let out a loud yawn, and repositioned his backside on his bench seat to indicate he was going nowhere.

"I have no wish to see that woman again," he said.

Yonder knew better than to press the matter. He buttoned his coat and tucked his book beneath his arm.

"Very well. I'll go alone." As he left, he made a point to call over his shoulder. "Remember, though. If you're not at the table, you may be on the menu."

CHAPTER EIGHT

"Do not let the locals become privy to our portals and windows. It can only sow disorder and cause consternation."
— Wherestone's *Commentaries on Custom*, page 23

The courthouse stood in the middle of an avenue that had, until fairly recently, been known as Queen Street.

It was brick, stately, and nearly empty, which was not at all uncommon for a government building on a Friday. This Friday, though, lamps shone through a lone window of the smallest office on the ground floor, a wan glow behind a cracked, frosted glass. It came from a shabby little room situated far from the main halls, near the building's gutter spouts, which meant the place was rarely dry in the winter. It could have been a serviceable storage room. As a courtroom, it left much to be desired.

Yet Yonder stood as if he were about to address the Chief Justice of the Supreme Court himself. He brought his small stature to its fullest height, held the pose, along with a demure smile that he was certain would exude both pleasantness and assurance. His coat was brushed and buttoned. A raft of important looking papers was shoved beneath his arm – on his way to the courthouse, he had picked them, happenstance and higgly-piggly, from a bookbinder who had no more use for them.

The only other occupants in the courtroom were a sleeping grocer's helper who apparently earned a penny a day working as a bailiff and the justice of the peace, Mr. Robert Onions, who was, Yonder knew, the grocer who employed the bailiff. A wobbly table served as his bench. Yonder listened as a hall clock ticked the time away.

Clink, clink, clink.

From a worn leather chair, the grocer justice screwed his wrinkled face into what was surely a well-practiced expression of disdain for those who came before him. A threadbare wig perched on his head slid a fraction of an inch forward. He pushed it back and returned his attention to the papers on his bench, leaving Yonder on his feet, to await His Honor's pleasure.

Clink, clink.

"May it please the court?" Yonder offered politely.

Onions kept his eyes fixed upon his sheet and replied.

"It does not."

He dipped a quill pen into an inkwell and began to sketch a picture. The justice's nose hovered just above the table's surface. He turned his paper at odd angles as he thrashed long, flourishing strokes across the page in a way that could not possibly have made any coherent lettering. Had he been able to see the justice's work for himself, Yonder would have found a credible rendering of a dragon. One that was breathing fire down upon a clutch of fat attorneys. His Honor kept at his drawing for another five minutes, and only when he seemed sufficiently satisfied with his composition did he deign to give Yonder a smoldering glare.

"State your business, then."

With a deep, reverent bow, Yonder introduced himself.

"I am John Yonder, Esquire come before the court on behalf of my client, Captain John Far."

"Don't give a damn about your names." Onions shook the feather pen, sending a shower of black from the table. "Which case you here on?"

"The Matter of Mary Faulkner, your Honor."

"Never heard of that one." He glanced quickly at the page he had been drawing upon and thumped it with an angry finger. "It isn't on the docket. Which means it weren't set for hearing. Which means you're wasting the court's time, counselor."

"Forgive me, your Honor, I should—"

"Talk to Petersen." The justice jerked a thumb toward his bailiff who made no pretense of hiding the fact that he was napping. Onions seemed untroubled by the snoring, for he rose from the table as if to leave. "He keeps the docket. Peterson'll give you a day. Likely won't be 'til the summer, though."

"Pray, forgive me, but I—"

"Tell it to Peterson," Onions repeated brusquely. At the sound of his name, the bailiff gave a slight start from his stool, a bleary eye started to crack open, then closed again.

"Forgive me, your Honor," Yonder pressed on, "I should have explained myself more clearly. We are here in response to a legal notice. One in this week's *Gazette*."

That froze the justice in his tracks. The clock's pendulum swung back and forth several times before he turned and blinked at Yonder questioningly.

"Did you – do you mean to say you actually . . . you read a legal notice in a newspaper?"

"Yes, your Honor."

Onions' hand swept across his face, moved his wig about, and scratched an itch on his chin. Apparently, His Honor felt compelled to sit back down at this news.

"See here, Mister – what did you say your name was?"

"Yonder, your Honor."

"Yonder . . . peculiar name. Look, Yonder, those notices aren't for reading. No one ever *reads* them. It just isn't done."

Yonder acknowledged the unusualness of the circumstances as he fished through his papers and relayed yet more apologies. He found what he was looking for, the copy of the *National Gazette* Far had lent him.

"Ah, here we are." Yonder flipped the paper to the back page and read aloud, "'A woman who has been identified as one Mary Faulkner was taken into custody by the constable last Monday on complaint of her disturbing the peace. Said M. Faulkner has been deemed feeble-minded, deaf, dumb, and/or a maniac, to wit: she is dressed in soiled clothing, can give no account of her person or actions, and is highly agitated. She is being held as a public invalid. Anyone with connection or interest in said M. Faulkner shall appear forthwith to the Court of Common Pleas, give presentment of his claim, and will at once be heard.'" Yonder concluded with a meaningful pause. "Your Honor, I have come to give presentment of a claim."

The justice of the peace gaped at Yonder. From his chair, he let out a succession of huffs. A withered tongue clicked thoughtfully behind his teeth, as his face grew dark.

"Oh-ho-ho." Onions wagged his finger at Yonder. "I get your game . . . you're here for the bursar. Come to shake me down, eh? I should have Petersen throw you out on your ass. Y'hear? Claim, indeed! Bugger him, bugger you, and bugger your claim!"

Yonder held his hands up in defense, but the vent the

justice had launched into would not be staunched. Even Petersen came to attention.

"You can tell that fat, crooked whoreson, I don't give a damn how much the constable charged him to pick this woman up. That's the bursar's expense, not mine! Public dole's the bursar's responsibility. Everybody knows that. I've got expenses enough to manage without reimbursing his flights of fancy!"

Yonder saw his chance to sneak a word in. "We're not here from the bursar."

"Eh?"

"I've nothing to do with that gentleman, your Honor. My client wishes to relieve the government of Miss Faulkner's care. Captain Far would take charge of the invalid, as her guardian. At his own expense."

The justice leaned across his table and eyed Yonder suspiciously.

"You mean . . . he's going to take someone *off* the dole?"

"Precisely," Yonder smiled.

The wig came off. Onions rubbed his bald scalp in apparent amazement.

"Where is this fellow?"

"At the moment?" Yonder reflected. "Either at leisure or engaged in hostilities. Those seem to be his favorite activities."

"Hostilities? What, is he fighting those French pirates?"

"Um – indeed," Yonder nodded gravely. "The very ones."

"Good. Frog bastards are due for a thrashing. But here now. How's your client going to serve as a guardian if he's at sea?"

Yonder thought quickly. Fortunately, he had his ream of documents, which he pretended to sort through and name.

"He is a man of considerable means, and I have with me

113

his power of attorney, an affidavit, bill of attainder, *coram nobis*, the usual forms. Captain Far has made all the necessary arrangements for me to act on his behalf to see that the lady is properly cared for."

"And, just so we're clear . . . he'll take full charge of the invalid, without recourse?"

"No recourse is asked, and none will be given."

"Well," the justice remarked, chewing his fingernail, "this is an oddity, that's for sure. Usually, I'd tell you to come back later. But as you're here to pay for – um, take charge of – a public invalid, and without recourse, I suppose that changes the matter around. You should've said something from the start, Yonder."

"I do apologize, your Honor."

Onions called the bailiff over, hissed in his ear, and off Petersen shuffled to fetch Miss Faulkner from her jail cell. He soon returned dragging an irate woman by the arm.

She was much gaunter than when Yonder had last seen her and looked as bedraggled as a beggar. What had been her wild shock of brown hair hung in damp, dead clumps. She berated Petersen mercilessly as he escorted her into court, stringing expletives upon him like a longshoreman while the bailiff pulled her across the far aisle of the courtroom.

No question, but that this was Blessed Mary, the fortune-teller of the South End. She was still dressed in the same ridiculous cloak she had worn at the séance, though it was much filthier, and stained, and, Yonder suspected, swarming with lice. He slunk down in his chair and turned it a bit so that she couldn't see his profile.

"Leggo of me, you sodding, impotent ass!" Mary hissed at Petersen. "Fucking whoreson! Leggo!" She must have noticed that she had been brought into the courtroom, but instead of composing herself, Mary simply turned her tirade upon the justice. "Hey, magistrate. You can't hold me here.

What about my rights? I want a plea, and a demurrer, and — and habeas corpus!"

"You are a ward of this town," Onions cut over her in a bored, officious tone, "held for your own protection due to your madness."

"I'm not mad! Who said I'm mad? I've a chatter-mouth that won't stop talking to me, and who won't stop playing the goddam flute! That doesn't make me mad!"

"Miss Faulkner," Onions warned.

"Day and night he's tooting, hammers and tongs. It's pretty, but I've got to sleep. All I want is for him to shut up. Just order him to stop, and I—"

At a prompt from the justice, Petersen clapped his hand hard over her mouth. Mary parted her lips, started to press her teeth into one of his fingers, but a warning tap against the side of her temple gave her pause. Petersen had brought out a leather truncheon. Likely the one he used to keep the drunkards on good behavior. Mary fell silent, while on the other side of the room, Yonder kept his face hidden from her view. Hopefully, she wouldn't recognize him before he could finish this hearing.

"Right," the justice said. "Now what did you say your client's connection to this woman was?"

"Captain Far is Miss Faulkner's husband," Yonder replied hastily. "They were very recently wed."

Onions gave a satisfied nod. "That'll work. So, Mrs. Far will—"

Suddenly, a horrible shriek rent the courtroom.

From across the courtroom, Mary pointed a skeletal finger straight at Yonder, trying to scream through the muffle of the bailiff's hand. Her eyes were aflame with recognition. She struggled to free herself, twisting wildly in his grasp, and clamped her teeth hard on the bailiff's thumb.

"You!" She charged toward Yonder, shaking a fist.

"Green bag *bastard!* You're the one that did this to me! What did you—"

A soft thud landed on the back of her skull. Mary went limp, her eyes rolled back, and she fell to the floor in a heap, unconscious. A line of spittle ran across the floorboards from her gaping mouth. Petersen stood over her, staring down dumbly. In one hand, he held a small truncheon; his other hand had her bite mark, swelling up pink.

"Woman's madder than King George," Onions muttered. "She seemed to recognize you, though," he said to Yonder, as he made a note of some sort in his record. "Good enough for public work . . ."

The justice scratched his signature across a document and blew the ink dry.

"Court's adjourned," he announced. "Petersen, better get some leeches on that thumb so it don't get infected."

Onions rose from his chair abruptly. Yonder was not at all certain of the legalities of what had just transpired.

"Um, what about Miss Faulkner uh, Mrs. Far?" he inquired. He cast a worried glance at the body lying on the courthouse floor, wondering how on earth he was supposed to move her, and whether she was entirely safe to touch. "What shall I, or um, I should say, how shall I—"

"Do whatever you have to with her. She's your problem now." The justice flicked his hand toward Mary, as if she were a pile of rubbish that should have already been removed. "Take her to this Captain Far. Or out to sea. Or to New York. Just see that she don't come back here."

Yonder peeked around the makeshift screen he had set up among the clutter of Mary's apartment. Mary was still in the cauldron, as wet, and naked, and angry as the day she was born. Steam twined about the folds of her skin, milk pale from her days in a cell, and curled around the strands of brown hair that floated about her head like kelp. The rugs and floorboards beneath the cauldron were soaked. Her garments burned in the hearth.

Despite the awkwardness of Yonder's proximity, Mary seemed to be in no hurry to finish her bath. Much to Yonder's annoyance.

It had cost him two and a half dollars to have Petersen transport Mary back to her home. Once inside, Yonder had drawn a bath in the only thing he could find that would serve as a tub, stripped her, and set her in the cauldron, hoping the warm water would both awaken her and at the same time calm some of her prior agitation. It succeeded in the former, less so in the latter.

"Would you care for a brush?" he inquired mildly.

"Go to hell."

Yonder let out a sigh. If only she knew . . .

"Here you are." Yonder reached around the lattice panel of the screen to hand her a wooden scrubber. A wet hand whacked his knuckles sharply, sending the brush clattering to the floor. Yonder sucked on his throbbing finger. It tasted like soap suds. "Still feeling a little off, then?"

Bathwater sloshed to the floor followed by a pair of feet tromping through the puddle. In a nick of time, Yonder was on his feet, doing his best to avert his eyes from the soaked and naked fortune-teller who stood before him.

"A little *off*?" Mary poked a dripping finger into his chest. Rivulets of water cascaded down her body. Yonder worried it would leak through the floorboards and into the rooms below, but at the moment Mary seemed no more bothered by that than by the fact that she had not a stitch of clothing on her. Her nostrils flared and her reddened eyes burned at Yonder. "What did you do to me?"

"What do you mean?"

Her hands waved in a flurry about her head, sending a spray of water everywhere.

"I-I hear things . . . all the time now. In here." She tapped the side of one of her temples. "Murmurs and music. All the time. It's so . . . sad, and awful," she paused, as if listening, "but – but beautiful."

She rounded on Yonder and started to back him into a wall. He stumbled over piles of cutlery, newspapers, a broken signpost, and nearly lost his footing as Mary jabbed an accusing finger at him with the fervor of a rapier. "Don't you *dare* tell me I'm mad!"

Yonder calmly shook his head.

"You're not mad, Mary."

Her eyes darted from side to side. She cast a wary glance at Yonder.

"It's that – that *thing* you did at the séance," she said under her breath, "whatever it was . . . what almost killed me. That's what this is, isn't it?"

There was no way for him to explain what he scarcely understood himself, and no point trying with Mary in her present state. She was still too riled. Yonder spotted a gray folded blanket on a shelf in the cupboard next to him. He handed it to Mary, who, to his relief, began to tie it about her person like a towel. Yonder clasped his hands and, remembering a bit of advice he had received long ago about a woman's wrath, spoke to her as gently as he could.

"First, why don't you tell me what you're feeling."

Mary's anger seemed to retreat a step. She finished knotting the blanket around her bosom and slouched onto a nearby sofa.

"I'm tired," she said at last, as her chin fell into her chest.

"I'm sure you are," said Yonder.

"Ever since the séance . . ."

"Tell me what happened."

118

A tremor shook Mary. She brought her knees in tight to her chest and shivered.

"When I . . . when I looked in the mirror, the one you had me set up, I-I was thinking of a line I'd use, something mystical sounding, and . . ." Her eyes shut tight. "It was like a gate had slammed shut inside my head, and then there was this hand, like ice, and it – it grabbed me – all of me," she held out her hands and gestured at her chest, as if to show Yonder her very soul, "it had me, and it squeezed all the warmth out."

Yonder leaned forward intently. "Go on," he urged her.

"Then it stopped. Squeezing, I mean. But the cold was still there. And I could hear a man's voice, he was laughing – from miles away, but I could just make it out. And he was playing a flute. I don't know how I know it was the same person, but it was. So beautiful. I just wanted to hold onto it, but it kept slipping away, like – like . . ." Mary blinked, as if she were starting to come awake. She rubbed the wetness of her arms. "Like holding onto water," she finished.

Her voice sounded stretched and hollow and still raw from rage. Yonder settled his back against the cupboard and gazed into Mary's eyes. What he saw in their reflection was more or less what he expected – confusion, affront, a bit of shame, some of the other base appetites of her kind – but there was something else in there. Almost like a light shining beneath a bushel . . . At least her faculties seemed to be intact.

"The good news," said Yonder, "is you've not lost your wits. You're alive, and you are in your right mind. Take comfort in that."

She turned to Yonder and in a steady voice asked him.

"What did you do to me?"

Yonder drew a long breath through his nostrils and let it out slowly.

"The best explanation I can give you at this time,

madam, the only one you can possibly understand, is that I used you."

She nodded slowly. "How?"

Yonder pursed his lips. What to say? Not the truth, of course. That was out of the question. But some modicum of candor would be necessary – if he hoped to make any further use of her, he would require her cooperation. For her to do what he required, she would need to know something about what she could do. His gaze began to wander across Mary's apartment. The painted mobiles still hung limply from the ceiling, the bottles and boxes were scattered in their piles and foothills and the garishly-colored cow skull marked the wall. The sign for Blessed Mary's services, the slate board that had listed her fees for prophesying and soothsaying, had been wiped clean. And rinsed. The mirrors he had had her arrange at their first visit were also missing. Not even a shard remained.

"Have you ever looked out a window for someone?" he asked her.

Mary's forehead crinkled. "Of course."

"This is a terribly crude analogy. But think of a window." He pointed toward a cracked pane of glass in the wall behind the cupboard. Less than a quarter of it showed, and that part was hidden behind a moldy, floral drapery. But a faint bar of sunlight still shone through, illuminating a small cloud of dust specks floating in the air. "A window is a vista," Yonder explained. "A way to view that which is beyond. They're not always as clear as we should like. Sometimes they're hidden by furniture. Or curtained. Or both. But the essence of a window is that it can let one see what he otherwise could not. If one should use it. Do you follow me so far?"

"I know what a window is," she said irritably.

Yonder drew a step closer to Mary and bent over so that he could meet her face fully. "Imagine if a window could be cut within the walls of your mind," he said. "So that you could see . . . outside. That was what I did to you. I made a window. And I opened it up."

Mary's face turned pale. She shivered and hugged her legs tight. He was about to offer her his coat when she suddenly recoiled. Her eyes fluttered, and she breathed feverishly. Sweat trickled from her forehead, mixing with the drying bathwater on her cheeks. Her bottom lip hinged open. Something in her hands seemed to have frightened her.

"Mary?"

She had her fingers splayed as wide as she could spread them.

"I see," she breathed. "Hands. Only . . . they're – they're *dark*. Two dark hands. They're not mine. Oh, God . . . What's happening to my hands?"

Yonder knelt before the couch, as close as he could dare without touching her, so as not to break her spell.

"Don't be afraid," Yonder whispered. "They're not your hands. They're his. Mr. Wylde's. He's a black-skinned gentleman. Do you see anything else?"

Mary wiped at her eyes and slowly turned her wrists around.

"I see . . . Chains. Manacles. God . . ."

Her body shook from a sob. She doubled over, clutched herself and began to weep. Whether it was from the sight she had just seen, or the strain she had borne in jail, or just the want of sleep, Mary fell into a bout of crying.

All the while, Yonder smiled, and, eminently satisfied with what he had heard, gave Mary's arm a soft, possessive squeeze.

Two days of gray sleet. The morning of the third broke

cold and languid, but clear. The last remnants of the doddering storm gasped its final wintry breath. A tin light marked the sun's ascent from behind a curtain of steel-colored clouds that had settled over the sky. A few flurries of snow drifted along aimlessly to find ridges and broken juts in the roads to settle upon. Just enough to lend a deadened sheen of white around Merchants Row.

Horses and townspeople were out, bundled in scarves. They shuffled along the street, clomped through the frosted puddles and slush, and kicked up muck on one another. There were more than the usual number of curses in the air, and at an unusually boisterous volume for morning time.

Yonder grew bored with watching and closed the curtain in his office window. In his arms he held a folded blanket. He wore slippers and crept quietly, not making any sound, as he approached the couch he had set next to his office's stove. The cheery fire he had built up was still burning behind the grate. On the sofa, half buried in cushions and tapestries, lay Mary.

She snored loudly.

Yonder spread the blanket on top of her, covering the last part of Mary's shins. He watched her for a while and let out a sigh as he returned to his desk.

His Wherestone was on one of the curved table edges. Yonder had left the green book there, a paperweight kept it pried open at the page he had read all morning. He glanced down at it and frowned. His people's letters were ornamental compared to Doldrums languages; in Wherestone's hand, they were almost acrobatic.

"Such pretension," Yonder murmured under his breath.

He made a slow circumambulation of the page and pinched the bridge of his nose.

" 'A curious variety of reactions,' " he read softly, " 'may attend the Doldrumite's exposure to our realm, which, in some instances, could prove fatal. Repetition of the exposure could serve to hasten or amplify these effects, whatever they may be. On the other hand, some of these folk seem to acclimate.' "

He let out a frustrated groan and glared at the page with irritation. He addressed the book directly, as if its author were sitting there within its pages.

"A variety of reactions *may* attend . . . in *some* instances . . . *could* prove fatal . . . *Whatever* they *may* be . . . What a chary writer you are." He closed the cover with disgust. "What I find curious, Mr. Wherestone, is how you can claim to have written a comprehensive work that is so utterly bereft of certitude. You should have been a lawyer."

"Oh, no, there's quite enough lawyers in this world," Far's voice boomed from the doorway. "Though there's one less of them now. Ha!"

"Shush, shush," Yonder hurried over to the foyer. "Keep your voice down."

"Now that I think on it, he might have been a money changer. Or maybe a banker? No matter. Whatever he was, there's one less of 'em!"

Far was in one of his moods, Yonder could tell straightaway. And judging from the smell of drink about him, perched on the edge of inebriation. He was booted and his clothes looked weathered. Yet there was a gleam in Far's eye, and a terrible glow shining about his face as he tromped into the office.

"Where have you been?" Yonder whispered.

"Reveling in Quincy," he replied airily. "Fine place. Miserable people. Had to settle an affair of honor with one of them. Here, something for the till." He dropped a wad of banknotes and coins, leaving Yonder to scramble after them on the floor. It was a small fortune. Yonder looked up at Far questioningly.

"The lout actually placed a wager on his own duel.

Typical merchant." Far was about to toss his coat onto Yonder's sofa when he noticed Mary. "And what the devil is *that* doing in your chamber?"

"Hush." Yonder left the rest of the money on the floor and led Far by the elbow into the adjacent room of Far's office. Once inside he kept his voice low even after he had shut the partition door.

"I got her from the courthouse," Yonder explained. "I cleaned her up and brought her here. She's been asleep all day, and I would prefer she remain that way so she can recuperate."

Far pulled a sour face. He glided across his office to the liquor cabinet for his bottle of port.

"I never cared for pets in a house," he said, as he pulled of his boots. "When will she be gone?"

"Yes, about that . . ." Yonder sat down, tapping his fingertips together. He cast a nervous glance at that terrible portrait of the Visigoth and wondered whether Far would look much the same once he learned of Yonder's plan. "You'd better have your drink."

Far's eyebrow arced quizzically, but he never needed an invitation or an excuse to imbibe his port. He brought the bottle and a glass over to an armchair, stretched his stockinged feet on the floor, and took his ease.

While Far drank, Yonder recounted his tale of how he had gained custody of Mary from the justice of the peace, how she had survived her brush with Custom, and the strange voices and melodies that had haunted her days. Unlike Far, Yonder always told orderly, sequential stories, though he did have a weakness for extraneous detail. This account was no exception. By the time Yonder had reached the point where he had brought Mary to their building, Far had finished off the bottle.

"So the short of the matter," Far cut in, "is that the woman's stuck seeing and hearing things. A pity for her. It's nothing to me." His words were slurred with a hard edge about them and were punctuated by Far waving his empty glass in such a way that it nearly went hurtling in Yonder's direction. Yonder measured carefully what he said next.

"If you'll hear me out, I'm afraid that is not the short of the matter at all."

"But I don't care," Far growled. "Don't you understand? I don't care what happens to this woman."

"You should."

"Why?"

"Because . . . because I believe she is beginning to understand what we are."

Far clapped his hands on his knees.

"I'll get my knife—" he said, rising.

"No, no, no, no." Yonder tugged at his shirt.

"Can't have her bleating about us to the other sheep. We'll never get a moment's peace."

"That's not what I mean. Listen to me – have a seat, I beg you. Listen. I can't say for sure. But I suspect her senses have been changed in some way. When I last spoke with her, just before she fell asleep, the way she looked at me . . . It was almost as if she was trying to peer through something. I think . . . she nearly saw me, as I am."

But Far tottered on his feet, scarcely listening. He grasped the back of his chair to steady himself, his face pinched with an irritation that, Yonder could already see, was well on its way toward a foul temper.

The drink may have been a mistake, Yonder thought glumly. He rose, walked over to Far, laid a hand on his shoulder, and spoke to him soothingly.

"We've nothing to fear from her. Everyone here believes she's a maniac. They'll never listen to her. She isn't, though. She sees more clearly than anyone in this realm. What's more, she can see Wylde – she can *feel* him. Almost like a compass. With a little encouragement, I think Mary could take us straight to Wylde. And we'll have my client's—"

"To hell with you and your client!" Far bellowed. He flung his empty bottle to the ground and stood over the broken pieces with his fists on his hips, his nostrils flaring. The temper billowed like a dark cloud about his head. "You're a *fool*," he spat.

Yonder lifted his chin but said nothing as his partner rounded on him. Best to let this fire burn itself out, he decided. It had been building for some time.

"A fool running 'round on a fool's errand." Far waved his hand at Yonder. "Look at yourself, pretending to be a lawyer. You've a shingle on a door and a book. That's all." He barked a laugh. "But you think your counsel is so valuable our people will come flocking to you – in Doldrums? What was it you said when you started this nonsense? We'd grow so rich in favors from your advice, we'd come home as kings."

"Like dukes," Yonder corrected. "I said we could set ourselves up like dukes."

"Fool!" Far made a disgusted noise, almost fell over, but righted himself at the last moment. His speech was heavy and dripped with disdain. "As usual, there was a flaw in your plan. Two, actually." He warbled on his feet and extended a finger. "First, you're not a lawyer. You never were."

The words hit Yonder like a blow. He shut his eyes and squared his shoulders, as if to help him bear the weight of Far's insult. Far turned his back on him and stumbled over to a desk where he began to search through a drawer, spilling out all its contents.

"Second," Far called over to him, "there's no one here to counsel. Or maybe you haven't noticed that—" He found what he was looking for. A long, serrated dagger that gleamed with a blue light. With each word, Far slashed at the air. "No one. Ever. Comes. To Doldrums!"

Yonder withstood the imaginary evisceration in silence.

Far panted, his voice fell low, "I'm finished with this farce. I've had enough, counselor." Far slipped the dagger through his belt. "You want to pretend you're a lawyer and slog across Doldrums for a shriveled old bitch's empty promise, I'll not stand in your way. But you're on your own. Meantime, I'm not going to let that—" He jerked his chin toward Yonder's office, "jeopardize what peace and quiet I can find in this realm. Since she knows what we are, I'm going to silence her."

Far started toward the partition door. Before he could pull it open, Yonder drew a deep breath and spoke with the cold, calm, pitiless detachment of a creditor settling an account.

"I'd prefer you not do that just yet," he said.

Far froze in place, swaying slightly from side to side. He tried to lurch forward, but like a hound that had reached the end of a leash, he seemed to be tethered. Far's breaths still fell like bellows of a furnace, but the fire was cooling.

With a solemn quiet, Yonder walked around Far, and placed himself before the doorway. Though he scarcely reached the bottom of his companion's chest, he lifted his stature in a way that he appeared entirely capable of barring the captain's way. He held Far's gaze.

"My friend," Yonder said softly, "my dear friend. How can I begin to express the depth of my gratitude to you? Your companionship, your aid, your patient indulgence of my proclivities. For a year you've dwelled with me here." He shook his head. "In this realm where a month can feel like a millennium, and with hardly a word of complaint. You've been like an oasis in a desert. A partner in the truest sense of the word."

Slowly, as if in a daze, Far returned to his seat, the tip of his dagger poked out from under his belt loop. Yonder sat next to him, so close they touched.

"And for that reason," Yonder continued, "in all our

time in Doldrums, I've not needed to remind you of the courtesy I extended to you when you faced her Majesty's judgment. Of the sacrifice I made on your behalf. That it is solely because of me, and my intervention, that you were banished, and not beheaded. That you are obliged to me for your life."

Far stared hard at Yonder, grinding his jaw. His eyes blazed from behind two narrow slits. His mouth trembled slightly, as if a torrent of retorts were frothing at the end of his tongue, trying to burst through the seams of his lips. Far forced them down, though, swallowed every one of them. For it could not be denied that Far was obliged to him.

"I've preferred that your debt has been left unspoken," said Yonder, "because there is no reason to speak of it. 'Gratitude is the first mark of a gentleman,' they say. And you, Captain, are above all else, a gentleman."

Far shut his eyes, tilted his neck, letting his hair billow over the back of his chair. He blew out an exhausted breath.

"I—" he started.

"Need not apologize," Yonder finished for him. "As your friend, I have no need of it. So long as we have an understanding."

Reluctantly, Far gave a tired nod.

A calm silence enveloped the office, so quiet they could hear Mary snoring in the room beyond. The shadows from the furniture grew long, and a blood-colored twilight filled the space, framing the darkness around Far, who rested his head on the back of his chair. Not to sleep, for that was not in their nature, but to settle thoughts that had perhaps grown too wild. As he sat in stillness, Yonder crouched on the floor to pick up the broken bits of glass and tidy the mess Far had made, his own thoughts churning on.

CHAPTER NINE

"A man of no renown once observed that in Doldrums the shortest distance between two points is a straight line. Perhaps. But how does one find the two points? That is the question to which one should attend . . ."

—Wherestone's *Commentaries on Custom*, page 2

In a way, Mary recovered.

She awoke early afternoon in a strange room feeling rested, almost pleasant. Warm biscuits and strong coffee were at hand. A fire in the stove flickered. The couch, the breakfast, the blankets, the rug beneath her bare feet all felt rich and comfortable. Certainly better than what she was used to.

She stretched her arms and got up from the sofa and began to meander about, the way one does when first going into a hotel room. Her fingers glided across the polished edge of a queerly shaped desk (it reminded her of a clover, of all things). As she walked, she looked at nothing in particular until she came to a beveled glass window. The drapes were partly opened. A soft light filtered through the frost that had accumulated on the panes. She leaned in to study her reflection in one of the glass squares.

What she saw was – off. That was the only word that came to mind.

She tried to pin down what it was that troubled her when the sound of the front door shutting interrupted her musing. Yonder had come in through the foyer with an armload of packages and boxes.

"Here we are, Mary," he said much more brightly than was necessary. "A little bit of home away from home, so to speak."

It would have been proper to thank him – after all, he had gone to the trouble of fetching her things from her apartment – but the thought of expressing gratitude to this man was repugnant. She turned to look at him, nodded, and returned her attention to her image in the window. Yonder seemed unfazed.

"So I've brought you fresh clothes." He laid out the packages and sorted through their contents as if they were his luggage. "A pillow, some womanly accoutrements, jewelry – I know how vitally important that is, some curtain cloth should you wish to make yourself a handbag, needle and thread, your Tarot cards . . ."

Mary broke away from the picture she saw in the window and sat down on the sofa.

"I want to go home," she said.

Yonder was about to untie another parcel. He paused and frowned at Mary.

"I'm afraid that's impossible. You're my ward now."

At that moment, the voice returned. Like always, a bodiless murmuring, somewhere between Mary's forehead and inner ear. She closed her eyes and sighed to herself, and though she knew there was no point in trying, she strained to listen to what was said. It was a torrent of words that perpetually remained just beyond her hearing. Like conversation from behind a door. But she had a vague feeling that this time the gentleman (for some reason, she felt certain the voice in her head belonged to a refined gentleman) had a complaint about his accommodations. It was a complaint with which Mary could commiserate.

"Your slave, you mean," she muttered.

Without asking, Yonder took a seat next to her. "If slavery is living in an opulent room on Merchants Row, with free room and board and a courier at your service, well . . ." He gestured at their surroundings and shrugged. "You've a strange notion of slavery."

"I can't go where I want."

Yonder made a troubled, helpless expression. "I had to bring you back here because you cannot remain at liberty. The constables would take you up. That is out of my hands, Mary. You were declared a lunatic."

The gentleman's voice – the one within Mary's head – was growing shrill with indignance. Mary's temper rose with it.

"That's a lie." She punched a sofa cushion. "You know I'm not a lunatic."

"Of course you're not," Yonder said soothingly.

She turned on him, her cheeks growing warm.

"And the only reason they think I'm mad is because of what you did to me. You," she jabbed her finger into his shoulder and tapped the side of her head, "you're the one who put this-this . . ."

"Window," Yonder replied.

"You're the reason why I hear – whatever it is I hear now."

Yonder studied her. She could not tell what it was that interested him, or why his liquid blue eyes gleamed with a light that, Mary sensed, was not entirely pure. Slowly he folded his hands on his lap.

"That is true. Though I should point out, you were a

willing participant in the affair."

Mary was about to let fly a sharp retort, but Yonder held his hands up and spoke over her.

"Here nor there, here nor there. My point is the milk has been spilt. And like the false label of your lunacy, that, too, is out of my hands. But—" He held up a finger. "All is not lost. I've a proposition for you."

The voice in her head still droned on, but it had become more muted. She tried to clear her senses so that she could listen to Yonder closely. She would be on her guard this time. Yonder had his legs crossed and reclined against one of the pillows. A placating smile glowed from his pumpkin cheeks.

"What is it you want?" she asked him warily.

"A trifle bit more of your assistance. Along the line of what we undertook at the séance."

"You must be joking," she snapped. Mary narrowed her eyes. "After what I've been through, how can you possibly expect me to help you with that again?"

"Actually, my dear, we shall be helping each other. With a little guidance from me, and a little more effort from you, we can use the window that's in that remarkable head of yours. And catch my man in the bargain. That is our common aim, you see."

"What do you mean?"

He leaned closer to her, so close that she could catch the scent of his breath – it was almost odorless but for a faint smell of tea and tilled earth.

"Your window was opened to find Mr. Wylde," he explained. "That is whose voice you hear, whose senses you feel, whose music you long after. Don't look surprised, you talk about it in your sleep." She felt him take one of her hands in his. "My point is, once we find him, the window may be shut. I suspect you'd like that."

Her heart gave a flutter in her chest. But whether it was

from the prospect of being rid of the din that seemed to be constantly rumbling in her mind, or something else, she was not completely sure. She took her hand back and examined the fingers: thin, pale, hers, for the moment.

As terrible as the past few days had been, and as unsettled as her poor brain had felt, Mary still had her shrewdness. She had gained an instinct in her life never to trust anyone at their word. That instinct told her, more clearly than any voice she heard, not to believe for a moment that any interest of Yonder's aligned with hers.

"Who exactly is this Wylde, anyway?" she asked. "What is it you want with him?"

"Oh, he's just some poor fellow who's gotten himself into trouble here." Yonder waved absently. "I've a client who wishes to help him. Free him from his bondage."

"So he's – he's a slave?"

"In a manner of speaking." Yonder thought for a moment. "Don't overconcern yourself with the particulars, Mary. Just trust me in this: once we find what you've been set to look for, once we reach Wylde, everything should settle of its own accord. The sensations will cease. You'll feel like your old self again. The trick is setting your focus aright so we can find him. But I can help you with that. Should be a simple affair. If you are willing . . ."

The strange, round shaped lawyer with the sapphire eyes and the pearl teeth tried to sound lulling, assured, confident. It was a lie, though. Or, at best, a kind of half-truth he plied. Mary was sure of it. She also knew she had no choice but to throw her lot in with this pettifogger. He had an edge on her. All Mary knew of this window (if that's really what it was) was that it was more, much more, than the sum of the strange sensations she felt. It was a thing in itself, and it was *changing* her down to her very thoughts.

So that in a way, Mary would never recover.

A week passed in the law office on Merchants Row. And as such things often unfold, the occupants of the building fell into a domestic routine of sorts – albeit an unusual one.

Far, who made no secret of his loathing for Mary, spent considerably more of his time out of the office and in the taverns by the wharfs. He only ever returned to Merchants Row at night, while Mary slept, when he would clomp about angrily in his room for an hour or so, change his clothes, drink himself into near stupor, and storm out the front door into the night. By week's end, an alarming number of mariners were reported to have gone missing.

For his part, Yonder busied himself with the task of figuring out what to do with the window he had opened in Mary's mind. His first experiment in Custom was so tantalizingly close to success. The portal was there. Open. In a live person. Such a thing had never been done before. The window was connected to Wylde, just as he had wished. If only the woman's feeble brain could be made to focus instead of garbling about in the muck of her feelings. If only he could draw back the curtains a little more and force her to *see* what was right before her. He would have to dupe her into thinking right.

So it was that Yonder began the work of "guiding" Mary's thoughts. Each morning after breakfast he read his Wherestone book, culling it for ideas. Around lunchtime one usually came to him, and he seized it with a sudden burst of energy. He enjoined Mary to stop whatever it was she was doing and follow his instructions carefully.

He had her stand on one foot, focusing all her attention on the bodiless music and voice in her mind, and try to lift the other foot. He told her to both fill and empty her mind using a swimming motion with her hands.

"Envision a rounded square," he told her. "Now draw it.

Find the midpoint of infinity on this piece of paper. Imagine clouds made of granite, stones made of breath, tea made of woe . . ."

At the end of each exercise, Yonder would press her. "Where is he?" "Where is he now?" "Do you see where he is? You must see him now, surely?"

But every response was just a variant of her continued ignorance. "I don't know." "I've no idea." "No." "God damn you to hell, leave me alone!"

As for Mary, her prediction that she had traded one jail cell for another did indeed come to pass, though it was not quite so bad as she had feared. The food in the foyer's larder was always plentiful, and the lawyer's funds seemed to be inexhaustible. There was good wine and fresh flowers, which seemed to spring up in vases of their own accord. The rooms were spacious and comfortable – those she was at liberty to visit, the foyer, the stairs, the attic, and Yonder's room. She had been warned in the coarsest terms by Far never to trespass into his quarters. She passed the hours reading her astrological charts, playing solitaire, looking out the window. She even tried her hand at sewing and surprised herself by making a serviceable handbag.

But her only company was Yonder, a man she had no reason to like, and who, in a week's time, had given her no reason to change her mind. He was insufferably snobbish and fussy, even for a lawyer, without a drop of humor. And for a lawyer, he had surprisingly little news. She longed for Mrs. Petersen, the franklin's wife, to spend an hour with her over Tarot cards, or a few minutes of Miriam the barmaid's gossip. Even a parson's sermon would have been welcome. She became terribly lonely in a few days' time.

And also – taut. Not from Yonder's "exercises" (which she thought were stupid, but harmless), but from these new senses in her head constantly swirling about with the old ones of sight, and smell, and sound. The unrelenting noises left her tired, strained. The gentleman's voice, his music, they were so maddeningly close, as if he was just down the road and around the corner from her. And impossible to ignore, like being made to chase after the wind without any rest.

Every so often, the sounds she heard in her head would suddenly come to a stop. A sight would flash before her, like a crack of lightning crossing the clouds – brief, startling, too quick in passing to study. The dark pair of hands. A wooden plank, like the inside of a wagon, or of a ship's hold. The color purple. Sometimes she smelled sweat in the air for no apparent reason. Or blood . . .

But she had no idea where any of them came from.

Ironically, it was Far who would come upon a solution.

It was late Thursday evening, and Mary sat at the shamrock desk, working through a series of increasingly bizarre exercises that, for some reason, revolved around St. John's Revelation. Yonder hovered just over her shoulder, sniffling and coughing upon her neck, loudly mouthing the words at a pace well ahead of hers. Mary had come to reading later in life, and the printed gothic lettering of Yonder's Bible gave her a headache. She had reached the part where all the fowls had been filled with the flesh of the remnant, and like the suffering believers she was reading about, Mary was exhausted and exasperated. As she rubbed her temples with her fingertips, she read aloud in a halting voice.

"And I saw an angel come down from heaven having the key of the bottom-bottom . . . Goddammit, what's the point of this?" Mary thumped her hands down hard on the desk.

"Recall that you were supposed to pivot," he explained

in a tone that indicated he, too, was nearing the end of his patience. "As you picture the persons and places herein." He gestured toward the scripture. "You quickly turn your attention to your window." He pointed to her forehead. "And thereby gain a clearer view. That was the idea, at least. Obviously, it's not working."

"Obviously," she quipped.

Mary slid back in the cushion of her seat and ran her fingers through the knots in her hair. The light had nearly died from behind the office window. The translucent curtains were still drawn, but all she could see of the outside world was a pane of beveled magenta and dark silhouettes. Some of them seemed to stir silently, which brought a chill to her neck. Yonder took a match to the stove's fire and lit the candles in the wall sconces.

The front door opened loudly. It was followed by the sound of Far's boots stomping on the foyer's wooden floors and a string of murmured curses. He was earlier than usual. Mary felt a knot of worry pulling tight in her stomach. She glanced behind her chair where Far stood tall and dark in the shadows of the room's half-light. He glared at Mary with bloodshot eyes and undisguised contempt. Though the sight of him made her quiver, she refused to let the lout know it. Mary glared back at him icily.

Far snorted.

"Still at it, then?"

"She's finding it a bit of a challenge," Yonder admitted. He finished lighting a small candelabra on his desk, shook the match out, and sat down across from Mary. "She senses him clearly enough, she feels his movements. But we can't seem to orient her to a particular place."

He talked as if she were some farmer's whelp stuck on her school lessons, Mary thought angrily, and with her sitting not three feet away. Mary rolled her eyes.

"I told you, you're wasting your time with her," Far growled.

He headed to the partition door for his office. The reek of gin hovered alongside his person. As he walked by, he threw his hat atop a coatrack, seemingly intent on retreating to his chamber without any further words. But as he went into his room, he grunted back to Yonder.

"Why not just try a map."

The door slammed shut, and Mary let out a soft sigh of relief. When she looked over at Yonder, he was frozen, the bottom of his mouth hanging open. His eyebrows had crescendoed to the top of his brow. He dropped his head into his lap and began punching his kneecap, as if to punish himself.

"What's the matter with you?" Mary asked.

Yonder let out a muffled laugh.

"I am a simpleton!"

He hopped to his feet, dashed around to Mary's side of the desk, and without asking her permission, pulled her chair back from the table. While Mary steadied herself, Yonder fumbled a key out of his vest pocket, chuckled when he dropped it, and managed to unlock a narrow, hidden drawer in the desk.

As he opened it, Mary caught a glimpse of what lay inside. Broad, shimmering pages of vellum hanging from a little silver rod that had been cunningly screwed into the panel. Each sheet a perfect, unblemished alabaster square. Yonder fingered through the stack carefully. He drew one out and laid it on the table before Mary.

He grinned at Mary, and to her shock, gave her a wink.

"If this works, I'll never hear the end of it from him," he said. "Never. But it will be worth his teasing, oh, will it be worth it."

"Wha-what do you mean?"

"Here I've been so caught up in Wherestone's

pontificating, and hypothesizing, it simply never occurred to me . . . never thought . . ." Yonder actually blushed. "Sometimes, we lawyers can overthink a problem. Complicate the simple. Look for the roundabout when there's a straight path right beneath our feet."

He swept his hand across the page he had laid out before her.

"Have a look at this, Mary."

Spread out upon the oaken tabletop was a map.

It was quite large and ornate, and heavy enough that Yonder needn't have bothered with the marble obelisks he used to hold down its corners. The paper had a velvet, milky luster, and it carried a faint, musky scent. Mary knew nothing of cartography, and little about illustrating, but she could tell this was an object of high art.

Her eyes danced across the page, taking in the sights.

"It's a bit dated," Yonder allowed. "But it should serve our purpose."

"It's beautiful," she breathed.

She stared, unblinking, at the wondrous drawing for a long while. It must have been an ancient map, perhaps a century old (though the paper looked nowhere near its age), for while she recognized the outlines of her native country's land, none of the names were familiar. In the center, the shoals of America Septentrionalis blossomed with colonies and harbors set alongside the Mer du Nord vel Mare Septentrionale. The map's creator, Messr. de L'Isle, had signed his work with an extraordinary hand. Every town, byway, and pond in half of a continent had been dutifully marked in his tiny, precise script. And such marvelous pictures of people, plants, beasts, and birds . . .

Slowly Mary began to recognize a few of the names despite the foreign spellings, and eventually spotted what she thought was her home.

"We are here." Yonder pressed a fingertip that covered

much of Massachusetts and Pennsylvania. "Let that be your orientation. Start there . . . and turn your mind loose, Mary. Let the window simply be."

Yonder leaned back in his chair and watched in silence, while Mary studied the small section of "Britannia" where Boston would have been situated. She looked at it from different angles, until all the words began to blur together.

Mary blinked to refocus. At last, she found "Boston" and bored her sight into the word. She read the letters one at a time: "B-O-S . . ."

That was when the drawing began to change.

Mary drew a sharp breath. Her eyes grew wide, as she bent over the map. The tip of her nose grazed against the leathery surface.

Yonder leaned in with her. She heard him whisper into her ear.

"Do you hear him?"

His breath felt hot against the side of her face, yet he seemed to be speaking from across the room.

"Yes," she shook her head slightly. "But it's not that. Do you – do you see . . ."

"What?"

She shut her eyes tight and opened them again quickly. It was still there.

"Those waves in the ocean." She pointed to the eastern edge. "All those crests. See? Where it says Tropicus Cancri?"

"The Tropic of Cancer. Yes, I see. The waves are an artistic flourish—"

"They're moving."

"Are they, now?" he asked calmly.

She bit down on her bottom lip and felt the blood drain from her cheeks.

"Am I—"

"No." He patted one of her hands. "You're not going mad. And you've nothing to fear." Yonder tried to reassure her, but Mary could not break her gaze from the picture that undulated before her eyes. "You're focusing," he explained. "Just as you ought. Keep searching. What do you see now?"

But how could Mary explain what was unfolding? How the world within an ink drawing was slowly coming into being of its own volition, a world with its own physics, its own interior logic, its own life. There were breakers frothing white across the shore of Florida. A miniature storm churning along the Antilles. Deep in the paper Atlantic, where the sun never shines, where all is dark and eternally cold, a beautiful leviathan thrashed in a death throe. A kraken had it locked within its tentacles, pulling it down, farther and farther into a papery grave. Mary thought she should help the whale. It was so majestic. She could free it, keep the poor creature from drowning, if only she could dive deep enough.

"Tell me what you see," Yonder repeated.

Tears welled in her eyes, when a figure near the top of the map caught her attention. She puckered her mouth in disapproval.

"Much help *you* are," Mary murmured.

"Who?"

"That man. He's just standing there, doing nothing." Yonder seemed perplexed as she pointed at the map. "The grousy king with a spear."

"It's a trident. I believe that is supposed to be Neptune."

"He's just waving it around. He should help that poor creature."

"Perhaps he is waving to you."

Mary hadn't thought of it that way. She looked more closely. He did seem eager to gain her attention. A saucy, belligerent-looking fellow, with a stern, angular face and a body that seemed suited only for hurting people. He reminded her of Far. No, Mary did not like the look of him at all. But the tiny, shaded lips were parted in a smile. He was mouthing a word.

It was her name. Mary.

She watched the black-and-white figure pull himself free from the gilded crest and scripted epitaph he stood before. Neptune stooped to hoist his naked legs around a fish, a carp that had, until that moment, been playing about underfoot. Once straddled, he smacked the fish's side like a horse, and he rode it down the Atlantic Ocean.

The fish swam hard against the current. Ink waves parted before the ink god's mount. Holding onto its gills like reins, Neptune rode due west. Black flecks of the ocean's spray drenched his face. All the while he beckoned for Mary to follow him.

Mary told Yonder what was happening. Yonder's voice answered from a mile away.

"Keep following him . . ." he said.

The carp reared to a halt. Neptune slid off from its back, kicked the fish away, and waded toward the shore. As he pressed forward, he grew smaller, more proportioned to his surroundings. He tromped south along the shoreline, pausing every few steps to make sure he still had Mary's attention. The names faded as he passed each land:

Terra Nova.

Acadia.

N. York.

Pensilvania.

Mariland.

Chesapeack . . .

There, the god turned, hoisted his trident overhead, and made his way northwest. He waded through a tiny bay. When he reached the shore, he shook his feet dry and fixed his hair. He continued his march inland, following roads and trails so tiny only he could see them.

Until at last, he stopped.

Mary held her breath. For some reason she had one of her sewing needles. Yonder must have slipped it into her hand.

Yonder whispered again. "Put this where he tells you."

The trident caught a glint from some hidden star. Three bars of pale white, three prongs with three barbed endings. With a mighty heave, he cast it high into the air. The trident leveled and plunged to the earth. Its shaft rattled.

Mary slid the needlepoint into the center hole the trident made. She drew back from the table and exhaled.

The trident was gone. The waves that had crashed along the coast curled one last time and froze in place. The ocean becalmed. The kraken and its prey faded back into vellum. The ancient sea god returned to his repose atop a map of his world.

It was only a map, once more.

Marked by the prick of a penny needle.

The smell of the harbor almost brought Yonder to retch. An awful admixture of stenches – kelp, rotting fish, piss – all carried along together, tumbling over one another in the jumble of a constant, biting wind. The grasshopper on Faneuil Hall's weathervane had his antennae pointed northeast. The stars and stripes nearby fluttered noisily against a flagpole. But no matter how hard the breeze blew, the foul smell lingered.

Yonder sucked in a breath, tucked his mittened hands deep in his pockets, and bumped through the crowd that milled about on the dock. He no longer bothered asking anyone's pardon; that was clearly not the etiquette among seamen and dock workers. These loud, leering men of every shape, color, and language, whose only commonality was liquored breath, salt-starched hair, and rapacious language.

They cajoled and cursed in equal measure, and the volume of all the haling, and shouts, and laughter had left Yonder's ears ringing.

For the dozenth time, Yonder chided himself for forgetting his earmuffs. He pressed his chin into his chest against the cold and did his best to stop the noise. His mouth was drawn tight, but no matter how hard he clenched, his teeth chattered. The wooden planks beneath his feet felt like they were moving (which they were), which only served to turn an already unsettled stomach sour.

How the devil did one get one's bearings?

Even on his tiptoes, Yonder found it hard to discern where the wharf ended, and the sea began. The dock's wooden planks were festooned with tables and customs booths that were, in turn, piled with crates, barrels, and miles upon miles of bundled rope lines. Propping it all up, weather split pilings encased in droppings and barnacles stood like haphazard sentinels among the waves. From these, an armada of rocking ships was somehow held together by a spangle of lines, stretched out in a hundred different directions, like a great cobweb. Everything was packed so tightly, he began to imagine that one could hop from the dock to a crate, to a warehouse, to a piling, to a boat's deck, and recreate the miracle of walking across water. Yet, everything also moved, constantly and in different directions. Back, forth, to the side.

Yonder swallowed down a bit of breakfast that tried to resurface. He trundled along the length of the dock, trying to keep his balance as he moved within the current of a busy crowd. Every so often, he paused and strained to raise himself another inch to gain an unobstructed view. But a mass of sunburnt, weather-beaten heads always seemed to loom around him. Between the shoulders, he caught a glimpse of another boat slip.

A rowboat had been hoisted up with pulleys and hung

upside down over the dock's edge. Next to it, a legless old African dangled from a separate line, a pot of paint clenched in his teeth. He feverishly worked a brush to spread a fresh coat of cobalt on the boat's underside.

"Would that be the thirtieth?" Yonder asked himself.

The man he had met at the Bunch-O'-Grapes had told him to come to the thirty-second slip of the Long Wharf. He had claimed to be a captain. What constituted a "slip" had been left as a point of assumed understanding.

Yonder frowned. The press of bodies pushed him on.

"Long Wharf, indeed," he muttered irritably. "Should've christened it the Endless Wharf. It'd be more apt. But surely, that's a slip. Yes, I'll count it. Thirty-one—"

His foot accidentally struck against someone else's.

"*Come mierde!*" A man bellowed.

Yonder spun around. When he stopped, the sun had been blotted out from the shadow of a colossus. The man was a head taller than Far and at least two stones heavier. Shirtless, the man must have kept warm from his covering of coarse black hair that ran from his navel to his nose. The fur – that was Yonder's immediate impression of what it was – abruptly ended with his bearded chin, for he kept the remainder of his face as well as his scalp cleanly shaven. A scar ran from the crown of the man's head, down his left eye, and past a mottled nose, where it curled into the corner of his mouth, a line which somehow imbued both perpetual rage and pleasant surprise into his countenance.

The knot of men in his company instinctively drew back, leaving Yonder and the man alone in a tight circle. From the growing chatter, it seemed the crowd expected some manner of martial entertainment, presumably at Yonder's expense.

"*Me hiciste soltar la moneda!*" the man growled and pointed a hairy finger at the deck near Yonder.

145

"I–I." Yonder scanned the entirety of the wharf, confused.

"*Mi moneda.*" He screwed his mouth into an odd shape, and to Yonder's astonishment, he addressed him in a slow drawl.

"That's my coin, you hit from me foot." He spoke with a strange accent, equal parts Catalan and Cockney. "You cost me. You dead. Bastard." His brow furrowed in waves around the equator of his scar.

"I'm terribly sorry, sir, I—"

A voice rang out from among the onlookers.

"*Oye, Correa! Dejar a este tonto solo. Él es mío . . .*"

"Oh, thank goodness," Yonder breathed. It was the ship captain from the Bunch-O'-Grapes.

The captain pushed his way through a line of mariners, stooped to pluck a coin from one of the planks, and walked straight to the hulking man he had called Correa. He flicked the brass coin away and proceeded to berate the man in what, to Yonder's ear, sounded like flawless Spanish. Correa stood before the wiry captain's tirade, mute and glowering, until the captain wound down and turned to face Yonder. The little throng had already dissipated among the larger crowd of the dock, the men murmuring their disapproval of being deprived of a beating.

The captain's face flickered with a thin smile, something that clearly pained him. He inquired after Yonder as pleasantly as he could, with a gravelly voice that seemed most attuned for shouting orders at idiots.

"You done past the slip, governor." The captain jerked his chin behind Correa. "By 'bout a hundred yards."

"Oh." Yonder felt embarrassed for some inexplicable reason. "My apologies, Captain Grimmette."

"No harm, no harm." Grimmette spat from a considerable wad of tobacco lodged in the side of his mouth with no consideration for where it landed. He scowled at the bare-chested Spaniard. "Correa. This here's our new client. What'd you say your name was, guv?"

"You may call me John Yonder."

"Give your respects to Mr. Yonder here," the captain said it much louder than Yonder would have preferred. Correa clasped Yonder's hand, wrist, and a part of his forearm within his grip.

"A pleasure," Yonder croaked through blinding pain.

"You like see again?" Correa asked brightly. "Place your bet?" Mercifully, Correa released his grip as soon as Yonder nodded. Grimmette cut over him.

"This gentleman's here on business. He's no time for your capers. Run back to the slip an' clear out all that flotsam they've got piled up. Good an' clear now. I'm bringing Mr. Yonder over to get a look at his charter. Go on, now!"

As Correa sprinted ahead, barreling through the mariners, Grimmette led Yonder down the dock and whispered at a volume that could have hailed a barkeep in a crowded tavern. "Don't think too ill of him. Correa's a handy one to have on board. Good first mate, knows his business and knows how to make a crew mind theirs. Fights like a bear. But he fancies himself a performer. That's why he was out here playin' with coins. It's his act."

"You don't say," Yonder rubbed his sore hand as he scurried around a locker to keep up with Grimmette.

"Aye. Man can juggle just 'bout anything, and with any part of his body. Hands, feet, knees, that shit sty he calls a nose. Even his prick. Hand 'o God, I seen him do it once. His game is to bet folks how many coins he can juggle. They toss 'em up to him, one at a time, and whichever ones he keeps in the air, he gets to keep. Whoever throws the one that makes him drop the juggle, gets a quarter of the take."

"My . . ." Yonder struggled for something appropriate to say. "How entrepreneurial."

"Aye."

Grimmette led Yonder in a backtrack down the dock, around clutter and crowds, through the middle of a heated argument between a cargo inspector and a purple-faced skipper, who to Yonder, looked as if he was about to draw a blade. Grimmette hardly gave them any notice.

"You said there'd be three of you," he remarked.

"There will. They entrusted the hiring to me. As their lawyer."

Yonder had left Mary at the office, locked up tight, while he managed this business. Business which Yonder wanted nothing more than to finish quickly and quietly. A wave coming off a nearby shoal trickled around the pilings. Yonder felt his feet begin to slide underneath him, and without a word, Grimmette' hand was at Yonder's side to steady him.

"This'll be your first time at sea, then." Grimmette said it as an observation, not a question.

There was little point denying it, but Yonder could not bring himself to concede his ignorance.

"It's been a while," he allowed, "but I'm familiar with Ole' Blue's wiles."

"Ole' Blue, aye. Follow me, an' mind you don't run yourself through on that hook there. Or Ole' Blue'll be good an' red."

They walked on a ways until they reached what looked like a solid wall of stacked crates. Grimmette found a space between two columns and slid between easily, leaving Yonder, with his more rotund belly, to wriggle and worm through. When he emerged, Yonder found Grimmette waiting for him at a section of dock that had been lowered several feet from the main pier. There were more crates and bins piled there, but a little space along the water's edge had been cleared.

"Mary's teats," Grimmette spat another brown stream

of tobacco juice, "if someone don't pick up this tea, I'm goin' to hoist it off myself. Even if it starts another war. Here, governor. Lemme step down first, then I'll help you."

With Grimmette's hand, Yonder managed to reach the platform without accident. Down there, closer to the ocean's brink, where the waves lapped against the planks and nothing blocked the wind, Yonder could feel the full chill of the North Atlantic. It cut through his clothes like a knife. Within moments, he was shaking all over and a dull ache began to spread from the stitches in his stomach.

"You'll need a pea coat this time of year," Grimmette observed.

Yonder nodded absently, his gaze pulled toward the expanse of water before him.

Boston Harbor was not especially large compared to other ports of call. In most weather, its blue waters stayed fairly calm, and today was no exception. Whitecaps crested every so often, breaking the monotony, but mostly the water shone like a mirror's glass. A procession of sloops, sails flashing white in the sun, entered the bay from the east, winding their way through the bevy of ships that were already at anchor. An impossible count of ships of every shape and size. Like wooden hamlets built across a watery valley. Their timbers creaked, their lines sighed, their bells *tinged.*

To Yonder, who seldom ventured near waters larger than a pond, it was both intoxicating and dreadful to gaze upon. He began to fidget with his jacket buttons. He felt Grimmette near him.

"So that there's the *Snuffbox,*" Grimmette gestured toward a cluster of boats.

When Yonder's eyes had finished darting everywhere, Grimmette explained in a gratingly condescending clip.

"She's the schooner over there abaft of that Dutch convoy. Got a quarterdeck, two masts, square rigged fore top sail, yellow trimming, naked woman carved on the bow . . . Christ, she's right *there*." Grimmette muttered a curse and forcibly turned Yonder's head several degrees to the left. A crooked index finger appeared in Yonder's vision, pointing a line straight to a small – and even to Yonder's untrained eye, miserable looking – vessel anchored in the shadow of a group of much larger and more commodious ships.

"Yes," Yonder said slowly, "The sun was in my eyes. But I can see her now."

He tried his best not to make a face, but the *Snuffbox* looked to be little bigger than his office. And far more squalid. Even from a distance, he could see the contrast between her shabby rigging and warped railings and the polished gleam reflecting off the ships around her. As if sensing his thoughts, Grimmette assured his potential customer that looks can be deceiving, never to judge a book by the cover, still waters run deep, and so forth. Though Yonder knew precious little about sailing, he recognized a lame horse sales pitch when he heard one. Once the conversation had reached more familiar territory, he decided it was time to assert his position.

"Let us be candid, Captain Grimmette. Your ship can neither hold much, nor is much to behold. I suspect that's why you found yourself scrounging for passenger charters in a tavern." Before the captain could respond, Yonder waved his hand dismissively. "It makes no difference to me. My clients and I can endure meager accommodations, so long as the journey is brief."

"Oh, it'll be brief. That there's the fastest ship in this harbor."

Yonder scoffed and made an affronted laugh.

"Come, sir. That is a wild boast. I can see plainly that she has but two of those logs to hold sails."

Grimmette squinted. "You talkin' 'bout the *masts*?"

"Indeed. Many of the ships out here have three masts." He scanned to make sure there might not be a vessel with four, or even five, but seeing none, he let the point suffice. "Surely, the additional mast and sails would make those ships much faster than yours."

For a moment Yonder feared Grimmette might slap him. But instead, the captain bit his tongue and stretched his mouth back into a grin of half-rotted teeth that, for him, must have passed for pleasantness.

"It ain't the number of masts that gives a ship speed, governor. It's the hull. That's what a ship sails on, an' what the sails have to haul." He heaved a thumb at a long, regal looking vessel anchored near the *Snuffbox*. "You take that frigate there. See? That there's the *Adriana*. They call her the *Baltimore*, now that the government's bought her into service. Which'll make for a blot of bad luck right off the start, but whatever the hell she's named, that there frigate an' her three masts will never get windward of a French corvette. Never. The Frogs'll scoot circles 'round her. Turn her into matchsticks before she ever comes about with her three masts."

Yonder tried his best to appear like he studied whatever ship it was that Grimmette was talking about. Once more, Yonder's head was jerked in the right direction.

"*Adriana*'s a couple more points to larboard. See?"

"Ah, yes." Yonder squinted his eyes and blinked several times. "That dratted glare again."

Grimmette let a wad of spittle fly.

"She may look prettier than my *Snuffbox*, and she might throw up more canvas. But that tub ain't ever breaking seven knots. 'Cause the *Adriana*'s got a fuckin' lead belly for a hull. An' everyone knows it. Now, you take my *Snuffbox*, she's got a nice, thin, narrow hull. Give her a fair wind, she'll reach fifteen knots like that," he snapped his fingers. "She's got a hull that's built for speed."

"If you say so," Yonder replied in a way that was sure to convey how unconvinced he remained. "Can she be ready to embark tomorrow?"

"She can. If you can."

"And we'll reach our destination within the time we discussed? No delays?"

"I'll get you to where you're heading in three days, or my name ain't Simon Grimmette." The captain spat the wad of tobacco from his cheek and licked his lips. "So what do you say, Mr. Yonder. We have a charter?"

A tremble passed through Yonder's bones, and he fell into a small coughing fit. As he recovered, he made notes to himself of the luggage he would need to pack. The flowers Otherly had brought him, for certain. All of them. It seemed he would be in need of that remedy sooner than he expected. He frowned at that thought.

"Well?" Grimmette pressed.

Yonder reached into his front pocket and produced three small coins. Each one was made of solid gold. They sparkled with a light of their own, with a luster as deep as midnight. The coins sent gleaming tongues of flame reflecting across the captain's leathery face. His jaundiced eyes burst round at the sight.

"If we reach Norfolk in three days," Yonder said softly, "you'll receive double this."

"That'll work, governor," Grimmette nodded, unable to suppress a chuckle as he palmed the money into a drawstring pouch. "That'll work just fine."

"What time shall we set sail tomorrow?"

"Any time you like." A sly grin spread to the corners of Grimmette's mouth. His face twitched with a mirth that quickly devolved into a hacking laugh. Grimmette patted his money pouch fondly. "Any time at all. So long as you don't miss the tide."

CHAPTER TEN

"The sea is a strumpet. Tempestuous. Inscrutable. Ungovernable. Neither Neptune nor Custom has a firm hold on her. Best avoid the sea altogether."
—Wherestone's *Commentaries on Custom*, page 55

It was midafternoon, a half-lit, dreary sky was mottled with clouds, and a languid mist hung in the air above Long Wharf. But the dock was bustling. To Yonder it looked like every boat in Boston Harbor moved in every direction at once. A cacophony of shouts, shrieks, clanging bells, washing waves, and groaning timbers echoed across the bay. Launches and barges overfilled with men and freight scurried between the pilings and the ships. Everyone on the wharf was in a hurry in what seemed to be a collective mood of vital urgency.

Amidst all the thrash and thrum of the busy dock, Yonder, Mary, and a scarecrow of a porter named Clive Stallings wound their way in a staggered line toward the thirty-second boat slip. Stallings lagged with their luggage, while Far pulled ahead. Yonder caught a glimpse of his companion's bottle green coat shoving through a newly arrived crew of Dutch sailors. Yonder glanced behind anxiously, wishing the old dotard he had hired would hurry up (and that his partner would slow down), as he tried to catch sight of Far again.

"Come, Mary," Yonder urged, but like everyone else in his little company, she seemed intent on walking at her own pace. He pushed forward a few yards when Yonder nearly ran headlong into Far who scowled down as a river of humanity flowed around him.

"Where the deuce is he?" Far huffed.

Yonder scanned their surroundings, perplexed.

"Should be right around – here ... somewhere. Hmm ..." His eyes swept the whole dock, but he saw nothing except an undulating press of bodies, pilings, and boxes, none of which looked remotely familiar.

But amidst the constant hum of ships and mariners, arose a familiar voice, Grimmette's. He was perched atop an overturned crate. With a shout that sent an albatross flapping off in fright, Grimmette leaped down, bellowing a string of curses.

"Bleedin', shittin' Christ, governor! The *tide*! We're gonna miss the fuckin' tide!"

The captain stormed across the dock planks, his face red with temper, looking as if he would heap burning coals over Yonder's head, but when Far stepped in front of his path, Grimmette stopped short, his shoulders fell, and all the color drained from his cheeks. Like an angry wave dashed apart on a shoal.

Far stood at his full height with his hands in his hips. He narrowed his eyes at Grimmette.

"You're the one who'll take us to Norfolk?"

"I – aye, sir," Grimmette licked his lips. "I'm Cap'n Grimmette."

"Call me Far."

"And this is Mary," Yonder motioned for Mary to hurry along. She was using her handbag like a plow to push her way through the crowd, pausing every so often to swat at the hands grasping after her bosom.

"Goddam lechers," she straightened her blouse with an angry snort.

"Ma'am," Grimmette bobbed his head perfunctorily.

Mary had decided to wear a garish yellow and purple dress and a small coterie of her cheap jewelry. There were shadows underneath her eyes, hollowness in her cheeks, but to Yonder she looked much improved. Almost like the old Blessed Mary, the fortune-teller.

"So here we all are," Yonder smiled in half-apology. "A tad delayed, I know, but we had a devil of a time finding a porter. Thank goodness Stallings was between jobs—"

"Between jobs, my ass. No one hires him 'cause he's as useless as a nun's teats." Grimmette cupped his hands to his mouth. "Here! Stallings! Shake a leg you worthless whoreson!" Giving Far a wide berth, Grimmette jostled back through the crowd until he found the dawdling porter and grabbed him hard by the shoulder. To Yonder's surprise, Stallings seemed not at all surprised or concerned by the manhandling. Grimmette yanked at Stallings' arm like it was a mule's bridle, which improved Stallings' shuffling to about a mule's pace. The old porter chewed his teeth and pulled the luggage in silence, oblivious to Grimmette's bellowing in his ear, while Far, Yonder, and Mary followed close behind.

They hurried through a maze of clutter and people packed tight along a small pier until they reached Grimmette's launch, a small rowboat with flaking white paint and four anxious looking oarsmen who sprang to their feet at the sight of their captain.

"Stand clear, Stallings," Grimmette barked. "You men, stow this gear! Mr. Yonder, you and your friends come down these steps here. This way. Smartly now. Gear's stowed in the aft, passengers in the bow. You're in the front, Mr. Yonder. Sit here, dammit. Cast loose! Let fall your oars and give way together! *Smartly!*"

The oarsmen groaned as they pulled hard to clear the boat from the slip. Packed with cargo and passengers, the little boat slowly gained speed, while Grimmette roared at his men and thumped them on the side of their heads to hurry up. At one point, he stood on the bow, frowning at the movement of the water before him, and made the sign of the cross.

"Lads, you better pray Jesus'll lend you a hand, or hold the fuckin' tide for you. Otherwise you're goin' to be rowin' a hell of a bigger boat than this one."

Either luck was with them, or the oarsmen's prayers found an ear, but the *Snuffbox* weighed anchor and set sail with the last ebb of the outflowing tide. The current carried her all the way to the edge of Boston Harbor where she let loose a flurry of sails from her foremast that sent her racing toward the open sea.

From the aft rail, Yonder watched the skyline of the town begin to fade into the gray horizon. The company of barges, sloops, and cutters that had packed the harbor gradually dissipated, each ship headed off on its own course. A few bands of sunlight broke through the cover of clouds and lit the sea around the ship as she veered south. A hard, brisk wind began to blow out of the northwest, and the first cresting waves of the open Atlantic broke against the *Snuffbox*'s port side, so that her deck pitched about like a wild horse.

A spray of icy droplets hit Yonder like a slap to the face. He clasped hard onto the railing, barely keeping his feet under him while he tried to hold his line of vision with the disappearing shoreline. He reached for a handkerchief and mopped his forehead with it, managing only to move the saltwater around. His belly roiled with each heave of the ship.

"I should not have indulged in that second helping of eggs," he moaned to himself. A sour taste of half-digested butter and sauce rose in Yonder's throat, and it took a considerable effort to keep his breakfast where it belonged. The frenzy of noise and motion across the schooner's deck did little to settle his stomach.

Moreover, no matter how hard Yonder squeezed himself against the wooden rail, he invariably seemed to be in some person's way. The crew, he had learned, numbered no more than a dozen, but the deck was so close and cramped and the men were so boisterous in their appointed tasks, there was not a sliver of space left above board for one to simply stand and remain in place. It was like trying to find stillness in the midst of an Irish reel. Somehow the sailors avoided colliding into one another, though not without an ample measure of shouts and curses in the colorful patois of seamen.

"Make a lane, if you please, sir!" a hurried, high-pitched voice hailed Yonder.

"Eh? Oh."

Yonder managed to suck in another inch from his waistline just in time for a short, bow-legged Polynesian fellow to slip by him, crouch down, and slam shut a hatch nearby.

"Wouldn't want you slipping in the head," the Polynesian smiled up at him.

Yonder felt his legs slipping from a sudden dip in the ship's movement, but the Polynesian reached out and caught him easily. The man couldn't have weighed more than ten stone soaking wet, but his arm felt like the trunk of an oak tree. He introduced himself as Cod.

"Pleasure to make – did you say, Cod?"

"It's what everyone calls me," Cod replied. His speech held an islander's cadence alongside a Celtic lilt. Yonder found it not unpleasant to listen to. Cod latched the lid down and gave it a tug to make sure it stayed in place. "Not my true name, though. It's one of the pictures, see?"

Yonder blinked at the swirl of blue and green tattoos that blanketed Cod's face. Cod pointed to a pattern just beneath his left cheek, which, once Yonder had stared at it long enough, seemed to vaguely resemble an ocean fish.

A wave of nausea swept over Yonder. He swallowed hard and shifted his weight.

"And – and what was it you said about that device there, that I should mind my head?"

"No," Cod laughed, "that there *is* the head." He propped up on his tiptoes, and, swaying in perfect rhythm with the waves, explained in a confidential tone, "It's where you'll make your water. Or whatever other humors nature compels."

"Oh."

Cod offered what appeared to be a sympathetic smile. His namesake momentarily disappeared within the creases of his weather-baked skin. "You know, you might find it more comfortable in your cabin, sir. I've stowed your gear for you. It's all lashed down now."

"Thank you, but I found the air below somewhat disagreeable."

He might have added that he had nearly concussed himself rocking into the cabin walls, but he worried he had already betrayed enough maritime inexperience.

Cod nodded. "As you like, sir."

Yonder brought out his change purse to compensate Cod for his troubles, but the affable Polynesian gestured for him to put his money away.

"That's very kind of you, sir," said Cod, "but I'm squared away." He scanned the length of the deck and dropped his voice low. "Bit of advice, sir. Best not to show your coin out here. Keep it stowed away." He glanced around. "It's a decent enough crew. But the open sea has a way of bringing out the pirate in a man. If you catch my drift."

The cabin room was soaked. The floor was overrun with foul smelling seawater, the walls were warped and moldy and slick with moisture, and the low ceiling dripped like a sieve. A miserably dank and dark chamber no bigger than a broom closet, separated by a door from an equally dank and dark galley of the *Snuffbox*'s lower deck. Save for a candle guttering in a horn lamp that hung from the ceiling, Far would have thought he was in a cave.

Thankfully, he had commandeered the only dry space in the cabin.

He lay in a net hammock strung between the corners of the ceiling, a bed just long enough for him to stretch his legs their full length, so long as he kept his feet tucked in. His body swayed with the movement of the ship. The noise of creaking planks, moaning beams, the thump of waves smacking the hull outside, and water sloshing around the floor inside reverberated within the room. Far laced his hands behind his neck and felt his hair caked stiff from saltwater. He watched the bottom of the lantern sway on its hook.

Back and forth, the milky glow spread across one side of the cabin, illuminated a patch of squalor and left it in darkness to shine in another corner. To and fro. Back and forth.

With each rotation, Mary's face grew more consternated. She sat atop her locker in a corner, her hands pressed against the walls to keep her balance, her knees bunched up to her chest in a vain attempt to keep her feet dry. Far had not acknowledged her presence, though he was lying less than three feet away from her.

An especially hard knock from a rolling wave made the whole cabin pitch. Mary tumbled headlong into the floor, and when she rose, she blew out a spray of seawater.

"Dammit!" she spat more water out. "You're taking up the whole cabin."

Far did not bother to look at her. His hammock rocked, the lantern bobbled. Up on the deck, a muffled bawl of laughter erupted. Something about a winch that had struck someone upon the head.

"I said," she repeated louder, "you're taking up all the room in here."

He exhaled a long sigh and addressed the ceiling.

"Then leave."

That seemed to shut her up; unfortunately, not for long.

"Worse than the jail cells," she complained. He heard her tromp through the water to reach a different corner. "At least there you've got some room to yourself. But you're nice and cozy, aren't you? You know, a real gentleman would see to a lady's comfort before his own."

That brought a smile to Far. He half turned in the hammock and gazed straight at Mary. Crouching in a shadow, with her hair plastered to her skull and her pouting lips quivering, she looked much like a sheep in need of sheering.

He replied lazily, "A real gentleman would – for a real lady." To twist the barb, he added, before he rolled back over, "so if one should come around, do let me know."

Before she could formulate a retort, Yonder staggered through the cabin's doorway. His face was as pale as a canvas except where it had been marred by an angry-looking welt swelling up from his cheek. He had a soaked handkerchief pressed against the wound with one hand as he tried to hold himself steady in the doorway with the other.

"Oh, thank goodness," he huffed, "I've finally found you both. It's like trying to squeeze into a rathole down here, and – oh, my!"

The cabin suddenly shifted from another roll and sent Yonder splashing across the flooded floor.

"Mind the water!" Mary snapped.

Yonder pulled himself upright at the last moment, narrowly avoiding bashing his forehead into the hanging lantern.

"Mind the light," said Far.

Yonder wiped his hand down the length of his face. The cabin pitched once more. Mary hoisted her skirts above her knees and grabbed onto the netting of Far's hammock to give it an impotent shake.

"Could you help me, please, Mr. Yonder? This isn't right!"

Yonder harrumphed awkwardly, and somehow managed to glance at just about everything in the cabin other than Mary, Far, or the miserable space of room they stood in.

"Why . . . whatever is the matter?"

"Just *look* at him lying up there," she snapped. "And me soaked to death down here. It isn't right. He's a goddam son of a bitch. I'd like nothing better than to slap some manners into him—"

Far whirled about in his hammock so that he sat with his legs dangling and Mary's enraged face no more than an inch from his lap. She gave a startled shriek at his sudden movement. She tried to recoil but the confines of the cabin gave her no avenue of retreat. Far bent over to address her directly and was mildly amused that she was unable to look him in the eye.

"You'll never lay a finger on me," he warned her. "No one here can touch me." He settled back in the netting and grinned at the Doldrums woman cowered before him. "But since you brought up the subject, let me tell you what I'd like nothing better than to do to you—"

"Now, now, Captain, Mary," Yonder interrupted. "Let's be civil here. We've three days on board together. We must try to get along."

A loud knock in the doorway interrupted Yonder's mediation. A smiling, tattooed face peered around the edge of the wall and offered a cheerful greeting.

"Mister Cod!" Yonder sang. "What a relief."

The deckhand addressed the cabin in a formal voice.

"If you please, sirs. My lady. Captain Grimmette sends his compliments and would be honored to have you join him as his guests for dinner this evening. He shall expect you at eight bells in the mess." He paused, smiled at Yonder, and added meaningfully. "I should say *promptly* at eight bells."

Yonder had to admit, however uncouth he may have seemed, whatever his faults in character, Captain Simon Grimmette could set a good table.

They were seated in the ship's mess, a communal eating hall that had been cleared, swept, scrubbed, and adorned with fineries that were almost passable for a low-end private club. A set of swinging doors that led to the kitchen was festooned with curtain sashes, and the wooden grate windows had been unshuttered to let in a brisk draft of ocean air. Glass lanterns burned bright all around.

In the center of the room, a linen was spread across the rectangular tabletop that ordinarily served the *Snuffbox*'s crew. Cushions were placed on the two benches that spanned the table's length. Far took up one, Mary and

Yonder the other. At the head of the table sat Grimmette in a worn gentleman's jacket and a faded white waistcoat. Opposite him at the other end was Correa. The first mate seemed to swallow his chair with his girth, but he rocked back and forth as merrily as a child who had been offered a second dessert. He wore a silk trimmed shirt that made Mary's yellow outfit seem a drab and meager thing by comparison.

They had just taken their seats as the last clang of the ship's bell reverberated outside. Grimmette beamed at the table and wished everyone a good evening.

"And right on time, too," he added, dipping his head to Yonder.

Yonder felt a blush coming on but took the jest in stride.

"I'd be a poor passenger indeed," Yonder replied, bowing, "were I to twice transgress upon a ship captain's punctuality." He looked up and smiled affably. "Why, I might find myself walking the plank."

The captain barked a laugh. "Oh, now we wouldn't go that far. Would we, Correa?"

From the far end of the table, Correa shook his head fervently and replied, "No, sir. Keel haul 'im, maybe. No walk the plank."

A ripple of nervous laughter arose from the guests, all except for Far, who sat in a shadow, twiddling his steak knife and looking dour. Yonder gripped his own utensils nervously; his companion's promise to remain "on his behavior" for the duration of the dinner had been rather coy.

"It's true, though," Grimmette observed benignly, "we sailors go hammer and tongs after our tides. No hard feelings for crackin' the whip, governor? You look a mite drained."

"I'm quite alright, thank you, Captain. I only hope we did not cause too much trouble from our tardiness."

"Well, it was a near run thing, but we caught the ebb.

That's all that matters. Like they say, all's well that ends well." Grimmette arced his eyebrows in recognition of Mary. "And how're you settling in, ma'am?"

"As well as you'd expect," she replied with a knifing look at Far, "given the company."

"Very good, very good. Just so you know," Grimmette dropped his voice, "I had the boys rig up a sheet aroun' the head for you. To, um, give you some privacy."

"Thank you, Captain." Mary turned to Grimmette and smiled. "That's very – gentlemanly of you. And thank you for inviting us to dine with you."

"Not at all." Grimmette waved his hand. Without warning, he flipped his head around and bellowed over his shoulder in a voice that could have hailed the crow's nest. "Cod! Where the fuck are you? We're starvin' in here!"

One of the kitchen doors flung open, and Cod hurried into the mess. He was dressed in an oversized-shirt and trousers and sweated profusely from the stove. Five pewter plates loaded with food were balanced down the length of his arms. In his hands he held a teapot, a clay jug, a decanter, and a glass jar filled with a burgundy liquid. It was an extraordinary display of butlery, and if Yonder weren't still wincing from the captain's roar, he might have applauded the little fellow.

"Is that port?" Far perked up in his seat.

"And is that tea?" Yonder added.

Grimmette *tsked* at Cod and gave him a rap on the side of his head. "See that? They're starvin' *and* parched."

"Beg pardon, sirs, m'lady," Cod said hastily. Somehow he bent a knee to Mary without dropping anything. He set each of the plates down in rapid succession around the table, starting with Mary. Fillets of white, flaking fish were still sizzling in the metal, flanked by piles of peas, onions, and celery, a generous chunk of cheddar, and a piece of hard bread smothered in butter. Cod flipped over each of their glasses. Yonder's was a chipped teacup.

"I have ale," Cod announced, lifting the clay jar with his pinky. "A madeira I just finished chilling overboard. And at Mr. Yonder's request, I've brought out a bottle of tawny port for the other gentleman."

For the first time that evening, Far smiled. He gestured for Cod to fill the glass to the brim.

"Good choice, Mr. Far," said Grimmette, clapping his hands. "That'll pair up nice with the halibut. Pour a glass for me, too."

Cod served beer to Mary, wine to Correa, and the port for Far and Grimmette. When he came to Yonder he paused and murmured in his ear, "You're certain you wouldn't prefer something stronger, sir? I've already got a pan of rum simmering on the stove. Just a squeeze of lemon, a stick of cinnamon, and a pinch of sugar, and you can have the finest grog in the Atlantic."

Ordinarily, Yonder would have enjoyed a warmed rum. But the rattle in his chest had started to bother his breathing, and his stomach still turned small somersaults every time the ship rocked.

He pulled his mouth into a contented expression and replied, "A cup of tea is all I require, thank you."

Yonder caught an embarrassed grimace flicker across Cod's tattooed face. Reluctantly, Cod poured a steaming brown liquid into Yonder's cup.

"The thing is, sir, we don't get many requests for tea. I had to scour the hold to find this little bit. I can't say as I can vouch for its quality."

"I'm sure it will serve my needs."

When the plates and napkins were settled, and all the cups and glasses filled, Captain Grimmette rose from his seat and cleared his throat for everyone's attention.

"M'lady, gentlemen, welcome to my mess. It's a captain's duty to host his guests their first night at sea. So here we are. Hope you like the food. Now, um, I don't know whether any of you practice a particular religious persuasion?" Grimmette scanned the table inquiringly.

"Episcopalian," answered Mary.

Yonder thought a moment. "Deist, I suppose."

"Indifferent," Far grunted from behind his glass.

"Those're all fine churches." Grimmette nodded. "But it falls to me to say a grace that'll cover the lot of us. So, uh, here goes." He made a sign of the cross, which Correa quickly followed, and Grimmette closed his eyes as he began reciting a blessing. "Bless us, oh Lord, and these, thy gifts. Of these, thy gifts . . . of thine bounty . . ." His thin lips puckered, struggling for the rest of the prayer. "Um . . . An' give us this day, our daily bread, clear skies, and smooth sailin'. Amen."

"Amen," the table answered.

Without further ceremony, they tucked into their feast.

It was a sumptuous fish, and its preparation was something absolutely masterful. Every taste held a fresh delight, a mystery. Cod had learned his cooking well. Before the plates were half finished, a cheerful spirit had descended over the room. Soon the hum of jokes and private conversations surpassed the clink of forks and glasses.

At the end of the table, Correa leaned on his hairy forearms, cracking his knuckles, and flashed dark looks interspersed with manic twitches, and tics, and wild gesticulations. All of which were meant to convey the message to Far: I am menacing. The first mate drained his cup and brought it down with a hard thump, barely missing Far's finger. With a glare, Correa's lips curled, and he laughed, as if daring his table companion to take umbrage.

The usual show, Far thought. The instinct of martial

men whenever they came into one another's presence to unfurl their feathers, puff their chests, snort and stamp. He had seen it many times, in many realms. Correa's performance was more than a bit overwrought. And his babbled, disjointed tales of past battles, skirmishes, and fistfights were embellished beyond fantasy. At Correa's urging, Far had shared one war story of his own, his favorite, though he scarcely bothered with the details.

"So this flesh flag you say you fight with," Correa's voice was thick with skepticism as he twirled a fork between his fingers. "What this is?"

"My banner, you mean." Far shook his hair and turned to look out of the window grate behind Correa's thick head. The sun's last amber light had settled beyond the horizon, but the waves of the ocean still undulated with crests of orange fire and troughs of magenta shadows. "It's something of a work in progress."

"So you say. And every man you ever kill is in it? You say you kill thousands at this Mad Queen's fort. The flag, she must be a league long, no? How you fly this thing?"

"Not every man I've killed." Far broke his attention from the window. "That would make it a cheap and sorry thing. No. I only keep the skins of those who fought well. Only my worthiest foes are sewn into the banner. Everyone else gets left to rot."

"Ah." Correa nodded knowingly. With a mischievous gleam, he leaned across the table's corner and clasped Far's forearm in his grip. He squeezed it hard and spoke in Far's ear with breath that reeked of wine and onions. "I not be in your flag, no."

"Probably not." Far drank his glass down and grinned at the first mate. "But if you fight as well as you say you can . . . who knows?" He shrugged and freed his hand easily and bit off a piece of bread. "Perhaps I could find room for you."

"No, señor," Correa shook his head. "I don't think you have a chance." He fixed Far with a steady gaze and with a sudden flash of movement, Correa swiped the knife from the side of Far's plate. He pointed the tip at Far's wrist.

Far simply stared at him, uncaring, until Correa's mouth transformed into a showman's smile. With a fluid motion, Correa flicked the pilfered knife high into the air. It arced, then tumbled down where he caught it easily with his other waiting hand. A fork and soup spoon followed its flight.

Round and round, the utensils flashed above the table. Correa twirled them in a succession that grew steadily more rapid. Fork, knife, and spoon became a whirling circle of metal. Far had to allow that the impromptu feat, though silly, was mildly impressive. Correa leaned back in his chair, heedless of the crumbs he was scattering everywhere, and grinned at Far.

"I'm quick. See? Faster than you, I think."

Far watched him juggle for a while, swirled his glass in his palm and lifted his port high in a mock salute.

"I've never seen your match with cutlery."

From the other end of the table, Grimmette called out, "Uh-oh, watch your utensils, folks. An' your purses. Correa's at his capers again. Here, Correa. Avast that. Give the gentleman back his knife already."

The knife came to a halt in Correa's palm. Its tip pointed straight at Far's heart where the mate kept it poised, meaningfully, somewhere between playfulness and mortal threat. In his breast, Far began to feel his pulse stir in the old, familiar way.

"He really has a knack for that," Yonder remarked to Captain Grimmette.

"That he does," said Grimmette stuffing a forkful of onions in his mouth. A rosy blush had spread from the captain's forehead all the way down to his neck.

"So tell me . . . what takes you folks to Virginia?"

It was a question Yonder reckoned would arise at some point in the evening. The question the captain had charitably avoided discussing during their prior negotiations. But polite incuriosity could not be expected to withstand the length of a three-day sea journey in close quarters. So Yonder had an answer at the ready.

"We are looking to find a gentleman," he said tersely.

"Ah . . . Family?"

"A distant relation of Miss Mary's."

"One I'd just as soon be rid of," she muttered to herself and sipped her beer.

"Just so," said Yonder and cleared his throat in such a way to indicate that the captain should drop the subject. But the man was too far into his cups for subtleties.

"Interestin'," Grimmette grunted. He rubbed at the stubble of his chin. "She don't like 'im, but she's in a hurry to catch up with 'im. With a lawyer in tow. Interestin' . . ."

"My client," said Yonder with a loud cough, "would prefer to keep the details of this affair private."

The captain held up his hands. A set of stained, crooked teeth creaked into a cynical smile.

"Say no more, counselor. I catch your drift." But the leer in Grimmette's countenance made it clear he wished to say much more, and so he did. "Y'don't have to spell out your signals for ol' Cap'n Grimmette. God knows, I've navigated 'round my share o' knocked up women an' knobstick weddin's. Oh, yes. Probably got a dozen bantlings out there's somewhere." He motioned toward the window with his drink, spilling it on his sleeve. "Y'know, I had a bastardy suit 'gainst me once. Down in Charleston. Couldn't set foot in the port for nigh on three years. But I don't blame you for takin' this poor sod in Norfolk to the law. Whoever he is. Woman's got a right to be supported. Hope it goes smooth sailin' for you, ma'am."

Yonder's chest became seized with a fit of coughing. By the time it passed, Mary's face burned as red as an apple. She turned to Yonder, her voice quivering with barely suppressed anger.

"It had better," she said evenly.

Over the course of her life, Mary had become immune to most jibes and snubs. Fortune-telling was not a particularly reputable avocation; being a spinster certainly wasn't – but Grimmette's accusation stung. Not because of his innuendo that she was unmarried and pregnant. That would have been no concern one way or the other. She had never accepted that a man should enjoy any more license to carnal pleasures than she. No, it was what he had accused her of needing – that she would have to beg for aid from anyone was . . . offensive.

Fortunately, Grimmette did not press the insult further. It was time for the pudding. The captain snapped his fingers and hollered for Cod to bring out dessert, an announcement that was immediately met with a murmur of approval from the entire table. Forks, spoons, and bowls were soon stacked to make room for the final course.

As Cod hurried around the table to pick up the settings, in the bustle of all the movement, Mary happened to notice Yonder furtively reach into his pant pocket, as if he were fishing for something. It seemed odd to her for some reason. While Cod cleared her plate, Mary kept her bench mate in the corner of her eye.

He held still, watching Grimmette. The moment the captain turned around in his chair to yell for Cod to hurry up, Yonder's hand came out from underneath the table and quickly brushed across the top of his teacup.

He had dropped something into his tea. She caught only a glimpse of what it was he had palmed, but she had no doubt about what she had seen.

A withered old flower. With crumpled leaves as black as coal dust.

Mary blinked.

When she looked again, Yonder's eyes went wide and locked onto hers. He froze with his cup poised against his lips. In the span of that moment, a mask fell away, and Mary could sense Yonder's thoughts as vividly as if she read them on a page. There were two feelings.

The first was shame. The second, profound sadness.

Yonder's hand trembled, but he forced the mixture down in a quick draught. By the time he had set his cup back on the table, his old visage had returned, the façade of amused pleasantry perfectly restored. He smiled as if nothing more than a lull in conversation had just passed between them. While Mary wondered what had just happened, Yonder hailed Cod in a jovial voice that, to Mary's ear, rang completely false.

"My dear Cod," he said, "if it's not too much trouble. I believe I'm ready for that rum now."

CHAPTER ELEVEN

"There is a long-standing and quite vulgar 'custom' among Doldrums folk in which they strive to pin a name upon every jot and tittle in Creation, no matter how high above their station or far beyond their comprehension it may be. Places, Powers, even Persons (even infants who have never uttered a word or performed a single deed, the poor dears), become festooned with labels that were neither asked for nor, in most instances, deserved. I do not know why, but the locals are simply beguiled with the puffs of sound they can make with their mouths. So they take it upon themselves to name things they know nothing about. Custom takes no notice of their impertinence.

"Unfortunately, you can't so much as hail a coach in Doldrums without appending at least two names to your person. So when you arrive, after you've donned your form and garb, you'll have to choose a first and surname. 'John' is the customary first name for men in this realm; 'Jane' if you're a lady. Select whatever surname you like. 'Forest,' 'Strange,' 'Lostsoul.' Anything you happen to see or think about will suffice."

—Wherestone's *Commentaries on Custom*, page 112

Mary nestled into the folds of a canvass sail that had been left in a heap on the forecastle deck tucked underneath the captain's launch boat. There was just space enough for her to sit upright with the boat hung upside down from its chains above her, almost like a market booth. She brought the edge of one of the sails over her head and shoulders, though it smelled old and felt as stiff as a boot. It kept out the worst of the night's chill. Though not the wetness.

A breaker sent a tall spray into the air that wafted up all the way over the highest deck on the bow. Mary winced from the stinging cold drops raining down the back of her neck. The bowsprit lurched down. The ship smacked against the trench of another wave. Another splash came down on her.

Mary blew the water away from her lips, wriggled her back against the starboard railing behind her, and pretended to study the hairy, callused palm she held clasped between her hands.

The rigger whose hand the palm belonged to watched Mary's face with mounting worry. He glanced over his shoulder, not for the first time, probably to make sure no one else was about, and he shuffled a little nearer to Mary, who kept herself hidden within the shadow of a masthead.

He was drenched to the bone, though he seemed not to notice it, and his breath reeked of grog. Yet he rolled easily on the balls of his feet with the ship's motion, no matter which way it pitched or rocked. Mary listened to his hushed voice with its strange, hurried staccato accent the origin of which she had already given up placing.

"Is bad, ain't it?" the man croaked. "*Es mal porque—*"

Mary held up her finger to indicate she was not to be disturbed while she was in contemplation.

Was he Catalan, perhaps? Or Portuguese? Impossible to say. Men of this sort, she knew, never remembered where they were born. In the span of five minutes, since he first cautiously approached Mary for "her advice," he had babbled phrases in four different languages and offered prayers from five different faiths.

"S-sorry," he whispered. A steady drip of water fell from his shaggy eyebrows. It created the illusion that he had been weeping.

She listened to the music the wind was making in the rigging. A low, somber note that Mary matched with her own softly whispered moan.

"Aaaoooowww . . ."

The rigger nearly leaped with fright. Mary clutched his hand tighter, all the while suppressing the urge to giggle.

"Woooaaa . . ."

"Oh, *mein Gott*, is bad for Gino. I know is. *Eu sei que.*"

Mary began to throw her head around in a circle to hide the smirk.

"Aaoowwll – show me! Show me, I pray. Show me!"

"*Ich kenne!*"

Mary made her eyelids flutter, as she twitched her head in spasms, sending heavy curls and droplets of water bouncing in every direction. She let out a long breath, opened her eyes wide, as if having just awoken, and gently curled Gino's fingers closed.

"I . . . have seen the fate within your flesh."

"Allah and Mary help me. Is-is bad?"

"It is complicated," Mary answered in a way that signified a large measure of foreboding, balanced against a glimmer of hope. "Yours is a complicated fate."

"Yes, yes," he practically panted. "Tell me, I beg."

"Very difficult. I need payment for such a difficult consultation."

Gino wiped his heavy hands down his face, down the

length of the frayed remnants of a shirt, and at last down to his pocket, in which he carried his money. He brought it back out quickly, secretively.

His fingers were gripped around the edges of a tarnished, worn coin. In a quick motion, he broke it in half with a sharp clink. He was about to quarter it, when Mary gave his hand a gentle smack.

"Four reales," she said firmly.

Gino's face darkened. She watched him swish his spit behind his teeth and shake his head, but he relented and agreed to her price. He handed half of the old coin over to Mary, who slipped it away.

"You and the sea are one," Mary declared, "and so you shall remain. That is clear in your bloodline, and from the influence that Neptune had in the stars when you were born."

Gino nodded along thickly.

"The sea is where your fortune is to be found – and I see a great fortune for you. It's in your destiny, even if it's not quite in your grasp."

"Money? Jewels?"

"Oh, yes. All that and more . . ."

Mary began to lay out a long, meandering, and vivid account of a fabulous store of riches Neptune and the stars had compiled for Gino, along with an impenetrably obtuse set of endeavors he would have to undertake in order to lay claim to his lucre, this fabled fortune of Mary's invention. Heracles himself would have been stumped to know where to begin or how to make any sense of it.

"But mind you," she warned, "once you reach the end of that endless road, the treasure will still be tied . . . to something . . . I can't quite make out what. It's like – like—" she searched about the deck for inspiration, "like it's tied to an anchor. Yes. A tied-up anchor. About to be thrown over. You'll have to untie the knot of opportunity quickly, or else your prize will disappear into the sea." She gazed at Gino meaningfully. "And beware. The fortune might still take you down with it . . ." Mary folded her hands across her lap. "That is the message I have been given. Heed my counsel."

The consultation was concluded, she had given him four reales worth of oracular advice. Since her legs started to cramp, Mary got up from her makeshift seat, stooping so as not to bump her head on the launch boat. As she flexed her knees, Gino thanked her profusely. A smile stretched the length of his grizzled cheeks. With a head that was no doubt filled with dreams of coins, and liquor, and women, he disappeared down the stairs to the main deck below to return to his post – and hopefully spread the word that a fortune-teller was on board and open for business.

Mary watched him leave and smiled to herself. Sailors were such a wonderfully superstitious breed. And it had been a treat to be able to ply her trade again. Gainful work always felt – liberating. She propped her elbows against the wooden slat of the rail and listened contentedly to the sounds of the forecastle deck – the hiss of the breaking whitecaps, the wind sighing through the yards and sails, the men on watch gossiping softly to one another. And Yonder chuckling from the shadows.

"Well, that was entertaining," he said wryly. "Knot of opportunity, indeed!"

She looked down the run of steps that led to the main deck and frowned as the familiar pear shape of Yonder emerged in the moonlight. He had his hands braced hard against the rails on either side of him, as if he might tumble overboard at any moment. He crept up the steps as slowly and as awkwardly as a crab that had been flipped onto its back.

"Here." Mary clasped onto Yonder's arm and hoisted him up to the relative stability of the upper deck. "Before you break your neck."

"Ah, thank you, my dear," Yonder said. He splayed his legs as wide as he could and balanced himself against the railing next to Mary. "Still getting my sea legs back."

"Mm."

"That was quite an inventive bit of claptrap you gave that fellow just now. Almost as good as your séance performance."

"He got what he paid for," she said.

"So he did."

In spite of his precarious stance, he grinned, teeth sparkling, with a rosy, orange glow shining about him. Yonder took in a deep breath and let it out with a satisfied expression. "Splendid night to be out at sea, don't you think?"

"Mm-hm."

"You're certainly looking better, Mary. The fresh air, I think. It's doing you good."

Mary studied him for a moment.

"That tonic you snuck into supper seems to have done you good."

It pleased Mary immeasurably that with a simple observation she had reduced the preening lawyer to stammering, and harrumphing, and flittering his hands like a nervous errand boy. The mirth blanched away in Yonder's cheeks. He looked about anxiously.

"Why – what – whatever do you mean?" he managed to ask her.

"Oh, please." Mary rolled her eyes. "We both know what I saw at the table. Don't pretend you weren't slipping something into your tea."

"I . . ." he started but closed his mouth. "Well, well. That window of yours, I suppose." Yonder said it in a way that almost made it sound like a portent. "Somehow it . . . it seems to have sharpened your other senses, too."

"Maybe."

Actually, the visions and the stirrings that had haunted Mary since the séance had settled as of late, ever since they reached the open waters beyond Massachusetts Bay. Still with her, still touching her thoughts, but somehow much farther away, as if blunted by the ocean's vastness. She had heard no flute for days. For the most part she enjoyed the reverie. And yet a small part of her, a tiny sliver of desire, had come to miss the company of the gentleman's wordless voice. It was not something Mary wanted to think about at the moment.

"You've nothing to be ashamed of," she said to change the subject. "I knew an alderman once who ate hashish every Sunday before church."

"It wasn't hashish," Yonder snapped. "I can assure you of that."

"Oh."

A silence fell between them. They stared out at the ocean, the ivory blur of the moon reflecting from its surface. It seemed to be galloping over the watery swells and crests. The wind backed and turned colder. Yonder let out a long, heavy sigh.

"It is a kind of flower," Yonder said quietly, "a temporary remedy I must take. A rather poor one."

"What ails you?"

"This place," he answered faintly. "Or, I suppose, my place within this place. I'm afraid I haven't quite found myself here, and it makes me feel off. My partner has been more fortunate in that respect. But I – well, I haven't . . ." He paused for a long while. When the words came, they were heavy, flat. "This place is weighing on me. Crushing me, slowly, a pebble at a time . . . I wish I could go home."

Mary turned to face him fully. For a brief moment, sitting there in the full light of the moon, she could see right into Yonder. And something occurred to her. As if she were meeting the man for the first time.

"Here, now . . . where are you from anyways? You and Captain Far. You've never really told me, and every time I think to ask you about it, I get distracted, or I start to hear the music in my head, or it's lunchtime, and for some reason I forget all about it. But this time . . ." she tapped the side of her forehead, "this time, I'm remembering. Isn't that strange? Why I should keep forgetting to ask you something so ordinary, but now I can remember to do it."

"It's not strange at all," he replied with a sad smile. "We – I mean, those from my country – prefer to stay unobtrusive when we're here. Keep to ourselves and talk about the weather, or concerts, or politics, what have you. Most of us are only passing through. So your kind seldom notices our presence . . . What was it we were talking about again?"

Mary shook her head. "Nice try."

"Ah, well. I suppose there's no avoiding it then . . ." Yonder folded his arms across his chest and closed his eyes. His expression drifted aimlessly, like the waves that broke beneath the ship, somewhere between wistfulness and regret. "From whence we came, from whence we came . . . It's hard to say precisely. A little ways east of here. Past where you can see. But only just. Far enough to be infuriatingly close. Any oak tree could bring you there, just like that." His fingers made a dull snap. "You'd only need to draw a door. And push it in. And then you'd be where we're from."

Mary stared at him.

"Are you drunk?"

"Slightly."

"I thought you'd say something like Hartford, or New York, or Manchester. Maybe Ireland."

"I'm sorry. We're not from any of those places. I gave you the best answer I can." He shrugged. "And it's the truth."

Mary brought part of the sail blanket back over her

shoulders. She spoke with a conviction in her voice that almost surprised her.

"You know . . . I believe you."

The wind ruffled her hair. She breathed in the scent of salt until it tingled in her nostrils. She could almost envision a forest glade in autumn, veiled in mist and creeping shadows, set deep in a valley within a wilderness that stretched on and on, all the way to the horizon. It was beautiful, foreboding, and, as he said, beyond reach. She asked him whether he missed his home.

"Terribly," Yonder replied flatly. It was, Mary sensed, the most bluntly honest he had ever been with her. In the milky light, Yonder stood quietly, staring at his knees with a forlorn expression. "I'd return in an instant if I could," he started, but he caught himself. His cheeks colored. "But, um, they've, uh, taken my – my traveling papers . . ."

It was plain to Mary he had spoken more than he had intended. And that he would prefer not to speak of it any further.

"Your traveling papers," she repeated to herself. Mary coiled a fold of her skirt, turning over the salt-stiffened cloth, lost in her thoughts. A sudden realization dawned on her. "Your name –you're not really 'John Yonder,' are you?"

"Of course not." He waved his hand dismissively. "I only call myself that to get about. For the sake of your convenience. You people can't make heads or feet of anyone unless you've pinned some puff of sound onto them."

She thought he was trying to evade her question, so she pressed him. "All right. What's your real name, then?"

Yonder stared at her for an uncomfortably long time. At last, he shook his head, and for once, seemed to struggle to produce words to his liking. "My true name is . . . me. All that I've ever been, or done, or seen. It's not a sound or a syllable, not something you can blow out of your lungs, or shape with your mouth. We name ourselves, Mary, and what we name ourselves is what we are." Mary squinted at him incredulously, but he only smiled at her. "Think of a fine, old, wood-paneled library, a comfortable place, filled to the rafters with the most wondrous books you've never read. Lend it an air of autumn, and a warming ray of sunshine, and a bit of smart conversation, and a thrill deep in the pit of your stomach that you're on the cusp of learning something you never could have imagined . . . Lay hold of that, Mary, and you'll have managed the first part of my name."

Mary pursed her lips. "Now I know you're drunk."

Yonder laughed. Though it sounded mirthful, Mary could detect a note of mourning lying just beneath its surface. "I suppose I am," he sighed. "Or I've grown acclimated to being John Yonder, Esquire of Boston."

The boat pitched hard so that they both had to catch their balance. Yonder tried to change the subject. "But enough about me. I am curious to learn more of you, Mary. Tell me. What brought you into the spiritual line of work?"

Mary rubbed her hands and brushed aside a strand of hair that was blowing in her face. "I hate children. I can't keep house. I tried midwifing once, did a little nursing in a plague house for a time, but that wasn't for me. Too much complaining. That left fortune-telling. Which suits me fine. It pays good. Gives me an excuse to collect things that I like to have about me. I get to learn up on rituals and religions, too, which I find entertaining. And it makes me feel good that I get to help people."

Yonder had tried to hide his face, but Mary spied him from the corner of her eye.

"I see you snickering," she said, "I know what you're thinking. Fortune-telling's just a caper, a shill. I know you look down your nose on me. But let me tell you, counselor – I actually give people something for their money, something they need that they can't get anywhere else."

"Indeed?"

"Indeed," she mimicked him. For a moment Mary felt an urge to slap the smirk from his pudgy face.

"Pray tell," said Yonder, wiping a tear from his eye, "what is this *pro bono publico* service of yours?"

"Here's an example for you. There's this mother that lives over on Brattle Street who came to see me last spring. She's got a daughter that's well past marrying age. Twenty-two years old. Boring as dirt. Got a mole on the end of her nose the size of a turnip.

"Now this mother wants nothing more than to match her girl with a lawyer's clerk or a banker's apprentice, but if worse came to worse, she'd settle for the grocer's boy. What can she do about it?" Mary began to tick off her fingers one at a time. "She can hope some gentleman will just come around and take a fancy to her girl. That doesn't cost her anything, but then hoping doesn't feel like she's doing much about the situation. She can pray. That'll cost her a few coins in the offering plate. But it doesn't feel much better than hoping. But what about a love spell? A real ritual. With candles, and smoke, and burning feathers, and a fortune that says," Mary began to intone in a deep, throaty voice, "*by the light of the three wands, the path to Artemis, to Mars and the line of the pentacle . . .*"

Yonder broke into a peel of laughter.

"That," said Mary, "will make her feel like she's actually done something for her daughter. Which she has – she's covered a risk. As best she can. It's kind of like insurance."

Yonder stared at her. His grin slowly faded into what appeared to be a mien of admiration.

"That sailor's no different," Mary continued, pointing to the aft of the ship. "He may not have as much money. But what he's after amounts to the same. All he wants is a little say-so with his fate. To hedge his bets. That's what I gave him. Same as I gave that Brattle Street mom."

Yonder nodded approvingly.

"You're not completely dim at all, Miss Faulkner. Quite unlike anyone else in this realm. Perhaps that explains how you managed to survive—" he stopped himself with an embarrassed grimace, "I should say *enjoy* this gift you've been given."

Mary felt her fists clench. She fixed Yonder with a hard look.

"What do you mean, gift?" she snorted.

"Why, the sights and the sounds from the window that's been opened in you. You can see things no one else can. I should think that would be thrilling. Given your line of work. Dare I say, even magical."

Mary glared at Yonder, her thoughts vacillating between anger and disbelief. It was obvious to Mary that Yonder truly believed what he had just said.

"Listen," she said quietly, "let's get something straight. I hate what you did to me. And I hate you for doing it. The only reason I'm on this god-forsaken boat heading to god-forsaken Virginia is because I have no choice. And I hate that, too."

The breeze that had been blowing steadily fell and died, and the ship began to pitch along in the swell. Dimly Mary heard a call from the main deck up to the masts to let out more sail. Yonder did not move, but replied coldly,

"Let us, as you say, be straight with one another." A hardness came over him as suddenly as the change in the wind. He never blinked. The stars that were splayed across the night sky seemed to descend into his eyes, a soft and intent glimmer from within a deep and dark nether. He lowered his voice to a whisper, and yet Mary could hear him clearly over the noises of the hands working in the rigging. "I've taken nothing from you. I've required no bargain of you. You're free to come or go, just as you are. It is your choice, Mary."

Mary turned away to look over the railing.

The *Snuffbox* lurched forward, slower than before, but gaining her way. Mary could feel the cold air, laden with emptiness, whistling past her. It made her feel tired. And sad, for some reason.

"Just as I am . . ." she sniffed. "I've got a stranger's thoughts wrapped up with mine like a tub of laundry. I see things that aren't there, hear words I can't make out." She paused, listening for the faraway voice that had grown quiet, the thoughts and feelings of a man she had never met, yet was coming to know as well as herself. He had not spoken all day, and that too, left her melancholy. "Maybe I am a lunatic," she sighed. "I don't know. But the choice you gave me isn't a choice. I can stay like this," she circled a finger around the side of her head, "for the rest of my life. Or help you find this man."

Yonder held up his hands.

"Fortuna is a cruel goddess. Except when she's kind."

Mary ignored him. She wiped her nose with the back of her sleeve, dried the tears from her own eyes. "Whatever you did to me," she said more firmly, "it's not a gift and it's not a choice. I don't know what you did to me . . . But, then, neither do you. Right?"

Before Yonder could respond, a bell rang from the aft of the ship, signaling the changing of the watch. A half dozen groggy sailors emerged from a hatch to replace the hands who lumbered down to their hammocks.

In the commotion, Yonder rose, somewhat stiffly, obviously glad to take his leave.

"I'd better return to the mess. I left Captain Far playing a game of chance with that Spaniard. Something to do with knives. I fear the wagers could take a dangerous turn at the rate they're drinking. We shall talk more on this soon, I promise. Will you be all right up here?"

The sound of approaching footsteps on the stairs to the forecastle deck drew their attention. They turned together to see a young, scarecrow of a man creep up the steps. He was unkempt, outfitted in a cheap set of clothes that were much too large for him, and the first wisps of a moustache were only beginning to sprout underneath a hooked, pock-covered nose. As he approached, he kept his eyes on the deck and pulled a threadbare hat from his head.

"B-beggin' your pardon." He gulped, and a billiard ball of a lump went tumbling down the pipe of his neck. "Um, which of you's is – is . . ." He swallowed again. "The Blessed Mary . . . the one that told Gino's future fer 'im."

For a moment, Mary's mind went blank. But as if by reflex, they alighted, the lethargy that had been weighing her down dissipated, and she felt the calm renewal of one who returns to a familiar craft.

"My dear child," Mary sang as she opened her arms. "The stars have led you to me. What is your name, again?"

"Um, Jones, ma'am. Henry Jones. I was wonderin' if – if – if maybe, you could, um . . ."

Mary laced an arm through Henry's and gave his hand a reassuring pat. She spoke softly, in confidence, as if the worries of a teenaged schooner's hand were matters of cosmic importance.

"You seek counsel, Henry. About your future. I can help you with that. For a very, very small price, I can reveal the secrets of what is to come in your life, show you the path you should take. You've a special future ahead of you, I can tell. I have a sense for special people like you." Mary smiled at the boy and cast a poignant look at Yonder. She added, "Some would call it magical."

CHAPTER TWELVE

"I have also noticed a tendency among men when out at sea. They become as wild as wolves. It leaves one with the disquieting notion that the sea somehow makes Doldrums folk—a bit more like us."
—Wherestone's *Commentaries on Custom*, page 55

The moon had crept her course across the heavens, the stars still twinkled in her wake. A scattering of clouds began to appear, one by one, as a predawn light drifted up from behind the horizon. All was gray at first, but the colors slowly returned, reluctantly, as if they had just been forcibly roused from a good sleep to begin a hard day's labors. So, too, was the crew of the *Snuffbox*.

The wind had turned, and the sailors clambered up the rigging and across the yards of the masts to adjust the schooner's sails to harness it. Massive canvass sheets, hundreds of pounds of them, had to be unfurled, tied off, or folded up against the yards. Lines had to be run back up and down the length of the masts. It was heavy, ponderous work for so early in the day and before breakfast. The crew tasked with performing it was rife with complaints. So, too, was their captain.

Grimmette stumped heavily across the main deck. He paused a moment, scowled at the world, and continued his walk. Each step came with a dull thud of pain that rumbled from stem to stern inside his head. His limbs ached, his mouth tasted vile, and his tongue felt as dry as a holystone. He smacked his lips and flexed his jaws, hoping the salt in the wind might clear out the leavings from last night's festivities. A bottle of port, a dram of grog, and numberless cups of ale had almost dismasted him. But he had made it through the night (though he remembered almost none of it). He was upright, walking about as one in a fog. Still wearing his best shirt, though it was terribly wrinkled and bore a prominent stain of dried vomit all down the length of the starboard sleeve.

Grimmette passed his hand down the length of his face, muttered to the Virgin to kill him, and craned his head to search the main deck.

"Cod!" Grimmette snapped. Raising his voice sent a piercing stab through his temples. "Mr. Cod," he repeated a little more quietly.

"Aye, Captain?"

The tattooed little dodger appeared so suddenly and so quietly, it gave Grimmette a start.

"Where's Correa? 'S'pposed to be his watch."

Cod's eyes fell and he wrung his hands. "Well, after he gave the order to make sails," said Cod hesitantly, "I believe Mr. Correa said something about the casks in the hold not being situated rightly. That they ought to be stowed more aft, I think was what he said . . ." his voice trailed off.

It was an old lark of hired mates and masters. Whenever a mate needed to nod off for a spell during a watch, he would say he was going to reposition the stores to help balance the ship. Most captains would rather wink at shirking than sojourn into a bilge-watery, foul-smelling hold to find a missing mate. Correa did it more often than most. No doubt the Spaniard was among the casks deep in the ship's recesses – sprawled out on his face, most likely.

Grimmette growled under his breath. Correa had left everything in shambles. Who knows how much time had passed, but the sails weren't even half set, and the crew was all sixes and sevens. The third mate had tied and untied the same knot at least a dozen times. A man who was supposed to be a rigger climbed the lines at a pace that fat lawyer Yonder could have bested. Another working high on the mainmast had accidentally dropped his corner of a canvass sheet and nearly fell to his death trying to catch it again. He hung by his knees helplessly. Lord, but a pack of drunk monkeys could have done a better job. And all the while, the precious wind was whistling by the yards, wasted.

That was not what troubled Grimmette most, though. They had reached the trade winds safe enough, with no incidents besides a rudderless crew, a sotted mate, and a hungover captain. There was something more, though – a tension about the ocean, an ominous feeling that seemed to be drifting in from afar. It was pricking at Grimmette's stomach, making it flutter, sobering him up much quicker than he would have liked. Whatever the feeling was, he didn't like it. He had lived at sea long enough to know better than to ignore such things. Grimmette narrowed his eyes and scanned the horizon's length, from the dark void where night still held, to the first glint of orange day, and all across the long vastness of gray nether in between. All he could see was an endless succession of bowling waves and whitecaps, marching along quietly beneath the dawning sky. There was not a flicker of a sail out there.

"We got no lookout, Cod," said Grimmette at last. He gestured toward the tiny crow's nest way at the top of the mainmast. It was still shrouded in a gray shadow. "Up ye' go. An' on your way, lend a hand to Jones. Idiot's got himself fouled on the yardarm."

Cod was the only crew member who could fit within the space of the miniscule basket perched fifty feet above the deck. He also was the only one who could withstand the wild ride of sitting atop a rolling ship's mast without getting sick. It always fell to Cod to serve as the *Snuffbox's* itinerant lookout – whenever anyone thought to post one. At least he didn't complain about it.

Grimmette watched the little man scamper up the mast. After he had helped Jones back to safety, Cod climbed up until he was no more than a brown and blue dot, peeping over the brim of a basket. Grimmette turned his attention to the rest of the hands and getting his ship righted. The sails were as twisted as bedsheets in a brothel. He hocked over the rail. Though it liked to burst his forehead, Grimmette began to roar a succession of orders and oaths at the hapless crew, which had the effect of making them move a little bit faster in their shuffling.

As the last set of sails were unfurled and backed into their proper places, Grimmette heard the door to his cabin swing open. Out came Yonder and Far, faces fresh, hair combed, coats buttoned, stockings on nice and straight. Neither man seemed a lick off their keel, nor any worse for the wear of having spent an entire night drinking and carousing. It was the first mark in the lubbers' favor, though Grimmette was begrudged to acknowledge it.

"Devil take 'em," Grimmette muttered, wiping his hand once more over his brow. He smacked his lips a few more times, faced the wind, and let out a belch. He went over to the helm and rested his hand to get a feel for how his ship was handling the sea. The helmsman clicked the heavy wheel an inch starboard, and Grimmette felt the *Snuffbox* thrumming softly in response. A jerking, unsteady vibration. Almost as if she were nervous . . .

"I say, Captain Grimmette?" Yonder hailed.

Grimmette ignored him and kicked at the helmsman to get the hell below and work the pumps for being a worthless sod. With the helm cleared, Grimmette curled his fingers tight around the handles of the ship's wheel, and concentrated. She was sailing fretfully, and not just because of the mess the hands had made of her sails.

"Captain?" Yonder repeated.

"What?"

"Might we have a word?"

Grimmette buried his face in his hand and swore, but as Yonder had more money yet to pay, he forced himself to put up the pretense of a pleasant expression.

"Whachya need, governor?" he answered, his gaze fixed on the bow. "Bit busy at the moment."

As Yonder and Far approached, Grimmette had to let go of the wheel to help grab a hold of Yonder, who toppled over on his feet. Far had the other elbow, and between the two of them, they were able to keep the fool from pitching headlong and splitting his face on the helm.

"Steady there," Grimmette chided. "We're in open waters. Gotta keep a hand on the rails."

"Yes, yes, thank you," Yonder replied. He was splayed out like an octopus trying to find its purchase, but with Far's aid, he managed to draw himself more or less upright. Yonder straightened his shirt collar. "That's actually what we wished to speak to you about," he continued. "Now I certainly do not mean to tell another man his trade . . . but, um, well, it appears we're traveling rather far from the coast." Yonder lifted himself on his tiptoes and, as impossible as it seemed, began to look eastward for the land. "I can't see so much as a rock out there."

Grimmette couldn't decide if he wanted to spit or to smack the man for stupidity. Instead, he croaked a sarcastic laugh.

"Y'mean you can't make out Portugal from here? Somethin' must be wrong with your peepers."

Yonder blinked at him.

"You're lookin' the wrong way," Grimmette explained as slowly and loudly as if Yonder were a foreigner who had just been kicked in the head by an ox. "Coast's off the starboard, that-a-way, 'bout eight miles or so," he extended his finger directly beneath Yonder's nose to get the fool oriented.

"Oh," Yonder said sheepishly.

Far piped up next to him.

"But why are we heading out to sea? You're taking us away from where we want to go."

Grimmette narrowed his eyes at the dark-haired hulk standing there, cocky as a lord, with his arms crossed and his locks billowing about his face. With a snap of his wrist, Grimmette turned the wheel.

"That's why," Grimmette jerked his thumb in the air.

The ship tilted and shifted slightly in her course. The sails were set, and they could drink their fill of the wind. The canvass sheets began to billow with great heaves of thrust and rustled in a way that everyone, sailor and lubber, could recognize as something stronger, more fulsome. The *Snuffbox* lurched forward with a new burst of speed, swifter than she had sailed thus far in her journey.

Grimmette smiled at his silenced passengers.

"This time of year," he explained, "the trade winds are roarin' out here. But you gotta come out a little ways to catch 'em . . ."

They seemed to fly through the waves, the hull crashing over the breakers. Off the port beam, the top of the sun crowned its head above the horizon, bringing the deck from haze into a soft, pink-tinged light. The riggers and seamen began to descend from the masts and make their way to the mess for breakfast. As the commotion on board gradually settled and his ship raced on, Grimmette's worry began to subside a little.

"It's like this," he continued, "if you was ridin' a racehorse, and you was in a hurry, which would you rather? Take a cart path that's close by, but where he can only go at a trot? Or head out a bit to an open field where he can break into a gallop, where you can let 'im run loose?"

"We do seem to be making better speed," Yonder allowed.

"If the trades keep blowin' . . ." Grimmette paused to touch a knuckle against a wooden spoke in the wheel. "An' we don't run into any unfriendly visitors out here, we'll make Norfolk a little past nightfall."

Yonder's eyes rounded at the news, and even Far appeared impressed.

"And you, governor," Grimmette added with a meaningful wink, "will owe me a certain bonus, eh?"

"I should be glad to incur the debt," Yonder replied.

"Aye, an' I'll be doubly glad to be paid it."

Grimmette leaned against the wheel when a shrill, distant call from high above fell down to the deck and caught his attention. Faint, but tinged with an earnest excitement – and, to Grimmette's ear, a hint of worry. It was Cod, in the crow's nest. Even from there, Grimmette could see the little man hopping up and down and waving his arms. He pointed aft, to somewhere far behind the ship, and shouted so loud his voice cracked.

"Sail ho! Sail ho! Three points aft the port quarter! *Sail ho!*"

Mary jumped up with a cry of pain.

She swayed in the hammock of the cabin, panting. All the blankets had been kicked off. The little horn lantern had gone out. Though the air inside was chill, her face was mopped with sweat. She twisted over in the rope netting and reached behind her neck to feel for her shoulder.

A sound had pierced her ears, a crack, like a peal of thunder. Searing pain coursed across her back. As if . . . as if she had been whipped.

Mary prodded at the skin and checked her fingers for blood. There was no cut, no wound. Yet it felt as if a piece of her flesh had been flailed off. She pressed her hand against her chest, felt the rapid flutter of her heartbeat, and tried to catch her breath.

The sting was already subsiding, fading into the memory that it was. Along with the dream. Dissipating fast.

And yet one part lingered. Over the din of the groaning timbers of the ship, Mary still heard a muffled noise. The faraway sound of a man wracked in pain. Sobbing.

It was Wylde.

Mary was certain of it.

She drew a sharp breath, held it, pinched her eyes shut tight, and ran her fingers through her hair. Such an awful, mournful sound! She tried to think about other things: her rooms on the South End, necklaces, a Tarot card (for some reason, The Tower came to mind), the taste of Cod's halibut, Yonder's nose, anything to block out the noise in her head. The melancholy was sharp as a blade. But slowly, very slowly, his moaning cries dimmed, faded, and fell away.

She was alone again, swaying softly in the quiet dark of the schooner's cabin.

Mary hoisted her legs over the side of the hammock. She slid down, her bare feet squishing on the wet floorboards. With her hands spread out to find the walls, she made her way over to the door and let out a loud yawn.

Three hours of sleep at most, but Mary had cherished every minute of it, despite the vision that had woken her. With Far out playing cards, and Yonder preferring to remain above, she had had the cabin – and the hammock – all to herself since she had retired. The clink of coins from last night's consultations jingled in her bosom (eleven reales, two dollars, and a half-crown). Her first thought was to find the head and perhaps something to eat. She pushed the door open and squinted at the bright shaft of daylight that illuminated the stairs leading up to the main deck. Hopefully, she hadn't missed breakfast.

No sooner had she emerged through the grated hatch, though, when Mary knew something was amiss. The wind roared in the rigging, as the ship raced fast and steady across the waves. And yet the hands scurried about every which way, as quick and as quiet as roaches, running up and down the masts, hauling in heavy rope lines, battening hatches. Their faces blazed with intent. One of the reefers squatting near her swore under his breath, the way a man does when he can't spare the effort of bellowing a proper curse. Correa's voice boomed from the quarterdeck behind him.

"Quiet fore an' aft!"

Mary turned around and saw the first mate, Captain Grimmette, Yonder, and Far gathered around the helm. They all stared behind them, at something far beyond the *Snuffbox*'s wake. Grimmette had a telescope wedged into his eye. None of them uttered a word. Mary crept aft to join them.

"It seems," Yonder whispered at her approach, "that we are being followed."

Mary looked out, squinted, and soon caught the shimmer of sails breaking over the waves. A good many sails, she noted.

"She's gainin'," Grimmette muttered. "Fast. An' that last tack cut off any run for the bay. Which we'd have missed her if you'd gotten the fuckin' sails set 'stead of nappin'.'"

Correa said nothing, but stared, unblinking at the ship

behind them. Grimmette thrust the telescope into Correa's chest roughly.

"You got sharper eyes than me. What colors is she flyin'?"

"Showin' Dutch," Correa replied. He shook his head and returned the telescope. "Is a lie, though."

"She's 'bout as Dutch as you are," Grimmette agreed. He shouted at the bow to let out the jibs some more and returned his attention to their pursuer. Mary watched as well, joining their silent vigil. Even from this distance, it was clear the ship behind them was bigger, and faster, and intent on catching them. Grimmette heaved a long, contemplative breath. "Well. No use pretendin' she can't see us. Correa, set the American ensign on the mainmast. Then run down in the hold with four or five strong 'un's and start jettisoning. Everything goes. I want us floatin'."

"The rum, too?"

"Goddammit," Grimmette snapped, "I said everything, didn't I?"

The mate hesitated. "How I get my cut then?"

"You want to save your sixteenth of cargo? Or your skin?"

Correa grunted and shouldered past Mary, shouting out names for men to come help him below. Grimmette shouted more orders to the crew working the masts. More sails blossomed from the beams, so that there wasn't an inch of the *Snuffbox*'s sparring that wasn't festooned with canvass. Correa and his men emerged from the hold, hoisting barrels, and crates, and boxes, which they heaved into the ocean. Mary knew she ought to make herself scarce, to stay out of the way, but she found the spectacle morbidly fascinating. So she stood quietly, pressed against the wall and watched. Far was quiet, too. Only Yonder seemed completely unapprised to what was so obviously happening.

"I wonder what the hullabaloo is about," he remarked

to Mary and Far. He turned to Grimmette, "I beg your pardon, Captain. But you seem concerned with that vessel back there. Is there something especially untoward about it?"

Grimmette's lips were already drawn tight, and Yonder's question seemed to set them aquiver. The creased lines in his forehead and cheeks were furrowed as deep as canyons, ones on the verge of an avalanche.

"As a matter of fact, governor," he replied archly, "yeah, there is. That there's about as *untoward* as a ship can be." He tapped at Yonder's shoulder and gestured aft. "That's a corvette. With a Dutch flag. But Dutch merchantmen don't sail corvettes, so she's flyin' false colors. She's givin' chase and overbearing us, which means sooner or later, she's goin' to steal our wind. And I'd bet your last gold coin she's carryin' at least twenty—"

Grimmette was interrupted by an eruption in the water not twenty yards from where they were gathered on the quarterdeck. It made a loud splash and a cloud of spray descended. A few of the drops reached as far as the helm. The report of a cannon shot quickly followed, like a distant murmur of thunder. Behind them, a thin wisp of white smoke trailed from the corvette's bow.

"Cannon," Grimmette finished.

"Good gracious!" Yonder cried as he covered his head with his hands.

Instinctively, Mary dove for cover, crouching underneath the wheel, and cursed as vehemently and as violently as any of the sailors on board.

Only Far had stood his full height. When Mary got back up, he was still unmoved, glaring straight at the corvette, a ferocious, defiant grin on his face.

"That'll be the bow chaser," Grimmette observed, wiping the wheel's handle dry with his shirt sleeve. "A long nine."

"Wha . . . why-why the devil did they fire upon us?" Yonder stammered. "We've done nothing to harm them!"

Grimmette kept his eyes fixed on the ship pursuing them as he replied, "To get our attention."

Yonder quivered on the deck, his face pale.

Far gripped the handle of a dagger he had tucked in his belt.

Mary spoke in a flat voice, "And to let us know we're in range, right Captain?"

"You got the drift." Grimmette leaned hard into the wheel to keep the chase going.

Miles off the Atlantic coast, on a cold and blustery ocean, a strange, intricate *danse à deux* unfolded between a corvette with a red, white, and blue banded flag and an old, diminutive schooner flying faded red and white stripes. Each movement began with Captain Grimmette who, whenever he pleased, barked out an order to change course. The schooner's crew raced around the deck and up into the yards. Grimmette turned his wheel, and the *Snuffbox* would alter her direction. Sometimes hard to port, sometimes a little starboard, sometimes changing so imperceptibly, it was hard to say whether they were still moving in a straight line. In the schooner's wake, a lengthening trail of flotsam, crates and boxes, planks and casks, spars, beams, and even dishware, were thrown overboard to help hasten her pace.

For the rest of the morning and into the afternoon, Grimmette played the mouse. With every course change, though, the corvette would match him, step for step – as slowly the cat crept closer. Every half hour or so, the corvette lashed out with her claws and fired on her prey. A puff of smoke and an iron ball would come plink across the waves or spelunk within a patch of ocean and rend the water into a fantastic fountain., Everyone on board the schooner would gasp and cower. But Grimmette suspected the cannon fire was just toying, for every one of the shots landed almost precisely fifty yards from one of the *Snuffbox*'s sides.

"Hard about," Grimmette called. The crew groaned in answer but lumbered back up into the masts to trim the sails, yet again.

The *Snuffbox* was still ahead. The lift from the trade wind and the lightening of her load made the whole ship feel as if she were some great, oaken seabird about to take flight. But the corvette that gave her chase was faster still. She inched closer.

Grimmette peered aft and frowned. He could make out the movements of the corvette's crew. She was full to bursting with hands. Probably all armed to the teeth. The tri-color flag had been hauled down, replaced with a black one.

"You don't want to blow up your precious prize now do you?" he murmured, as if the warship were an old friend he could persuade. "Of course you don't, that's why you ain't fired—"

At that moment, there was a loud whistle followed by the crack of timbers as a cannon shot ripped straight through the heart of the *Snuffbox*'s rigging. The sailor who had nearly been decapitated let out terrified shriek as the spar beside him crashed down into the water, followed by a tangle of lines and canvass.

Grimmette shook his head sadly.

"So much for that then. Ah, well. Least we did it proper . . ."

It had been an exceptionally well-placed shot across the bow. And it confirmed what Grimmette had suspected about the corvette's gunnery: the wide shots were deliberate, meant to herd him. But the herding was finished. This was his last warning. There was nothing more to be done.

Grimmette pulled himself upright behind the helm, squared his shoulders, put on his most dignified face, and called out for his first mate.

"Mr. Correa," he said. "Avast any more jettisoning, if you please."

Correa set down a small barrel he had been about to hoist over the railing and cast a furtive glance aft.

"Aye, cap'n," he answered glumly. "They got us. She's showin' her true colors now."

"Strike ours," Grimmette ordered.

As the *Snuffbox* ceremoniously lowered her tattered American ensign, Grimmette brought the wheel around, turning the ship about hard so that the wind fell out of her sails. A series of moans could be heard across the ship. Everyone knew, or must have had a pretty good notion, of what was about to happen – almost everyone.

"Oh, we appear to be slowing down," Yonder remarked innocently. "Are we arranging to meet with the other ship, then?"

"Weepin', pissin', fartin' Christ . . ." Grimmette muttered. If he weren't pressed for time, he might have thrown Yonder overboard. Instead, without a word to Yonder or his passengers, Grimmette sidled around the helm to a space where he could view the length of the main deck.

"All hands!" he called out. "All hands to the quarterdeck!"

The order echoed up and down the yards, through the hatches, and down into the ship's hold. Slowly, the motley little crew of the *Snuffbox* emerged. There was Cod, leaning from one tiptoe to the other to get a better view over the taller shoulders surrounding him. And Gino the rigger, an old hand who had been to this dance before, though he seemed especially sour faced about this one. Young Henry Jones held his knees into his chest and trembled. A wet stain was spreading across the crotch of his baggy pants. The rest of the men ambled about the mainmast. Grimmette blew a shrill whistle for quiet.

"Listen close, Snuffies!" he bellowed. "There's no easy way to say this. We're caught. She's flyin' the black flag now, so it looks like we're gonna have to pay the toll."

That was met with a loud barrage of curses.

"I don't like it any more than you," Grimmette raised his voice over the throng, "but there's no givin' her the slip. Now, most of you've been through this before, so you know what to do. First come, first serve on hidin' places. Your ass'll work in a pinch, but only for a coin or two. Don't get greedy. If they see you listing when you walk, they'll make it real uncomfortable for you, believe me."

"Fuck the money!" Gino bellowed. "I no want get pressed!"

There was a loud roar of agreement. Grimmette had to wave for quiet.

"I hear you. There's no knowin' how many of you they'll wanna take up, an' how many of you they'll just drop off somewhere's." The truth was, better than half of this miserable lot weren't worth pressing and wouldn't be missed if they accidentally fell overboard or had a knife brought across their throats. But Grimmette kept that to himself. "All I can tell you is, they're givin' quarter. So if they press you, don't fight 'em. It'll only make it worse for everybody. Ain't the end of the world, after all . . ."

But the mood of the *Snuffbox*'s crew had already degenerated into a general panic. There were angry, frightened shouts, as men scrambled to save what few valuables they possessed. A few tried to wriggle into spaces between the beams, as if they could somehow make themselves disappear, but there simply was no place to hide on a ship that was not much bigger than a glorified cutter. Some of the old-timers leaned back on the railing to smoke a pipe and enjoy a few minutes of relaxation before they were put to harder work. Henry Jones curled into a ball and began to sob for his mother.

That was that, then. The only ones left to deal with were the passengers. Grimmette turned to the three of them. The lawyer and his lady friend still rooted near the helm, faces as pale as cream. The big one stared ahead like a bull in a pen. Grimmette tried his best to sound apologetic.

"Sorry 'bout how this has turned out," he said to them. "But these things happen, y'know. No use cryin' after spilt milk."

"So – so we're to be taken by pirates?" Yonder squeaked.

"Afraid that's the look of it," Grimmette nodded.

"And what will become of us?"

"Well . . ." Grimmette thought aloud for a moment, "can't say for sure, but I suspect since you're a gentleman of means, there'll need to be some kind of payment made on your behalf. By which I mean, you'll likely be payin' out the better part of your worldly goods. That might cover you an' Mr. Far. As for your woman . . ." He could not bring himself to meet Mary's eyes, so he tried to make himself sound more cheery. "Here, but let's not fret too much about the future. There's some talkin' to be done yet. And I'm as good as a lawyer when it comes to talkin' ships and stores. Let's just see what I can't work out with their captain. Always hope for the best, eh?"

"Well, as to that, sir." Yonder licked his lips and tapped his fingertips. "As to that, I've no doubt you're competent, in your own way. But let me, um, well," the lawyer lifted his chin, "I should like to offer my assistance in any, uh, talking, that might concern my person or my companions. I am a well-regarded negotiator."

Far must have found something funny, for he bit his tongue and let out a harsh laugh. Grimmette simply scoffed.

"Look 'ere, Yonder," he explained, "this ain't playin' whist in a parlor. These are pirates 'bout to come aboard. They'll kill you as soon as look at you."

"Of course, I just thought, perhaps . . ." Yonder's voice trailed off.

"No, sir. I'm the captain. It's me'll be doing the talkin' for my ship – though I appreciate the offer."

Yonder swallowed and met Grimmette's gaze with a terse nod.

"I trust," Yonder said evenly, "you will negotiate vigorously on our behalf."

"Eh? Oh, of course. 'Course I will."

"Then I shall leave you to it. Pray do not hesitate to ask if you should need my aid. I'll be only too happy to help you."

"Sure."

There were a hundred matters that needed his attention and he had little time, but at least he had shut the damned lawyer up. Grimmette tied off the wheel, checked to make sure it wouldn't spring loose and looked over his shoulder toward the corvette to gauge how much more time he had before she came within hail. No more than half an hour, at the most. "Now if you'll excuse me," Grimmette said hastily to his passengers, "but I got some papers to attend to. Get the manifest in order an' all that . . ."

But before Grimmette could leave he heard Far's gravelly voice, and the sound of it startled everyone. There was something foreboding in the way he spoke that made Grimmette pause mid-step.

"I have no intention of surrendering," Far said. There was a calm detachment about him that was completely at odds with the mayhem on the main deck just beneath him. "My person and my property – are mine."

Grimmette eyed him warily. "Look here, lump-muff. That's a sure way to end up in Davy Jones' locker."

Far stretched his long arms and inhaled. A trace of a smile parted his lips.

"I've always wanted to try my hand at ship fighting."

"Ship fight— Why you addled son of a bitch. Are you lookin' to get us slaughtered? I've got a pistol and a couple of rusted axes. That's it. They've got a whole battery of cannon. They'll rake us stem to stern!"

"All the better."

Grimmette was caught between fury and stark terror, but before his temper could turn into a tempest, Correa happened by. His mate took him by the shoulder and murmured into his ear.

"I know how talk to this kind," he said. "Leave 'im to me . . ."

Far felt pleasantly surprised with how this trip had turned out. A dreary beginning, to be sure, followed by a tedious evening of enduring Correa's boasts, but the end was shaping into as fine a one as he could have hoped for. The wind, the chase. The boom of cannons. The picture of a cannonball careening through the mast, blasting it to splinters, held steadily in his mind. As well as the sight of all those men crowded on the deck of the corvette, all those swords, gleaming in the sunlight . . .

But there was that pest Correa again, interrupting his reflections. As the captain scurried off into his cabin, no doubt to work on falsifying the *Snuffbox*'s records, Correa spoke to Far as if he were a fellow confidence man that needed to be let in on an inside angle.

"You need listen to me."

"Do I now?" Far answered.

"*Si*. This no game. No gamble." He nodded toward the ship that swiftly moved up on their port beam. "See the flag she flies? Is death's head and an arm. That means pirates. But is black. You know *that* means?"

Far hunched his shoulders. "That they're not fond of colors?"

"Is black means they give quarter. No fire on us, no kill. So long as we no fight. They just take your money." He glanced at Mary. "An' your woman."

"They're welcome to the latter," Far replied, "not the former."

Correa chuckled. "They'll take what they want, but least you live. If you no fight . . ." He gave Far a long, penetrating stare. "If you try fight, they fly red flag. Red means no quarter. No mercy. *Es fuego y sangre.*" Correa made an explosion with his fingers and blew out a loud puff of air. "There nowhere to run from cannon, my friend. *Todos muertos.* So we no fight today. Tomorrow, who knows? But no today."

Far listened indifferently and turned his attention to watch the waves lapping up against the side of the schooner. Like long lines of emeralds cracking apart, dying upon the wall of this one, tiny firmament. Farther out, a three masted warship had drawn alongside the railing. Far could see her plainly. No more than a hundred yards perhaps. Long, sleek, her sails drawn in to slow her progress, a machine that was well run and well commanded.

And so wonderfully lethal.

He could feel it in the glint of iron cannons, ten in a row, all pointed straight at him. The distant shouts of the corvette's crew echoed across the water. Jeers. Laughter. A white painted launch lowered from her side.

Far had never been to sea before, and yet he knew what was about to come, knew it like an old prelude he could sing by heart. Correa gaped dumbly at him, as the lord captain began to whistle a familiar tune.

CHAPTER THIRTEEN

"The study of Custom should especially delight those of a legal bend. For in many ways the system of Custom is a close cousin to the Contract, that sanctum sanctorum, in whom Perfect Freedom and Divine Order draw close and kiss blessings upon each other."
—Wherestone's *Commentaries on Custom*, page 3

It was near the end of the afternoon. A stiff breeze blew out of the north by northeast, sending flecks of white froth across the breaking waves. A calm, orange hue had begun to settle over the small corner of the Atlantic Ocean where two wooden ships laid across from one another's beams.

A white yawl, her oars shipped, was latched onto the stern of the smaller of the two vessels. A length of netted rope laddering had been cast over the side to allow the yawl's men to come aboard. Only five had bothered to make the crossing to claim their prize. Captain Grimmette tried to be philosophical about it. An empty, creaking American schooner was, in the maritime hierarchy, pretty small fish.

But Grimmette made up his mind to present the

Snuffbox with proper ceremony and, as best as he could manage, to give the ship her due. Most of his crew had scattered and cowered like frightened rats. The ship's rigging had been left in an embarrassing mess. The decks and rails were in dire need of scrubbing and a fresh coat of paint. Still, it was his ship.

"Was," he reminded himself glumly. She would only be his for a few more moments.

Grimmette swayed with the motion of the deck, a sheaf of papers to present to whomever came aboard tucked underneath his arm. Some of the pages had smeared from where the ink was still wet. Cod stood across from him clutching an old boatswain's pipe.

Boots thumped against the hull, a metal clank, probably a sword, and a gloved hand appeared. A finely stitched, ermine glove.

Cod brought the pipe to his mouth and blew the whistle.

As the note lingered, a somewhat surprised-looking gentleman's torso emerged over the bulwark rail. He was dressed in white and, though he had just crossed a wind-blown, choppy length of water, his dark hair was still combed to perfection. An oiled beard and moustache graced a finely chiseled olive face, a face that announced the man's aristocracy better than a calling card. The white-clad gentleman climbed aboard with unhurried grace, removed his gloves, adjusted the coat buttoned across his chest, and glanced down at Cod. His lips remained drawn, but Grimmette could see a hint of bemusement – and something else, dimly familiar.

"How very gracious of you." The man dipped his head at Cod. His English was a rich baritone and held only the slightest remnant of a French accent. He turned to Grimmette, and his eyes lit up in genuine delight.

"Ah!" the man exclaimed, "*mon Dieu!* Of all the ships in

all the seas! Surely this cannot be Captain Simóne Grimmette's?"

Grimmette almost gasped. "M-Mathieu Mercier?"

The gentleman burst into laughter, loud, ringing, carefree and infectious. Grimmette caught a scattering of eyes cautiously peep out of hiding places throughout the *Snuffbox*. The momentary levity was quickly smothered, though, as the rest of Mercier's companions climbed up over the side of the railing to join him.

Four men had come with him, all heavy set, with broad, scarred faces, and thick arms. Each one had a cutlass at his hip, two pistols tucked in his belt, and a musket with a bayonet slung over his back. The closest one to Mercier brought his musket around, but Mercier checked him with a sharp word.

Grimmette had sailed long and wide enough to have a passing hold over French. He strained to catch what Mercier murmured, but he thought it ran along the line of: "*No need for that. I know Monsieur le Captain. He's a mouse.*" While Grimmette still puzzled out what he had heard, Mercier turned to beam at Grimmette and reverted to English. "But this is amazing, Simóne. To run into an old shipmate here in the New World. The odds are imponderable. Truly fate is indeed a strumpet!"

"Glad to see you, too, Mat," Grimmette said, wiping a line of sweat from his forehead. "Right damned glad."

"So." Mercier's eye discretely scanned the decks and rigging of the schooner, as if he were a first-time houseguest entering his host's parlor. "This is a spritely little vessel you have here. Beautiful lines. Tacks like a boxer. Sails close to the wind. Pitches a bit overmuch, but with the right placement of ballast, that could be easily compensated I should think . . ."

Some further trifling observations followed, each of which Grimmette answered with what he thought was appropriate nodding and smiling. He was still so overcome with surprise, the customary formalities that should have attended the seizure of his ship had fallen completely out of Grimmette's head. But when a lull fell over Mercier's conversation, Grimmette recollected his duty and started to stammer a few words.

"So," Grimmette began, fidgeting with his buttons, "I hereby request quarter for myself and my crew and present to you, Monsieur . . . um – I should say, Captain—"

"Lieutenant," Mercier corrected. He smiled benignly. "I am honored to hold a private commission in the corvette *Niaiserie*. We've not yet received our formal *lettre de marque*. This new Republic we have in France is utterly incompetent with papers. But since you've surrendered, we shall give you and your intrepid crew quarter, food, and water, under the usual conditions."

A gust of wind blew across the deck, stirring the sails that had been haphazardly furled. He would have preferred privateers over pirates, but at least it was a pirate he knew.

"Who's your captain?" Grimmette inquired.

"An idiot of no importance."

Their eyes met, briefly, and when Mercier's fell it was as deliberate as a semaphore signal. There was an inquiry scratching behind that glance. An opportunity. Grimmette saw it and seized it straightaway.

"Well, at least we made him work for his prize," Grimmette said with a wink. "What's left of it."

Mercier chuckled. "Yes, you gave us a good run, captain. A creditable showing – for an American ship. I find myself quite exhausted."

"Can I offer you a chair in my cabin?"

"I'm surprised you have furniture to offer, with all the flotsam you threw in the sea."

"Got some wine, too. If you'd care for some."

That seemed to genuinely shock and delight Mercier.

Grimmette continued, "I'm sure Cod here squirreled away a bottle or two somewhere. He's a schemin' little devil. We could share a glass, go over my papers an' such. If you're not too pressed for time."

"For you, my dear Simóne, I shall make time."

Mercier gave his men their orders to spread out around the *Snuffbox* to post a guard at the helm, the hatches, and in front of the launch to prevent anyone or any more cargo from leaving the ship. As Mercier's men jostled about the main deck, Mercier followed Grimmette through the door beneath the quarterdeck, into his private cabin. Though they were lingering just above him on the quarterdeck, Grimmette did not spare a glance at his passengers before he disappeared.

When the captain's cabin hatch had been shut and latched and the voices within had fallen to a muffle, Yonder let out a relieved sigh. For the first time, he felt as if he had returned to familiar grounds. Beneath the thin planking, just feet away, men were negotiating, which, for Yonder, was the very craft of hopeful prospects.

He turned to Far and Mary.

"Well, this is rather better than I expected," he said as if he were assessing how a court proceeding had turned in their favor. "Indeed, we are in a much better bargaining position now than before."

Far rounded on him with a questioning eye. "How the devil do you figure?"

"Did you not see how well the gentleman knew our captain? Why, they practically embraced as cousins. You mark my words, their acquaintance can redound to our benefit. With a little aid."

Far simply glared at him while Mary shook her head.

Her curls bobbed around what looked like a worried frown.

Why were they both so sullen? Yonder wondered.

"You really believe Grimmette will be an honest broker?" Mary asked.

Yonder blinked at her. Before he could respond, Mary answered her own question.

"You shouldn't."

She tightened a shawl around her shoulders and withdrew down the steps to the main deck to lose herself in the crowd of seamen who slowly emerged from their hiding places.

"She's right," Far agreed. "For once."

He, too, left. Yonder was alone, on the quarterdeck, leaning on the helm and listening to muted laughter welling up from the captain's cabin.

There was some needling point in what they had said, an unsettling truth, though Yonder did not wish to dwell on it. Instead, he bit at his bottom lip and balanced his aching feet against the roll of the ship.

The table in Grimmette's cabin was covered in crumbs and a sheaf of papers. A single lantern cast a wan, greasy light from the aft wall. There was a hammock left strung up on a nail, a chest, and two rickety chairs separated by the table, each one set against the port and starboard walls respectively.

Grimmette leaned back in one chair, Mercier sat primly in the other. A cluster of documents was spread out before the lieutenant alongside a plate that held gray, broiled meat, a weevil infested biscuit, and a cup of weak red wine. It was shabby fare by any account, but it was the best Grimmette could scrape together under the circumstances. A fishing boat would have held better stores. But Lieutenant Mercier expressed his gratitude all the same.

Grimmette pushed a jar of old mustard across the length of a board.

"Something for the beef?" he offered.

"Thank you, no," Mercier smiled. He stroked at his moustache and regarded the dripping, salted lump of flesh before him. "Mustard with beef is an English innovation. I've not yet found a taste for it."

"Suit yourself." Grimmette shrugged, dipping his finger to the bottom of the jar. He spread a thin line of brown across the lukewarm flank of meat and wiped his finger clean on the plate's edge. "Lord knows, I'd never tell a Frenchman what's the right way to eat."

Between sips of his wine, Mercier studied the *Snuffbox*'s manifest, log, and muster roll. The official papers were supposed to catalogue the schooner's hands, mates, and passengers, as well as every stick, crumb, or jar of cargo she carried, where she had come from and whither she was traveling. As the Frenchman read, Grimmette prayed he would overlook the pages that had been inked within the past hour – which was better than half of what lay before him.

"If I read this correctly," Mercier let the segue float for a prolonged moment, "you've set sail for Chesapeake Bay with a skeleton crew of landsmen."

"And my first mate," Grimmette added.

"Yes, this Monsieur Correa. Whom you've rated an able seaman but, you note, 'he is prone to thievery, mutinying, and may be a pederast.' My, my."

Grimmette held out his hands. "I can only work with what's at hand. All the good 'uns have gotten pressed."

"And apparently your only cargo is . . ." Grimmette could see he was squinting at a blot of ink that ran down the length of a column. ". . . a crate of wooden buttons and a half ton of animal feed."

"Southern cows gotta eat, too."

Mercier *tsked* softly, his lips pursed with mild disapproval.

"My dear captain. I expect a measure of liberality will show up in a ship's documents once I've run it down, but this." He waved his hand across the splay of pages. "This is outright fantasy. Even for you."

"You saying that's a false muster?"

Mercier replied with a disarming smirk. "I am incredulous."

Grimmette softened his tone, since his bluff had been called.

"Well," he allowed, "I might not have been as careful as I should've with my papers. I don't have a bookkeeper. And you know I was never good with figures."

The lieutenant's smirk turned into a grin and ended in a chortle. "*Au contraire*, my friend. Your figures are the stuff of legend. That caper you pulled when you were clerk of the *Lutin* is still whispered about, with awe and reverence."

"Ah, good ole' *Lutin*," Grimmette sighed.

"However did you manage to make six tons of lead disappear?"

Grimmette smirked. "Bad scale's prone to make a bad weighing."

"Bad scale, indeed. You old scoundrel!"

When their laughter subsided, Grimmette continued,

"So it may be – *may* be, I say – that between not having a proper bookkeeper and being in a rush to catch the tide, that muster *may* not be as shipshape as I'd like." He paused. "Or maybe it's fine as it is. If you'd prefer to leave it the way it is."

Grimmette took a slow sip from his cup, all the while keeping his eyes on Mercier. The lieutenant settled back into his chair. It was time to broach a proposal – of a private nature.

"I've got passengers," Grimmette murmured in a low voice. "The kind that prefer to keep their business to themselves. An' can afford to do it. I'm to drop them off in Norfolk. They ain't on the muster."

"What is their business?"

The captain drew in a long breath through his nose, as if that were a mystery he had been unable to solve. "Can't say for sure."

Mercier rolled his eyes and began to drum his fingers on the table edge.

"All right, all right," Grimmette said. He leaned across the table to drop his voice lower. "It's a woman, an' her lawyer, an' her bodyguard. They're bringin' the law down from Boston on a gentleman who's worth bringin' it down on. These folks are willin' to pay anything to get to this man."

Grimmette raised his eyebrows meaningfully. Mercier, however, seemed to be growing impatient.

"And?"

"And one of 'em's a goose . . . that lays this for eggs." Slowly, he brought out one of Yonder's faceless, featureless golden coins. He pinched it between his thumb and forefinger, letting it catch the gleam of the lantern light. It shone with a brightness of its own, as if someone had knocked in a window to let the daylight inside the cabin. Grimmette carefully slid the coin to the other side of the table. It made no sound in the passing.

A strange silence fell over the cabin. Mercier looked at the smooth façade of metal with seeming indifference. He dabbed at his mouth with his napkin, then deigned to pick the coin up.

"Quite heavy," he remarked casually. But Grimmette noted the coin's edge tremor in Mercier's palm, as if from a tiny jolt of electricity. The lieutenant set it down again and took a drink of his wine. "A pretty little thing. But not enough for what I require. Not nearly. My debts are . . . well, much the same as when we last saw one another. Unfortunately."

"I figured," Grimmette said soothingly. "You were havin' a bad run with the cards for a while there. An' I'm sure they're squeezin' you for a bond before they'll give you a letter of mark. It's no wonder you're stuck as first mate to a pirate. No, I suspect you need a right square sum to clear the decks, get a fresh start as a privateer, with a ship of your own . . ." He drew Mercier's attention back to the glimmering coin on the table and whispered, "There's more where that came from. Lots more." Grimmette brought out another, and another of the coins. Mercier could no longer hide the desire shining within his eyes. "This goose is stuffed, I tell you. An' ready to be plucked."

Grimmette smiled to himself, for Mercier simply could not pry his gaze from the luster of the three golden circles lying on the dingy tabletop. The lieutenant did his best to maintain a pretense of disinterest, but it was no good. Grimmette could almost hear Mercier's thoughts turning over weights, and gold prices, and exchange rates. *The longer, the better*, Grimmette thought. But conscious of how he was watched – and marked – Mercier let his napkin fall over the small treasures, as if to break their spell.

His chin tilted up, and Lieutenant Mercier addressed Grimmette in a formal, commanding tone.

"You are wasting my time," he declared.

Grimmette arched an inquiring eyebrow.

"Not to put too sharp a point on the matter, Captain, but I already have these passengers and their fortunes. And yours. You surrendered this goose when you surrendered your ship."

"Perhaps so, Mat. Perhaps." Grimmette nodded. "But, see, there's two things to consider. This goose is pretty sickly, and it's prone to trip over its own shadow. Could be it'll have an accident, or maybe just up an' fly away. Closest port for you to claim prize money would be Bayonne. That's a far sail. Who knows what could happen between here and there?"

"Who knows," Mercier echoed flatly. As it happened, Grimmette and Mercier shared a well-informed notion of how easy it was for a man to have an accident, or slip overboard, or simply disappear while crossing the Atlantic. "What is the other consideration?"

"At the moment, you an' me are the only ones who know about this goose."

"Ah . . ."

Mercier nodded. No doubt, the smudged pages of Grimmette's manifest took on a whole new light. In a hurried whisper, Grimmette explained his proposal. Mercier would present the *Snuffbox*'s papers to his captain and confirm that, after thoroughly inspecting the entire ship from stem to stern, they were accurate in every respect. With such a meager prize, the captain of the *Niaiserie* would assuredly order Mercier to sail the *Snuffbox* —alone – for France so that *Niaiserie* could keep hunting the coast for bigger fish. And once Mercier reached Bayonne . . .

"I keep the goose," he said.

"An' I keep my ship," said Grimmette, slurping down the last of his wine.

A calm dusk light fell and purpled the sea. Long shadows stretched down from the masts and beams across the length of the *Snuffbox*'s deck. The wind backed off somewhat, so that the waves no longer crested, but lolled by in lazy progression. Most of the sails were furled, so that the ship meandered with the current. The deck lanterns were lit. Though the air was cold, it almost felt pleasant to be above deck.

Certainly, the mood onboard had lightened considerably.

The Snuffies went about their duties, chatting quietly, some even laughing, smoking pipes, and sipping grog they had fetched back out from their hiding places. Were it not for a corvette's cannons that were still rolled out, manned, and aimed directly at them, someone might have struck up a jig on a fiddle.

Captain Grimmette and the French lieutenant emerged from the captain's cabin and made a show of expressing their good spirits. Grimmette shared a wink and a quick whispered word with Correa, who would spread the good news to the hands. They might – just might, mind you – come through this capture with nothing more lost than a few weeks to make Bayonne and back.

"So tell 'em to mind their manners," Grimmette grunted to his first mate, "do like they're told. Keep sailin' with the wind, an' it'll take 'em all home."

Lieutenant Mercier and his guards gathered at the port rail. The French yawl was already being lowered. A rope ladder was cast down after it. Mercier had a parcel of papers tied up and clutched in his hands. One by one, his men descended, took their places in the boat, and outed the oars.

"Monsieur Captain Grimmette," Mercier announced, grasping one of the rope rungs, "if you will prepare to set sail on the course we discussed. I'll return after I make my report to my captain. I shan't be long."

"Sure thing, Lieutenant."

In a much lower voice, Mercier added, "Better make sure that goose doesn't fly before I return. It would be very unfortunate for you if that were to occur."

"I'll see his wings are clipped," Grimmette assured him.

Mercier climbed down the ladder but came to a halt. Peering up at Grimmette, he murmured another warning, "And do not even think of – how do you Americans say it –

making a run for it while I take care of matters on my ship."

It was almost comical, but Grimmette tried to sound offended. Why, nothing of the sort had passed his mind. It would be against his honor as a gentleman to strike his colors and run. Doubly so, since he and Mercier had a bargain. Grimmette pressed his hand against his heart and swore on his Savior, the soul of his mother, and the souls of his children (whoever they may be), that he wouldn't dream of trying to cut out on him.

"Very good," Mercier nodded. "I only worried that the coming darkness and my temporary absence might prove to be too much temptation for you."

Mercier went down the last ropes of the ladder, ordered his men to shove off, and the yawl began a measured beat over the hundred-odd yards that separated the *Snuffbox* from the *Niaiserie*. Once the sounds of the oars' rhythmic splashing had faded, Grimmette turned on his heel and called for Cod.

"Cap'n," the little crewman reported.

"Where's our guests?"

Cod only had to reflect for a moment before answering that when last he saw them, Mr. Yonder was pacing on the quarterdeck and apparently talking to himself, Mr. Far was sitting underneath the mainmast, sharpening a knife, and Miss Mary was in the cabin below. He could not say for sure how she was passing her time down there, though he suspected she may be trying to find a suitable hiding place.

"I'll have a word with Far on the quarterdeck."

"Aye, Cap'n."

"An' Cod." Grimmette grasped Cod's shoulder firmly. He dropped his voice low. "See if you can't persuade him to leave the knife behind."

"Is there – a particular reason he should disarm himself?" Cod ventured.

Grimmette snarled and squeezed his shoulder hard

217

until the little devil's masked face showed a proper measure of fear.

"Here, you questionin' my order?"

"No, sir! Never, sir."

"That's the same as mutiny."

"I only—"

"Look here, you lil' painted heathen bastard. I'll see you *swing* before you square my deal!"

Cod held up his hands imploringly.

"Captain, please. Of course I will follow your order. I only ask because the gentleman may be disinclined to follow my suggestion. He seems fond of his knives, I've noticed."

Grimmette relaxed, but only a little.

"Oh." He was momentarily distracted by the clinking sound of iron chains crossing the main deck. Grimmette looked over as Correa smile crookedly at him. "Tell Far whatever the hell you want, just see that he comes to the quarterdeck, alone, and unarmed."

"I – aye, sir."

As Grimmette tromped away up the steps that led to the quarterdeck, Cod fretted over what he ought to do. He had never been one to shirk from an order, even orders from wicked captains like Grimmette, but this one made him feel especially uneasy. There was some malice – more than the usual amount – in the captain's cold, dead eyes.

Troubled by those thoughts, Cod began to wander a long, circuitous route around the rails toward the mainmast. He brushed past his crewmates ambling about the main deck. They greeted him in a friendly enough fashion, but it bothered Cod to see men so idle in their occupation and ignorant of what was happening around them. The more he considered it, the more his gnawing anxiety grew. Cod was so lost in his musing, he nearly tripped over Far. The gentleman sat at his ease with his back against the mast.

The dusk sun and the ship's lanterns kept the deck alight, but somehow Far, with all his height and bulk, was completely immersed in shadow. So fully, he might have been a part of the darkness. There, but not there. Cod gave a slight start at the sound of his name.

"Cod," said Far without ever looking up. "You've the face of a man who's seen a ghost." The soft scrape of a whetstone brought against a blade punctuated his words. "Or fears he may become one."

"S-sorry, sir. I was actually looking for you."

Far rose, stood at his full height and slowly came into Cod's view. He had a sardonic smile and held a long and lethal-looking dagger.

"You've found me," he said.

"If you please, sir," Cod brushed his braids behind his neck, "Captain Grimmette sends his compliments and requests that you join him on the quarterdeck. Mr. Yonder is there already."

"What does he want?"

"I suspect it pertains to our recent capture."

"I suspect it does." Far glanced aft at the quarterdeck and made a long, sweeping search of the ship. "Tell me, Cod. Why did our enemies return to their ship? I find that strange. And a bit unsettling."

"I – I'm sure the captain knows."

"I'm sure he does." Far's eyes narrowed. "I'll learn what's afoot." He started to head aft, but Cod begged his pardon.

"If you please, sir. Before you go . . ." Cod swallowed and shifted his weight from foot to foot. He had thought through how he could broach this, but when it came to it, once he was before Far's presence, he found it hard to start. "It, um . . . it is generally considered uncouth, even improper, to address the captain of a ship on his quarterdeck – while one is armed . . ."

Far growled. He brandished the dagger menacingly. The blade was almost as long as Far's forearm.

"I shall bear whatever arms I damn well fancy wherever I damn well wish."

Cod did his best to keep his voice from breaking. "Of course, sir. I mention it because – well, only because you might wish to consider *concealing* that particular weapon. For the good of all concerned. If you take my meaning. Perhaps in the side of your boot?"

Far paused and stared at Cod for an uncomfortably long time. Cod did his best to meet the gentleman's gaze, but Far's was a dark and dour presence, like a monsoon on the horizon. And Cod already treaded in dangerous waters. Though worlds separated them in language and temperament, Cod hoped he had made himself understood. For he could not say any more in good conscience.

"Good idea," Far slipped the blade into the space between his boot and his stocking, so that only the upper tip of its black handle was showing. "Thank you, Mr. Cod."

CHAPTER FOURTEEN

"There is no more potent venom to the spirit than submission. In Custom, it is downright lethal."
—Wherestone's *Commentaries on Custom*, page 42

Far ascended the steps leading to the captain's quarterdeck just as the last rays of the setting sun slipped behind the horizon and died away. Deepening shades of cobalt and gray painted the small sweep of the elevated platform in the aft of the schooner. The falling shadow was held at bay by two lamps burning atop the corners of the taffrail.

The quarterdeck seemed unusually crowded. Three men were huddled beneath the port side lamp. Their faces were grim.

Far announced himself by clearing his throat.

"Oh, thank goodness you're here!" Yonder sputtered. "I-I don't know what's possibly gotten into—"

"Shut it," Grimmette growled. He drew a step back so that Far could see for himself where matters stood.

Correa and Grimmette had Yonder backed into a

corner. Yonder's coat was torn open and his shirt askew, and he trembled like a dandelion. Which was perhaps understandable, since Correa had a pair of flintlock pistols, full-cocked and leveled not more than a few inches from Yonder's chest. As Far took a step toward them, one of the pistols swiveled to find its mark on Far.

"No closer," Correa warned.

Far halted and casually folded his hands behind his back.

"Why, Captain Grimmette," said Far with mock indignation, "whatever is the meaning of this?"

Grimmette had two sets of heavy rusted chains and padlocks slung across either of his shoulders and a pistol of his own tucked into belt. He licked his lips and glared straight at Far, as if in challenge. "You really need me to lay it out for you?"

"No." Far shook his head.

"Thought as much."

Beneath the taffrail lantern, Yonder quivered, and squirmed, and muttered miserably to himself. He tried in vain to put more distance between himself and the barrel of the pistol that was trained on him. But from where he was, cornered in the back of the quarterdeck, the only way further was overboard and into the sea. Yonder stole a glance at the dark, impassive waves breaking below in the stern wake and turned to Far.

Yonder was pallid, sweating, as he spoke quickly, "You know that I'm not well. If I should be shot – it could-could actually . . ."

"I know," Far replied quietly.

"Here now," Grimmette interrupted, "Correa don't really want to shoot you, do you, Correa?"

"No," Correa answered. "That break my heart."

"Like I told you, governor," Grimmette continued, "nobody's goin' to get shot, nobody's goin' to get hurt."

"Then-then why the chains?" Yonder asked.

"What? These?" Grimmette gave the chains on his shoulder a rattle, as if he had just discovered their presence. "They're for show. So the frogs'll think you won't try to cut an' run on 'em. Like a ruse, if you catch my drift."

Yonder eyed the fetters with a disgust that was both wretched and despairing. Grimmette started to unwind one of them.

"So we'll start with you, Mr. Far," Grimmette said, taking a step toward Far. "You just stick those big paws of yours out, nice an' slow, so I can chain you up a little bit, an' then Correa can put away the guns."

"Don't do it!" Yonder warned. "You mustn't. If you submit to chains, Custom will chain you. You'll be in his power. Wherestone's clear on this—"

"That's enough o' your lawyer talk!" Grimmette gave a hard rap across the side of Yonder's head with the end of a chain link. Yonder doubled over, whimpered and clutched his ear.

"Custom," Yonder repeated softly. "Custom. You mustn't . . ."

"It's quite alright," Far assured him. "I know what to do."

"See?" Correa laughed and gave Far a long, meaningful wink. "I told you, Cap'n. He not so dumb."

Grimmette joined his first mate's cheerless snigger, while Yonder whispered four words to Far, "Do what you do."

A warning rattle of the chain stopped Yonder from saying any more. Grimmette scowled down at him.

"Y'want another?"

Far studied his companion, cowering and holding his head miserably. He turned his gaze to the darkness mounting on the port beam. The flickering lights of the *Niaiserie* twinkled benignly, like stars piercing the gloom of a wintry night sky. He could hear the French voices, muffled, carrying across the small expanse that separated them.

Following Far's attention, Correa spoke, "She not goin' nowhere. Nor them cannons. No use fighting it."

"But fighting is all I know," answered Far.

Grimmette snapped at him, his patience finished, "I'll have your hands, Far."

Far stood unmoved. He watched the corner of Correa's mouth curl into a wicked smile.

"Look, *come mierde*. Is chains on your hands. Or a ball through your heart." He gave the pistol aimed at Yonder a slight bob. "And then another ball through your friend's head. One for each, see?"

"Here I thought you brought those out to juggle," Far quipped. "I was looking forward to a show."

The grin fell from Correa.

"Hands. Now. Is no game I play here."

Slowly, Far brought his hands out from behind his back, but before Grimmette could clamp the chains around his wrists, Far stuffed them deep into his pockets. He looked from Yonder, to Grimmette, to Correa, and let out a long, contemplative sigh.

"But I want to play a game with you. Here."

Far brought his left hand out in a flash of noiseless motion. A quick flick of his thumb, and an old penny he happened to have went tumbling through the air toward Correa.

Correa's face did not have time to register his surprise. He had to have seen it was nothing but a penny, that was plain enough even in the failing light. An absurd thing to have thrown at him. Which was precisely the point of it. Correa's slow and feeble mind could not grasp what Far was doing. And since he could not comprehend Far's action, Correa could only react to it.

A reaction entirely dictated from habit, from the shows

and capers he had boasted to Far he had performed in ports around the world. Two objects were in Correa's grasp. A third was suspended in the air. An audience was watching. Correa's hands turned, as if of their own volition. To start the juggle.

And in the span of that moment, Far shot his right hand down the side of his leg.

A gleam of light flashed from the penny's twirl, another shone from Far's dagger. Far made the blade follow the path of the penny – but with the force of a battering ram.

Correa's lips parted in protest and breathless surprise. His eyes dropped as Far pulled the long line of metal free from his chest, from where he had plunged it deep. A spread of crimson gushed like a fountain through Correa's shirt. The mate's legs crumpled. As he fell, Far stepped on him casually, the heel of his boot crushing Correa's face, forcing him down, like the deadwood he was.

A single stride was all it took for Far to reach Captain Grimmette. One of the chains the captain had been holding fell with a loud, heavy clank to the quarterdeck. With his hand free, Grimmette had just time enough to grasp for the butt of his pistol in his waistband. Time enough to garble an oath as he reached for it. But not enough time to do anything to repel the storm of violence that Far brought upon him.

The dagger, still slick with Correa's blood, pierced deep into Grimmette's breast. For good measure, Far stabbed his man twice more.

"Oh . . . God . . ." Grimmette sputtered.

He clutched his arms tight around his chest, as if embracing himself, and his eyes darted about sightlessly. He dropped to a knee and collapsed beneath Far's shadow. The quarterdeck rocked gently beneath them. A break of waves, a skirl of a breeze, a lonely cry of a gull – all the sounds of the ocean's breath – mingled with Grimmette's dying breath. As the man lay on his back, leaking the last stream of his life's blood, a smile broke through his pain wracked face.

"Least – least I-I'm on m'ship . . ."

It was, perhaps, a better ending than Simon Grimmette deserved. But such is fate.

Not that Far spared a moment's thought upon the justice he may have meted out. With a simple, practiced swipe, Far cleaned his dagger's blade on the captain's shirt sleeve and, glancing aft at his companion, asked if Yonder was at all hurt.

Yonder was still huddled on the taffrail corner, shaking badly, his face as round and pale as the moon.

"I – I am unhurt," he said before he fell into a fit of wheezing.

For his part, Far felt fairly pleasant, though a little unsated. It was like he had been given two sips of decent port at the end of a long day, only to find it was the last of the bottle. He combed his hair with his fingers, untangling it in the wind, and hoped that more enjoyment would follow soon. As he pulled Yonder to his feet, his companion spoke to him with what Far could detect was a hint of admiration and a hint of jealousy.

"I suppose that was well done."

While Captain Grimmette sojourned the uncharted waters of the afterlife, Far stuck his dagger in his belt and considered where matters stood. There was little time to waste, he was certain of that. The *Snuffbox* had a dozing, drunken, dreg of a crew, but sooner or later, *someone* was bound to notice that their schooner's captain and first mate had both vanished. Once they did, there would be a hue and cry. Followed by disorder. Followed, no doubt, by a pillage of the officers' cabins and the ship's stores. Some fighting, some score-settling. Perhaps a mutiny or two. The ship would quickly devolve into bedlam. And when the French returned – which could be at any moment – and saw the sorry state of affairs that had overtaken the *Snuffbox*, the bedlam could turn downright nasty.

That was the usual course for these affairs, in Far's experience. An idea had hatched though, as to how he might turn it to their advantage. He helped Yonder gather himself, buttoned his partner's coat, straightened his belt, and brushed at some of the blood that had spattered his shirt.

"How quick can you find Cod?" Far asked.

"Quick enough, I suppose." Yonder coughed and looked at Far with raised eyebrows. "What do you want of him?"

"Tell him to lower that little boat – I think it's called the launch – and to make it ready to sail. If anybody asks what he's about, he's to tell them the Frenchman's orders were to send over the passengers come nightfall. That we're going to be held on their ship."

"Why would he—" Yonder started. He paused as comprehension slowly dawned on his face. "A plausible ruse." He nodded approvingly. "What of our luggage?"

"No time for that. We'll have five, ten minutes at the most."

"And what of Mary?"

Far rolled his eyes and uttered an oath.

"We need her—" Yonder began to plead, but Far cut him off.

"Fine. Fetch her, too. But if she slows us down, she'll be following these two gentlemen. Off you go."

As Yonder bustled down the steps, Far crouched down to examine Correa's hairy, blood-soaked hulk. Whatever skill the Spaniard may have had in life with his juggling, in death the stupid oaf had managed to drop both his flintlocks over the side after Far had struck. There was nothing else worth taking from the corpse. With a shove and a heave, Far brought him up and over the ledge of the quarterdeck's taffrail. The body fell quickly, with scarcely a splash in the turgid wake of the *Snuffbox*. Far did the same with Grimmette, pausing only to remove the pistol the captain never had a chance to fire. With the corpses gone, Far did his best to push their pooled blood over the aft with the side of his boot, but soon gave up the effort. Too much gore had seeped into the planks. If anyone came within sight of the platform, there would be no concealing the recent violence.

So far, though, his luck held. The soft murmur of the men milling below remained unbroken and unchanged. No one had ventured near the quarterdeck's stairs. No one had called above for orders or bothered to check on their captain. But, Far had come to learn, a ship's quarterdeck at sea was something akin to a general's tent in the field – a place men only entered when bidden or when needed. For the time being, he had Grimmette's quarterdeck to himself. And the crew was oblivious.

He tucked the captain's pistol behind his shirt and into his belt and listened.

It was not long before Far heard the distinct plunk of a small craft's hull dropping into the water below. He allowed another minute to pass. He smoothed out his hair and fixed a casual, serene expression on his countenance as he made his way down the run of steps to the main deck. As he walked the deck's length, he was greeted with a curt nod from a rigger and a look that might have passed for sympathy from the ship carpenter. Far almost made it to the forecastle deck when Henry Jones begged Far's pardon as Far went by.

"Please, sir, and – and I don't mean to add to your troubles, but as you've come down from the quarterdeck . . ."

"Yes?" Far arched his eyebrow.

"Well, what – what does the Cap'n want us to do?"

The look in Jones' face reminded Far of a calf – one that

had broken its leg and been left behind for the wolves. Far gave him what was meant to be a kindly, sympathetic pat on the shoulder, though it seemed to cause the boy some pain for he winced beneath the weight of Far's hand.

"I suspect," said Far, "if he's not told you otherwise, you're to carry on. Follow your orders. But whatever you do, I wouldn't trouble him on the quarterdeck." Far leaned closer. "He's in a pretty foul temper."

"Oh." Jones dropped his gaze, crestfallen. He stuck his knobby hands in his pockets. "Yes, sir. I mean, no sir. I'll not do that."

"Best of luck, Jones."

Far edged his way past the boy and made it to the forecastle deck, where Yonder was standing by the chains that had held the captain's launch. Far glanced over the rail.

Below them in the water, Cod was in the hold of the little boat, working to hoist a mast that looked like a toothpick in comparison to the ones aboard the schooner. Mary was already halfway down a rope ladder that reached the launch. She had her curtain purse clenched in her teeth, but, thank the gods, she had left that ridiculous trunk in the cabin.

"You go next," Far said to Yonder.

"I . . ." Yonder eyed the swaying set of ropes and the tiny rocking vessel he was supposed to climb down into and swallowed. "I shall do my best."

A tentative foot probed for a hold in the rope ladder, and Yonder made an ungainly, ignoble descent over the side of the *Snuffbox*. But he had scarcely cleared the gunwale when it became evident to Far that Yonder carried far too much ballast in his backside for his delicate arms and legs to hold steady. Even if the Atlantic were perfectly becalmed (and it never was), Yonder would never have the strength or dexterity to negotiate his flabby mass down twenty feet of cold, slippery rope into a heaving, bobbing launch boat.

As Far looked down, gritting his teeth at Yonder's incompetence, he watched what he knew was bound to happen. Yonder flipped over, his whole portly body, bottoms up, breasts down. There was a painful-sounding thump against the schooner's hull. He dangled by his ankle in the rope webbing. Back and forth he swung, like a well-dressed cuttlefish hung out for sale in a fishmonger's booth.

"Oh! Oh!" Yonder cried.

"What are you doing?" Far hissed at him.

"Hang on," Mary called up from the launch. She reached out her hands to try to help guide him back to the ladder. "Grab that knot with your hand, the one over there – no, not *that* one!"

"Wooaahh!"

A rolling swell lifted the schooner away from the launch and brought them back together. Yonder twirled around in the ladder. He did a half-twist before returning to his previous position. Mary grabbed onto the bottom ropes to keep him from flipping again. From Far's perspective, he looked like a marionette, upside down yet rising and falling with the water's motion. He was sure to draw attention.

"Get him in there!" Far whispered hotly.

"I'm trying," Mary snapped. She said to Yonder, "Grab – the – knot."

Another wave brought the two vessels apart, and Yonder let out a terrible cry, "My pocket!"

In all the commotion, it must have come inside out. Yonder shifted to reach for it. Before he could bring his hand to save them, four things fell from his person. Far watched as they tumbled down, one after another, to disappear into the water's gloom.

Three gold coins Yonder carried, the last of their traveling money. Followed by a pouch.

"No!" Yonder wailed. "No, no, no . . ."

The pouch had opened. From the railing, Far could see

a small posy of shriveled stalks and petals floating on the surface of the waters between the launch and the schooner, their unearthly blackness almost seeming to shine within the space of darkness. They started to spread out. A lap from a wave top crashed over the bunch of them, and the flowers were gone.

Yonder hung limply from the ladder, as if he had been speared.

Some of the hands on the *Snuffbox* noticed Yonder's predicament. They let out a loud guffaw.

"Look what Cod caught in his net!"

"Here, I didn't know we was fishin' for lawyers!"

"Ha!"

"Dammit all," Far muttered. He swung his legs over the side, secured himself on a rung, and grabbed onto Yonder. He quickly worked the ropes from around his companion's caught ankle, and he lowered Yonder's weight down to Cod and Mary, who waited below to catch him.

"Watch his head," Mary warned.

"Easy does it, Mr. Yonder," said Cod gently as he let Yonder's weight slide onto his shoulders. "You're safe on board now. All's well that ends well. There we are."

Carefully, Cod guided Yonder down to the launch's middle row next to Mary. Yonder sank upon himself. His face was still red from having been upside down, but otherwise he looked as lifeless as a corpse. Far climbed in after him and found a place near the bow.

"Where to, Mr. Far?" Cod whispered.

"Take us around the back of the ship – but do it casually. We're going to make a run for the coast. When we do, I want the *Snuffbox* between us and the corvette."

"Aye, sir."

Cod put his arms to work, rowed a few yards out from the side of the *Snuffbox* until the current began to carry the launch. The little fellow put on a ruse of pretending to be fuddled with setting up the sail's rigging. He let the lines fall askew as he kept tying and untying the same knot over and over. Slowly, the launch boat began to drift toward the rear of the schooner. It turned its bow toward the *Snuffbox* and Cod shouted a theatrically loud curse.

It was an admirable performance. The men on board the *Snuffbox* began to jeer again.

"You're headin' the wrong way!"

"Fucking painted little lubber's fouled his lines."

"Stick to cookin'!"

A chorus of laughter cascaded down, but Cod beamed a smile at his shipmates and held up his hands in helpless resignation.

"Almost got it," he called out to them.

Slowly, Cod began to pull on the ratline he had been holding all along. The first rustle of canvass elicited mocking cheers from the Snuffies. The launch's little sail rose slowly, haltingly.

"You're still headin' the wrong way!" came a voice from the schooner. "Corvette's lyin' eastward. Y'need to tack. Tack your sail, you idiot!"

Cod's foolish grin widened. From the side of his mouth, he addressed Far, "Sir," he said, "won't the French see this, too? If they think we're running, they might open fire."

Far peered at the *Niaiserie* expectantly. The silhouette of her long, slender form rose and fell. Her tall masts pierced the sky. The cannons were there as well. All run out. Far could sense their presence. Ten empty eyes gazed at him steadily, hungrily, like watch dogs. Were their masters paying attention, though? Perhaps Cod had a point.

"I should hope they would," Far remarked, rising from his seat. He balanced his feet on both sides of the bow's rails so that he could stand as tall as he could. "Better make sure of it." The moment the launch had rounded the *Snuffbox*'s stern and Cod tacked the sail to set their new course – away from the *Niaiserie* – Far bellowed a loud, challenging cry that seemed to echo to the end of the horizon.

"*Look here!* We fight to the death! You hear me? Over here! To the *death!* No quarter! *No quarter!*"

He reached for his belt, brought out Grimmette's pistol, steadied its weight, and aimed the barrel straight at *Niaiserie*'s beam. He squeezed the trigger.

There was crack of sound, a puff of smoke, an acrid whiff of gunpowder. Not even Far's keen eyes could follow the miniscule ball of lead his pistol had fired across the expanse of darkness; most likely, the shot had died, an infinitesimal ripple in the ocean's indifferent bosom. Not a splash or a sound marked its passing. Which only made Far chuckle. The show of force was so paltry it was comical.

But it accomplished his purpose. For there was no chance that the corvette, crowded as it was with hands, could have missed the report of a pistol from their prize's launch. From the schooner that had struck her colors and been given quarter. The men who remained aboard the *Snuffbox* had certainly seen and heard it. By the time the breeze had cleared the pistol's smoke, the Snuffies' cries and curses filled the air.

"Quickly, Cod!" Far yelled over the noise.

With a swift tug of the line, Cod brought the sail to its full height. He tied off the end and grabbed at an oar to row them faster. Far found another oar and joined Cod. With the better part of the wind in her stern and two sets of arms at the oars, the launch glided over the water. The pointed bow burst through the waves, sending clouds of frigid spray to drench the launch's passengers.

Far paid the damp and the chill no mind. While he rowed furiously, he kept a steady eye as the *Snuffbox* fell away behind them and the *Niaiserie* just beyond her. The sounds of desperate, crazed men quickly faded, overtaken by the steady thump of rollers crashing hard against the launch's hull. He blinked at the seawater dripping in his eyes. Far could make out in the distant darkness a wispy trail of smoke, the slow match circulating among the corvette's gun crews.

From off in the distance, a lone word, laced with fury, somehow reverberated across the waters, "*Tirez!*"

Far looked at the corvette and noted, with some detachment, that the *Niaiserie* had not bothered to replace the broad, fluttering black death's head flag with a red one. As the first roar of cannons rent the night, he found himself wondering whether Correa or Grimmette would have considered it a *faux pas* on the corvette's part to have opened fire while still flying a flag of quarter. There were so many odd, sundry customs among seamen. Not that it mattered. No one on the *Snuffbox* would live to recount an impropriety in their slaughtering.

Orange flames sliced through the darkness. Uncorked thunder pierced the sky. As they slipped away, the corvette began to pummel the schooner with round after round of merciless cannon fire.

"By the Gods . . ." Far breathed exultantly.

One of the *Snuffbox*'s foremast sails had caught fire. It glowed as bright as a bonfire.

"Keep rowing, sir!" Cod urged. "We're still in range of that grape."

At that moment, a piece of hot shrapnel arced over the *Snuffbox*'s deck, somehow missing the schooner's blocks and rigging to come whistling past Far's ear. Far grinned after it. Reluctantly, he sat back down to row.

The wind backed yet even more, and the launch practically galloped over the swells. The glow of the burning schooner was soon gone, vanished within the horizon. When they had put a sufficient distance between themselves and the corvette, Cod and Far stowed the oars underneath the benches.

Cod went aft to steer the tiller, glancing up at the

flickering stars every so often to adjust their course. Far stretched his shoulders and settled his back against the mast to have a rest. Yonder had his knees clutched tightly to his chest. Next to him, Mary was snoring. And so the little company aboard the launch arranged themselves fore and aft to find what comfort could be had in an eighteen-foot-long array of oak planks sailing across a darkened ocean.

A crescent moon broke through a cloud. It made a meager, marble pool of light in a patch of water that seemed to flee before the launch. The waves smacked beneath the hull in a hypnotic rhythm. Three men and a woman were spread about the little boat. They said nothing, though they were all filled to bursting with thoughts.

Far's were fixed on that wondrous din he had heard, that glorious noise, almost magical. That lovely, marvelous growl of cannons . . . He swore to himself he would have a battery of his own someday.

Mary's were troubled. She had awoken with a start (and a sharp ache in her neck) curled in the launch's corner. She had heard a sound. Distant but familiar. She buried her chin into her chest and listened. The farther they sailed, the more Mary became certain she was beginning to sense the soft, relentless murmurings of Wylde. Spinning in her head again. Like a window opening once more.

As for Yonder, his thoughts were singular and bleak. He hacked into his handkerchief, sniffing miserably, feeling wracked and wretched, and stared at the tops of his scuffed shoes. He was unable to free his mind of anything except an image. The frail petals of his Baby's Death, his one remedy in this world, swallowed up by a wave.

Only Cod was thinking in the present. He kept his attention on the stars to hold his course steady.

CHAPTER FIFTEEN

"Certainty is a rare a coin in Custom. This subtle science trades in speculation, inclination, and conjecture. It is a bartering of hunches."
    —Wherestone's *Commentaries on Custom*, page 2

Snowflakes drifted through the air. A few dozen perhaps, falling softly, sometimes trailing sideways, or round in spirals, only to suddenly be cast back into the sky from a passing breeze. Eventually though, inexorably, gravity pulled them down, every one of them, where the currents of a meandering, brown river would claim them. A continual patter of quiet annihilation.

Yonder cast a brief, uneasy glance at the snowfall.

He stood, half stooped, half leaning against a dock piling, pulling at the ends of his coat in a vain attempt to increase what little warmth the soaked garment could provide. His legs wobbled, though the weathered planks beneath his feet offered the firmest ground he had stood upon in days. It should have been a welcome change from pitching, heaving schooners and launches, but Yonder was exhausted, aching all over, and feeling out of sorts.

Cod had sailed them up the Elizabeth River for about a mile before he tacked south into this secluded estuary – just beyond sight of the hamlet of houses, churches, and shipyard of Norfolk. The only sign of settlement was the dock spurring out from a forested embankment and a tumbled down cottage that was covered in moss. Though surrounded by running fresh water, the air still carried the tang of ocean salt from Chesapeake Bay. But there was the hint of something else in the breeze, a harsher scent. Almost like a distant remembrance of burnt timber.

Yonder would have welcomed some conflagration right about then. He rubbed his hands together and tried to blow some warmth into his fingers. The arrival of morning had brought no relief from the winter chill. In fact, it had the ominous feel of a day that was bent on growing colder. He felt his spine shiver and quickly pressed his finger underneath his nose to stifle a sneeze just as Cod bustled by.

"Beg pardon, Mr. Yonder," Cod said. "I don't trust these overmuch."

He lugged a heavy rope over his shoulders, which he began busily tying around the post Yonder had been leaning upon. It was the third line he had used to secure the launch to pilings that bore the look of having weathered more years than pilings ought.

Yonder returned to his reflections, when at last he noticed that Cod had finished tying off the launch and that his tattooed face was watching him expectantly. Cod cleared his throat. It was difficult, but Yonder mustered the energy to smile at the little fellow in acknowledgement.

"Well, sir," Cod began brightly, "we've arrived, more or less on time. Though probably not in the manner you expected."

Cod tittered at his own joke. Yonder said nothing. He

felt the dampness in his clothes sticking to his skin and shuddered.

"I apologize for having to dock out here," Cod continued. "It's an old smuggler's berth, but I thought it wise to avoid the port. There's always some inspector, or tariff collector, or harbormaster hovering around. And I assumed you and your companions would prefer, well . . . given the nature of your charter, and what's transpired . . ."

Cod's words drifted into a polite silence. But Yonder felt so drained, he could not be stirred to take up what was obviously called for, a compliment. He should have praised Cod's yeomanly work and shrewd forethought. Instead he gazed at the dimpled lines stirring across the surface of the water near the dock. The eddies of river and ocean currents mingled together with the wind. The snow began to fall a little heavier. The whole world seemed to be weighted with a cloak of wet, cold grayness.

"Anyway," Cod pressed on, "it's only a short walk to Norfolk proper from here. I trust you and your companions are in suitable shape to reach town?"

Mary had gone off into the woods to relieve herself and freshen up her appearance. Far waited impatiently at the end of the dock. Yonder gave Cod a curt nod.

"Very good, sir."

Another silence fell between them. Yonder feared he was being rude, and that snapped him out of his lethargy. With a heavy voice, he thanked Cod for all his help, smiled wearily, and added, "You have been exceedingly dutiful, Mr. Cod."

"Not at all, sir."

"I wish I could compensate you for your troubles. But you must believe me when I say that I find myself bereft of funds. I'm afraid that in our flight I suffered – a considerable loss."

"I am sorry to hear it. Don't worry about paying me, sir,

I'll make do." Cod paused for a moment, his dark eyes darting from the launch boat and back to Yonder. "I would only ask . . . whether you intend to make a claim."

"A claim? On what?"

"The launch, sir."

The idea had never occurred to Yonder. Cod, perhaps sensing as much, explained, "What with the *Snuffbox*'s recent misfortune, her launch would be considered salvage. Under the laws of the sea, any man could claim it as his private property so long as he – but forgive me. Here I am presuming to tell a lawyer what the law is."

Yonder brought his knuckle to his bottom lip and pretended to carefully study the dismal-looking contraption that knocked against the dock, a tub of a boat that had brought him to this weed infested inlet in a wilderness six hundred miles from his home. He remembered a long, harrowing, and terribly uncomfortable night sitting in that hull. The sight of it only reminded him how much his back was aching.

"Consider the salvage yours," Yonder smiled. "It's the least I can do."

Cod trimmed the sail of his new possession to head eastward for the bay. The other three walked northward along a winding cattle path that led through the woods outside of Norfolk. It was quiet, except for the sounds of their feet crunching in the dirt. The pine trees rustled whenever a breeze gusted overhead. Flurries of snow were beginning to gather into piles of white along the ground between the forest's shadows. The path stayed level and smooth enough, save for an occasional fallen tree limb or a cluster of leafless brush that they had to pick their way around.

This commonwealth's roads were no worse than the ones back home. Yet Yonder found himself struggling to keep up.

Far was well ahead, taking his usual long strides, while Mary bustled a few yards after him, holding her bag before her chest. It bothered Yonder a little that he couldn't offer to carry her luggage. Couldn't because he feared she might accept his show of gentlemanliness as if it were genuine, and Yonder had no real desire to ease the lady's burden. But it was all he could do to keep his own feet moving forward. His legs felt as heavy as anchors, and his head swirled. He thought he could actually hear, as well as feel, the rattling in his chest.

He trudged along in silent suffering, sniffling and rubbing his eyes. He wondered at Cod's notion of what a "short walk" entailed when he lost sight of the path before him and tripped over a tree root. His knee hit the hard ground, and he cried out in pain.

Far paused for a moment to glower at him. Mary dropped her bag and hurried back.

"You don't look well," she said. She pressed the back of her hand against his head. She held it there no more than a moment, tugged at the skin beneath each of his eyes, and immediately announced a diagnosis.

"You've caught a chill."

"Don't be ridiculous. We do not get sick—"

A powerful sneeze burst forth like a cannon shot. As soon as it was expelled, Yonder felt his nostrils plug up, as if a gunner were wadding another round into the cavities of his nose. In the blurriness of his close vision, he could see his nose's tip glowing pink. "At least . . ." he felt for his handkerchief, but that, too, had apparently been lost in the flight from the *Snuffbox*. "I've never been sick before."

"You never had a cold?"

"Of course not."

She fished out a spare bit of cotton cloth from her handbag for Yonder.

"Use this," she told him, "while you catch your breath."

There was nowhere to sit, so after Yonder wiped his nose, he leaned over, put his hands on his knees, and tried to make his breathing come more slowly. Far still lingered on the path ahead, aloof and impatient. He blew his lips with an exasperated flutter.

"He should be lending you a hand," she said disapprovingly.

"It's not his way," Yonder replied without looking up.

"Then you should be more strict with him."

Yonder rubbed at the dull throb in his forehead and sighed. With some effort, he was able to hoist himself upright.

"The gentleman is in my debt, not my service."

"All the more reason why you should be strict."

Yonder was in no mood to argue, so he tried to change the subject.

"And how are you feeling, now that we're ashore?"

He caught an angry glint flashing from within Mary's eyes. Her eyebrows creased.

"I'm fine," was all she said.

On the surface, she seemed not at all fine; she was bedraggled and obviously bothered, though no more than usual. Buried deeper, however, there was a distraction. More so than ever. Which was a curious development, and perhaps auspicious.

He asked her gently, "Having visions again?"

"I don't know." She waved her hand, as if to shoo away a bothersome discussion. But Yonder pressed her, delicately but firmly, by insisting that he might be able to offer some comfort and guidance. It took a little further prodding, but she slipped into the simple, disjointed idiom Yonder had come to recognize as Mary's view from her window.

241

"I'm hearing him again," she admitted, her voice flat and heavy. "Only now . . . it's clearer. Like a curtain's pulling open. It's still there, the curtain I mean, but the sounds aren't so muffled. I can make out his words every now and then. Big, buttery words. Like how you talk."

"Indeed." Yonder regarded her closely. "I detect there's something more."

She narrowed her eyes and let out a long breath.

"Yes," she said. "Ever since we started on this cattle path, I keep seeing this light. Way out there, from the corner of my eye. It's like it's trying get my attention, but when I look at it, it runs away."

"What kind of light?"

"Like . . . like a leftover. From a rainbow. A bit of the purple band. It's . . . sad. I think it got left behind or abandoned."

Mary frowned, her bottom lip pouting, as she gazed pensively into the distance.

Yonder nodded with satisfaction.

"Very good, Mary," he said, patting her shoulder. "Very good."

Yonder had recovered enough of his strength that he could resume walking, so long as an elbow remained close at hand to help him. He and Mary toddled along together on the path, while Far, seeing them on the move, clambered off to roam ahead among the thinning pines and heath rows. The rest of the way to Norfolk, he kept far enough ahead so that he was just within Yonder's sight, while whatever light may have been guiding Mary stayed just beyond hers.

A sheet of gray blotted the sun and the sky. The snowfall stopped. A layer of frost caked with dirt covered a maze of narrow, cobbled roadways that ran like rabbit warrens from a small, dingy square of modest lodgings and buildings. On the edges, the snow had already turned to slush from a steady stream of animals, people, and wagons. A cracked church bell tolled the noon hour for those who may have been interested.

Far leaned against a post and opened his mouth slightly to taste Norfolk.

Sweat. Earth. Rust. Manure. There was a great deal of toil in the air. And a whiff of violence. The latter brought a faint, half-smile to his lips.

Far had wandered aimlessly through the outskirts of Norfolk, waiting for Yonder to catch up, until he came to the town's square where he decided to stop. Across the way was the town hall with its lead-colored dome and what looked to be a courthouse. To the north, a warehouse had one of its sides badly burned.

It was quite unimpressive. The buildings were cruder, smaller, not nearly as stately as those he had become familiar with in Boston. The same could be said of Norfolk's people.

The ten score of men and women he watched going about their business were all folk who had the look and smell of the plow about them. It was most prevalent with the black-skinned servants (of whom Far counted more in this town square than he had seen in all of Boston), but even those that ruled – the aldermen, the shop owners, the lawyers and plantation stewards – they all reeked of the land, too. As if no one in this place could rise above the stench of digging in the dirt.

"Animals," he muttered to himself.

Far crinkled his nose and made an affronted sniff. He glared disapprovingly at the whole of the town about him, which, in its entirety, disgusted him.

He brooded over whether he would ever find any amusement, when Yonder and Mary came upon him. Mary appeared to be carrying the better part of Yonder's weight in a slow, ponderous limp that did little to mitigate the lawyer's propensity to stumble. They made their way around an overloaded wagon cart, through the throng of the black workers loading it with cotton, and across the square to where Far stood.

They both looked as bad as the townsfolk. Yonder grasped his chest, huffing and wheezing. His cheeks were streaked with a pallid sweat, dark circles shadowing underneath his eyes. Though Mary seemed in better shape, her dress was stained and stiff from saltwater, her hair stood almost straight, and she seemed to have something of a twitch that kept her swatting at her ears, as if a fly, or a noise, badgered her.

"Well?" Far said to Mary.

"Well, what?" she snapped, disentangling her arm from Yonder's.

"Where's Wylde?"

"Prattling like an old maid," she craned her head as if listening intently. "Something about the food, or the tables – he doesn't like the setting . . . He's close, but I don't know where."

It was exasperating.

"What do you mean you don't know? That's the reason we brought you along."

"My friend, please," Yonder murmured. "Let's not draw attention."

With his eyes Yonder indicated a group of local gentlemen who were mingling at the other end of the square. They made no secret of staring at the three of them disapprovingly. Mary tried to brush some of the dirt from her skirts and hastily ran her fingers through her locks.

Yonder cast an uneasy glance at the gentlemen in the square. He lowered his voice.

"Perhaps we should retire to more private quarters to continue this discussion."

Mary nodded. It made no difference to Far.

"We could all use a drink," Yonder continued, "and a meal, and a bath. I suspect Mary would like a bed as well."

"You need one more than me," she said pointedly.

Yonder wiped his brow with a handkerchief and pressed his hand to his chest for a moment. He turned to Far.

"Is there an inn nearby?"

"One right there." Far pointed to a white, wood-paneled home with a lamppost by the front doorsteps and a dirt path that led around the side to a stable. It would have been indistinguishable from the houses were it not for three oversized shaded lamps, red, white, and blue, glowing in the front windows and a newly painted sign of a bald eagle swaying from one of the gables.

"I suppose it will do," Yonder said.

Far started to cross the street, but he heard Yonder groan. Far turned and saw his partner hang his head. His whole body seemed to have deflated.

"What's the matter now?" Far demanded.

"I forgot," said Yonder sadly. "I've no more traveling money. I lost it all. In the sea, with my flowers . . ."

Far gave it only a passing thought. The loss of funds was irksome perhaps, but a minor problem that was easily solved. He had always found it quite easy to reap the coins and bits of paper Doldrums folk traded. With a quick glance, Far began to take the measure of some of the better dressed passersby, ones who would likely have Doldrums money on their person. He plotted how he might lure one or two into the forest outside of town. Perhaps a fire? That felt a tad ungentlemanly. Too much like herding deer into a pen.

"That is annoying," Far sighed. "Let's just push on until

this one," he said, jerking his head at Mary, "gets her bearings and finds our man."

"Don't be ridiculous," Mary scolded. "Yonder can't go another step, and he's in no shape to stay out in the cold. Here."

Mary sidled between Far and Yonder, shot a quick look around to make sure no one was watching, and plunged her hand down her blouse's neck to the bottom of her bosom. With a wince, she brought out a palm full of metal coins, a collection of reales, shillings, reichsthalers, and dollars.

Yonder's face brightened.

"Your fortune-telling on the *Snuffbox*! Ah, bless those poor, dead fools who paid you."

Mary clasped her fingers into a fist and held the money before Yonder's nose.

"This is a loan," she proclaimed. "Whatever gets spent you'll repay me with interest. Once this business of yours – of ours – is finally over. Agreed?"

"Fine, fine," Yonder nodded.

They set off for the inn together, Mary wedged between Yonder and Far. Far stole a glance down at her. Though he loathed the sight of this woman and could scarcely abide her presence, he found himself admiring how adroitly Mary had managed to put his creditor into her debt.

The Eagle Inn & Tavern (Lieutenant Samuel Fee, Proprietor, R.I.P.) catered to a particular clientele of Norfolk. It was a place reserved for the middle class of Virginia, as dwindling as they were. Men of modest means could gather around the inn's fireplace to do business, or grumble about their families, or gossip about their betters. The Eagle catered to America's yeomanry, and proudly so.

The inn had ten rooms spread across two floors that

were connected by a stairwell and a chaotic run of narrow hallways. Cramped but clean, each room had a straw bed with sheets, a chair, a rug, a dresser, and a wash basin. Some might sniff at such accommodations. But where the late Lieutenant Fee had been frugal with the lodgings, he had splurged on the Inn's capacious parlor. There was a wide, high-ceilinged space filled with comfortable armchairs and sofas, an oversized granite hearth topped with a bronze eagle statue, a bevy of mirrors hanging over wallpaper striped with crimson and white bands, and a fine royal blue billiard table.

Out-of-town, peculiar-looking gentlemen like Yonder and Far would have been given the guest book to sign at the Eagle without much ado. Mary, however, was made to feel less than welcome.

In fact, the clerk on duty (who called himself Mr. Elliott), stared down the end of a beak nose at her. He made no pretense of being anything other than affronted by her appearance. A scarecrow of a man, bespectacled, with pouting eyes and a fulsome set of lips, he drew himself even taller when he spoke to Mary. His voice drawled and dripped, like sour honey.

"The Eagle, madam," he informed her, "has never let rooms to unmarried women."

His bony fingertips flittered and tapped themselves before his chest. They reminded Mary of a spider's legs, scurrying around a fly that had been caught in a web. Unconsciously, Mary folded her hands to cover the absence of a wedding ring. She tried to assume the assured, authoritative voice she used for fortune-telling, but it sounded paltry in her ears. She knew what she must have looked like to Mr. Elliott. The mirrors were as ubiquitous as they were merciless. Nevertheless, she arched an eyebrow and made a go of it.

"What do you take me for?"

Mr. Elliott seemed intent on letting the silence stretch for some time before he replied mildly,

"I'm sure I wouldn't know. I've not had the pleasure of making your acquaintance, Miss . . ."

"Mrs. John Yonder of Boston."

His eyebrows lifted a fraction of an inch. He peered over her shoulder into the inn's parlor. Mary looked, too. Far was strolling around the billiard table, absently rolling a cue ball against the rails, while Yonder had collapsed in the chair closest to the front door. She and Far had almost had to carry him through the doorway.

"One of those gentlemen is your husband?" Elliott inquired.

"Of course." She gestured at Yonder, who was too tired to look up.

"You'll forgive me." Elliott brought his hand before his lips in a poor effort to hide a skeptical smirk. "But it's somewhat . . . unusual for a gentleman to leave his wife to pay for their lodgings."

"Oh, that? Well. It's just that he doesn't feel well, you see—" Mary stopped herself short when an idea came to her. She spun about fully, giving Elliott her back, and jammed her hands into her hips.

"Dear," she chided, "the man's right. If you're that sick, let's send for a doctor. I'm sure there's a reputable one in this town."

Yonder lifted his face just enough to frown at her. "No doctors," he waved from his chair. "I'll be fine."

She turned back around to Elliott again, pretending to be exasperated, and offered the best imitation of a harping, old church wife she could.

"Every time we travel, it's the same," she complained loudly. "He'd rather stay seasick than send for a doctor. Because Heaven forbid he should take medicine—" she threw her voice over her shoulder, "which would make him feel better." Mary heaved a theatrical sigh, one that conveyed the suffering of Job, and put it to Elliott: "Why is it you men are so averse to being physicked?"

Elliott studied Mary quietly, but whatever reservations he may have carried, he kept to himself. The silver dollar coin Mary had quietly laid on the table before him may have helped assuage the last of his doubts about her station. He cracked a restrained, but sufficiently polite, smile at her and scribbled a name into a guest book.

"I'm sure I don't know – Mrs. Yonder."

Mary returned the smile.

"We should like a hot bath drawn before our luncheon."

"Certainly. But now what is the other gentleman's connection to you and Mr. Yonder?"

He pointed over at Far who had racked a set of billiard balls and twirled a cue in his fingers like a quarterstaff. He settled in over the table's edge and leveled the stick to line up his shot.

"Oh, that's just Far. He's in our service."

"Ah. Unfortunately, the Eagle does not maintain separate servants' quarters. I could let an adjoining room – at a reduced cost, of course . . ."

Mary could not suppress a mischievous grin. She heard the hard crack of a cue ball collide into a billiard. One of the porcelain balls fell to the floor and rolled away, as Mary replied to the innkeeper,

"He can sleep in your stable."

CHAPTER SIXTEEN

"What is bound in Custom is bound by Custom . . ."
—Wherestone's *Commentaries on Custom*, page 68

Yonder blinked in the sunlight reflected through a frosted square window. For a fleeting moment he believed he was back home in his Boston office. It might have been a pleasant fantasy, for as long as it lasted, but the prickled feel of the bed beneath him immediately gave away the lie. He shifted his weight to the sound of straw crinkling. A quilt had been tucked in around his sides. Someone had hung his jacket and waistcoat on a coatrack and taken off his shoes and stockings. And left him a metal bathtub full of water, along with a towel.

He remembered none of it.

Yonder surveyed his surroundings. It was a small room. Wood board walls recently painted with whitewash. A lone window. A writing desk. A chair. There was a drawing on the wall, a charcoal apparently, of shirtless African men serenely carrying their baskets of cotton under the gaze of a kindly white overseer whose whip hung benevolently coiled from his belt. Beneath the charcoal on a bench there was a jug and a pewter mug.

Nothing looked at all familiar. Though the room had no clock to tell him the hour, Yonder knew, as if in his bones, it neared noontime, and that an entire day had passed.

"Was that sleep, then, I wonder?"

Yonder laid his head back against a pillow and thought for a while but found he was unable to piece together any memories between walking through the woods (interminably, it had felt like) and looking out this window. Very strange to have lost his time. A bit unsettling, as well. At that moment, though, the labor of thinking about it seemed more bother than it was worth. He blew out a heavy breath and shook his head.

"Rather underwhelming if that's what it was. With all the fuss they make about it here . . ."

Slowly, Yonder got up out of bed and stretched. His knees creaked, and his feet protested bearing his weight again. He was still tired, but it was a dull, pleasant kind of grogginess, the kind that a splash of water and a good cup of tea would dispel.

He washed himself and dressed and went down a narrow flight of steps that led into the parlor where he found Mary. She was in a new outfit (a muted green affair, he noted with approval; she must have procured it while he had slept), and her hair was relatively tamed by some strategically placed ribbons. She sat at a table, a half-eaten bowl of grits before her, chatting freely with an elderly man in a gray frock coat. The man appeared to be giving her directions.

Mary's face lit up when she saw Yonder. She begged the old man's pardon, floated to the stairwell, and clasped Yonder's hand.

"Dearest," she greeted him with a meaningful look. "I was beginning to worry you'd sleep through our whole vacation. How is your seasickness?"

"I – my. My what?"

"You looked so peeked, I simply didn't have the heart to wake you – *dear*."

She squeezed his knuckles hard and stretched a smile that was so arched and implying, it probably pained her. Why the deuce was she carrying on like this, Yonder wondered.

"Dear?" Mary repeated, stretching the word a furlong's length.

Yonder was on the verge of asking if she wasn't feeling well, when her prompting jarred a piece of yesterday's events back into place. He let out a startled gasp of recognition and quickly recovered himself.

"Right! Dear. Thank you . . . my dear." He hurriedly leaned in to kiss the air next to one of Mary's cheeks. Under the circumstances he thought it an appropriate embellishment, based on what he had seen of other husbands and other wives in this realm. Mary seemed to relax and released his hand. "I feel much restored, thank you."

Turning to the man who had been giving directions, Yonder bowed.

"I'm called John Yonder, of Boston."

The man dipped his head and spoke with a Virginian drawl.

"William Sprowle, originally of Richmond. At your service, Mr. Yonder. I was just explaining to your lovely wife where the slave market is situated from here."

"Mr. Sprowle is in the business of slave trading," Mary explained.

"Is that so?" Yonder took a chair and called for tea.

"Well, um . . . not quite." Sprowle's thin lips quivered and curled, as if uncertain how to broach an awkward conversation. "I should say, not at all. Begging your pardon, ma'am, but I should've explained myself better. My company merely *insures* the ships that engage in the trade. We underwrite the cargo. But I've nothing to do with slave trading, as such."

Mary scrunched her eyes, and even Yonder found himself somewhat perplexed.

"That's not a part of trading slaves?" she asked.

"Oh, no, ma'am," said Sprowle with his liver-spotted hand before his heart. "Far from it. You see slave traders . . ." the words seemed to hold a caustic taste in the gentleman's mouth, "are those who actually deal with the slaves themselves, in some fashion or another, strictly speaking. Most hold it to be a low line of work. Not that I'm casting aspersions. I mean, I'd lose my livelihood if the traders ever stopped sailing – or stopped buying insurance. But that's as far as it goes. My company's business is completely unconnected to theirs."

Yonder would have had to confess that he utterly failed to discern the distinction Sprowle had just drawn but did not give a thought to pressing him further on it. They were, after all, guests there.

A manservant came by the table carrying a tray that held a steaming kettle, milk, cups, and a small plate of breads and cheeses. Yonder thanked him and invited Sprowle to join he and Mary for breakfast. To Yonder's delight, the food and tea were not displeasing. Sprowle appeared to share that assessment and ate greedily from Yonder's plate.

"If you don't mind me asking," said Sprowle, helping himself to a third seed roll, "but why do you want see the market? I would've thought northerners would prefer to steer clear of the place. Given you all's sentiment about the institution."

Yonder shot a quizzical glance at Mary, who replied with a somewhat exaggerated indifference.

"Just idle curiosity. A woman's passing fancy. Something to see since we're passing through the South."

A second embarrassed expression passed over Sprowle's face.

"I only ask, Mrs. Yonder, because you might find the spectacle of the market – distressing. Mrs. Sprowle avoids the place entirely. It can be a bit rough, if you take my meaning."

It seemed his meaning was not taken, or at least not in the way Sprowle intended, for Mary lifted her chin indignantly.

"I'm sure I'll survive the spectacle," she said firmly. "Or do I look that frail to you?"

Sprowle held his hands up in apology.

"No, ma'am. Of course you don't. I meant no disrespect. It's just that . . . well, if you all are only passing through, it'd be a pity to miss out on the best our fair city has to offer. There's a lovely park on the river that Mrs. Sprowle is fond of, fishing for the gentleman – the trout'll bite no matter how cold it is, you can depend on it – whist games, pianoforte concerts, lectures. In fact, now that I recall, I read in the paper just the other day where Mr. Marshall will be delivering a talk at St. Paul's this evening. He's that Federalist who's *against* the Alien and Sedition Acts—"

"Anarchist," Yonder muttered under his breath.

"Beg pardon?" Sprowle broke off.

"Forgive me, I coughed," Yonder waved, "pray continue."

"My only point is if you all are searching for entertainment, you might find a dreary old slave market a bit disappointing, despite the novelty."

Yonder passed another roll to Sprowle, whose appetite belied his thin stature and filled a cup of tea for himself.

"We appreciate your concern." Yonder puffed into his cup, blowing off a film of steam. "But I think that Mar –

rather, Mrs. Yonder – is quite set on what she wishes to see while we're in Norfolk?"

"She is," Mary nodded.

"There, you see? Her mind is made up, and far be it from me to thwart her." He took a long sip of tea and winked knowingly at Sprowle, as one married man to another. "You know how wives can be when they've set their minds to something."

The slave market of Norfolk was an oblong plot of colorless, trampled earth bound by a tall, crumbling stone wall behind the courthouse in the center of town. It was treeless, shrubless, cheerless. Indeed, except for the smattering of merchants clustered about, almost lifeless. Which gave the place the feel of being colder and darker than it should. The air was windless, and the courtyard's stones were all hard and pitiless. There was a collection of brick huts with tiny, barred windows scattered about, a livestock well, and a row of wobbly desks and chairs that were all weathered from having been left out in the elements. Most of the chairs were filled with businessmen who talked in whispers to one another. Somber men with gray clothes and sharp faces that seemed to prefer the cover of shadows. They studied their sheets, and counted their coins, and couldn't be bothered to greet Yonder.

He walked aimlessly about in a vain search for assistance. Not one of the gentlemen would so much as acknowledge his greeting. They all turned their shoulders rudely away. Mary might be able to help (she was a woman, after all), but something seemed to have begun to trouble her. She lingered near the wall closest to the courtyard gate, clasping her hands and pouting. He considered whether he ought to try a sterner, lawyerly approach with these traders when Far groused behind him.

"A slave market. A Doldrums slave market. Truly, we've hit the bottom."

Yonder turned around and made a face at Far to keep his thoughts to himself. He wished, for the dozenth time since they had set out for the market, that he could have prevailed upon Far to take a bath. He wore the same garb he'd had on since their flight from the *Snuffbox*. Gauging by the black stubble sprouting on his jaws, he was in need of a razor as much as a clean change of clothes. Apparently, Far had passed last evening not in the Eagle's stable, but on Norfolk's wharf, drinking and reveling. Yonder thought it most likely, given the state of his partner's trousers, he'd been fornicating. He had only returned to the inn an hour before for a pot of coffee, cutting a shabby and foreboding figure.

Thus far, though, his partner had not grumbled overmuch. And for that, at least, Yonder had been thankful. But it seemed Far's familiar taciturn mood was returning.

"I'm already plagued with one of these people," Far flicked his chin back in Mary's direction, "why the devil would I purchase another?"

Yonder answered him in a hushed voice.

"Don't be ridiculous, we're not going to buy anyone. We're only here to look."

"Eh?"

"I wish to see if Wylde came through this market."

Far looked at Yonder incredulously. "You think they mistook him – as one of their *own*?"

"I'm sure of it. Remember, he is entirely in their power now. He's bound by Custom. And since he's dark skinned . . ."

It seemed to take a while for Far to sort out what should have been a rather obvious implication. No doubt he was still addled from his evening of port and lechery. But at last he nodded.

"They'd think him a slave and bring him here. A plausible notion."

"It was Mary who seized upon the idea, and it makes a great deal of sense. If Wylde came through Norfolk, there's certain to be a bill of lading here, or an invoice, or a receipt of some sort, something we can use to pick up his trail. These people are quite meticulous in recording their oppression. If I can just find where the records are kept . . ."

Yonder propped up on his tiptoes and made a sweep of the grounds until he spotted a cottage in the far corner that was set apart from the other structures by its seclusion and its coat of paint. He could see a message board posted outside the doorway and a low, smoking chimney

"Ah, here we are," Yonder brightened.

He motioned for Mary to come over. She seemed reluctant to leave the gateway, but at last she trudged out to the grounds to join them. As she approached, her gaze kept straying to a point near the courtyard's center.

"That's sure to be the auctioneer's office." Yonder gestured to the cottage he had found. "Let's see if he's in. Come, Mary. Captain Far will lead us."

They followed Far across the courtyard through a throng of traders who did not even deign to notice their passing. Midway to the cottage, they came to a small wooden platform with a post set in the middle and a set of rusted shackles. Yonder turned to see where Mary was, but she was frozen, rooted in the post's shadow. Mary stared at the chains, an unblinking mask of horror on her face.

"Mary?"

She let out a grunt of pain. By the time Yonder reached her, she was doubled over, clasping at her sides. Her face writhed in agony.

"He's been here," Mary gasped.

Yonder took her by the arms and tried to keep her upright, while inwardly he cursed Far for not coming back to lend a hand. She trembled, and panted heavily, and Yonder feared they were surely making a scene. But no one else in the courtyard seemed to notice her. Or perhaps they did and were so callous to suffering, that a woman's momentary discomfort engendered no concern. Regardless, it was an astonishing level of obliviousness, even for Doldrums folk.

"Are you all right?" he asked her.

"He was here," she repeated, pointing at the post. "Look . . ."

"Let's keep walking," Yonder whispered, "but tell me what you see."

He led her past the platform, and Mary quickly regained her strength. She could walk on her own and shirked off Yonder's offer of his elbow. She cast wary glances over her shoulder.

"That post," she said. "It was bleeding . . . his blood."

Yonder stole a look at it. The old round piece of timber had probably stood there since the courtyard had been built. The wood was split and had turned light gray from decades of weathering, but to Yonder's eyes, it looked clean of any gore.

"I'm sure it was," he said to her.

They made it the rest of the way to the cottage without any further incident. Far waited for them by the door. Yonder gave him a curt nod, and Far pounded the announcement of their presence.

From within, a man's shrill voice barked back at them, "Sale don't start 'til *four*. It's in the court notice. Can't ye read?"

Far's face darkened, and he started to growl an oath, when Yonder intervened to give a more polite greeting.

"Good day to you, sir. We're not here for the auction,

but we do have important business. May we trouble you to let us in?

A latch sounded, and the door squeaked on its hinges just enough to open a crack. The smell of burnt wood and cigar smoke wafted out. A yellow-tinged eye buried within a wild brush of white eyebrow studied him. Yonder smiled at it.

"What kinda business?" the eye demanded.

"The paying kind," replied Yonder pleasantly.

Without a word, the door shut in their faces. Something was moved across the floor and a drawer was opened and slammed shut. The latch was worked once more to give them entry.

An elderly man dressed head to toe in an ill-fitted black suit, stepped aside for them to enter. A shriveled butt of a cigar dangled from the old man's bottom lip.

It was a small room, cramped all the tighter for the rows of old, broken barrister's cabinets that spanned every inch of its walls. These were filled to bursting with rolls of documents, ledgers, books, and loose papers all stacked higgledy-piggledy on top of each other. The man who had admitted them stumped around the desk on a wooden leg and sat down in the only chair in the room to glare at his guests.

His blue eyes were beginning to cloud from cataracts, but they were still penetrating. He took each of their measures quickly, an ogle at Mary, a scowl at Far, and, Yonder could sense, a genuine admiration for the cut of his coat.

"State yer business, then," the man drew a puff of tobacco.

"I am called John Yonder. You may call him Far. She's Mar – or I should say, this is my wife, Mrs. Yonder."

A wreath of smoke twirled about the man's eyebrows. He neither rose nor extended his hand at their introductions but responded with a puff of smoke.

"Mr. Beverley. I run this here market. An' I'm very busy. What've you got for me?"

Yonder looked around unsuccessfully for someplace to rest his legs but resigned himself to leaning against one of the barrister's cases. Far found a place where he did not have to stoop from the low ceiling, while Mary went over to the fire to warm her hands.

"We are looking for a gentleman who may have been sold in your market some days ago."

"A *gentleman*? Can't say as I've sold many of them. Though there's a few out there in the courtyard that I'd like to!"

Beverley guffawed at what must have been some private joke. Yonder pressed on.

"The individual we're after is traveling under the name of Wylde. He's about my height. Plays the flute. Very fond of the color purple. Oh, and I should mention he has dark skin."

Beverley dropped a load of cigar ash to the floor and exhaled a cloud of smoke that caused Mary to cough.

"Last week's auction," he replied archly, "sold two hundred sixty-one slaves. Week before, I topped three hundred, That was a damn good week. I got another hundred an' eighty I'm gonna trot out this afternoon. There ain't no way I can remember anythin' 'bout who I may've sold or to who."

"Of course not," Yonder agreed. He eyed the reams and volumes of yellowing papers that surrounded them. "We were only hoping you might assist us with your records."

"If you're askin' for a look through the ledger, well, that's an official court document. You'll need a lawyer to file a court petition to see it, but first you gotta pay the filin' fee, a dollar, the clerk's fee, another dollar, the record search fee, that's two dollars, schedule an appointment—"

"Yes, yes." Yonder nodded impatiently. "I'm familiar with the customary forms for such matters, but, um," he let a pause stretch for a meaningful moment and dipped his voice lower for added effect, "I find myself rather short of time . . . short of time, not funds. If you . . . catch my drift."

The auctioneer squinted at Yonder shrewdly.

"Might be I can help y'all cut through some of the red tape. For a price."

"I would be pleased if you would . . ."

Yonder pasted a pleasant grin across his mouth, though he dreaded what was coming.

Alas, there had to be some haggling with Beverley, whose initial idea of a "reasonable expedience price" was quite astronomical. But the negotiations were mercifully brief, for, after all, Beverley was an auctioneer. Some back and forth, some haggling over details, but in ten minutes' time they had reached an agreement. Mary had to forfeit the last of her reales, while Yonder had to execute a brokerage agreement in favor of Mr. Beverley, one which included a commission (should Yonder choose to purchase Wylde) that bordered on usury.

"Just the usual cut is all I'm after," Beverley assured Yonder. "An' it'll come from the seller, not from you."

Yonder bit his bottom lip so that he would appear sufficiently tepid about signing the document Beverley had drawn up, while Mary glared hard at Yonder. The debt he was into her had nearly doubled.

"Alrighty," Beverley clapped his hands and hopped out of his chair. He scoured through the rows and shelves of papers like an old, hobbled hound on the scent of a fox. It didn't take him long to corner his quarry. He fetched down a heavy book with a tattered cloth cover that, Yonder suspected, had been known to him all along.

"Let's see if we can't find your man in here . . ." he murmured through his cigar and opened the book to a place marked with a tattered business card.

As Yonder, Mary, and Far watched, Beverley began flipping through the pages backward, his cold eyes swirling like ball bearings around a gun barrel, searching for Wylde, up and down across the pages, over and over . . .

Mary felt her thoughts tumble in her mind. The book's pages leafed by under Beverley's thumb with a rapid flutter, and yet, she felt each one falling, one at a time, with a heavy thud that reverberated in her chest.

"An' here we are," Beverley announced triumphantly.

Mary had to steady herself. Thankfully, none of the men paid any attention to her. When her balance settled, she followed Yonder and Far's gaze to the open page where Beverley had his fingertip pressed against a column of crimped names. The list was offset on either side by two more columns of miniscule numbers.

"Here's your man," said Beverley. "Came through with the last batch . . . Funny. I kinda recollect this one. Mouthy fella, tried to act the dandy. Had to give 'im the whip to knock that nonsense out of his head."

Yonder leaned over the auctioneer's shoulder and stared intently at the book. Mary went over and joined him. As soon as she glimpsed the letters, she felt a change come over her.

"Is it . . ." Yonder started to ask Mary.

She gave him a quick nod and brushed her hand across her forehead. A cold sweat had broken on her brow.

The words and numbers on the page twirled before her eyes, like water flowing down a drain, but one row remained fixed. Just beneath Beverley's tobacco-stained fingernail. The entry looked like a jagged scar cut across the skin of the paper, infected and inflamed, weeping light down into the spine of the book:

Jan 1799 – W-I-L-D-E, m. – $175

Beverley's voice broke her vision.

"Well, ain't you in luck," he said. "Looks like it was Mr. Harris that bought him. Lives just up the road a couple miles, near Tanner's Creek. Fiery old codger, richer than Solomon, but he's always lookin' for a stone to squeeze." Beverley craned his head around to flash a knowing grin at Yonder. "I happen to know him personally."

"Indeed? How soon could you arrange a meeting?"

At that, Beverley positively leered with lucre.

"For an extra five percent . . . tomorrow."

Supper was winding down in the Eagle's parlor, and Far enjoyed the head-swim from a fine cognac. The tables had been cleared. Dusk light was turning to candlelight as a servant went around to attend the sconces and build the hearth fire up bright and cheery. At the end of the room, Yonder and Mary sat huddled around the fireplace for warmth. They hadn't spoken a word for a quarter of an hour.

Which seemed strange. The meal had been warm and filling, the ale and wine both stout and plentiful. The day's errand had apparently gone well, from what Yonder had reported. And yet neither Yonder nor the woman seemed at all contented. Both stared listlessly at the same log, silent and sullen as men about to face an enemy's charge. They sat in their chairs, gaping like two hooked guppies, as Mary gripped her handbag. Yonder clutched an ever-present handkerchief in his hand for that damned cough he had acquired. Their mood irritated him.

Far swirled his glass and frowned at his companions.

"What are you two so glum about?" he asked.

"Everything," Yonder sighed. He dabbed the kerchief to his mouth. "This meeting tomorrow will be a delicate business."

"How so?" Far leaned back in his chair. "When Harris brings Wylde to the market, I'll take him." He swiped a hand through the air like a club. "If anyone gets in my way, I'll kill them. What could be simpler?"

"Don't be ridiculous," Yonder snapped. "How many times do I have to tell you? Wylde is *bound*. You can't just *take* him. Any more than you could take a mountain range, or an ocean, or the wind. He freely gave himself to chains. According to Custom, the only way he can be freed is if the one he's bound to freely gives him back."

"Well," said Far musingly, "if we can't take Wylde, let's just take what we need from him."

"And how should we go about that, I wonder?" To Far's surprise, Yonder dipped into a rare bout of sarcasm, pretending to converse with a new acquaintance. "A pleasure to meet you, Mr. Harris. Thank you for coming out in the cold on such short notice, but if you don't mind, might we have a word with your slave, in private, so we can barter with him over something you can't be privy to?"

Yonder fell into another coughing fit. When it passed, he continued, "Besides, Wylde may not be carrying it on his person. Assuming he even still has it. No, I need to get Wylde alone – so he can get it for us."

Yonder's assurance stirred a dark remembrance for Far, one that grated in his breast. He countered Yonder's earlier acerbity with a blow of his own.

"Do you remember what happened the last time your plans relied on someone getting something for us?"

It pleased Far to see Yonder blush from the recollection.

"Forgive me, my friend," said Yonder. "Now that we're so close to our goal, I find myself fretting and irritable.

Wylde is cut from a very different cloth than the fellow you're referring to. And this time there's Custom to help keep the bargain. Wylde will stay bound to us. If we can just come up with the money to buy him. Which I could manage if I still had my coins . . ." Yonder chewed a nail. "I might be able to persuade Harris to accept a deposit or a promissory note. But if he paid $175 to buy the man, I don't know how I shall ever haggle him down to . . . well, whatever currency we have to work with." Yonder shot an awkward, questioning look at Mary.

"Two dollars," she answered flatly. Her eyes never left the flames as she spoke. "That's all I have left."

"Ah," Yonder's shoulders sagged ever so slightly. He stifled another cough.

Mary said nothing. The fire began to play tricks of light, washing out what little color was in her cheeks, and making the pea-green wool she was wearing almost gray. The log crackled and collapsed in a fit of embers, and Mary broke her gaze from the hearth.

"The food, the drink, the lodging, the bribe, this thing." She pulled at one of her dress sleeves. "It all adds up. My fortune-telling money's gone. Gone away . . ."

She fell into silence. Her eyes drifted back to the fire, and she began to hum. It was a paltry noise to Far's ear, but yet he could detect a sad, bodiless tune in her croaking, one that sounded distantly familiar. It brought to mind a flute for some reason. Yonder patted the top of her hand.

"Not to worry, my dear. Every pence and farthing shall be repaid the moment we return home. In fact, I'll double what you've advanced us. And I shall buy you the finest, most garish, wardrobe in all of Boston. I promise."

Mary rose from her chair. She slipped some coins into Yonder's hand and told him to use the money however he liked.

"I'm going for a walk," she said quietly.

"Excellent idea," Far replied with a swig of cognac. It seemed the evening would be off to a promising start. "Take your time. But stay clear of the wharf. That's my quarter."

"A walk?" Yonder asked her haltingly, "Now? Well, do take care. It's dark after all. Wouldn't want anything to happen to you. I may require your help tomorrow." As soon as the door had shut behind Mary, Yonder turned to Far. "I must ask that you delay your debauchery for just a bit."

A faint twinkle gleamed from Yonder's beetle eyes. He slid his chair close, and Far had the irksome feeling that this would have something to do with Custom, and that he was about to be subjected to another one of Yonder's insufferable lectures. Far started to leave, when, as if sensing his thoughts, Yonder rested a hand on Far's elbow and bade him to stay.

"I promise," Yonder assured him, "I will refrain from scholasticism. But I've just had a notion how Custom might serve in place of money with this Harris fellow. It's just an idea, mind you, but it's one I think you will like. It will require some planning, though."

CHAPTER SEVENTEEN

". . . And this holds true in all Affairs in Doldrums, for all stations, Nobles, Courtiers, Esquires, Travelling Fellows, Soldiers, Serfs—yes, even Affairs with the locals (as unseemly as that would be) . . ."
—Wherestone's *Commentaries on Custom*, page 68

She could hear him singing.

Mary walked briskly up a rutted path along the outskirts of town. The chill was brutal, and the night was damp. Her toes were numb beyond all sensation and her hands shook with cold, but she held her skirts high above her ankles so that she could walk more quickly. By the crow's flight, she headed due north into the dark, coastal wilderness that straddled Norfolk and the bay.

The strain of music in her mind had grown louder throughout the day, drowning out all the other annoying noises. She gave up resisting its call. Like a moth chasing after a lantern, Mary knew she was being pulled closer and closer to a flame. Whether for comfort or oblivion, she did not care.

The streets had been quiet and nearly empty. She hurried past the last periphery of house lamps twinkling from behind frosted windows, from warm, amber light of hearths into the harsh iron glow of the moon, and never slowed her step.

She hummed aloud, the tune he was singing. The farther she walked, the clearer it became.

The moon had crested above a line of treetops, full round and watching. She plunged into a little glade and had to shield her eyes from the aura of jarring contrasts that met her. Pine needles blazed with light, while the limbs that bore them sent down long, jagged shadows across the ground. Stones jutted out like hoar-frosted fingers, knobbed and gnarled, clutching pools of darkness around them. Mary paused, panting. Her breath rose in a cloud of silver. She smiled.

She could almost make out the words. Sung in a bass so deep, so enigmatic and graceful, and so filled with sadness, as if a leviathan had washed ashore only to sing of his dying. It was a music Mary could have never imagined. One voice, somehow harmonizing of its own accord, blending a sonata with a spiritual.

Her heart still raced, but it was almost exhilarating. Like a child on the verge of winning a footrace. She set out again, jogging past trees and through brush, heedless of the nettles and the stinging cold that bit into her lungs. A clearing emerged, a long stretch of clay, where the moonlight seemed to sear the earth with whiteness. The moment she set her foot within its blaze, the words that had eluded her for so long, the whispers that were always around the corner, began to ring like a bell, true and clear, within Mary's mind in that wonderful tune:

> The corn has turned from red to gray,
> Dead seed, dead shoot, dead god

Drear food, like dust, drear world, drear cage,
I pray it all gone—
Gone away.

Her feet felt as if they would take flight beneath her. The ground dipped and became soggy. Freezing mud squeezed between the straps of her shoes, but it only spurred Mary to run faster. Once she tripped and twisted her ankle. But the voice was so close, she could almost hear it with her ears.

The babe has crawled from womb to grave
No child, no dream, no god.

She limped on, her foot screaming in an impotent protest. The earth leveled, gradually rose and a gray, sandy path appeared. It was marked by a signpost. She didn't stop to read it but kept along the pathway, curving around clumps of bush and stunted trees until she reached a wide, sweeping field. It seemed like a sea of grass that grew as tall as ship's masts. The blades rustled in the breeze. Beyond the field was the bay; beyond that, the sea. She could hear its waves crashing in the distance in a steady hiss. Mary hobbled up the path.

The brush and weeds were thick all around her, but the path was well worn, and level. Along the way, she saw signs of livestock tracks peeling off through the vegetation, an empty animal pen, a water trough. The path stopped and became a quarried road, and there she came to a halt.

Mary's breath was a painful rasp. Her chest heaved, and her hurt ankle throbbed. And yet neither the pain, nor the sound of her heartbeat thumping madly in her head could drown out the music. She grew calm, her pulse slowly sliding into the rhythm of the song.

Mary looked about. A quarter mile ahead the road ended in what appeared to be a bowling green, which led to the front porch of a modest manse. It was a quiet, severe building with a porch roof held aloft by four plain, unassuming columns. All the gables were awash in shadows. Nothing stirred. A little to the right, perhaps a hundred yards from the bowling green's edge there were a cluster of decrepit shacks, the servants quarters, and beyond them, as if keeping watch, an old and lifeless magnolia rose from a flattened patch of brambles. It reminded Mary of a mausoleum. Tall, desolate, its knotted bark shone in the moonlight with an alabaster gleam. A passing breeze sighed through the creaking limbs.

A man lay cradled in one of the tree's boughs. He sang softly to himself.

It was the voice she had heard since the day of the séance, the one she had traveled through Boston and down the coast of the Atlantic to find. It was a bright voice, though it sang of a pain, keen and cutting.

> My life, a husk, my soul, my name,
> I pray it all gone—
> Gone away.

She crept closer toward the base of the tree. The grass seemed to part before her. Mary's lips parted with it. The wind hushed, expectantly. Mary's tongue, her throat, her lips were loosened. She was carried along, her voice joining his.

> My prayers are all gone—
> Gone away.

The man in the tree jolted upright at the sound. He peered down from the limb, squinting, and when his eyes met Mary's, his face brightened, his legs swung around, and as gracefully as a cat, he slid down to join her. The man was black and dressed in rough-spun gray, and he looked as stretched and forlorn as the magnolia's bark, but his voice, so familiar, rolled forth like a rainbow.

"Can it be I have a visitor?" The breeze echoed with his laughter. "Can it be . . . a friend has come from home in my hour of need? My dear, dear lady."

He made a courtly bow.

"You may call me Wylde."

Mary couldn't help but laugh with him.

They wandered amiably up the pathway through the grass covered field, Mary's hand nestled in the crook of Wylde's arm. A chill breeze kissed her cheeks. As they walked, Wylde carried on an allegro of conversation. Much of what he said, though it came as rapid as rainfall, left Mary with the impression that Wylde thought he knew her already. That they were old acquaintances. Innuendos, inside jokes, allusions to frightful people she would never wish to know and fantastical places she could only dream of visiting. Somehow he believed her to be a dear friend.

Mary had no desire to disabuse him of his mistake. His words were all so lovely, his thoughts so lofty, she could have listened to him prattle on until daybreak. That would have been enchanting.

He never wasted a movement. He never stumbled or paused in his step. He never let a hair become blown out of place. And never was there so much as a trace of hesitation in his speech. It was as if Wylde's conversation came to him, ready formed, to be delivered perfectly in perfectly metered prose.

He was also, Mary reflected, profoundly conscious of his beauty. His languidness was precise. His face just the right degree of bemused. On anyone else, the clothes hanging from his slender body would have looked ragged, dirty, ill fitted, but he bore them like a royal mantle.

When they had nearly reached the signpost that marked the start of the path, Wylde came to a stop. He invited Mary to sit next to him on a spot of soft, dry grass shielded from the wind by a hawthorn bush. He lounged there at his ease beneath a leafless branch as if he were in a parlor. His hips brushed Mary's.

The stars glistened through the clouds, the moon blazed bright and cold. An apologetic smile from Wylde dimmed them all.

"I am sorry I can't invite you inside. Or offer you refreshment. All I have in this wretched world is a drafty old shack that is already filled to the rafters with field hands. So, of course, I never set foot within. Don't misunderstand me, they're all decent enough fellows. But I want you all to myself. You're a treasure too precious to be shared!"

Mary held her hand to her mouth to keep from tittering.

"And what do you call yourself here?"

"Mary."

The sound of her name seemed to simultaneously perplex and amuse Wylde.

"Really?" He propped himself on an elbow and raised an eyebrow. "What a plain and earthy appellation you've adopted. You must have a taste for irony. But now I've jabbered on enough – Mary. Let's have it. What's the news from home?"

"The-the news?"

"Spare no detail, no trifle. I'll relish every tittle and tattle you can spare – this is sustenance to me."

She could only blink incomprehensively at Wylde. After all she had been through, all the miles she had crossed to chase after him, and all he wanted from her was *gossip*? As if she were some eavesdropping old neighbor come to pay a visit? Mary became conscious of how foolish her grin must have looked, but she could think of nothing to say. Nothing at all.

Wylde tapped his fingertips together playfully and giggled.

"Oh, you're hiding something. I can tell. Something *juicy*! Something from her Majesty's court. I'll never tell a soul, I swear, but you simply must tell me what's happened!"

"I-I'm sorry, but I wouldn't know," Mary stammered. She felt her cheeks growing flushed. "You see . . . I'm actually . . . I'm a Bostoner."

Wylde stared dumbly at her.

With a single fluid motion, he leaned over her, his hands braced on both of her sides. The smell of lilac spilled from his lips. His eyes bored into hers. Never in all her life had Mary felt so naked, and so delighted to feel that way. The weight of his body, the intensity of his gaze, was intoxicating, and yet at the same time a little harrowing.

He studied her the way a fox might peer down a rabbit hole.

"What – is – *this*?" he breathed.

"What?"

Wylde drew back, as if indignant.

"You are not from my country at all. You're from Doldrums."

She nodded. "I'm sorry."

"I could have sworn . . ." He peered again into her, and for a moment Mary became lost in the dark wells of Wylde's eyes. "By the Grove . . . I must have been looking at my reflection. But how can this be?"

Wylde took her by the shoulders and began to scan the entirety of her head. His fingers drifted to her forehead, caressingly, and parted her hair from her brow. He let out a startled gasp.

"Someone opened a window . . . in you!"

His eyes dropped. He shook his head sadly. When he

looked at her again, his pity was so profound it brought Mary to tears.

"That was a cruel thing to do," he whispered. "And I know something of cruelties. We draw portals in trees, because that is what trees are for. And we are taught from our fathers' knees to always shut our doors behind us. To open one in a *mind*, and then leave it open, that . . . should not have been done."

"I . . . I . . ."

Mary's tears blotted her sight. Between the strain she had borne and kept to herself all these days, the flurry of feelings tumbling in her chest, and the aura of this man's tenderness, Mary felt her senses overcome. It was as if the knots that had held her together were, one by one, coming unwound. As if through a fog, she heard him ask her,

"Do you know how this happened?"

She bobbed her head once. A rivulet of tears ran freely down her cheeks. Mary despised herself for falling apart this way, but she could no more withhold her cries than she could will her hair not to curl, or her cuts not to bleed. After a while, though, with some encouragement from Wylde, Mary recovered herself, enough that she could tell him her story.

At first, it came out all in fragments, garbled impressions in no particular order. But as she went on, the pieces slowly came together. The more she spoke, the more Mary could sense the threads – the séance with Yonder, the mirrors and the visions, Faneuil Hall, the *Snuffbox*, Norfolk – were all bound together into this man. By the time Mary had finished, the moon had reached its zenith, Venus had slipped into oblivion, and a weight she hadn't known she had been carrying slowly slipped from her shoulders.

Wylde held a contemplative finger before his lips, tapped it, but said nothing for a long while. His eyes narrowed into slits. The air seemed to grow cold from his pensiveness, and Mary shivered in her shawl. At last, Wylde emerged from wherever his private reverie had taken him.

"I've met this fellow who calls himself Yonder," he said. "I know of his companion by reputation."

"They're from – wherever you're from."

"Oh, yes. Those two were quite infamous. Though you'd never know it with Yonder. He's a bit of a milk puddle."

"He wants something from you," Mary said, a hint of alarm creeping in her voice. "I don't know what, but that's why he did – what he did to me. That's why he's come here, and why he wants to buy you tomorrow."

"Then I'm afraid he shall be sorely disappointed. As you can see, I am bereft of worldly goods." He brushed his hands caressingly down the length of his rags and paused when he reached a recently healed scar on his chest. "My captors – were terribly cruel. They took everything from me. Even my flute. Though I made sure she'll never play a note for them. Your friend will find me a very poor purchase. I am as destitute as I am broken."

"No, no." Mary shook her head. "That's not what I mean. I think he wants you to get something. And I – I don't know how I know this, but they're desperate."

"I've no doubt they are."

That gave Mary a bold idea. She spoke with an excited hush.

"Then let's leave. Now." Mary rose to her feet and held out her hand. "Come with me. I don't have any money, but if we can make it to Richmond, I can earn some. It's a big town. There's lots of travelers coming and going. No one will notice us. Once we've saved enough, we can charter a boat back to Boston, and then—"

Wylde burst out with laughter. It was a dazzling, ringing sound, gilded with music, like the first birdsong in spring, and it seemed to float up into the air and catch a cloud that happened to pass overhead. Mary was smiling.

With a mirthful solemnity, he got to one knee and clasped the hand Mary had offered.

"Fair maiden, you've come to rescue me, your trapped prince! Oh, Mary. Mary. I'm savoring this. I'm feasting. You've no idea how this is restoring me." He let out a long sigh and smiled sadly. "I would fly away with you, carry you, ravish you (don't blush so, my dear, you'll make the dawn jealous). If only I could. But alas. Watch . . ."

Wylde hopped up and started at a brisk walk toward the glade of woods beyond the path. The moment he reached the signpost, though, his foot seemed to catch on something, almost like a snare, that nearly brought him to the ground. No matter how hard he pulled at it, Wylde could not seem to shake himself free from whatever it was that held him. Mary hurried over to help, but when she reached the post, she could see nothing but grass and frost by his feet. He jerked his leg helplessly and, to Mary's eyes, he did indeed seem to be bound by an invisible chain. She grasped by his arms and pulled; she grappled his legs and tugged. She clasped him around the chest. She groaned from trying to push him from behind, but all her efforts were wasted.

There was no moving him.

"It's that Custom devilry, I'm sure," he punched at the post with the side of his fist.

Mary had no idea what he was talking about, though she thought that the force holding him captive, whatever it was, had to do with the sign. The tall, polished board nailed to a post looked like nothing out of the ordinary. A tad ornate for where it was situated, but an ordinary road sign like dozens of others she had seen in Norfolk. There was no reason why it should give Mary such an uneasy feeling. And yet the painted white wood with the black, gothic lettering seemed to quiver in the force of the moonlight. It read:

Harris Manor
Private Property

Wylde could not pass an inch beyond its boundary. He slid down to the ground resignedly, sitting his back against the post like a prisoner resting against the bars of his cell. Mary sat next to him and let the frost seep through her clothes.

"I'm sorry," she said after a while. Her eyes settled upon a scar and a run of bruises visible through his tattered shirt. "For everything that's happened to you. Did they . . . did they hurt you much?"

Wylde's face darkened. It was the first time she had seen anger cloud his features. He tugged at the cloth of his shirt to hide his wounds.

"I would prefer not to talk about that," he murmured.

"All right."

They sat quietly together in the weeds beneath the sign, straddling the border of a frigid, invisible barrier. The breeze died, and the grass blades stopped their whispering, and the night's silence seemed to mount and roll over upon itself, until Mary could feel its weight pressing down upon her. She shuddered and turned her head. Wylde studied her intently. His voice broke the stillness in a perfectly timed measure.

"Let's talk about something else, Mary."

"Let's."

"I know," he said, brightening. "Since you've brought me news, I shall do the same for you." He shifted from where he was sitting to look at her fully. "I gather from what you've told me, your Mr. Yonder has never confided in you *why* he is trapped in Doldrums?"

"No," Mary shook her head, "he never has. He's very close about – well, everything, actually. But, no, he's never told me what brought him here."

"I'm not surprised." Wylde let his hand fall gently on her knee, and the reassuring warmth shot through Mary like a jolt. He leaned close to her, his voice a conspiratorial whisper. "Because the story was a most salacious scandal."

"Really?" Mary felt a wolfish smile spreading across her cheeks.

"Mind you," he cautioned, "I heard the account second-hand. I was traveling at the time. But the one who told me was in the very thick of it – and her word is as true as gospel. Would you like to hear his story?"

"Nothing," Mary replied, "would please me more."

Wylde settled into a more comfortable position and started a tale, and from the first words of its telling, Mary felt as if she were being lifted to a faraway realm.

"Now you must understand," he began, "that in my country there are only two queens. Or I should say, were. Her Majesty of the Grove," as he spoke the title, Wylde dipped his head in homage. "And Her Feral Majesty," he dropped his head again, "her late Feral Majesty – she who was sometimes called the Mad Queen. They were sisters. So naturally they loathed one another. And, naturally, they made war. Fairly regularly, and often brutally.

"Not long ago – it was springtime, I believe – their majesties were engaged in an especially nasty bout of battles along their borderlands. During the fighting, one of Her Majesty's captains, a man of no particular renown, was somehow able to slip undetected behind the Feral Queen's lines. Most likely, the blunderer just got lost. Regardless, however he managed it, this captain and a band of his warriors found themselves deep within the Feral Queen's realm. Since the Feral Queen's son and all her warriors were fighting at the border, the captain was able to march unmolested all the way to the Sacred Knoll where the Feral Queen held her court.

"Well, the arrival of a mob of swordsmen caused something of a stir at Her Feral Majesty's court, as you can imagine. There was a great deal of shouting and running about. She sent her swiftest messengers for the Feral Prince to come to her aid. But it was too late. The captain accosted the Feral Queen, even as she sat seated upon her Throne of Thorns. And there, before her own court, without so much as a beg-your-pardon or a by-your-leave, the captain slew her. I'm told he did the deed in a decidedly gruesome manner."

"Far," Mary whispered knowingly.

"That is what he calls himself here." Wylde nodded. "He did not even attempt to conceal his regicide, so news of the murder spread quickly. What was rejoiced throughout the Grove was lamented in the land of the Knoll. The ranks of the Feral Queen's army became baffled and filled with dread. Order fell to pieces, and her soldiers began to turn on one another. Some of the Queen's less trustworthy lords, in hopes of saving their own skins, laid their hands upon her son, the Feral Prince, and put him in chains, and handed him over to Far as a prisoner.

"All of which greatly pleased her Majesty. As soon as she learned that the Feral Queen was slain and the Feral Prince was her prisoner, she let out a delighted squeal and came from her Grove to claim her sister's queendom. Her vassals, and knights, and choristers, and ladies-in-waiting came with her, for it was Her Majesty's desire that they should all feast together at Her enemy's table.

"There, on the Sacred Knoll, as the Feral Queen's pyre still smoldered, her Majesty of the Grove held a banquet. After the first toast, she arose from the Throne of Thorns and called for the Feral Prince to be brought out. It was, of course, her intention to kill the poor fellow in the customary manner. That is, the Prince was to be bound and gagged and then thrown naked upon his mother's pyre to burn slowly as fuel for a roasting, spitted pig. But when Her Majesty called for 'The Royal Tinder' to be brought out, and the laughter subsided, there was a long silence. It seemed no one knew what had become of the Feral Prince or where he was to be found. Her Majesty was starting to become annoyed, when at last, Far rose from his seat and had to confess.

" 'Your Majesty, he escaped,' was what he said. 'When I gave him parole.' "

Wylde paused in his story and slowly shook his head.

"I heard – heard, mind you – that when Her Majesty learned she was deprived of her most triumphant moment at her own banquet . . ." He shuddered. "Well, they say that day on the Knoll there was fire and hail and thunder and tornadoes. And, well . . . the family resemblance between the Mad Queen and her sister became readily apparent."

Mary was confused.

"Why was she so angry? All Far did was show someone some kindness. For once."

"It wasn't kindness." Wylde wagged his finger. "It was folly. He had been duped. And now he was done for. For as the Prince's captor, the responsibility for the Prince's escape fell on Far's shoulders. Everyone in the court was whispering that this was the end of the hapless brute. Her Majesty would surely call upon his oath to her.

"But then someone else spoke up. The one who had actually been responsible for the Prince's escape, the one who was the true source of this mischief. It was he who told Her Majesty what had happened."

Mary's eyes widened in recognition.

"Yonder," she breathed.

"Indeed." Wylde nodded. "It seems that while the good captain was busy gutting Her Feral Majesty, Yonder had been gallivanting about the lower outskirts of the Knoll. For some time, he had been cavorting with the lesser gentry and ne'er-do-wells of the Feral Queen's court under the pretentious claim that he was a royal counselor 'between patrons.' The truth is, Yonder is nothing but a Traveling Fellow, as I am, though he seems rather ill suited to the calling. Anyhow, Yonder confessed to Her Majesty that when he heard the news of the Feral Queen's demise, he made straightaway for the prison where the Feral Prince was kept captive. He hoped to insert himself into affairs as they unfolded. In secret, Yonder made contact with the imprisoned prince. Yonder met and had words with His Feral Highness, which is a perilous thing for anyone to do.

"You see, His Highness has a tongue of honey when it suits his need. He was able to convince Yonder that there was a great treasure of some sort buried in the borderlands, one that only His Feral Highness could find. The Prince claimed he would be only too happy to fetch it and bring it right back. Her Majesty would bestow half her queendom to have it. Such was the splendor of this treasure. All the Prince said he needed was for his captor to unlock him from his chains, and only for the briefest spell. Surely Yonder could help him broker such a simple, and profitable, arrangement . . ."

Wylde shook his head again. "Yonder was hooked like a fish. Off he ran for Far. With promises of easy lucre and certain reward, he brought the captain before the Prince, and, well, it didn't take long before the captain, too, was under the Prince's spell. The Feral Prince is as mad as a devil, but, like I said, he can be a charmer when he needs to be. And what a charm he wove!

"Oh, he made promises, of course. The Prince swore, again and again, that he would be faithful in his undertaking. Yonder drew up the most punctilious of contracts, and the Prince signed it, readily, willingly, without a single objection. With gilded words in their ears and a contract in their hands, they both lost all their senses. For it was no surprise to anyone – other than those two, perhaps – that the Prince proved utterly faithless. Why wouldn't he? The lowly can't hold the great to their promises. Everyone knows that. The moment the Prince's fetters were unclasped, His Feral Highness ran away. He disappeared into the dusk, where no one could find him.

"When Yonder finished telling the Queen what had happened, and the unwitting part he had played in the Prince's escape, her anger began to quell."

Mary had been staring into the sky, watching a silver-lit cloud drift from shape to shape, until it had found a new form. One that reminded her of a gourd, which brought to her mind an image of Yonder, smiling to himself in his office with the sunlight falling on his shoulders, reading that green book of his, a steaming cup of tea at hand.

"It was good of Yonder to own up to his mistake," she said.

Wylde chuckled sardonically.

"You give him too much credit, my dear. In all likelihood, he simply reckoned that his part in the affair would come to light sooner or later, so he had better just come clean on his own. It was a shrewd calculation, not a mark of goodness. No different than the Feral Queen's lords betraying the Prince."

For the first time, something in what Wylde had said rang false to Mary. She thought he might be mistaken. But she did not dwell on it long, as Wylde continued.

"No, Her Majesty was not moved by Yonder's confession, but rather by his news. You see, the truth was, Mary, there really *was* a treasure. In that respect the Feral Prince spoke truly. I came to learn (don't ask me how) that this treasure may have even been the source of the sisters' feud. Anyhow, it had assuaged Her Majesty's vexation to learn that it might still exist, for she had thought it long lost.

If her nephew knew of it, he might also know where to find it. And that prospect brought her a small measure of comfort.

"Still, two of her servants had been incompetent and more than a trifle conniving, and that had to be dealt with."

" 'Come forward, both of you,' she commanded.

"They did as they were bidden, Yonder quaking in his knees, Far staring dumbly.

"Her Majesty spoke gravely, 'We had scarcely tasted from the cup of victory,' she said, 'before the servant who brought us the cup gave it away. Today we've been brought joy, then tears, then . . . news. 'Tis a strange turn. We could claim you had broken your oath, Lord Captain – and forfeited the Breath of your body – for what you have done.'

"Far bowed his head but said nothing. Then Her Majesty turned to Yonder.

" 'As for your Traveling Fellow, you've worked a great harm in our realm. We could justly claim a right to the head whose foolish counsel led our servant astray. Indeed, we could kill you both. But we have something else in mind . . .'

"At that, the Queen of the Grove parted her royal lips and opened wide her mouth. She craned her head back and let her hair fall like stars from the heavens upon her shoulders. Her breasts heaved." Wylde smiled faintly for a moment, as if lost in a memory, before he recollected himself. "And then, from within her chest, a breath from among the myriad stirred. It came forth at her summons, twirling like a tiny vortex in the space between her royal countenance and the men beneath her. With a puff, she blew the breath upon them, along with her judgment.

" 'Take back what you gave and go,' she declared. 'In reward for your services, you are released from my service. In punishment for your foolishness, you are banished from my lands. Both of you. Go hence from here, and do not return. Away with you.' "

Wylde paused, inhaled through his nostrils, and blew the air out slowly, making a puff of silver mist in the dark. The tiny cloud hovered in the space between them until Wylde tapped it with a finger and it disappeared.

"The breath," he said softly, "began to swirl before the two men, and it grew wide and tall, until they both found themselves wrapped within a vortex of wind, and twigs, and leaves, like a cocoon. They could not escape it. The courtiers gave a cheer as the Queen's breath lifted the soldier and the would-be counselor high into the air. The vortex carried them away from the Knoll, past the borderlands, past the forests, and over the mountains. Took them far away. All the way to Doldrums."

When Wylde finished his story, Mary began to feel a pang of sympathy. It was strange, she thought to herself. There was little to like in Yonder; and she absolutely loathed Far. And, yet, from what Wylde had told her (and she believed every word of his tale), she found herself unable to bury the tiny grain of pity she felt for the two of them. It was a hard thing not to have a home. Harder still, she imagined, would be to have one taken away.

"I want to help you," she said at last. "However I can. Because . . . because . . . whatever they did, whatever Yonder and Far may have done, they shouldn't be held here forever, and you shouldn't be held here at all. That's just . . . wrong. I'm going to help you get away."

Wylde's smile broadened and reflected the moon like a glimmering string of pearls. In his light, Mary felt a tingle, followed by a warming thrum. It coursed through her body, spreading like liquor from her heart, to her shoulders, to her hands. His fingers had somehow become laced through hers.

"I know you will, my dear," he cooed in her ear. "Soon. Very soon, you will help me." Wylde moved closer to Mary, and the world seemed to recede into the sound of his voice, until all that Mary knew was the scent of his hair, and the press of his weight, and the warmth of his body, and his hands enveloping hers.

"Meanwhile," he said, "we are here. While 'soon' is still out there. And I can only enjoy you here . . ."

CHAPTER EIGHTEEN

"Thus, beware of your dealings in Doldrums. For the Bargains we make and the Bonds we give in this realm are as binding as they are at home – indeed, more so. For some reason, Custom both amplifies the terms of our agreements here and then twists them with an almost venomous poignancy. So watch your Words."
—Wherestone's *Commentaries on Custom*, page 68

A dead clank of metal banged five times from the church steeple. Yonder glanced up at the sound fretfully. They were running late.

The sun pinpricked a curtain of lead-colored clouds high in the air, shedding dapples of light across the town of Norfolk. The streets hummed dully with the half-hearted business of tradesmen and merchants. Knots of people huddled close together or hurried to finish up their affairs. The temperature was dropping as suppertime neared, and no one wanted to linger outside much longer. Through the dispersing crowd, Yonder, Far, and Mary made their way toward the courthouse.

Far strode fast and purposefully ahead, while Yonder hobbled back alongside Mary. His feet ached, his head felt stuffy, and his nose was running like a stream.

"If only I had thought to ask for a handkerchief," Yonder chided himself. Mr. Elliott could have procured him one. But Yonder and Far had spent all morning and much of the afternoon in the Eagle's parlor immersed in their planning. They had worked through lunch, coffee, tea, supper, and drinks without pausing. When he checked, Yonder was aghast to see the clock on the mantle showing five minutes before the hour. Yonder had time only to fetch Mary and his coat and scarf. He had let the time slip right past him, and for that, Yonder also chided himself.

Yonder and Mary limped as quickly as the sickly lawyer could manage through the streets of Norfolk. Yonder made a pretense of holding his arm for Mary, when, in fact, he leaned most of his weight on her. The cold, acrid air bit his lungs. Yonder's chest seized with a spasm of coughing. How he wished for the Eagle's hearth, and a bowl of stew, and another glass of warmed wine . . .

The last reverberation from the church bell faded. The first lanterns were being lit in the windows of the public houses. They were surely going to be late for their appointment. He could walk no faster. So, Yonder thought with resignation, he might as well collect himself.

"Mary," he said, "would you mind slowing down a bit?"

Mary had remained unusually quiet since they had scurried out from the inn. She said nothing but did as she was asked. Up ahead, Far turned and made a face.

"Thought you said we had to hurry?"

Yonder waved at him to push on ahead. "Send my regards and tell them we are not far behind. And my friend?"

Far paused mid-step.

"Do remember what we agreed on about a signal."

Far dipped his head once in acknowledgement before

he disappeared around a corner. Yonder and Mary shuffled a few steps farther. Yonder was about to ask Mary if she would mind lending him the entirety of her shoulder, when he noticed something in her face.

"You seem . . . different somehow," he observed. She wore her new dress, which was already thoroughly tousled, her eyes were a trifle puffed, but still the same color. Her hair bounced with its usual lunacy.

She met his gaze impassively. Yonder squinted.

"Perhaps it's just I haven't seen you all day," he continued, "but you seem . . . I don't know. More alert than usual. Did you have a coffee?"

"No," she replied.

Yonder dropped his voice.

"You do still sense him?"

"I do." Mary paused and seemed to think to herself for a moment before she added with the faintest hint of a smile. "He's closer to me than ever."

"Good." Yonder nodded approvingly. "So Harris is bringing Wylde along. Very good. And you've brought your funds?"

Mary rolled her eyes. "So you mean to spend my last two and a half dollars?"

"It will help me in my bargaining." He patted her elbow reassuringly.

Mary came to a halt under the shadow of a gable. Yonder felt her arm tighten in his. She turned him to face her.

"You need me for this business of yours," she said flatly.

"I . . ." Yonder found himself faltering. What she had said was entirely correct, but why mention it now? "You've been a tremendous help," he said in the most cheerful voice he could. "I appreciate all you've done for me. And you have my promise, I shall repay all your funds with interest."

"Do I have your breath?"

Yonder felt a chill. He stared hard at Mary. There it was again. A change had come over her features. No. It was her lighting. There was a dull, pulsing shimmer just behind her eyes – one of lavender. It was very peculiar.

"How do you . . . know about that, Mary?"

Her hair fluttered from a passing breeze.

"I've learned a lot," she answered, "in the past few days."

Yonder studied her intently. What she asked of him was, of course, preposterous. He was a Traveling Fellow. He had no intention of swearing such an oath to anyone, let alone a ridiculous Doldrums woman. But that she had even asked such a question troubled Yonder and left him with a mounting apprehension. It was like having a faithful sheepdog who one day, inexplicably, found a voice and used it to demand a fair wage. Yonder decided he had better broach the matter tactfully.

"Well, well," he said, clicking his tongue, "you have learned a lot. It seems your window has also made you privy to my people's business. We had better get it closed. Your request is quite . . . blunt, Mary, so I will respond as bluntly. What you ask is impossible. I cannot give you my breath. I can't give you what you could not hold."

Mary scrunched her eyes at him warily, and, for a moment (to Yonder's relief), began to look more like her old self.

"So you, so you won't—" she started.

"No, it's a patently unreasonable demand." Yonder held his hands before him to appear both reasonable and conciliatory. "And honestly, even if you could keep my breath in pledge, do you really expect me to give up my life for the scraps of paper and metal you people bandy about? My *life* for your money? That's hardly a fair bargain."

"I . . . suppose." She eyed him with suspicion. "But,

then, how do I know you'll do what you say and not just leave me in a poor house?"

"I've already promised I'll repay you."

That should have sufficed, Yonder thought. It had before. And yet Mary did not move. She stood resolute within a shadow, her arms crossed across her chest, her shoes planted firmly on the ground. A group of fishmongers elbowed their way around Yonder and Mary, and when they had passed, she said to him, "The lowly can't hold the great to their promises."

Another jolt went through Yonder and set him to shivering. He felt like he had been doused with ice water. He was bereft of words, and that, too, made him uncomfortable. He did not at all like the tenor or the tone of this conversation. The sooner it ended, the better.

"It pains me that you've suddenly come to mistrust me," Yonder said and heaved a sigh. "After all we've been through. All I've done for you. Are you really asking for a bond, now, when we're so close?"

"I am," she said firmly.

Yonder's face drew taut. His eyelids fluttered shut, and when he spoke, it was with obvious distaste.

"All right, Mary," he murmured as his eyes opened again. "I give you my . . . word." His shoulders trembled slightly. "When I've concluded my business with Wylde, I give you my word I shall repay my indebtedness to you. That is the only surety my kind can give to yours. I trust it will suffice."

It was Mary's turn to study Yonder. Yonder had the impression she saw more of him than she ought. He drew his coat about his chest and rebuttoned it. Thankfully, she must have been satisfied with his pledge, though she had one last term to add.

"With interest," she said.

"Damn you for a shill," Yonder muttered irritably. "Fine. With interest."

Mary had always prided herself on her tirelessness. She could plow on late, night after night, telling fortunes whenever a ship came into port, or the farm hands finished bringing in the corn. If a customer called at two in the morning for a spell to break a fever, she would give the same performance she would if it were two in the afternoon.

But the past night had left her exhausted.

Pleasantly so. Her head felt a little bleary, and reeling, as if she had taken a glass of wine too many.

She smirked at the private recollection, held her free arm out to keep her balance, and trudged her tired legs up the three steps that led into the Norfolk courthouse's walled courtyard, grateful to have arrived. Yonder was still in tow, huffing and sniffling. Before them was an old iron gate, half open, groaning on a rusted hinge. Yonder leaned against the stone wall to catch his breath. Which was a wonder, since she had all but carried him through the town. Beneath his pallor, there was a fresh nervousness – as one who, already overwhelmed with worries, had suddenly remembered one more.

"Listen to me, Mary," he said briskly, "you might feel somewhat . . . unusual . . . when you come into Mr. Wylde's presence."

"Oh?"

"Yes. You see, your window," he said, gesturing at her forehead, "could begin to close once you are in his presence. I can't say for sure. But I need it – I should say, I need you to remain open to him, open to his presence. In case he is taken away again."

Mary felt an overwhelming urge to snicker but managed to keep it in check.

"I'll do my best to open up to him."

"Above all," he continued, "You must remain calm while I bargain with his captor. However strange you may feel, just sit quietly. It will pass. And if all goes well . . ." Mary was surprised to see Yonder reach for a nearby birch sapling and rap his knuckle against it. "I can set you free. No more romps inside his head. Won't that be nice?"

Mary had to turn her face for fear he would see her blush. At that moment, she glimpsed through the flaking, rusted bars of the gate two figures come out of a hovel in the courtyard, one leading the other on a chain. The one being led was dressed in rags, and dark, and walked stooped with a slow, limping gait.

As if sensing her eyes upon him, Wylde suddenly halted and stood erect in the center of the courtyard grounds to his full height. Taller than the one who held him, and infinitely more beautiful. For just a moment, in the midst of a shabby dirt yard, a chiseled statue, exquisite and graceful, radiated with a light that only Mary could see. He squared his shoulders and flashed a brief, knowing grin at her. It was a grin as salacious as a tomcat returned from his prowl. He bowed his head, shuffled to where he was taken, and looked like a slave again.

Yonder sat upright in the rickety chair he had been given and did his best not to shiver beneath the shawl Mary had placed about his shoulders, but the cold was relentless. It did not help that neither Mr. Beverley, the market's proprietor, nor Mr. Harris, the gentleman seated across the table from Yonder seemed inclined to discuss this business indoors. Both men, apparently, had assumed that the sale of a slave should be conducted in the same manner as the sale of a horse or a mule. A transaction one made outside, so the property could be thoroughly tested and inspected.

So there he sat, with Mary at his side, in the dusty, featureless courtyard behind the Norfolk courthouse with nothing between his person and the elements but the outer wall of a slave hut at his back and a tree limb hanging over his head. Yonder forced a pleasant expression, but Harris only glowered at Yonder and continued to drum his fingers impatiently on the table's edge. The gentleman had already been kept waiting and plainly resented any further imposition upon his time.

Yonder liked the look of Harris. The gentleman had an erect, severe bearing, and crisp staccato voice. Small, fierce eyes darted constantly, never lingering overlong on any person or thing. It was as if he was too pressed for time to find everything that affronted him. His demeanor demonstrated beyond a doubt that he was of a military trade, and that he would have, as reported, an exceedingly short temper. He was a tall, spritely man, Mr. Harris, with wide shoulders. He had a nose that listed left before it bent over into a crook, two dark and bushy eyebrows, and a perpetual blush. Immediately behind Harris stood Beverley. He was dressed in a heavy coat and held a chain.

The chain was attached to the manacles that bound Wylde's wrists.

Yonder reached for his pocket, but remembering there was no handkerchief, discretely rubbed his finger beneath his nose. But it was too little, too late. The sneeze came out as loud as the church bell. No one gathered in the courtyard offered a blessing.

Far still hovered about Wylde, poking at his hair, tapping his shins with his boot, smelling his breath, and otherwise offering a paltry performance of a potential buyer inspecting Wylde's condition. Yonder made a note to himself not to overplay his companion's ability to act his part. He cleared his throat.

"Well? How does he look, Captain?"

"Terrible," Far replied, a trifle too vehemently.

Harris turned slowly in his seat and cast a tight, perturbed smile at Far. "Whatever do you mean, sir?"

Far lifted his eyebrow mockingly. "Terrible? It means something is worse than very bad, but better than horrible."

Before Harris could respond, Yonder struggled to his feet, walked around the length of the table, and said he would like to have a look at Wylde for himself.

"I suspect Captain Far's eye finds fault with your servant's obvious physical limitations."

"Well, he's looking at him wrong, then." Harris let out a frustrated sigh. "I already told you Simon's a domestic. He's not built for the fields. But you assign him to work as a footman, or a butler, or a parlor boy, and he'll be first rate."

"One of the best domestics I ever sold," Beverley added helpfully.

"I'm sure he was," Yonder nodded.

He stifled another coughing fit and drew closer to Wylde who, thankfully, played his part to a tittle. Wylde had not uttered a sound, but kept his shoulders sufficiently hunched, with his eyes riveted to his feet. His patched, soiled clothes were more than adequately rumpled. No one besides Yonder or Far would have seen anything other than a man enslaved, one whose fate was about to be bartered. Not "terrible" (that was a tad overwrought), but the poor devil certainly looked much worse for the wear since the last time Yonder had seen him. He was thin to the point of gauntness, and the light about his person shone more dimly.

Yonder addressed Harris.

"As you can no doubt tell, Mr. Harris, I am not in the best of health."

"He's practically at death's door," Mary added. Though

she made a show of patting Yonder's arm, her eyes were fixed on Wylde.

Harris sniffed, shrugged, and muttered something that could possibly have been construed as his sympathy.

"So we require a servant," Yonder explained, "who can not only discharge the duties of a domestic, but who can also follow the particular instructions of my physician. My care will depend upon it."

"Simon'll do whatever your doctor tells him to," Harris replied.

"Unfortunately, my personal physician is a Parisian, and as such, rarely deigns to speak English. I don't suppose your Simon understands French?"

Wylde stirred slightly, lifting his head enough to shoot a quizzical glance at Yonder. Yonder smiled at him placatingly. Harris, however, was obviously annoyed by the question.

"I've no idea what Simon's native tongue is," he snapped, "he's got the queerest accent I ever heard. I can tell you this, though. With the right whip he'll learn to talk however you need him to."

Yonder turned his smile to Harris and dipped his head.

"I've no doubt. Would you mind if I spoke to your servant for a moment?"

Harris waved his hand to indicate Yonder could do what he liked, so long as he was quick about it.

"I say, um, Simon?"

Slowly, Wylde lifted his head and faced Yonder fully. His features were a perfect mask of deference, but Yonder could see the two lavender candles burning brightly within the pools of his eyes. Yonder asked him,

"*Tu parles français?*"

Wylde nodded demurely and answered, "*Bien sûr.*"

Just as Yonder had suspected, Wylde's tastes had, at some point, guided him in Doldrums to that wonderfully elegant and profoundly wicked republic across the sea. He continued his conversation in French as hurriedly as he could, while trying to appear as if he maintained a casual chat with a servant.

"I hope you've not been mistreated."

"I have been robbed, whipped, starved, and beaten with an iron bar."

Yonder kept his smile steady.

"I'm very sorry."

"The food I am given is dreadful," Wylde continued, "so I do not eat it. The quarters are not fit for a hound, so I do not stay in them."

"And Harris?"

"A witless brute. A Philistine. I am in bondage to a man who cannot tell the difference between his salad and bread plates. No matter how I arrange them. I should like to eat his liver."

"Would you like to be free of him?"

"Need you ask?"

"I can help you."

Wylde made a pretense of being amused by what Yonder had just said.

"How? I'm bound to the bastard. I don't know how it happened, but I am."

"You're bound by Custom," Yonder explained. "I happen to be learned in Custom."

Wylde moved his hands, causing the chains of his manacles to rattle.

"You're trapped here, too. How can you help me when you can't even—"

"I don't have time to explain the details. Do you want my help, or not?"

Wylde nodded. "Yes."

"All I ask in return," Yonder continued quietly, "is one service. When I have freed you, you will get something for me here in Doldrums and bring it to me."

"What?"

"Something you brought with you. Something which I believe – which I know – you can still get."

Wylde shook his head. "They took everything from me."

"Do I have your Word?"

His shoulders sagged slightly. For once, he was not acting, Yonder could tell.

"Do I have a choice?" Wylde asked.

"No."

"Very well . . ." Wylde shut his eyes, and drew a deep breath, let it out, and gave Yonder his Word. "I give you my Word I will bring to you whatever is in my power to bring to you."

"Excellent!" Yonder clapped his hands together and spun on his heel to address Harris, who, until that moment, had been squinting at their discourse with mounting impatience. "His speech is as flawless as His Christian Majesty's, rest his soul."

Beverley let out a low whistle.

"A genuine French domestic."

Harris' face began to shine with greed.

"He's worth two – no, three hundred."

"At the very least, sir," Beverley nodded vigorously.

"Yes, yes." Yonder made his way back around the table and resumed his seat. "We'll pay whatever he's worth. Captain Far will take care of that."

At the sound of his name, Far's eyes pricked up expectantly. He was in a good position, standing in the vicinity of the table, close enough for the conversation, but not so close that he might scare off Harris too quickly. As long as Far stuck to the script they had rehearsed . . .

"So," Yonder continued, keeping his voice as casual as he could, "once you furnish Captain Far with Simon's papers, he'll see that you're paid."

The courtyard fell silent. No one sniffed or shuffled their feet. No dogs barked outside. Not even a breeze stirred the leaves in the trees. The quiet drew long and became tight as a hangman's knot. The hue in Harris' cheeks spread and deepened from raspberry to plum. It was better than Yonder could have hoped.

"*Papers!*" Harris spat the word out with revulsion. "What the hell are you talking about?"

"His title, his bill of lading, the usual recorded documents."

"Always a lawyer," declaimed Mary, lacing her voice with a hint of exasperation. She held up her hands to Harris. "He so loves his legal papers."

Harris cursed loudly and thumped the tabletop. "Look here, Yonder. I don't know what you're going on about papers for. Simon's mine. I bought him with my own money. I got him in chains. He's mine to sell."

Yonder spread his palms out soothingly above the table.

"I have no doubt you bought this fellow with lawful tender, Mr. Harris. But I must have proof of his servitude to take him back to Massachusetts with me. My commonwealth has a somewhat, shall we say, stricter view of these transactions than yours. Suppose he were to claim . . . I don't know . . . that he was a freeman who was wrongly taken and shipped down here where he was unlawfully sold. "

"He'd be a liar," Beverley growled.

"Of course he would. But in Boston, where I live, such claims are not uncommon. I may be called upon to show the magistrate proof of his status. Failing which, he would be set free. And I would be fined. Perhaps even jailed. Why, I couldn't possibly purchase a man without proper papers. If I did that, I'd be a – I'd be a—"

"You'd be a fool," Far delivered his line perfectly.

"Just so," Yonder agreed.

The sound of a chair crashing to the ground was followed by a string of curses. With surprising quickness, Harris was on his feet. He shoved Beverley aside grasped Wylde by the hair and gave his head a frightful shake.

Mary let out a gasp. Yonder gripped her arm firmly and shot her a glance to hold her tongue.

"Goddammit, Yonder!" Harris roared, "I tell you, he's mine. This here's the fifth slave I've bought at auction and none of them ever came with papers!" He gave Wylde a hard shove, sending him to his knees. "He's a slave. Anybody with eyes can see that. Now are you going to buy him or not?"

"Please, Mr. Harris," said Yonder soothingly. "Please, sir. There's no need to shout. Of course I shall buy him. For three hundred dollars. If we can be provided with a certified copy of his papers—"

"Which I told you, I don't have—" Harris growled.

Yonder laughed breezily.

"But I wouldn't expect you to be holding his official records, Mr. Harris. Such things are kept in court files. In courthouses." He leaned back in his chair and craned his head to look at the dreary, gray building at the end of the yard. "That is what courthouses are for. I'm sure Mr. Beverley can fetch the papers straightaway. Mr. Beverley?"

Beverley nearly jumped at his name, the color drained from his cheeks. "Eh?"

"Would you kindly retrieve the official records for this slave? I should like to make his purchase." Yonder raised an eyebrow at Beverley, who stood dumbly, still holding Wylde's chain in his limp hands. Yonder gazed at him pleasantly, Harris glared at him menacingly. Beverley gulped loud enough that everyone in the courtyard could hear it. He started to stammer.

"I . . . that is, I, well . . . the official records? That's kinda unusual. I mean, there's records, and then there's records, you know . . ."

It was Beverley's turn to bear the brunt of Harris' wrath.

"Just get him some fucking papers, Stephen, so I can close this sale."

"Yessir. Of course." Beverley clasped the back of his neck and rubbed it hard, "I will. But then there's the record search fee that's got to be paid—"

"Two dollars," Yonder interjected brightly, "I believe that was what you said that fee was. Here you are." He placed two of Mary's coins onto the table, and for added effect, crossed one leg over the other, as if, having paid his fee, he would be perfectly content to pass the time out there while Beverley did as he was bidden.

"Hop to it," Harris snarled, "do your job . . . if you want that commission."

Mumbling to himself, Beverley pocketed the money and walked glumly across the length of the grounds, until he came to the courthouse's back door. He shoved a key into the lock, shouldered the door open and disappeared within. He was gone for nearly twenty minutes.

When he returned, he moved quicker, furtively. Without looking anyone in the eye, he rounded the other end of the table. In his hand, he held a small, unfolded sheet of parchment, which he set on the tabletop, as far as he could from Yonder.

"There you are," Beverley announced brusquely. "Official records. How 'bout that three hundred dollars now, please."

A thin smile broke Yonder's lips. With his eyes, he indicated for Far to bring the paper over to him. Far nodded, went around to get it, pushing past Beverley's futile attempt to block him from seeing the parchment's contents. Far leaned over and started to chuckle to himself softly.

"What's so funny?" Beverley challenged.

Far gave the document a careless flick, sending it over to Yonder. It only took a moment for Yonder to read its contents, and he too joined in his companion's laughter. Beverley and Harris looked flummoxed.

"Come, come, Mr. Beverley," Yonder chided. "You've had your joke. Now let's have the real documents."

"Whadya mean?" Beverley's bottom lip quivered indignantly. "That there is the real documents."

Yonder let his face slowly fall from bemusement into the most lawyerly, solemn frown he had ever made. He looked from Far, to Harris to Beverley and slowly, disapprovingly, shook his head.

"You cannot possibly expect me to believe that this is an official Virginia record." Yonder peered at the paper as he began to recite.

"To all to whom these Presents Shall come unto the Commonwealth of Virginia, be it Resolved, for and in consideration of bona fides, caveat emptor, wheretofore, of said Party of the Third Part, once removed, being lawfully seized of said Negro, to have and to hold . . ." Yonder curled his lips. "Gibberish. Why, look—" He quickly stroked a finger across the surface of the page and held it up for all to see. His fingertip was stained dark gray, and a long, arching smudge marred the crimped and hasty handwriting on the parchment. "The ink's not even dry. To call this a forgery would be an insult to honest forgers."

Far shook his head and *tsked*.

But Harris had clearly had enough. He roared a curse at Beverley for being an incompetent ass, at Yonder for being a persnickety lunger, and at Far for being tall and in the way. He grabbed Wylde's chain and started to leave, but before he had made it a step, Yonder mused aloud, "You know, Mr. Harris, you have no right to keep that man."

Harris stopped and slowly turned back around.

"I got every right I need. Right here," he gave the chain a jangle.

Yonder held him with a steady, unblinking gaze.

"I am afraid you are in the wrong. There are no papers of this man's servitude. So he is considered stolen. Under the law, he should be set free."

For a long moment, Harris ground his jaw, and screwed his face in angry contortions until his cheeks vacillated between red and scarlet. At last, he let out a violent laugh and spat in the dirt near Yonder's shoe.

"This son of a bitch goes free," he said through his clenched teeth, "over my dead body."

Yonder's voice was steady and implacable.

"Sir, do I have your word on that?"

"Damn right you do."

At that, Yonder turned meaningfully to Far.

"Captain, what would you call a man who tries to barter with stolen property?"

Far took a few strides toward Harris and Wylde. A dark, menacing grin spread across his lips. He was only a few feet away from Harris when he answered, looking straight into Harris' eyes, the final line he and Yonder had practiced.

"Why, I'd call him a thief and a liar."

Harris' mouth dropped open. A few more hues raced across Harris' face, purple, indigo, until it was as black as Wylde's. The man's rage had grasped him so tightly, he was almost incoherent – almost. Fortunately, whatever discipline had been instilled in the course of his life enabled Harris to issue the inevitable challenge.

"Fucking . . . Whoreson . . . *Yankee!* You'll answer for that! Stephen, you're my second. Tomorrow . . . at dawn!"

CHAPTER NINETEEN

"To be sure, Custom affords our race a certain 'spring in the step' compared to how the locals lumber about in Doldrums. We are faster, stronger, and can suffer more hurts than they. Take care, however, for this boon of Custom is not limitless. We are all quite powerful here. But none of us are all powerful."
—Wherestone's *Commentaries on Custom*, page 13

F ar leaned over the edge of the billiards table to study the ivory sphere. A white ball with a red dot, lay on a blue field, almost – that was key – almost at a point that made a right angle between his cue ball and a red ball, some two feet away. If he struck it exactly right, with a bit of finesse, and with just the right force, the white could be propelled sideways to strike the red. Which would score a carom. A difficult shot from this angle, but possible.

Angles, forces, possibilities, hitting objects with a stick. A fine game, billiards. And a good distraction from Yonder and Beverley's bickering.

Far glanced over his shoulder and frowned. The two of

them were still going at it. Yonder lay reclined in the plushest chair of the Eagle's parlor, shivering by the fireplace, and guzzling down his precious tea. Before him, Beverley hopped from his good leg to his wooden one, droning on about whatever it was that had him in a tither, and throwing his hands about like an Anabaptist. Apparently, something upset him. The scene he was making seemed to have scared off most of the Eagle's usual customers. Which would have been fine. But as Far leveled his cue stick and pointed at his mark, Beverley's voice intruded on his concentration.

"That's all you got to say? Jesus! What kind of a goddam second are you, Yonder?" Beverley squeaked.

"One who knows his principal," Yonder replied mildly. "Captain Far is resolved. He will satisfy your principal's challenge. Tomorrow at dawn, in the field in front of Mr. Harris' manor."

"But you're not doin' what you're supposed to do, dammit. You're supposed to try to talk your boy out of fightin'. You're not even tryin'!"

"Because there is no point. Captain Far is very much looking forward to his duel with Mr. Harris."

Far heard Beverley punch the side of the wall.

"I brokered y'all a damn fine deal for a genuine, frog-talkin' domestic. Brought you a ready, willin', and able seller. I'm owed a commission!"

"The commission was Mr. Harris' obligation, remember? I suggest you seek it from him."

Beverley roared a profanity just when Far tried his shot. The cue scampered wide of the target, scarcely grazing the side of the other ball. The red ball bounced haplessly against the rail and rolled a couple of feet, never touching anything. A wasted shot.

"Bastard," Far snapped.

He threw his billiard stick down on the table and

marched over to Yonder's chair. Yonder pinched the bridge of his nose and did not bother to look up. Beverley began to quaver, his eyes bulging like a fish at Far's approach.

"I've had about enough of your noise," Far warned him.

The clerk stammered, and wrung his hands, and darted his head this way and that, as if looking for someone to come to his rescue in the empty parlor. The fire was at his back and had settled to a low crackling, leaving Beverley's face mostly hidden in shadow, but Far could see his forehead beading with sweat.

"You-you started a duel," Beverley blathered, as if Far had not grasped what had happened not a few hours earlier in the evening. "There's formalities. Forms. A code. We gotta—"

"Yes, yes." Far waved his hand absently. He strolled past Beverley to the hearth and peeked inside a kettle that was, unfortunately, filled with nothing stronger than boiling water for Yonder's damned tea. "I know all about your Code Duello and all the forms you people must follow before you kill one another. But it's getting late, and I've not had my supper, so let's be done with them already." Far began to count with his fingers. "I acknowledge that I insulted your man, Harris, in public when I called him a thief and a liar. I have accepted his challenge, and I've made Yonder my second in this affair. Harris made you his. And now the seconds have both met."

"Right." Beverley seemed to regain himself. "But your second's supposed to try to work somethin' out – that's what seconds do, 'least in Virginia. Which if he'd try, maybe we could all get back to business—"

"Mr. Yonder's never been much of a negotiator," Far said pointedly. He glanced at Yonder, who sniffed in his teacup, but said nothing. "Let us acknowledge that he's failed at his task and move on to the final points. There will be no apology. So we will have our duel tomorrow morning, and no quarter will be asked or given. There. We're finished."

"I . . . well . . . shit." Beverley wiped his mouth with the back of his hand and wagged his head dumbly. "You sure don't seem to care much over what you're about to do. I mean . . . one of you all's gonna die. An' I'll tell you what. You may be a big fella, but bullets is bullets, an' blades is blades." Beverley could not hold Far's gaze, but he worked his face into an almost comical mask of forewarning. "Just so you know. Stanley Harris is a crack shot, an' he can make a blade dance. He's dueled eight men on this coast, an' none of 'em ever touched him. He'll cut you down to size. I promise you."

The absurdity of Beverley trying to frighten him struck Far as rather farcical, but he kept his mouth steady, and even acknowledged what Beverley had said with a slight nod. For this at least was a form he knew, and honored, one that had come down from time out of mind. The boast before the battle. Far would respect the boast that had been made in the customary manner, by responding with his own. He smiled at Beverley.

"Your man can cut at me all he likes. I give you my word, he'll be dead and gutted this time tomorrow."

From the chair in the corner came a blustering, bothered sound, followed by a fit of angry coughs. Yonder's face contorted. He struggled to his feet, and if Far didn't know him better, he might have thought the old pumpkin was on the verge of having a temper.

"I think," Yonder rasped, "that there's been enough discussion. Let's have no more words." He glared at Far for a long moment before he turned to Beverley. "The time and place have been decided, sir. I believe the only remaining matter is the choice of weapons."

"Yeah," Beverley pointed toward Far. "Well. He's the one that was challenged, so he gets to choose."

Far thought on it for a minute, recalling all the crude weaponry he had come across in Doldrums. Pistols, poleaxes, grenades, that delightfully inventive, but preposterous device they called a morning star . . . Ridiculous trinkets, but in the right hands anything can be made deadly.

In the end, he decided he would stay with the familiar.

"I don't suppose you have any sabers lying about?"

The morning of the duel drew dark and blustery, and it brought with it a cruel wind out of the northeast, whipped along by a bank of charcoal-colored clouds from the sea. It had the look of a coming blizzard. Yonder took one glance through the Eagle's window curtain and promptly ordered a coach and driver. It would be a two-mile trek beyond Norfolk to reach Harris Manor, and as it was all he could manage just to dress himself, he felt the expenditure was justified, even necessary. It depleted the last of the funds they had on account at the inn, but, if all went well, there would be no need to spend another night there. If all went well . . .

A copse of dreary, leafless trees rolled past through the carriage window. The horses slowed. Yonder could hear their hooves squelching through muck. A shore breeze blew fiercely, sending the first flurries of snow into their cabin. Blinking back tears from the wind in his eyes, Yonder caught sight of the manor house in the distance.

He looked over at Far. His partner stared pensively at the distant bay, his broad, heavy hands resting on his knees. No coat or scarf, no hat, no expression. His hair blew loose behind him. Sullen and bored. The same as he ever was, Yonder reflected. Yet Yonder had a gnawing worry that something seemed off. He coughed into his handkerchief and asked, "Are you feeling quite alright?"

Far turned to him with a bemused expression.

"The kettle is fine," he said. "How is your own soot, Mr. Pot?"

"Don't jest. I only ask because – because I am concerned. I fear you may have done something foolish last night. I can't be certain, though."

"Oh?" Far replied without a hint of concern. He returned his attention to the horizon. "And what was that?"

"You gave your word."

Yonder fell silent. The coach made its way through a boggy stretch of clearing and picked up speed as they drew onto more level ground. They trotted down a gray pathway in the sand. Yonder looked past Mary's shoulder to the Harris Manor signpost and a dead magnolia tree, as a small field emerged from within the morning fog. Still veiled in haze, the manor house stood just beyond it. Three shadows were in the center of the grassy field, waiting for their arrival.

Yonder clutched his hand to his shirt and twisted the collar tight to keep from coughing. As the carriage slowed, Yonder felt his stomach churning, and a knot of worry began to tighten.

"Mary," he said, "best you remain in the carriage while we tend to this sordid business. And as for you, my friend."

"What?" Far grunted.

Yonder fixed him with one last, searching gaze.

"Best you remain silent until the business is finished."

The carriage lurched to a halt, and the driver announced that they had arrived at Harris Manor.

Far stood near the middle of the dew-speckled bowling green. The steady murmur of waves crashed in the bay, and a breeze stirred the branches of distant, leafless trees. They were the only sounds that broke the stillness. His partner, Yonder, had withdrawn to the far edge of the field along with Beverley. His enemy, Harris, faced him.

Harris was dressed in black pants, low, supple boots, and a loose gray shirt that he had buttoned to the collar and left untucked. The hue in his cheeks had subsided, for his face was as colorless as his shirt. He was clean shaven. No vest or coat sleeves to constrict his arms, no scarves or ribbons to become tangled upon, no belt to offer an opponent something to grasp. A proper outfit altogether, Far thought approvingly.

"Simon," Harris raised his voice and snapped his fingers.

Wylde came shuffling down the steps of the manor's porch, still barefooted and in rags despite the cold. He had cradled in his arms, a lengthy bundle covered with an oil cloth. Harris said nothing as he approached but unfurled the cloth to reveal two beautifully curved and polished blades. They caught the sun's light and held it greedily within their steel.

"You asked for sabers," Harris said. His speech was brisk, to the point, another mark in his favor. "Here you are. I've used them both before."

Far could hear a faint, tinny sound ringing in the air about the swords, like the distant echoes of men gasping in death throes. He cocked his eye and caught a glimpse of what looked like thin streaks of blood running down from their points. A steady trickle of scarlet, and lost hope.

"So you have," Far agreed. He had a talent for sensing which weapons had taken life and which ones were still virgins. These old blades had had their share of trysts.

"This one," Harris pointed to one of the swords, "is two and a quarter inches shorter, but it's a heavier blade. Balanced more on the hilt. That one's more your traditional cavalry saber. Take your pick. Doesn't matter to me."

Far felt a tiny thrill. These were no virgin blades or cheap costume props, like most of the trinkets that passed for cutlery in Doldrums. Harris had brought out two seasoned blood mavens, lush, blossoming, panting. In their prime and moaning for a kill.

"You wanna try 'em out?" Beverley asked.

"Like a menáge?" Far chuckled. "No, thank you." He considered his choice and made up his mind that he preferred his beauties to have some heft to them. "Since I've longer arms, I'll take the shorter blade. To even your lack of reach."

"I told you," Harris repeated, "it doesn't matter to me."

Far and Harris each took their blades and drew a couple of paces away to swish them through the air.

Such a note she could cut! Far quite lost track of time or where he was. He cleaved and hewed through a wall of imagined foes with his saber, swiping, stabbing, thrusting the sword faster and stronger. He reveled in the sound it made. A low, throaty growl, but with the crisp edge that warned of a deadly bite.

"So are you ready?" Harris prompted impatiently.

Far glanced about, as if from a dream. Wylde had already withdrawn to the manor's porch, where Yonder and Beverley were watching in rapt silence.

"At your pleasure," Far smiled.

"Then come *en guarde* and wait for my second to give the word."

Harris went into his stance. In a single moment, Far's eyes took every measurement of his enemy, every grain of dirt and dead blade of grass beneath his feet, every movement stirring in the field. A chilled, salted breeze kissed his cheeks. Harris' sword point hovered a few feet from Far's chest, poised to strike. As if in response, Far's heart reveled with anticipation.

From a distance, he heard Beverley's gruff voice calling out.

"Touch swords and go to it . . ."

Far started to lift his sword to meet Harris', but suddenly that lithe and lovely blade he had chosen, the one that had, but a moment ago, been singing for him, felt dead and ponderous in his grip. As if both his arm and his saber were mired in a bog. The weight seemed to mount. Far clenched his jaw, tightened his fingers until they must have been white, and struggled to bring his weapon to the ready. It took most of his strength, but the blade came up. To Far's horror, it quivered – Harris noted it, too.

Harris' mouth curled into a leer.

"Second thoughts, Captain?"

Far's mind raced. He changed his grip, locked his fingers together, pulled his thumb beneath the other knuckles. He pulled his elbow tight into his side to gain more leverage. He even brought his left hand over to aid his right (though fighting two-handed with such a wispy blade was folly). No matter what he did, no matter how he tried, he could scarcely hold his sword aloft. It was if he was not wielding a sword – but a millstone.

"The blade," Far muttered, "feels heavier than I thought."

The contempt in Harris' glare caused a blush of shame to warm in Far's cheeks.

"Here," Harris flipped his own saber end over end and clasped it by the hilt. He tossed it to Far, who caught its handle.

Somehow, this one was even worse. What should have been the longer, lighter blade, and what could not have weighed more than three pounds, felt like a leaden anchor.

Far grimaced. A line of sweat streaked down his temple. Harris' saber began to sink, the tip almost brushed the ground. That his enemy should see him in a state of weakness was intolerable, but to sully such a fine blade before the first blow had been struck . . . that would be unbearable. He forced himself to appear unconcerned while inwardly he groaned. With a great strain, he was able to hoist the proffered blade back to its owner.

"Thank you, no," Far replied. "I was – complimenting the quality of your steel. I am satisfied with my choice of weapon."

Harris gripped the sword Far had returned and gave it a terse wave, plainly unimpressed with Far's explanation. With another heave, Far was able to bring the first saber he had chosen just high enough to touch Harris' blade.

"*En guarde*," Harris said.

What happened next was surreal. For just a moment, Far's vision seemed to withdraw from Harris' sneering visage, and his sight became elevated, lifting higher and higher, until it settled far overhead. It was as if he were a falcon that happened to be soaring overhead, one that had spotted two men below. One looked broad, the other lean. Both were tall. Both intent. Only one moved his weapon. For Far, it was utterly maddening. He gave his head a jostle, slapped himself, and came back to the earth, and to the contest.

Harris feinted twice, a quick lunge and a jaunt to the left. Each time Far had to retreat a half-step to avoid the blow. Far crouched low and slowly stalked around Harris' flank. But it was a futile positioning. He could not strike. He could scarcely keep his saber from dragging through the grass. It was humiliating, but it had the effect of confusing his opponent.

"You going to dance, or you going to fight?" Harris snapped.

"Are you offering your hand for a kiss?" Far quipped.

Harris' cheeks blew out, his teeth flashed, his face reddened.

"You son of a bitch . . ."

Far could have played the poor fool perfectly. It would have been magnificent. If only he had the strength to lift his sword.

For in his rage, Harris had angled his elbow much too high. He was striking for a *coup de grâce*, and in so doing had left his breast as open and as welcoming as a dockyard whore's. Gods, he would have relished plunging his sword through the man's heart. But Far could do nothing but watch – and retreat.

Harris leaped headlong at Far, driving his saber like a flash of lightning. Unable to turn the blow with a parry, Far twisted around at the last moment, turning so that only his side showed. There was a gush of air from the flurry of movement, followed by a grunt from his opponent. Far heard the sound of cloth tearing and quickly stepped away to regain the space he had lost from his opponent's attack. As he moved, he saw that his shirt was torn on his left side. A gash had cut the flesh beneath his arm. A drop of blood, his blood, fell to the earth.

Harris said nothing. Though the gleam of triumph in his eyes was unmistakable. A shining of rage and rapture. He had struck first and struck true against a man, he must have realized, was faster and stronger than he. It pained Far to cede even so small a victory.

Far withdrew, pulled his sword along like a tethered ship, a ship that was fast drawing water. He could scarcely keep the point above his knees. Harris was *en guarde* and ready for another pass. As before, he studied Far for a while, testing flanks, feinting steps, as if still unsure whether his opponent was playing a gambit, and if so, what it might be. This time, though, the hesitation was shorter.

He struck again. With guile. Harris made a stuttering jaunt, and when he had come into range, he drew his arm high in a nearly perfect mimicry of how he had set up his earlier lunge. Far nearly fell for the ploy. But he had already given up using his blade to parry. Instead, Far leaped to the side, just as Harris turned the stab into a last-moment slash that would have gutted a slower, or less attentive man.

Far winced in pain. Harris had cut him again. A streamer most likely, he gauged from the flow that was rapidly soaking his shirt. Not deep enough to be mortal, but deep enough. In the field, he might have paused for stitches. Far had endured more and worse. There was still ample blood left in his body. He still felt strong. But he knew that once a foe saw running blood, once he smelled an enemy's life leeching from him, he would redouble his assault. And Far's only defense, it seemed, was to run – which was no defense at all.

Harris' attacks became relentless. He sensed that Far was incapable of offering any counter to his onslaught. For his part, Far who had never enjoyed practicing footwork, had scarcely worked on it at all in his time in Doldrums, had exhausted his meager repertoire of dodges. The fight, such as it was, went on for what felt like an interminably long time. At last, with Far gasping for air, and his shirt and upper body shredded by Harris' saber, he heard Yonder's ragged voice cut across the field through the pounding in his head.

"I say, Mr. Harris?" Yonder called out. "I've asked for time. Time, I say! My principal needs drink."

Harris blinked, as if coming out of a wondrous, violent dream, and made a face at Yonder.

"Did you just ask for . . . time?"

"I did, sir."

"What the – Goddammit!" Harris spat after a gulping breath. "This is a duel, not a summer hike."

"So it is."

Far craned his head. Yonder ventured a couple of steps out onto the field. From Yonder's worried expression, Far reckoned he must have made a pitiful sight.

"I've invoked Rule twenty-six of the Code Duello," Yonder announced. As impossible as it seemed, Yonder had come upon the field of combat and assumed his lawyer's pose. The condescending chin, the pedantic eyes, the hectoring tone. Far found himself grateful for it.

"The *what?*" Harris asked.

"Rule what?" Far huffed.

"Rule twenty-six," Yonder repeated. He approached Harris as imperiously as if he approached a hostile witness in a courtroom. "Of the Code Duello. Surely, you're aware of it." Yonder pretended he recited from a memorized passage; pretended, for Far knew he was making it up whole cloth. "Where the contestants have chosen swords," Yonder intoned, "and the contest has lasted longer than five minutes, or five passes, whichever is first, either gentleman or their respective second may call for time to refresh themselves before renewing the contest. So that the contest may remain one of swordsmanship and not constitution."

Harris shot a questioning scowl over his shoulder toward Beverley, but his second was plainly out of his element in matters concerning the finer points of codes and formalities. Beverley's mouth opened and closed a few times, he tapped his wooden leg in what passed for thought, until he held his hands up and shrugged. Yonder had positioned himself between Far and Harris, all but making it impossible for Harris to resume the fight honorably. And thereby left him with no choice but to acquiesce. Apparently, lawyers had their own kind of footwork.

Harris met Yonder's arrival, as well as his proposal, with undisguised displeasure.

"Ten minutes?" Yonder inquired.

"Two," Harris showed two fingers to emphasize the point. "I'll give you two minutes." He shot a mocking smile at Far before he turned his back on him, and added, "That should be enough time to teach your man how to swing a sword . . ."

"The Code Duello has only twenty-five rules," Far murmured once Harris had withdrawn. "But I like your invention."

"You be quiet!" He took Far's elbow and led him a few steps away so that they were well out of earshot of either Harris or Beverley. He sounded frustrated and worried, though he kept his voice at a whisper. "Why the devil haven't you run him through yet?"

"What, you're not enjoying the show?" Far felt a jarring pain from one of his cuts, the long gash most likely; it nearly bent him over. Yonder seemed too preoccupied to notice.

"We don't have time for this," Yonder continued. "Just stab him and be done with it already."

Far was too tired, and too hurt, to be annoyed with Yonder's impertinence. A sharp retort would have been appropriate, but he found himself speaking frankly.

"I can't."

"What do you mean?"

"The sword . . . I can barely lift it."

Yonder grasped the weapon with his soft fingers and gave it a feeble turn, but it seemed to require no more effort from him than if it had been a candlestick. Thankfully, Far did not chide him.

"I was afraid of this," Yonder declared. He handed the saber back to Far, who felt it sink from its newfound weight just as before. "This is Custom's work," he continued, "and it's your fault."

For some reason, Far found he was not especially surprised. In fact, he had suspected Custom was the culprit almost from the beginning, though he couldn't guess why it had chosen to intervene in such a decidedly unfair and untimely manner. Yonder motioned for Far to listen closely.

"Last night, at the Eagle, you gave your Word on this contest," he explained. "Custom bound you to that Word. To your precise Word."

"What?" Far tried to piece together what Yonder could have been talking about. "How did I do that?"

"You told Beverley that Harris could cut you 'all he likes.' Then you gave your Word. So now—"

"Harris is cutting me all he likes." Far shut his eyes as the memory, and the realization, settled on him. He felt his shoulders fall. From the other side of the field, Beverley chuckled at some jape of Harris'. It was beyond vexing. He looked at Yonder who asked him gently, "You're . . . still bleeding, then?"

"Yes." Far was gashed in at least seven places, his clothes were dyed brown and, where they were torn, bright red from the staunch of his blood.

"Are you badly hurt? Tell me truthfully."

"I . . ." Far had gauged countless battlefield injuries of all kinds; he could sort a mortal wound from a near death blow like a Dutch merchant grading gemstones. There was no reason to hold back what he knew to be true. "Two more cuts . . . and it will be my end."

Yonder, to his credit, kept his face unperturbed.

"Hey, there!" Beverley yelled. "Y'all've had your two minutes. Ready to beg pardon?"

Far grit his teeth. "I'll do no such thing," he murmured to Yonder.

"Of course not. But listen to me . . ." He made a hasty gesture in Beverley's direction to indicate that Far would be coming out momentarily. "There is no defeating Custom. You will have to win this fight within the boundaries that you've drawn." He paused meaningfully. "Can you?"

"Captain Far!" Harris' voice boomed in a tone that

sounded like he was at the height of merriment. "Come on now! It's bad manners to keep a thief and liar waiting!"

Yonder's fingers clasped Far's elbow.

"John?" he asked.

Far hoisted himself upright and slowly rose to his full height. Sharp, burning needles seemed to tear at his skin from the motion. His head felt dizzy. But he would not show weakness; no, not a glimpse of it. He made his shoulders square, lifted his chin, forced his feet to march. Without answering Yonder, Far trudged back to the center of the field, each step a new burst of pain and another foot closer to exhaustion.

The air felt colder, though the sun had already cleared the manor's rooftop. It was coming on to be a bright, clear day, he thought absently. When he had reached Harris, he took a deep breath and was able to inch his saber high enough so that it cleared an inch from the ground. It would come no higher. He stared straight into Harris' face.

"You've cut me as much as you've liked," he said simply.

Harris squinted at him, as if unsure whether Far had admitted failure, asked a question, or something in between. He licked his thin lips and replied, "You haven't put up much of a defense."

"No, I haven't."

The two stood before each other in silence, one *en guarde*, the other all but defenseless. From behind a saber's pommel, Far could see Harris' expression begin to soften, like the first drop of water rolling down an ice sculpture. Slowly, Harris lowered his blade.

"Don't know why the hell you chose sabers," Harris remarked, shaking his head, "when you're no swordsman." He took a step back and fixed Far with a look that vacillated between annoyance, and admiration, and almost – friendliness. "But you've got a set of balls on you, I'll allow that. Look here. It'd be murder for me to finish you off when you're just a novice. And I think you've paid enough for your insult."

Far warbled slightly on his feet. His blood felt frigid where it had dried on his skin.

"Here," Harris said and held out his hand, "let's get you stitched up. I'll even give you a drink to cut the pain. Simon! Go and fetch the parlor whiskey."

The salty warmth of blood began to fill Far's mouth. He hocked up the spittle and shook off Harris' hand.

"We agreed, sir," Far said quietly. "No quarter, asked or given. But I promise you. I give you my Word . . ." Slowly he lifted his face to meet Harris'. "As you're the only man in Doldrums to ever wound me, you will fly in my flag. I'll honor you for all time. You've been a worthy foe, Mr. Harris . . ."

In a single, swift motion, Far dropped his saber and, free of the weight, lunged forward to grapple his opponent. As he sprang, Harris tried to parry with his sword. But he had lowered his guard, so his blade landed well beneath Far's chest. The tip bit into the meat of Far's thigh where it became stuck. Far felt the tendons, the muscles, the veins, burst in a volley like cannon shots. A fresh, delirious pain brought stars to his vision, blinded him, making his stomach wretch. He couldn't see the indignation blazing from Harris' eyes, but he could feel his man's arm, his sword arm, and with one hand, Far seized his enemy's wrist, bound it as fast and firm as an iron fetter. Harris pulled hard against it, but he was powerless in Far's grasp.

"What the— What the hell are you?" Harris said.

The scent of fear was flowing from Harris' nostrils. It was intoxicating. Far laughed aloud and curled his other hand into a fist. He brought it high over his head and flexed his arm. A voice assailed him, Beverley's.

"Goddammit, Far!" Beverley screeched. "Y'can't do that! This ain't a tavern!"

319

"You-you . . . you . . ." Harris could only stammer beneath the shadow of Far's hand.

Whatever final insult Stanley Harris wished to hurl in this life was stymied, lost before his tongue could form it. For at that moment, Far began to pummel him. Four, five, six times, his fist smashed into Harris' face and the bafflement and displeasure that had been fixed there disappeared along with that final lost word. Harris' nose shattered into a ruined mess of crimson. His cheekbones cracked. He gasped once, made a pitiful noise, and fell dead. And still Far hit him, tired and bloodied as he was, as methodically as a miller grinding his flour.

"Come, Mary," Wylde whispered in her ear.

Mary gave a frightened start from where she sat in the carriage. The coachman, having professed his fervent desire to remain ignorant of any duel that "might involve Mr. Harris," had withdrawn the carriage to the edge of the Harris property to await the matter's conclusion. Mary had wrapped herself in a saddle blanket and watched the wind stir among the trees. Somehow Wylde had crept up to the side of the coach, to within an inch of her cheek, without being noticed. He took her hand and helped her down from her seat. Wylde told the visibly relieved coachman "neither gentleman had further need of his service," and off the driver clattered, not even awaiting a tip.

Wylde led Mary back up the gray, sandy path to the manor's yard. He seemed in a hurry.

"What's happened?" she asked.

Wylde picked up his pace, forcing Mary to run to keep up with him.

"I'm not sure," he said between breaths. "But I think you may be needed. Over here."

Mary had seen men's wounds before, had seen their corpses, heaven knows there was no avoiding that in this world, but never had she seen a man butchered. Far was sprawled upon the lawn, drenched in his own blood. At least a dozen gashes had left his shirt in tatters. A sword was still buried in his leg. Harris had cut Far like a hog. It looked like a horrible way for a man to die. Even a man as vile as Far. But when she saw what Far had done to Harris . . .

"It's all right," Wylde held her close.

"They killed each other," Mary shook her head against his shoulder.

"No. Far still lives."

"What – how?"

"Come. Yonder is taking charge of the matter now. We'd better join him."

Mary let him lead her across the field, walking quickly over the crinkled grass, crackling weeds, and a blood-soaked patch of earth that had been trampled flat.

Yonder crouched at his partner's side and rested his hand on Far's shoulder. The sun lit Far's head with a halo, the dark strands of his matted hair extending like rays from his countenance. He breathed in labored rasps, and his eyes seemed fixed, unblinking, on the clouds above. He was bathed in blood. But he lived . . .

"Rest, my friend," said Yonder gently. "You've done exceptionally well."

"I . . . know," Far breathed, and there was, Yonder could detect, a hint of that familiar, smug smile beginning to peek through his companion's pain.

Beverley had remained as far as he could from where the contestants had fallen. He stumped up and down the bowling green's periphery, running his hands through his hair and moaning to himself. To Yonder's consternation, Beverley had apparently come to remember his duties as a second, for he plodded out to join Yonder in the center of the field. As he approached, Beverley started to make a noise.

"Th-that – Th-that-that . . ." He sputtered over and over.

"That was unfortunate." Yonder nodded without looking at him.

"L-look what he did!"

Yonder spared a glance at Beverley's late principal. Harris' body seemed as fit and angular as ever, as if it might spring up at any moment and resume the violence he had been reveling in. His clothes still looked nicely laundered, unsullied from his recent contest. The collar was nice and stiff. But all that remained above Harris' neck was a lump of flesh. The contents of what had been his head were laid out and rolled flat, like an emptied sack. Yonder acknowledged the grotesquery with a furtive condolence.

"I should say," Yonder corrected himself, "that was very unfortunate."

"It-it's *murder*, is what it was!"

"It was no such thing," Yonder replied indignantly. He arose to assume the meme of an attorney defending his client. "My principal's behavior was beyond reproach. An exemplar of the Code Duello."

"Code, my ass." Beverley braved a step closer to jab an accusing finger at Yonder. "You all murdered Stanley Harris, right here on his own property. An' I got witnesses. I'm gettin' the sheriff . . ."

"Allow me."

Yonder spun around as Wylde strode calmly toward him. Mary was close behind, pale, shaken, but resolute. With a calm detachment, Wylde stepped over the corpse of Harris, and paused to regard Beverley as one might a yapping dog or a buzzing fly. Wylde bent over, pried Harris' fingers open, and plucked up the dead man's saber for his own.

"Here, boy," Beverley started for him, "that there's your master's."

Wylde flicked the blade in the space between them, bringing Beverley to a halt. Beverley's eyes went wide.

"Nonsense." Wylde smiled. There was a malevolent, pitiless chill in Wylde's expression as he turned the blade to flash with the day's light. Beverley cringed before Wylde, but he seemed unable to run. The smile never wavered as Wylde continued, "Haven't you heard? My master's gone away. Gone away . . ."

The saber came around with a flash. Mary gasped. Yonder flinched. From where he lay, Far nodded approvingly.

A long, red arc ran the length between Beverley's left jaw and his right arm pit. The artery in his neck was pumping out blood to the rhythm of Wylde's recitation.

"Gone . . . gone . . . Gone away."

Beverley stood for almost a minute, swaying raggedly in a pool of fresh blood. Wylde let out a long, joyful laugh.

"Why, I've never done that before!" Wylde's eyes roved the length of the saber, stained with Beverley's life. "It's a splendid feeling, isn't it?"

Beverley's body fell to the ground with a lifeless thud. Wylde dropped the blade next to him. From nearby came a tired, ragged sound. It was Far.

"It does . . . grow on one," he said.

Mary came to her senses. The clerk Beverley was curled in a heap, bleeding and dead. Wylde had . . . slain him. A whirl of competing sensations came over her. Whispers with shrieks, shadow and dazzling blaze, a window and a curtain. The thoughts and images she had – was still sharing with Wylde – became blurred between her revulsion and his rapture. Mary's spirit felt as light as a feather, but her thoughts were as heavy as lead.

"Are you, are you free now?" she managed to ask Wylde.

"Free as a bird, Mary!"

With a wink, he took off in a sprint, like a hare bolting a field, over the yard, down the road, past the dead magnolia and the servants' shanty with all the fearful eyes that surely watched from within. Down the gray dirt path he raced, his long, limber legs gliding untiringly. As Mary watched, he came to the sign at the end of the path. The manor's sign that had bound him the night before. He paused there, turned around and waved back to her. To Mary's delight, he took a long step past its border, walked a slow, deliberate circle around it, and slapped the sign's surface with the back of his hand. He trotted back up the road to rejoin her.

"The chain's broken," he said huffing. "Thank Gods and Grove, that blasted chain is broken! I don't know how I can ever repay you."

Yonder responded before she could,

"We'll have a word about that shortly. *Your* Word, in fact. So do stay put. Mary, if I can prevail upon you once more for your assistance. You, too, Mr. Wylde. Captain Far needs tending to . . ."

CHAPTER TWENTY

*"The garb we wear in Doldrums should not be cast
aside lightly. For the realm itself is flesh and bone. That is
all there is here. And Custom is our only costume."*
—Wherestone's *Commentaries on Custom*, page 111

With no other option for shelter at hand, and no one
to prevent their entry – for the servants had all
long since run away – Yonder decided they would
repair to the Harris Manor house. It seemed to him a
relatively minor imposition on the late gentleman, given
what he had recently suffered. Wylde and Mary helped to
carry Far, who was in no condition to walk, across the yard
and up the creaking steps that led to the front doors and into
the manor's parlor. It was, just as Wylde had warned, a
sparse and cheerless abode. Besides being a militiaman,
Harris, it seemed, was also a lifelong bachelor, and his tastes
in furnishings, without the warming influence of a wife or
children, tended toward the stoic. At first, Yonder wondered
whether he had stumbled into a monk's cell.

Inside he found a cold fireplace with the stump of a

candle melted on the mantle, a table with a lamp, a threadbare sofa, and two mismatched chairs. Dirty, gray windows kept the daylight at bay. Not a rug or carpet covered the dusty wood-planked floor. That was fortunate, as Far was unconscious and still bled quite freely.

"Lay him there," Yonder pointed to the sofa. He scanned the room doubtfully. "Mr. Wylde, can I presume you would know if needle, thread, and bandages may be found somewhere in this house?"

"You can," Wylde answered brightly, "and they may. I shall fetch them at once."

Off he flew up a flight of stairs and when he returned he had with him a black leather bag. In it was a mound of linen, a tiny needle, and a spool of black thread.

"Crude," said Wylde, laying them alongside Far, "but clean."

There was an uncomfortable silence, as Yonder looked at Wylde expectantly.

"I don't suppose you could, um . . ."

Wylde's forehead crinkled, his eyebrows curled with indignance.

"Surely you don't expect me to touch his person." He made a face at Far. "He's a mess."

"Well, I haven't the skill."

Mary let out an exasperated gasp. "Oh, for God's sake, I'll nurse him!"

Yonder expressed his deepest, sincerest gratitude. He had no doubt that Captain Far could not be in better hands than hers. As Mary began to untangle the linens, and thread her needle, Yonder led Wylde into a darkened hallway where he could speak to him in private.

It was a narrow space, as cold as a crypt, with peeling wallpaper and a stuffed buffalo's head that hung crookedly from a plaque at the far end.

"Now my friend," Yonder began, "my traveling brother, it is time to settle accounts."

The joy that had been radiating from Wylde's face, the exultation of a man who had been freed from prison, dimmed for just a moment.

"You hold my Word," Wylde acknowledged.

"I do. And now I shall call upon it."

Yonder studied Wylde closely. He had made no attempt to flee, had drawn no portals, had not attempted to disappear; but, he couldn't, as Yonder knew perfectly well, for he was bound by his Word. As surely as he had been bound by his unwitting submission into slavery. The bond of servitude had been broken when Harris gave his word to free Wylde over his dead body (which Far had dutifully obliged). Wylde's Bond to Yonder, however, had yet to be fulfilled. And it was time to collect the debt.

"So what do you want?" Wylde sighed. "I already told you, I have nothing in this realm."

"There's one thing you have," Yonder lifted a knowing finger, "I'm sure of it. Something you would never leave lying about. Or let be taken."

Wylde stared at him incredulously. The air in the hallway grew thick, and the light seemed to fail. Which suited Yonder's purpose. He pressed Wylde with a relentless glare.

"You were given a token of affection not long ago. A lock of hair. From a certain lady with whom we are both acquainted."

A startled gasp slipped from Wylde. His eyes rounded with surprise.

"Do not deny it," Yonder continued. "I know all about the affair."

"How—" Wylde started. But he composed himself. His face displayed a gamut of emotions, like an actor practicing his craft – shock, indignation, guile, anger, ennui and, at last, resignation. He dipped his head, and Yonder took it as a salute, of sorts. "All right," Wylde breathed. "I don't know how you could have . . . But, yes. I have it."

A warm glow began to spread inside Yonder. He felt his face warm for the first time in days. It was uncouth, he knew, to show one's triumph in dealings, but he could not restrain the smile that spread across his lips. At long last, after all he had gone through, despite the turns and wiles of Doldrums and Custom, he had what he was after . . . He steeled his voice with resolve.

"I want it."

The poor devil, Yonder thought. He looked tormented, and no doubt he was, for what Yonder had just asked of him was no small trifle. A lock of a lover's hair held power, everyone knew that. And a Traveling Fellow never knew when he might have need of power. Still, his reticence struck Yonder as somewhat overwrought. Wylde stood before him wringing his hands, shaking his head, and put forth such an unhappy performance that one might have forgotten the man had been liberated from slavery not a quarter of an hour ago. Apparently, his gratitude was as fickle as his taste in lovers.

"Who told you?" Wylde charged.

Yonder would be unwavering.

"That is a confidential matter between my client and me. Suffice to say, I know you have the lock of hair and," he paused and raised a triumphant eyebrow, "I know you have it on your person."

"You do?" Wylde's eyes darted fearfully. The fellow regarded Yonder as if he were some kind of a sorcerer.

"Yes," Yonder continued. "Only a fool would have kept such a priceless treasure in plain sight while traveling. And you're no fool." He leaned forward, narrowing his eyes. "You kept it safe, on your person – on your true person. I'm certain of it, so don't deny it."

Wylde let out a long moan. His hand went reflexively behind his head. "You don't understand. This is . . . special to me."

"I'm sure it is." Yonder nodded.

Tears, as clear and sparkling as diamonds, began to brim from Wylde's eyes.

"I-I never would have survived without this hair. It . . . sustained me. I know it did. It's what got me through my ordeal, how I survived this damned Doldrums air."

"The dead drear fare. Yes." Yonder waved impatiently and felt his lungs seize from the chill in the hall. When he finished coughing, he continued, "I'm familiar with the malady. No doubt the hair was a saving grace for you."

"I held it every night." A faraway expression came over Wylde and his voice seemed to drift. "In the magnolia, when everyone was asleep, I would – I would hold it, sing to it, warm myself in its light . . ." With a burst of renewed resolution, he crossed his arms across his chest. "No. It was given to me. As a token of love for me. It's useless to you. You'll gain no power from it. Ask for something else. Anything."

It was Yonder's turn to show his own resolve.

"I have no intention of using the lock for myself. But I will have it. As I have your Word . . ."

With that, Yonder drew in a deep breath, though it stung every inch within his chest, and as he exhaled, he began to search in his mind for the Word Wylde had given him. A smoke tendril slipped from his mouth; dragging behind it was Wylde's Word. Like a great, heavy chain, clanking up from the depths where Yonder held it, an anchor aweigh. One that Yonder could cast upon the man it was tied to, if he must.

He began to speak aloud Wylde's words, "*Je te donne ma Parole. Je t'apporterai tout ce que je peux.* I give you my

Word I will bring to you whatever is in my power to bring to you."

Yonder felt Wylde grasp his lapels.

"No, no, no. Stop it, I beg you." Wylde started to pat down the coat cloth he had just rumpled. "No need for that." His face drew into a pained smile. "We're brothers, after all."

Yonder let the chain of Wylde's Word slip back into the depths again.

"So we are," he agreed. "But I must hold you to your Word, brother. Give me the hair, and you're free to go." Yonder lifted his heavy head and tucked his fists into his hips; it was the best show of authority he could manage. "So let's have it."

This time, there was no contortion of emotions, no fretting, no feigning. Wylde simply let his chin fall to his chest, reached around to the back of his neck, and pulled. There was a sudden, dazzling glow, as if from a firework, followed by a steady, pulsing light. It seemed to hang in the air just above Wylde's head like a miasma, a fog of purple incandescence. It, too, was pierced when a strand of white brightness toppled out.

Between his forefinger and thumb Wylde held slender threads of sunlight, pure, blinding, golden as a summer's noon sun. They wavered in his grasp for a moment before he hastily pressed them into Yonder's outstretched palm. Yonder squelched the light and shoved it deep into his coat's outer pocket. Wylde spun on his heel and stormed off without a word.

For a few minutes, Yonder stood in the drafty, narrow hallway of Harris Manor, patting the little bundle in his pocket in disbelief. He let the smile spread into a self-satisfied grin. He had never been one to bask in his life's triumphs. In moments of honesty, he would acknowledge they had been rather meager. But this was one worth relishing. He had successfully prosecuted a replevin. He had retrieved his client's property, intact and without loss, from a Traveling Fellow on the run in Doldrums. And he had done it under the most trying circumstances by a deadline that bordered on the farcical. Quite an accomplishment, indeed. Since no one else was around, Yonder indulged in a little titter.

When he had waited what he thought a suitable length of time for Wylde to have taken his leave, he reached for another coat pocket by his breast. He carefully ripped open the stitches Mary had sewn to keep it shut and felt the two items he had kept hidden within. The retainer was the first thing his fingers came across, but he reached past it, and clasped what he was searching for.

A smooth bit of metal with a handle. Jane Otherly's silver bell. He waited another minute, brought it forth, and with a profound feeling of accomplishment, shook it hard a-ringing.

For a man who seemed perpetually annoyed and prone to offense, Mary found Far to be a fairly obliging patient. Certainly preferable to the handful she had worked with before she became a fortune-teller. No ranting screams or thrashing about. Not even a curse. He lay still on the couch with his arms at his side, breathing steadily. Every so often, he would wander toward the periphery of consciousness and murmur some disturbing utterance. One made Mary shudder, as it concerned skinning Mr. Harris' corpse for a flag of some sort. Otherwise, Far suffered the constant prick of Mary's needle and thread without so much as a stir. Sewing the gashes in his body closed had been no more difficult than mending a garment. He endured his pain impassively, quietly – not at all like a man.

What surprised Mary most, however, was how quickly

his flesh seemed to be healing. All the wounds she had ever seen were red, angry-looking things that would stay swollen for days until they healed, or, more often than not, until they become infected. But Far's skin folded neatly in place wherever she worked, as clean and white as a bedsheet. His bleeding had all but stopped. A quarter of an hour ago she had counted him as a dead man. However, she no longer wondered whether he would survive his duel with Harris, but how quickly he would be back on his feet.

She had just started winding the last length of linen around Far's stomach, when she felt a sudden anguish that caused her to stop short. Her heart sank in her chest. A trickle of tears came unbidden. It was as if she had been suddenly transported to a funeral and listened to the earth shoveled on a casket. Of one of her children.

The bandage fell from her hand onto Far's bare chest. She kept it from rolling off, and quickly tied off the knot. Her vision blurred. A sob shook her.

Far's eyes fluttered open. He started to speak, "What's . . . the matter . . . with you?"

"The window," Mary replied softly. It was the only explanation.

She felt Wylde entering the parlor. His footfalls had made no sound when he returned from the hallway, but she sensed his presence. Mary was on her feet in an instant.

"What's happened?" she asked him.

Wylde looked strained. And profoundly sad. But he tried to make a kind face.

"Nothing you need concern yourself over, my dear."

It was a poor deflection, and Mary took it as a reproach. As if sensing the offense he had given, Wylde reluctantly explained.

"Your companion – that is, Mr. Yonder – extracted a very high price from me."

"What did you give him?"

The loss shining behind his eyes was almost more than Mary could bear.

"Nothing you could understand," he said simply. Glancing at the couch behind her, he changed the subject.

"He looks much improved."

Far was asleep, his pale, bandaged body breathing steadily in the gray twilight that filtered into the room.

"Yes," she said. "Listen, I'm sorry for – for whatever he's taken from you."

She felt Wylde's hands caressing her shoulders, gently supporting her. He gazed fondly into her eyes.

"You've nothing to be sorry about. What he took – was freely bargained for. I gave him my Word. And he procured my freedom. And now I'm free, Mary. Truly free. I shall travel again."

The feeling of joy, hard-won and well earned, began to percolate from him like a warming fire. Mary wiped away her tears and smiled.

"I have you to thank for that," he said softly.

"I'm glad," she said, and meant it. Though she knew, without asking, that he would be leaving her. That this man whose thoughts and feelings she had held as her own would never return. It was strange, but she found the prospect more sweet than bitter. Like setting a deer free from a pen. An idea occurred to her.

"You know," she began, "maybe I can get back what you want."

"It's no use stealing it." He shook his head. "It must be freely given to be of any use."

"No, I wouldn't do that. It's just, well, Yonder is in my debt, too. He owes me one crown, six shillings, two reales, a reichsthaler, and eight and a half dollars."

Wylde chuckled to himself.

"You Doldrums folk with your coins and bills. Like children playing make believe. Alas, I cannot fathom that

Yonder would part with something as precious as he now holds in trade for your people's guilders. Your money is worthless to us."

Mary thought carefully and began to sense that Wylde's certainty on that point may have been more superficial than he realized, even naive. Bills and coins held a kind of power. One that Yonder had learned to make use of.

"You know more about your people than I do," she allowed, "but when it came to it, and I pressed him, Yonder gave me his Word for my money."

Wylde's eyebrows rose with incredulity.

"Really? You hold his – his Word? That can't be . . ."

But before she could reply, there was a blinding flash of blue light that burst through the windows and filled the parlor. It was followed by a boom that shook the glass panes and rattled the sashes. Wylde raced to the windowsill to look outside. Mary was right behind him.

The grime and dirt accumulated on the glass was thick, but she could still see clearly enough outside. She scanned the grounds of Harris Manor, but nothing seemed amiss. There was the dull, colorless heath. The slaves' cabin on the verge of tumbling down. The winding silt road. It was Wylde who spotted it first.

"That's strange." He pressed his fingertip against the glass pane and pointed to the magnolia tree. Its twisted, marbled bark was smoldering. A trail of smoke wafted above it and disappeared into the air. At the bottom of the trunk, just above a sprawl of roots, Mary saw – what she could only think of as a door. Its outline was a band of fading light, shimmering in the wood, fading with the smoke. She heard Wylde observe off-handedly, "Someone was in a hurry."

Yonder strolled the length of the hallway, occupied with

the pleasant dilemma of how he should present Otherly with her lock of hair, whether he should indulge in the flourish of a long, climactic story that would culminate with the hair's presentation, or have it out at the ready when she arrived, accompanied perhaps by a suitably dramatic pose. Both options had much to commend them. So long as she was sufficiently impressed, and impelled. His client had been quite anxious about the return of her token. Perhaps, Yonder began to wonder, with his present run of good fortune, he could extract a further concession from her. As it stood, Otherly was bound by her Word to commend his name and offer a good report to her Majesty on his behalf. Perhaps she could be persuaded to go a step further? The lengthier presentation. That would better serve his purpose.

He made his way into the manor's parlor, but his musings came to an abrupt cessation with the unexpected sight of Wylde. Standing by Mary, the two of them gazed through the window.

"Why are you still here?" Yonder demanded.

Wylde regarded him as one who had just suffered an affront on top of an offense, while Mary practically snarled.

Yonder quickly recollected himself.

"Forgive me," Yonder said. "I was simply – surprised to see you still here. I thought you would have made for the first oak tree you could find. Leave this terrible place behind. I know I would, if I could." He tried to sound deprecating, but it rang hollow, even in his own ears. Wylde's expression turned imperiously cold. He replied with a level voice.

"I was taking my leave of Miss Faulkner before I depart. Like a gentleman." He gestured toward the window. "When someone drew a door. In a magnolia. A dead one," he added meaningfully.

"Eh?" Yonder glanced through the glass at the burnt trunk and the haze of brown smoke that surrounded it.

"Well, it is the closest tree."

"Were you expecting a visitor here?"

Yonder's stomach churned. He should have checked to make sure Wylde was gone before he summoned his client. Once again, his over-eagerness had caused mischief.

"Look," Yonder approached him and spoke hurriedly. "You're free now. No need to tarry here. Off you go." He reached for his arm, hoping to usher him away. "I'm sure there's a back door—"

"Unhand me, sir." Wylde shook him off easily. He straightened his threadbare shirt. "May I assume the lady I see walking up the steps has some connection to my lock of hair?"

"Your what?" Mary asked. She looked from Wylde to Yonder. "Hair? Was that what this was all about? Why I've gone through all this hell? So you could get some damned hair?"

Yonder let out a groan.

"My brother," he pleaded to Wylde, "I beg you, leave. Out the back door, while there's still time. It will be – very awkward if you don't."

Wylde folded his arms defiantly. Mary joined him.

There was a knock on the front door.

And again, Yonder watched his plans go awry.

Jane Otherly burst through the doorway of Harris Manor without a pause, or a greeting, or even an acknowledgement of Yonder's invitation to come inside. She had been ranting since her arrival and apparently had no inclination to stem her displeasure for the sake of pleasantries.

"What a miserable, execrable dog's run of a place," she hissed as she stomped through the doorway. "Not an oak for a mile! Utterly wretched portals. Worse than that Boston town. If it weren't for – oh!" She paused when she noticed Wylde. Her eyes went wide for a brief moment, and the wrinkles around her mouth curled.

Oddly, it was not a scorned lover's indignation that Yonder read in Otherly's expression, but something more akin to . . . delight. Of an especially cruel variety. While for Wylde's part, although his bottom lip quivered, and his eyes glazed with shock, he did not at all seem the image of an embarrassed cad. Instead he looked more like a gentleman who finds himself disgusted by the unannounced intrusion of a vulgar street woman. Very strange, indeed.

Fortunately, Mary, whom Yonder had quite forgotten about, found her voice and posed the inevitable inquiry, and it served to break the unspoken tension in the air.

"Who is this?" she asked.

"Otherly," replied Yonder distractedly. "Or I should say, Lady Otherly. Lady Otherly, this is Mary Faulkner of Doldrums . . . I believe you're already acquainted with Mr. Wylde."

Otherly brushed past Mary, paying her no more mind than if she were a house cat, but lingered near Wylde. He gaped at her with undisguised loathing.

"I thought Mr. Wylde had already departed when I rang," Yonder apologized. "I hope you do not find his presence . . . uncomfortable."

"Why, not at all!" Otherly sang, and Yonder nearly stumbled from surprise. She fixed Wylde with a contemptuous glare and, again not bothering to wait for an invitation, she strode straightaway into the manor's parlor, a set of satin black dress skirts fluttering in her wake. Seeing Far sprawled on the couch, she took one of the remaining chairs and sat down. "I'm surprised you didn't have to kill him," she observed in a conversational manner. "I had assumed you would." She paused as her face clouded. "You didn't ring without having gotten it from him?"

"Of course not." Yonder shook his head. He glanced at Wylde again, wishing with all his might that the fool would come to his senses and just go away. And if he took Mary with him, so much the better. But for whatever reason Wylde seemed intent on remaining, gritting his teeth and huffing to himself, not at all caring that his presence cast a terrible pall over Yonder's moment. As Yonder was in no condition to force the fellow to leave (and Otherly seemed quite content to conduct her business under his nose), there was nothing to be done but press on. Yonder cleared his throat officiously and began the speech he had started composing in the hallway, recounting the sundry difficulties he had had to overcome, the twists and turns of fate, the exemplary service he had rendered that would merit the additional favor he would eventually ask of her, but Otherly cut him short.

"I can see with my own eyes you've had a time of it," she said uncaringly. "You're as pale as a corpse." Otherly craned her neck to look at Far, and the sight of him as an invalid was apparently not displeasing to her. "As is your partner. Did he die?"

"I don't believe so."

"Oh." She shrugged. "Anyway, I do not require a drawn-out recounting of your travails. Just tell me plainly without the lawyer's rigmarole. Do you have it?"

"I have it right here."

Yonder reached into his outer pocket and felt the tiny bundle of golden strands he had just taken from Wylde. The lock of hair was light, soft as down, but with a solid firmament, almost like a spider's web. As he curled his fingers around the lock's length, he found his hand seemed to become fond of its touch. There was a warmth he hadn't noticed when he had taken it from Wylde. It began to spread from his fingertips to his knuckles, up the length of his hand

and arm. The tightness in his lungs loosened and the constant, plodding ache that had plagued his temples subsided. Yonder drew a breath of air, and for the first time in days, it was whole and deep, without any pain. His eyes began to see more clearly. Slowly, reluctantly, Yonder brought out the lock of hair.

The golden glow filled the space of the parlor, illuminating every crack and crevasse, and revealing the hidden-most thoughts within each person in the gathering. Yonder's eyes took each one's measure in a quick succession.

Far's face showed pain and struggle – and indomitability.

Mary's was lit with an almost childlike wonder.

Wylde's was filled with horror.

And Otherly . . . Hers was a naked coveting.

Yonder started to extend his hand to her.

"No!" Wylde shouted. Everyone turned to him. He paced back and forth, gesticulating with his hands, his eyes never breaking from the lock of hair. As close as he was, and as much as he may have desired it, Yonder knew that Wylde was powerless to take it back from him. He had given it freely. He could still make a scene, however.

"You cannot give that to her!"

"It is mine now," Yonder answered. "I can do what I wish with it."

"But you never told me you were going to give it to *her!*" He struck the side of his fist against a wall breaking a piece of plaster. "I'd have stayed in chains if I knew you were going to hand my dearest treasure to that creature."

"I was not at liberty to divulge my client's confidences," Yonder sniffed. "I had given my Word to keep her affair secret."

Mary seemed to come out of her daydream. She tried to calm Wylde's distemper.

"What's the matter?" she asked him. "I mean – it's very

pretty. But it's just some strands of hair. Isn't it?"

"You don't understand," Wylde buried his face in his hands. "It is . . . beautiful."

"Enough of this," Otherly snarled. She rose from her chair. Her hand trembled with excitement as she opened her palm for the hair. "Give it to me," she commanded.

Yonder hesitated. With each passing moment, he felt his health restoring, his head clearing, his senses growing sharper, and with it, a vague, but mounting worry – that something was not quite right.

"Give it to me," she repeated, her gray eyes smoldering like storm clouds, "and I will sing your praises to Her Majesty. I'll flatter you to the heavens. When I'm done whispering in her ear, she'll welcome you home herself."

Yonder felt a desperate hand grasp his elbow, his body whirled around. Panicked, pale, Wylde's brow was doused with sweat.

"Is that the Bargain you made – with *her*? Don't be a fool, man! Don't you know who she's—"

There was a sudden flash of black, the rumple of silk cloth, and a thunderous clap. Wylde flew across the length of the parlor, his body smashed against the far wall, and he slumped to the floor. Mary lunged after Otherly with a cry.

"You bitch—"

The old woman flung her other hand as if she were flicking away a horsefly. It struck Mary across the face with the boom of a cannon shot. A mane of hair and a homespun dress somersaulted through the air. Mary landed with a thud next to Wylde.

When he turned back to Otherly, she had her fingertips steepled before her chest.

"Now," she said mildly, "give me my hair."

There was a low, painful moan from the floor.

"It's – not – hers" Wylde panted.

"Quiet!" hissed Otherly.

In that moment, with a sudden, inexplicable lucidity, Yonder came to a terrible realization. He let out a sharp breath. His hand shot inside of his coat to the hidden pocket he had ripped open earlier. A frantic rummage, and his fingers brushed against the other item he had kept hidden in the cloth space. His enameled box. He fumbled the lid open. Inside was another piece of hair, a single strand. Otherly's retainer. He snatched it out and held it up next to Wylde's lock.

Where the one was radiant with the gold of morning's promise, Otherly's strand of hair shone scarlet. Dark and red as a murdered man's blood.

He had been fooled.

Utterly fooled.

Yonder looked up, but he could scarcely see Otherly any longer, for in place of the prim, dour spinster in black silk skirts, there was a presence. A shadow fell over Yonder.

"I beg your pardon, Lady Otherly," Yonder addressed the darkness with the most dignified formality he could muster, "but I fear you've not been entirely honest with me, as your attorney."

A darkness rose where Otherly had stood and slowly expanded until it touched the ends of the room. The meager daylight from the parlor window seemed to bend, and bow before the terrible shade. Only the golden hair, and Otherly's desire for it, shone through, two flames contending against one another. A voice like flint scraping against a granite stone answered Yonder from within the void. It was Otherly's.

"Finally caught on, have you?"

"Yes . . ." It came out as a sigh. "I have."

But that was the extent of Yonder's self-censure. A spark of pride still smoked within his heart, growing hotter in his belly and stiffening his spine. He forced his chin up, fixed his collar, and fashioned his expression into the righteous (but impotent) condescension of culture over vulgarity. He had been duped, but so long as he could still comport himself, he would not be deprived of his honor.

"It appears, Madam," Yonder regarded both strands of hair, "that the hair I've labored to replevin for you was never yours to begin with. I can see it plainly now. Whose hair is this?"

"Give it to me!" Otherly shrieked. "Give – it – to – *me!*"

The whole house shook from Otherly's wrath. The few hangings Harris kept on the walls crashed to the floor. A cloud of dust and broken pieces of ceiling fell after them. From within the shadow, two grasping claws stretched forth. They reached for Yonder's throat. He stood tall before her, unflinching.

"I cannot give you property that does not belong to you," he replied. "That would be unethical."

"Give it to me or die."

Her fingers clamped fast around Yonder's neck. Like vipers, they slowly spread the length of his neck, freezing his skin, squeezing the life from him . . .

At the moment he thought would be his last in this life, the fingers were gone. Yonder bent over, gasping for air and clutching his burning throat. The room was still cast in a haze, but the shadow had coalesced into something between form and light, a dark, smoky substance that wore an infuriated mask of Jane Otherly.

"How *dare* you?!" she roared.

Far had her in a bear hug. His powerful arms grappled her shifting shape, pulling her back to the corner of the room. Half-naked, bedraggled and bandaged, but as wondrously fierce as ever Yonder had seen him. Every one of Far's muscles was taut with strain, and the veins on the side of his head throbbed.

The prim, elderly lady was a tempest, swirling farther and farther out from what had been her former shape. A hurricane unleashed itself from the elements. A column of darkness launched from its center and struck Far's face with the force of a battering ram. Far grunted, fell to his knees, but somehow he held his grip. She would overpower him any moment, though.

Wylde leaped into the fray.

"Are you mad?" Wylde screamed at her. A shadowed hand buffeted Wylde's head. He almost succumbed to the blow, but he was able to seize what remained of Otherly's form in his arms and hold on. The two of them, Wylde and Far, were like men trying to wrestle the waves of an ocean.

Wylde yelled at the pulsating shade, "Put your form back on! Put it on before you kill us all! Mary, run—"

Arcs of lightning streaked across a pulsating penumbra surrounding a shadow so deep, so bottomless, it hurt Yonder's eyes to look upon it. Violet flames twined like cobras, burning the walls, the floors, the ceiling of the manor to cinders. A chandelier broke free, fell, and incinerated in the inferno before it hit the ground. Yonder felt the floor pitch, as if he was at sea again. A maniacal voice roared from within the maelstrom.

"Give it to me!"

The storm hurled Far to the ground. He tried to rise, wobbled, and sunk back to his knees.

"The fire's too wild," he groaned. "She'll explode . . ."

Yonder knew what he had to do. But a pique of vengeance made him pause just long enough to make sure his client could see him do it. The strand of hair was still clutched tight in his hand. He lifted Otherly's retainer before him. Two slits within the darkness, Otherly's eyes, narrowed with suspicion.

"What are you doing?" she demanded.

"Lady Otherly," Yonder said, "your retainer is forfeit. Go hence from this realm. Now. Away with you."

He pinched the other end of the glowing red strand of

hair, pulled it tight, and snapped it in two.

"No!"

There was a burst of light.

A last rush of wind.

Otherly was gone, without an echo, without a trace of her passing, leaving only the silence of her absence to fill what remained of the manor.

The three of them, Yonder, Mary, and Wylde, walked together alongside a shoal, the breeze at their backs. The leafless brush stirred, and the sound of the ocean's breakers rose and fell rhythmically, like a pulse. The sun shone across the gray landscape, lending it a stoic beauty that had seemed hidden. They had left Harris Manor behind them. Far discovered the late Mr. Harris' private store of whiskey in a cellar, indicated he had had enough exercise for one day and would prefer convalescing indoors by himself.

Mary was glad of it, and she wished Yonder had followed suit. It would have been perfect if she could have had Wylde to herself.

But no, that would be asking too much. She smiled to herself resignedly and remembered a piece of advice she often dispensed in fortune readings. One should never set perfection against the good. And this was very good. Not even Yonder's noisy bustling could ruin the enchantment of this stroll.

She walked leisurely next to Wylde, sometimes slipping her hand through his waiting arm, while other times, she simply stole a glance that always happened to coincide with his. They made for a copse of trees that was still another quarter of a mile away.

"Then, am I to understand," Yonder asked Wylde, "that you were never Otherly's lover?"

344

"Certainly not," Wylde scoffed. "I only make love to beautiful people."

He regarded Mary appraisingly and, she sensed, with satisfaction. A feeling she shared. One of his hands lingered down her side and trailed across one of her thighs. It made her feel as warm as an oven. She gave his arm a fond squeeze.

"Indeed," Wylde continued, "I only knew that vile woman by her reputation – which is rather mixed."

"Oh?" Yonder seemed surprised. "I thought she was highly placed in the Queen's court."

"She was. But only so that she could remain under Her Majesty's eye." Wylde came to a halt. "But surely you knew her connection?"

"I . . ." It was apparent from the dumbfounded silence that followed, he did not.

"Oh, my poor brother." Wylde shook his head and clapped Yonder's shoulder. "If only you had been a little more forthcoming, if only you had told me of your true aim when we spoke at the lodge. I could have saved you a great deal of trouble."

Mary could tell Yonder was about to become indignant, though he tried his best to hide it.

"As a lawyer," he replied evenly, "I couldn't discuss the matter with you. It had been told to me in confidence, and I gave my Word."

A mocking grin was spread across Wylde's face. He laughed in a way that reminded Mary of a precocious child who had just caught his father telling a fib. Wylde wagged a scolding finger at Yonder.

"So you had no compunction about lying, cheating, and using my enslavement to wrest my hair from me, but you drew a line at divulging a stranger's chit-chat?"

"Now, see here—" Yonder huffed.

"Oh, he's only playing." Mary jabbed Yonder hard enough to make him wince.

"I am, I am," Wylde laughed. "It's just such a splendidly absurd mistake. You see, dear brother, that woman who called herself Jane Otherly, your client – is the Mad Queen's cousin."

The little color that had been slowly returning in Yonder's jowls drained away in an instant. Mary watched his thick bottom lip turn white and quiver like a carp on a fishing hook.

"Then . . . I-I was working for—"

"You were working for Her Majesty's enemies."

They resumed their walk, Yonder hanging back a pace, his head bowed from dejection. Wylde, though, quickly became magnanimous.

"But you couldn't have known," he said, "all this transpired after your banish— After your departure from Her Majesty's court. With the Mad Queen dead and her son absconded, there was only one relation of Her Feral Majesty that still remained, a spinster cousin of absolutely no account, your Lady Otherly. A shrewish old bitty who found herself with no friends and no patrons. So she entreated Her Majesty, begged her before all her courtiers, to take her under her protection. Which the Good Queen did, though everyone knew it was only because she had no choice. Otherly had never taken up arms against Her Majesty, so it would have been very bad form to kill her. But with the Mad Prince on the loose again, it would have been unwise to leave her to her own affairs."

Yonder nodded sagaciously.

"If you must live with a scorpion, keep it under a glass."

"Precisely. She made her a lady-in-waiting."

"Very sensible." Yonder became contemplative. "But then," he wondered aloud, "whose hair is this? Who gave it to you?"

"Sir, I am a gentleman." Wylde sniffed. "I am not at liberty to divulge the confidences of my lovers." He let the silence hang as they walked. After a while he spoke again, this time in a quiet, confiding tone. "But you're a clever fellow. Surely you can guess."

All of a sudden, Yonder's face lit with realization.

"Her Majesty!"

True to his honor, Wylde would not confirm Yonder's guess. Neither did he so much as make a peep to deny it.

"That's why she was so intent on obtaining it," Yonder continued. "Not to restore a part of herself she had given up, but to steal a part of Her Majesty that had been freely given. And if I had given it freely to her, she could have held it over Her Majesty, used it against her, perhaps even destroyed it. The fiend!"

Mary had been so enraptured with Wylde's presence, she had only been vaguely following their conversation. But there was something she wished to know.

"What's so special about your hair?"

Wylde smiled affectionately at her.

"It's essence," he explained, "it's you – a part of your true form. And when such a thing is given freely to another, it can hold great power."

"Yes, and Custom—" Yonder started as if he was about to begin another one of his lectures.

"Custom has nothing to do with it," Wylde cut him off. "It is true everywhere, under every law. It simply is."

"I was about to say," Yonder continued, "that Custom has no effect on the giving or receiving of such tokens. They are expressions of love," he said the word in apparent distaste, "which works by its own set of laws and statutes. I don't profess to understand them in the least. An impenetrable mess, if you ask me . . ."

Mary held Wylde's hand and walked the final steps by the shoal until at last they arrived at the edge of the little wood. A meager collection of maples, pines, brambles, and a lone, stately oak tree. Its bark reflected a soft, yellow glow.

"It's still a pretty thing," Yonder observed, tossing the lock absently in his palm. "But I wonder if Otherly didn't overestimate its transferability. Or longevity."

A revelation came upon Mary in that instant as a ray of sunlight. Though she scarcely grasped a tenth part of who these two men were, where they came from, or what they spoke about, Mary felt an overwhelming certainty on one point.

"I'm ready to be repaid," she announced to Yonder.

"What?"

"Your debt to me. I'm calling it in. You gave me your Word, remember?"

"Yes. But, Mary, I-I don't have any of your money here. It's all in Boston. As soon as we return to our offices, I'll settle our account. I'll pay you in gold if you like."

"No," she shook her head. "I don't want money. I want that," she pointed straight to the hair. "My repayment is that lock of hair."

Yonder's face pinched in disbelief.

"Do you have any idea what this is?" he squealed. "What it's worth?"

"I do, actually. A much better idea than you have."

A drop of moisture touched Mary's ear. She looked up as Wylde wept quietly. Mary brought her hand to his eyes, touched them each dry, and continued.

"I know that it will become worthless if you try to keep it. Look. It's dying in your hands already. Because the woman who gave it never loved you. She loved him."

She and Wylde watched as Yonder contemplated her words and the prize he still held. He chewed on his gums and rocked back and forth a while. The breeze ruffled his hair and coat. He was the picture of a learned mind baffled by the workings of the heart. Men like Yonder never understood such things, and Mary could think of no way to explain them. Wylde was right – some things simply are.

They stood in silence for a long while at the edge of the wood, until the quiet seemed to become a fourth member of their little group. The hair that hung limply from Yonder's grasp looked ordinary, plain, not unlike any other snippet of hair that might have been locked away in an attic drawer. An old, family memento whose story had long since been forgotten. Yonder sighed.

"You know, I think you may be right, Mary." He studied the blonde strands. "Whatever power was in this, it seems to be gone. Damndest thing. No doubt it's Custom's doing . . ."

Yonder went up to Wylde and dropped the lock of hair into the other's hand with all the ceremony of paying a coin to the grocer.

"Here," he said. With a meaningful look at Mary, he added. "I've now fulfilled my Word to you. We are, as they say, square."

"Yes," she replied. "We are."

Of course, Wylde was too well bred to celebrate the return of one lover's token when he was still in the presence of another. He discretely returned the lock to his shirt, close to his heart, his face beaming like the heavens though he tried his best to hide it. Mary could only smile.

"Mr. Wylde," Yonder began haltingly, "as you are in the Queen's good graces, when you return . . . if you could give a word on my behalf, and Far's, any good word at all, it would be most appreciated. I would love to come home . . ."

Wylde responded with an enigmatic expression that not even Mary could begin to interpret. His mouth drew tight, and his eyes seemed to find nothing they wished to remain fixed upon. He actually fidgeted, which Mary found particularly droll. Wylde muttered what was obviously an uncomfortable admission.

"I should like nothing better than to help you. But,

um . . . right now, well, I fear my recommendation may do you more harm than good. I'm afraid I no longer enjoy Her Majesty's favor. She is a bit irritated with me for the moment."

"What happened?"

"Well . . . one day she gave me her hair. The next day she asked for my hand . . ." Wylde held out both of his lithe and lovely hands as if to show their helplessness.

"I see," Yonder's shoulders sank an inch.

"You understand, Yonder. You're a Traveling Fellow. What was I to do? Marry her? Spend the rest of my days in court, in a cage?" Wylde shuddered. "It was an unfortunate misunderstanding of intentions."

The laughter came rolling out of Mary like a river, and was quickly taken up by Wylde, and even Yonder's serious mouth cracked a smirk.

"You're a cad," she said and thumped Wylde's chest playfully. "A beautiful cad. But a cad." Heedless of Yonder, she slipped her hand behind Wylde's head, brought his lips to her, and kissed him passionately. The heady scent of violet and lilac, and the thrum of his heartbeat, and the coverlet ruffle of the ocean breeze filled her head, made her tremble, but she held him fast, until they were both almost breathless.

Still holding her hands in his, he stepped back and made a courtly bow.

"My Lady of Doldrums," he called her, "upon that perfect note, I will now bid you adieu. Though it pains me. If I am ever in this realm again, I pray you'll allow me to call upon you."

"Of course," Mary smiled. With her window into him, she could see his intentions, his desires, read them like the words of a book. He would flutter with the breeze, wherever it led him, for all his days. Perhaps one of those days if it happened to lead him to Boston again, he would call upon her. Which for Mary was a good, if not entirely perfect, prospect to think about.

Wylde kissed each of her hands in turn, stood to his full height and said farewell to Yonder. As Mary watched, he held out his hand to the oak tree and made a curious gesture. He stretched forth his finger and traced a square in the bark.

The edges of where he traced began to shimmer a faint backlit glow. He gave the square a push, and it became a doorway. Shadows and lights swirled within its space, stars whooshed by, clouds passed, while the bark outside of the square's boundaries looked just as it had before, as if nothing unusual were there at all. Wylde crouched to fit within the space of his door, he cast a final, tender glance at Mary, and slipped through to whatever lay on the other side.

There was the sound of a door clanking shut, the portal disappeared, and it became an old tree again. A white oak rooted in the dirt of a cold Virginia coast, surrounded by scrub. The moment the door shut, Mary heard another sound.

The window in her mind had closed. What she had thought was a curse was gone, and its absence left her feeling – empty. The breeze cut through her clothes and made her shiver. She looked over at Yonder.

He stared at the tree longingly.

Mary's gaze fell to her hands. They were still clenched from when she had been holding Wylde's. Dirty, scabbed, plain-looking. Slowly, her fingers opened, and in her palm, slipped there in secret by her lover, was a token.

A single strand of his hair caught the sunlight like a pulsing ember, bright, gleaming like the feather of a peacock.

EPILOGUE

"It was while I was on sabbatical from my law practice and visiting the realm of Doldrums that I happened upon an area of study that was so bereft of critical analysis, so neglected in serious thought (and left so thoroughly muddled by one of my brethren), I resolved at once to undertake this Scholarly Work. For though my avocation was in the law, I am, in my heart of hearts, a Scholar."

—*A Modern Treatise on Custom*, Introduction
by John Yonder, Esquire, a Traveling Fellow

Yonder blew across the book's page and studied the letters. A fine, rich ink, the words were all evenly spaced, perfectly lined, flawlessly written, the curls embellished where appropriate. An exemplar of refinement, and intelligence. It was a marvelous first page – which was satisfying, since he had been its author.

He leaned back in the chair of his Merchants Row office, gazed at the words fondly, and when he was certain the ink had completely dried, he carefully turned the page, dipped his quill pen back into the glass inkpot atop his desk, and resumed his composition on a fresh page.

"With all due respect to my Brother Wherestone," he wrote, "but this author has weighed the gentleman's pronouncements upon the Science of Custom and found them wanting. They elide rather than illuminate. They obscure where they should elucidate. For when one has actually practiced Custom (as opposed to pontificate about it), one finds that Wherestone's platitudes often lead down a path of—"

"What's that you're doing?"

Somehow Far had walked through the front door of the foyer and into Yonder's office without his hearing him. Yonder looked up from his work. Far appeared to be dressed for hunting, a heavy wool coat and coarse brown trousers, topped off with a hat, and, of course, a weapon. Today he had chosen a dirk. Yonder shifted in his chair and made his best attempt to hide the annoyance of having his writing interrupted in the midst of a productive flow.

"It's a book," Yonder replied, hoping that would be the end of the conversation.

"Who are you writing it for?"

"Posterity."

Yonder returned to his pen and ink, but his companion seemed intent on vexing him. It was a bothersome habit of his.

"What's it about?"

Yonder smacked his pen down on the table and snapped, "Why do you care?"

Far grinned mischievously. He sidled around the partners desk until he was directly behind Yonder.

"I don't really," he said, reading over Yonder's shoulder. "It's just that you looked – I don't know – happier – than I've seen you before in Doldrums. Healthier, too. I haven't heard that damned cough of yours all day."

Something in what Far said aroused Yonder's curiosity. There was a tangent there, a clue, almost as if Far had stumbled unwittingly upon a whole new corridor in the labyrinth of Custom. He should make a note of it. Yonder began to chew on the feather of his pen.

"Now that you mention it," Yonder mused aloud, "I do feel better. Isn't that curious?" He shook his head. "And where are you off to?"

"Militia duty," Far said, beaming. "I've purchased a captaincy. Only a dozen men so far. Mostly jail dregs. But I'll get more. I'm calling them Far's Fell Fellows of Foot."

"How alliterative. Are we at war again?"

"There's always a war here," he gushed. "It's the one commendable feature of this realm. That and the alcohol. I've scheduled exercises for the rest of the month. I'll turn these Doldrums sheep into wolves – or I'll kill them. Either way. I think this shall be a nice diversion."

"No doubt it will. Well, happy warmongering."

With a grin, Far took his leave. He was almost through the doorway when Yonder thought of something else.

"My friend," he called.

"Yes?"

"On your way out, would you mind taking down that sign outside our door? The shingle I had hung for the law practice. I think I've found a more suitable occupation."

THE END

Acknowledgements

As always, I owe a big debt of gratitude to my patient and loving wife, Alexis, and our sons, James and William, who not only put up with, but enthusiastically encourage, this writing habit of mine. There's no greater blessing than family.

Thanks to Maer, Rob, Joe, and all the team at Ellysian Press who took a chance on this book and made it shine better than I could have ever imagined. You all have been a pleasure to work with.

A *merci beaucoup* to Nelly Khouzam who helped me out with the French language, and a big thanks to Steve Northcutt who somehow made my mug look better than it is.

Finally, thank you, dear reader, for taking a chance on this story. If you liked it, I'd be honored if you'd leave a favorable review wherever you can.

ABOUT THE AUTHOR

Matthew C. ("Matt") Lucas was born and raised in Tampa, Florida and lives there now with his wife and their two sons. He's the author of the dystopian epic fantasy novel, *The Mountain*, and shorter works that have appeared in *Bards & Sages Quarterly*, *The Society of Misfit Stories*, *Swords & Sorcery Magazine*, and *Collective Realms*. He is a graduate of Florida State University and the University of Florida Levin College of Law.

The historical fantasy, *Yonder & Far: The Lost Lock,* is Matt's first novel with Ellysian Press.

You can find out more about Matt's work at www.matthewclucas.com.

ALSO FROM ELLYSIAN PRESS

Fate Accompli by Keith R. Fentonmiller

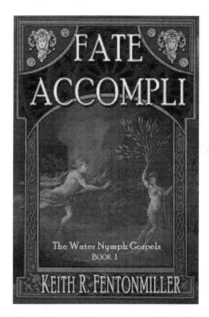

**Fate had one job. And she bungled it . . . badly.
Now only a cursed hatter and a tormented
water nymph can fix the damage.**

Tuscany, 1603

Andolosia Petasos dreams of being the next Da Vinci. Only Fate has cursed him to make hats.

It's not Andolosia's fault. After all, a Greek ancestor stole Hermes' teleportation hat and brought down all of Olympus. And the gods don't easily forgive that sort of thing.

In Olympus, Moira strives to weave a future that will fix the heavenly disaster. The very one she created.

Meanwhile, the rich and powerful Sansone de Medici hires Andolosia to create a fantastical hat. A job that will change the hatter's life.

At de Medici's Florentine palazzo, Andolosia encounters the feisty Carlotta Lux. She claims de Medici has kidnapped her because she is descended from Daphne, the legendary water nymph. Of course Andolosia has no choice but to rescue her using Hermes' hat. But instead of gratitude, she is furious. Carlotta had been within inches of killing her captor.

Because Sansone de Medici is not who he seems. He is driven by a supernatural urge that demands he never gives up the chase.

And Andolosia and Carlotta can't run far enough to escape him.

The Clockwork Detective from

R.A. McCandless

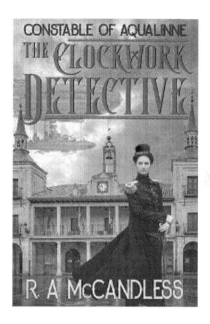

Aubrey Hartmann left the Imperial battlefields with a pocketful of medals, a fearsome reputation, and a clockwork leg.

The Imperium diverts her trip home to investigate the murder of a young *druwyd* in a strange town. She is ordered to not only find the killer but prevent a full-scale war with the dreaded Fae.

Meanwhile, the arrival of a sinister secret policeman threatens to dig up Aubrey's own secrets – ones that could ruin her career.

It soon becomes clear that Aubrey has powerful enemies with plans to stop her before she gets started. Determined to solve the mystery, Aubrey must survive centaurs, thugs and a monster of pure destruction.

"This is my kind of book: a wonderful, fully realized, utterly plausible Steampunk world with a dynamite plot, great characters, and the best dirigibles this side of anywhere. I hope there's more to come."— From James P. Blaylock, World Fantasy Award-Winning Author, Co-Founder of the Modern Steampunk Genre

Moonflowers by David A. Gray

I'm not like those other freaks. The kids who can look inside your head and bring your nightmares to life.

The weirdos who can steal your luck or make a thing true just by wishing it. The outliers born from the mess that followed Armageddon.

The ones you call Moonflowers, half mockingly and half afraid. They're the mistakes that humanity hates – and needs.

I'm not like them. I'm worse. And I'm the only thing standing between you and the legions of heaven and hell.

—Petal – The Armageddon-Lite Archives

About Ellysian Press

Ellysian Press has been bringing high-quality, award-winning books in the Speculative Fiction genres since 2014.

To find other Ellysian Press books, please visit our **website**: (http://www.ellysianpress.com/).

You can find our complete list of novels here. They include:

Fate Accompli Keith R. Fentonmiller

Evil's Whisper by Jordan Elizabeth

Beneath a Fearful Moon by R.A. McCandless

Time to Die by Jordan Elizabeth

A Forgotten Past by Tiffany Lafleur

Aethereal by Kerry Reed

The Soft Fall by Marissa Byfield

Motley Education by S.A. Larsen

Moonflowers by David A. Gray

The Clockwork Detective by R.A. McCandless

Progenie by Mack Little

Time to Live by Jordan Elizabeth

Before Dawn by Elizabeth Arroyo

Redemption by Mike Schlossberg

Kālong by Carol Holland March

Marked Beauty by S.A. Larsen

Dreamscape by Kerry Reed

The Rending by Carol Holland March

A Deal in the Darkness by Allan B. Anderson

The Tyro by Carol Holland March

Muse Unexpected by VC Birlidis

The Devil's Triangle by Toni De Palma

Premonition by Agnes Jayne

Relics by Maer Wilson

A Shadow of Time by Louann Carroll

Idyllic Avenue by Chad Ganske

Portals by Maer Wilson

Innocent Blood by Louann Carroll

Magics by Maer Wilson

The Ellysian Press Catalog has a complete list of current and forthcoming books.

Made in United States
Orlando, FL
08 October 2022